RULE BRITANNIA

"'Mad' is an admirable character, her courage and resourcefulness equal to any provocation . . . Imaginatively, plausibly, with delightful wit, Dame Daphne portrays the household that defends her heroine, and in Madam she has one of her finest characters."

The Atlantic Monthly

"A humorous, satirical, suspenseful story together with unforgettable characters and polished writing . . . a winner."

Columbus Dispatch

"The author of many bestsellers has written a sharp, suspenseful, satirical fable."

Publishers Weekly

Daphne duMaurier

RULE BRITANNIA

AVON
PUBLISHERS OF BARD, CAMELOT, DISCUS, EQUINOX AND FLARE BOOKS

AVON BOOKS
A division of
The Hearst Corporation
959 Eighth Avenue
New York, New York 10019

Copyright © 1972 by Daphne du Maurier.
Published by arrangement with Doubleday and Company, Inc.
Library of Congress Catalog Card Number: 72-86230.

ISBN: 0-380-0062-8

First Avon Printing, July, 1974.
Second Printing

AVON TRADEMARK REG. U.S. PAT. OFF. AND
FOREIGN COUNTRIES, REGISTERED TRADEMARK—
MARCA REGISTRADA, HECHO EN CHICAGO, U.S.A.

Printed in the U.S.A.

For Glads, a promise, with love.

Bean.

KILMARTH, *November 1971–March 1972*

RULE BRITANNIA

1

Emma awoke to the sound of planes passing overhead, but she was not fully conscious, and the sound merged with her dream. The dream was a recurring one, begun in childhood around the age of five and returning still at the age of twenty, so she knew it must have some sort of psychological importance, but what it was she did not care. In the dream she and Mad were holding hands, bowing gracefully to the audience and then to one another. The applause was deafening, and the curtain rose and fell several times but the clapping never ceased. As a child she had looked up to Mad in the dream, as her protectress, and there was a feeling of reassurance in the echoing smile, in the squeeze of the hand, as though Mad were saying, "It's all right, they can't hurt you, I'm here, now and forever." Then through schooldays and adolescence the protectress figure had shrunk, or rather it was that Emma grew, and now they were equal in power, she and Mad, they were identical faces on either side of a coin, and the applause was for them both . . . The last burst of clapping, the final fall of the curtain, and it wasn't the world of theatre any more but the dwindling sound of aircraft hum-

11

ming inland away from the coast, and she was in her own bed with the window rattling against the sill, the curtains blowing, and the smell of morning, cold and clean, seeping into the room.

Emma looked at her bedside clock—it was a few minutes after seven—and then switched on her radio to the local station. But there was no time signal, no announcer with the news, nothing but an interminable hum that must mean there was a fault somewhere, and it wasn't any better when she tried the national programme. The hum persisted, with crackling and spitting thrown in for good measure. "Oh, to hell with it!" She pushed the transistor aside and lay back on her pillow, her hands behind her head, transposing "To be or not to be" from *Hamlet* into a critical assessment of her own ambivalent life. To leave or not to leave, that is the question; whether 'tis nobler to continue living, sharing Mad's life, her home, her whole existence, or to break here and now with all dominion, cut myself loose, start on a separate road...

The trouble is, which road? That was the rub. No openings for girls with or without the right exams behind them. Secretarial pools all jammed with applicants. Men, women, boys, girls, jostling for position, scrambling to obtain the few jobs worth the holding, and ever since the government had backtracked and pulled out of Europe—dissension amongst the Ten was the official reason, and a national referendum had given the government of the day a thumping majority—things seemed to have gone from bad to worse. So Pa said, he ought to know, being a merchant banker.

"Travel the world," he told her. "I'll pay."

"I don't want charity," she replied. "I've turned eighteen."

And so the inevitable and abortive effort to make the grade on the stage. Mad's influence, of course. But despite the recurring dreams she had made no headway. And unless she could get to the top bang off, then there was nothing doing. Not after all those childhood years with applause sounding in her ears. T.V. commercials or regional announcing? No, thank you, ladies and gentlemen and viewers everywhere. Let us rather bear the ills we have than fly to others that we know not of.

Emma tried the radio again, with the same result, a prolonged hum. She got out of bed and went along the

12

passage to turn on the bath-water. Glancing out of the window she saw that the curtains of the little boys' room were still tightly drawn. Thank heaven for that—with luck they might still be asleep. The side door slammed, well, that would rouse them, if the sound of the planes hadn't. It was Terry, wheeling his bicycle out of the side hall—where he was not supposed to keep it—and careering away up the drive. Terry was a poor early riser as a rule, unlike Joe who was always up by seven, chopping wood or digging in the garden, and curiosity impelled Emma to throw open the window and call after him.

"Where are you going?"

He took no notice, of course, merely waved a careless hand, grinned over his shoulder and continued on his way. She was about to close the window again when she noticed that a slate on the sloping roof above the little boys' room had worked loose and was sliding down into the guttering. It was followed by a second, and then a third. Rage filled her. She knew what it meant. Andy had climbed on to the roof from his bedroom on the other side of the house and was squatting on the disused chimney that was his favourite spy-place. He must somehow have dislodged the slates. "I can't and I won't stand it." The memory of the dream, so different from reality, infused Emma with the sense of frustration that can only be appeased by instant action of a useless sort. Deliberately she let her tooth-glass fall into the wash-basin with a crash. The splintered fragments gave her satisfaction. "Serve her right," she muttered. Serve who right? Herself or Mad? The bath-water was tepid—the immersion heater must have gone wrong again. And this, she told herself, is what comes of living in a mad-house, rightly named after its owner, who, on retiring from the stage some years ago after a brilliant career, could think of nothing better to do than to adopt six parentless, maladjusted boys and let them run riot in her home, believing, by so doing, that she had justification for living when her carreer had finished.

"I won't help her any more. She must find someone else. I will not let my life be ruined. I'm far too young."

Emma bathed and dressed—same old tunic, same old jeans, no one here to care how she looked—and then went downstairs into the kitchen, to be greeted by the revolting smell of eggs and bacon. Dottie insisted that growing boys

13

must start the day with a good breakfast, otherwise they would lose their strength, and as she had the cooking of it she took responsibility.

Dottie had been Mad's dresser for forty years, and now, torn from the world of theatre she had made her own, was installed as cook, housekeeper, cleaner, nurse, or whatever else she might be called upon to do through the sudden demand of the employer she adored. You could hardly imagine, so Emma had decided long ago, the one without the other. If memory was a photographic plate, as she sometimes felt it must be, then her first memory was of the dressing-room at the Theatre Royal, with Mad turning round from the stool in front of the wide mirror, holding out her arms to Emma at the age of three or four and saying, "Darling..." with that radiant, wonderful smile, and Dottie bustling in the background behind a screen, putting some incredible costume on a hanger. Madam must have this... Madam must have that... Madam is on top of the world... Madam is in one of her moods. And so it was that Dottie's appellation of "Madam," which through the years spread down the theatre hierarchy, from director, author and leading man to call-boy and scene shifter, became shortened at some forgotten moment, on the lips of a child, to the Mad of today. It was significant, though, that nobody was allowed to use the name but Emma. If anyone else had dared... the heavens would have split asunder.

The heavens were going to split any moment, as a matter of fact, so Emma decided as another wave of planes passed overhead. There must be scores of them, probably some exercise or other, and perhaps that was what was causing interference with the radio. Dottie was trying to squeeze her rotund form into the narrow gap between dish-washer and kitchen sink, head uptilted to the window beyond.

"What's going on?" she said to Emma. "The blessed things don't give one a moment's peace. I didn't need my alarm clock this morning. It was one long throb-throb before six. They ought to have more consideration for the general public."

"Who do you mean by 'they'?" asked Emma.

She began laying the table for the boys. Plates, knives and forks, cereal bowls.

"Well," Dottie replied, returning to her fry, "the powers

14

that be, whoever they are. They've no right to do it. Now I've burnt the toast. It's going to be one of those mornings. The post's never come and I had to send Terry on his bike to look out for the van. If Madam doesn't get her post with her orange juice there'll be murder in the house. I've been expecting her bell for the past half-hour as it is. Get those boys moving, Emma dear, I'm all behindhand. And tell Andy to clean his teeth with the tooth-paste, not the soap."

A moment's respite from the droning overhead. A sudden lull. I ought, thought Emma, to be doing something truly worthwhile, like nursing old people with leprosy, or feeding famine-stricken multitudes after a tidal wave ... Oh hell, she thought, what a load of rubbish. This is what T.V. documentaries do to one, Mad is perfectly right. All judgement goes.

Deathly silence from the little boys' room. Surely they were not still asleep? She opened the door. The curtains were tightly drawn, but the light was on. Ben was sitting in the far corner of the room on an upturned chamber pot to serve as stool. He was stark naked except for a pair of gloves and a discarded hat of Mad's, sent to a jumble sale and never sold. He was ebony black and beautiful, and looked less than his three years. It was not only because of his colour that Mad had adopted him but because, so the authorities told her, there was something amiss with his tongue, he might never learn to speak. He rolled delighted eyes at Emma as she entered, held up two fingers, a gesture taught him by Terry, then gazed once more towards the uppermost bed of the double-bedded bunk which he shared with Colin.

Colin, six years old, was as white as Ben was black, blue-eyed, golden-haired—a director would have picked him from a million candidates for the role of the child Jesus. Found in a ditch after a Pop festival, his parents never traced. Mad, who was snobbish at times, swore he was of royal descent, but the devil had a hand in his making too, for he had a serpent's guile beneath an angel's hide. "If anyone can teach Ben to speak Colin will," Mad determined, and to Dottie's consternation she placed them together in the double bunk, from which moment Colin had become Ben's god, though speech had not yet materialized.

15

"What are you doing?" asked Emma suspiciously.

Colin was lying motionless on the top bunk with a sheet folded over him, his hands on his breast. His eyes were closed. Emma walked over to the bunk and prodded his cheek, and one eye opened.

"Go away, Emma. I'm doing a play for Ben. I'm Madam dying, and in a moment I'm going to gasp and choke and it will be the end of the play. Ben will then have to clap, and I shall jump up and bow."

"What a horrible idea for a play," said Emma. "Stop it at once and dress, breakfast will be ready any minute."

Colin looked aggrieved. "It's not horrible at all. It's realistic. Madam thought of it herself. We're rehearsing it for her. At least, I am—Ben's the audience."

Emma left them to it and went out of the room. The trouble was, as Pa was in the habit of saying—though she disliked agreeing with him where Mad was concerned—the trouble was that Mad was the last person in the world who should be permitted to give a home to maladjusted children. Happy they might be, but the world they lived in was unreal, a world of fantasy. Like mine, Emma thought, like mine, we're all tarred with the same brush, Mad's brush . . .

She walked along the narrow passage and opened the door of the middle boys' room. Andy and Sam, being twelve and nine, were known as the middle boys to distinguish them from their elders, Joe and Terry, who were nineteen and seventeen. The middle boys also had bunks, but their room was larger than the little boys' lair, and it had a distinctive smell. This was due to the wired-off portion, containing a very ancient grey squirrel which, Sam had decided, could no longer fend for itself. The squirrel had shared the bedroom with him and Andy for several weeks. Discarded nut-shells scattered the floor. Dottie had protested, practically in tears, that it was against all laws of hygiene.

"Hygiene my foot," Mad told her. "Sam will probably grow up to become a famous zoologist and win a Nobel prize. I won't have him checked."

Sam was kneeling on the floor when Emma entered the room, but he was not tending to the squirrel's needs. A new inhabitant, a pigeon, trailed a wing, while Sam endeavoured to coax his visitor to take seed from his open

16

palm. He glanced over his shoulder and motioned Emma to silence.

"Don't come too near, Emmie," he whispered, "you might scare him. Once he knows me for a friend he'll let me bind up his wing."

Perhaps. Perhaps not. Sam had saved wounded birds before now, but he had known failure too, and then there had been tears, and funeral ceremonies in the shrubbery, with Colin, invariably fascinated by death, performing his role as parson.

"How did it happen?" asked Emma, also whispering.

"He fell from the roof. He was disturbed by something." Sam had a narrow, thin face, and he had been born with the squint that was still his distinguishing mark, making those who did not know and understand him feel uncomfortable. Perhaps it was the squint that had discomfited his parents some years previously. Sam had been a battered baby, and when Mad saw the bruises she seized him for her own.

"What disturbed him?" Emma enquired. "Was it those planes?"

The crossed eyes spared Sam from many an admission. People could never tell from their expression whether he was speaking the truth.

"Yes," he said, "at least, I think so."

The open window and the absence of Andy suggested otherwise, but Emma knew better than to expect Sam to betray his room-mate.

"It's all right, you don't have to tell me," she said. "I know he's on the roof again, I saw the fallen slates from the bathroom window."

She crossed the room, and opening the window wider still, but holding it firmly, leant backwards, suggesting someone on the point of suicide. The square chimney at the roof's end, long blocked from within, had a rounded aperture, whence the smoke in ancient times had issued from a vast range in a basement kitchen. Today the opening made a splendid vantage spot for an adventurous boy, who, well concealed, his matted hair, which might have been a jackdaw's nest, the only visible sign of occupancy, could thus ensconce himself as lord of all he surveyed, occasionally to the disadvantage of those below.

17

"Come on down," called Emma authoritatively. "I shan't tell you again."

The jackdaw's nest moved. So did a weapon. How on earth, Emma wondered, had Andy managed not only to climb the dangerous sloping roof but to carry with him one of the bows which all the boys were forbidden to touch, and which should by rights be standing with its fellows in the entrance-hall?

"Given me by a field-marshal," Mad used to say. "Toxophily was his favourite hobby. He was one of my greatest fans for years."

"Completely untrue," Pa would whisper to Emma. "She bought them at the Battersea fun-fair."

True or false, the arrows that went with the bows were lethal. Andy's head and shoulders emerged from the chimney. He smiled engagingly at Emma.

"I only grazed the pigeon," he called. "I didn't mean to, I wanted to scare the aircraft, but they were out of my range. Several choppers came low, and if they'd only been a few hundred feet lower I might have got one of the pilots."

"Bad luck for you," scoffed Emma. "Now come along down, and put that bow back where you found it."

"But it's mine," shouted Andy, wide-eyed. "Madam gave it me, didn't you know?"

Emma shrugged, and withdrew from her precarious windowledge. It was quite hopeless to instill any sort of order. One of these days someone would be murdered, and it wouldn't be the fault of herself or Dottie or the boys. Mad would be to blame. As for Andy, you would think that a child who was the only survivor of an air-crash in which both father and mother and an elder sister had been killed—sabotage, a bomb had exploded soon after take-off—would have fought shy of the idea, however distant from reality, of bringing further aircraft and their crew to the ground in flames. Not so. Which only went to show . . . show what? Emma left the middle boys' quarters and returned to the kitchen.

"I told you it's one of those mornings," observed Dottie, dishing up the eggs and bacon on to a long trestle table. "The telephone's not working. I wanted to ring the butcher and the line's gone dead. I don't know what Madam will say. Will you take up her orange juice, dear? I don't think

I can face her at the moment. It's one thing after the other. Half a mo', I hear Terry with the post now."

The inevitable skid of the bicycle, as it was thrown on the ground under the kitchen window. Then the clatter up the back stairs and Terry burst into the room, his cheeks aflame, the same colour as his shirt. His looks were Byronic, clear-cut profile, tumbled curls, and, though barely seventeen, he was the heartthrob of all the girls within a ten-mile radius. The trouble was that his drug-taking mother, who couldn't name his father, had slashed her wrists in a moment of despair and left Terry to be discovered by a neighbour. He had scampered from every Home until Mad rescued him. This was several years ago, of course. He was Mad's first find, and didn't let you forget it.

"You've no idea," he said breathlessly, turning from Dottie to Emma. "I couldn't get further than the top of the lane. There's soldiers everywhere. They've got a great barricade across the main road. I couldn't get within twenty yards of them—they waved me back. And all the time those choppers overhead creating a hell of a racket. It's terrific, just like the real thing. Where's Joe?"

The sound of sawing from the basement told him that his room-mate was at his usual early morning ploy of filling log-baskets for Madam's fire. The skies could burst, helicopters land in the garden, Joe could carry on undeterred with his self-imposed task of ministering to Madam's needs.

"Barricades, indeed!" exclaimed Dottie. "Whatever next? Did you see the post-van, Terry?"

Terry stared at her and snorted. "Are you crazy?" he said. "Do you think a post-van could get past that lot? A bunch of them are up the telegraph poles, too, doing something to the wires."

He clattered downstairs once more in search of Joe, slamming the kitchen door.

"That explains why I couldn't get the butcher," said Dottie. "Madam is going to raise Cain when she hears of this. Here, take the orange juice." She gave the neatly-laid tray into Emma's waiting hands. "It beats me why she hasn't rung before now. Did you remind Andy to clean his teeth?"

Emma did not answer. Andy's teeth were of secondary importance compared with the strange happenings without, all of which must surely have a direct and disastrous effect upon Mad's early morning mood. She went upstairs slowly, disliking her mission, for untoward events, unless expressly designed to suit the purpose of the doyenne, could have unfortunate consequences for the household. She paused at the head of the stairs. The notice "Don't Disturb," which hung from the handle of the door, had been turned around to reaveal its reverse. This was the quote from Dante's *Inferno*, "All hope abandon, ye who enter here," which one of Mad's leading men, in days long past, had stuck up outside her dressing-room as a warning to intruders.

Emma coughed, knocked, and went into her grandmother's bedroom.

2

Mad wasn't in bed. She was sitting up in her chair by the open window that overlooked the bay, field-glasses to her eyes. She was fully dressed, if such a term could be used to describe her outfit, which was a combination of Robin Hood and the uniform worn by the late lamented Mao Tse-tung. It was certainly practical for early November on the Cornish coast, if the person wearing it was about to engage in an archery competition or clean a locomotive. Mad was destined to do neither, so far as her grand-daughter was aware, but then you never could be sure what the day would bring.

"Dottie's apologies," Emma began. "It's one of those mornings. I hope you haven't been awake for hours. Those infuriating planes, and now Terry reports there are road-blocks at the top of the hill on the main road and soldiers everywhere. It must be a hell of an exercise. The post can't get through, the telephone's gone dead, and even the radio won't work. Here's your orange juice, darling."

She put the tray down by the writing-table beneath the window. Mad did not answer. She was too intent upon the view through the field-glasses. Staring at the ships at anchor, before they entered port, was one of her favourite occupations. She liked to think she knew the nationality of every waiting vessel by its shape and design, quite apart from its flag, but today the test was harder. There were no merchant ships waiting to load clay. A warship was at anchor, too distant to decipher anything about it from its ensign, which was out of sight, or from its shape or super-structure. It was evident to Emma, even without the aid of field-glasses, that the helicopters which were passing to and fro hailed from the parent ship in the bay.

"I still don't see," she continued, "why a naval exercise should have to disturb everyone ashore, interfere with radio, cut the telephone and stop post-vans delivering the mail."

Mad lowered the field-glasses and reached for her orange juice. Emma wondered why, instead of the usual exclamation of annoyance or impatience which the morning's surprising events should have evoked, her grandmother seemed thoughtful, even grim. The clear-cut profile that in her youth, and indeed throughout her theatrical career, had stamped itself on postcards all over the world appeared suddenly aquiline and harsh. The cropped white hair, curling at the nape of the neck, gave her the appearance not of a famous beauty and actress who, when she celebrated her eightieth birthday in two weeks' time, would finger nose-gays and Interflora tributes with a graceful bow, but of an aged warrior, possibly a Roman legionary, who after long idleness and years of peace lifted up his head and scented battle.

"This isn't a naval exercise," she said, "nor even a com-bined forces exercise. If it was, we'd have heard about it. Jimmy Jollif would have rung me up days ago." Admiral Jollif was the C.-in-C. at Devonport, and because he was the son of an old friend of hers, long dead, he and Mad were on Christmas card terms. He had even been to lunch. Emma thought it doubtful that the Admiral would have telephoned her grandmother to warn her of forthcoming postal and telephone delays, but you never knew.

"Perhaps, darling," Emma ventured, "the exercise has to be realistic to make an impact. Otherwise it would be a waste of time. It's a good thing they picked on half-term, and the boys didn't have to catch the bus to school—they'd never have made it."

Mad turned and looked at her grand-daughter. Her sudden smile was confident, the blue eyes bright. "Tell Dottie to serve them double rations of eggs and bacon for breakfast. It may be their last square meal for the day."

"Oh, honestly, Mad . . ."

"I'm not joking. And keep them indoors. Not just the little ones, this goes for Joe and Terry too. Andy is not to climb the chimney, but he can help Sam clean up their room, as long as he doesn't frighten the squirrel."

"There's a pigeon as well this morning," murmured Emma, feeling like an informer.

"Oh, really?" Mad looked thoughtful again. "That's interesting. It might be a carrier. Had it a note under its wing?"

"The wing was broken. Anyway, trailing."

"H'm. Could be a sign . . ."

The trouble was, you never could tell whether Mad was acting or not. Her life nowadays was so frequently an elaborate game of make-believe, but whether to encourage the latent powers of imagination in the boys, or to amuse herself now the pulse of the blood was tame, Emma never could decide. Pa said it was neither, but from force of habit, like cleaning her teeth, his mother was obliged to give two performances daily to audiences long dead. Which was rather cruel, when you came to think of it, but then Pa, being a banker, had little time for sentiment.

"Look," said Mad suddenly, pointing to the ploughed field beyond the garden wall. "There are some men coming up from the beach, they must have landing craft of some sort, I've forgotten what they're called these days—they used to be dukus or dugs, or something. Run down at once and give my strict orders that no one, repeat, no one is to leave the house. I'll be down myself in a moment to supervise, as soon as I see where all these men are going. And whatever you do, don't let Folly out."

Folly was the Dalmatian bitch, now fourteen years old, blind in one eye and partially deaf, who lived on a chair in the corner of the library and seldom stirred, except to crouch, twice a day, on a plot of grass that had become dried and barren from her attention.

Emma flung one last look over her shoulder, and stopped in astonishment. Her grandmother was right. There *were* men, soldiers, wearing that idiotic camouflage they all wore

23

no matter what army they represented, coming up across the field, spread fan-wise, rifles at the ready, tin hats on their heads.

"I know," said Emma, and she laughed, because it suddenly seemed so obvious, "it's a film, they're making a film, they're here on location. And those men at the top of the road mucking about with the telegraph wires weren't soldiers at all but the camera crew. Oh no, they mustn't frighten the dog . . . !"

Spry, the farm collie, a wizard with his master's sheep but terrified of all explosive sounds, from thunderstorms to aircraft flying low, must have escaped from his safe lair at the farmstead over the hill, and was now running as if for his life across the field in front of the advancing soldiers. One of the men paused and took aim, but did not shoot. Then, as another helicopter roared low over the roof, Spry, in panic, turned at bay towards the advancing soldier, barking fiercely as was his wont with strangers upon his territory, and this time the soldier fired.

"God rot his guts!" cried Mad.

Spry was no longer the guardian of his master's flock but something bleeding and torn, not even a dog. Mad put down her field-glasses, rose from her chair and walked across the room.

"Did you say a film?" she flung at Emma, and preceded her downstairs.

It isn't true, thought Emma, bewildered. It can't be true. Soldiers don't shoot animals, they have them as mascots, they love them, and then before Mad had reached the bottom of the stairs Emma heard her call sharply, "Sam, come here!" There was the sound of the front door being thrown open, and from the top of the stairs Emma saw the small flying figure of Sam running across the lawn to the gate, out on to the driveway and the orchard and so to the field beyond. Sam had seen what had happened. Sam had gone to the rescue of his friend, the collie-dog Spry. Hysteria, panic, qualities hitherto unknown, seized upon Emma. If the men shot animals, they would shoot children too.

"Sam!" she screamed, tumbling down the stairs. "Sam . . ."

Then she felt Mad's hand in hers. Restraining, hard and cold. "Don't worry," she said, "they'll turn him back. The man who shot Spry won't repeat his mistake. He'll be in trouble anyway from his platoon commander, or whoever is in charge of this fantastic outfit."

The tears were coursing down Emma's cheeks. The sudden horror of seeing the dog destroyed, the dog they all knew, who came courting poor old Folly when she was on heat, and Sam running headlong into murderous fire, this did not belong to the world she knew, this was nightmare.

"How can you be so calm?" she sobbed. "How can you?"

She looked out across the orchard field. Sam had reached the gap in the hedge, and was about to climb through the gap when one of the men, approaching from the opposite side, came swiftly forwards and spoke to him. He put his hand on Sam's shoulder. Sam turned and pointed towards the house. The man appeared to hesitate a moment, then shouting some order to the soldiers behind, he climbed through the gap in the hedge, with Sam beside him, and both of them walked slowly across the orchard towards the house. The rest continued to advance up the ploughed field, some making for the woods, others for the paddock that led to the lane and the main road beyond. Raised voices, arguments, children's high-pitched questions arose from the kitchen. An agitated Dottie appeared in the hall, closely followed by Terry.

"What's going on, Madam?" she flustered. "We heard a shot and Sam said something about a dog. It's not Folly, is it? Sam went tearing through to the front and I couldn't stop him."

"I'll get him," interrupted Terry. "Those chaps are everywhere, just look at them crossing the paddock. Of all the bloody cheek! You leave it to me, Madam, I'll sort them out, I'll . . ."

"You'll do nothing of the sort," said Mad. "You'll do as I tell you. Get back to the kitchen and stay there. You too, Dottie. Send Joe to me. Sam is going to need someone to comfort him. There's been an accident. None of the other boys are to come through to the front without my permission."

Terry turned on his heel, muttering under his breath. Dottie hesitated a moment, murmured, "Yes, Madam," and retreated. Mad's lips were pursed in a soundless whistle, a danger signal to all who knew her. The soldier, Sam at his side, had crossed the orchard. Soon they would reach the

25

gate separating the front lawn from the drive. Emma felt someone touch her shoulder. It was Joe. He said nothing, but his eyes questioned her. Joe, now nineteen, was the eldest of Mad's adopted brood, and the most dependable. His open, honest face would have been handsome but for the irregular features and long upper lip and the scar beside his right eye. He was neither an orphan nor illegitimate. An only child, his fault had been that he had never learnt to read or write—a disability that was still little understood when he had started to go to school—and his parents, both schoolteachers, had been unable to cope with the situation and had emigrated to Australia, leaving Joe in the care of a grandparent who had since died. "If it were not for Joe," Mad sometimes said, "I would give up. He is the only person, except for myself, who can be relied upon." Mad never wasted a flow of words on Joe; he understood, and followed, all instructions.

"They've shot Spry," she said. "Sam won't understand, and will be distressed. I want you to take him upstairs at once to his room away from the others and stay with him there. Help with the pigeon that has the trailing wing. I'll deal with the man."

She seized a stick from the stack of walking-sticks in the hall, and for one terrible moment Emma wondered if her grandmother was going to attack the soldier, who by now had opened the gate and was walking up the garden path.

"Do be careful," she said involuntarily.

"Don't worry," replied Mad. "If they don't shoot boys they won't shoot old women . . . yet."

She descended the steps to the garden, Joe at her side. Emma, curiosity overcoming panic, stared at the man. Apart from his fighting gear and his gun, he looked quite ordinary. Strained, perhaps, a bit on edge. Sam wasn't crying. He seemed in a state of shock. Joe walked down the path, picked him up in his arms and went back to the house without a word. The soldier came to a halt. He even stood to attention and saluted. It must be basic training, thought Emma, because he couldn't have expected someone as old as Mad to come down the steps, looking exactly like Mao Tse-tung.

"Sorry about your pet, ma'am," he said. "An error of judgement on the part of one of my men."

Surprising. The accent was American. Then it *was* some sort of combined operation. Emma glanced at her grand-mother, who showed no emotion.

"It's not my pet," she said. "It belongs to Mr. Trembath, the farmer, and is, or was, a very valuable dog."

"The farmer will be compensated, ma'am," replied the soldier. "All reports of damage will be dealt with speedily and effectively. Meanwhile, I would advise you to keep indoors, and remain indoors until you have notification to the contrary. Thank you, ma'am."

He saluted once again, but his courtesy was wasted on Mad. She advanced a further step down the garden path so that the soldier, to save his dignity, was obliged to retreat.

"Would you mind telling me what this is all about?" she asked, her voice ringing loud and clear as though she was addressing the back row of a theatre gallery.

"Sorry, ma'am, I can only inform you that there is a state of emergency throughout the country. Keep tuned in to your local radio or television station. They should be on the air within the hour. Thank you, ma'am."

He clicked his heels, then turned and walked down the path, shutting the gate behind him, and walked smartly up the drive towards the main road. His companions-at-arms had all disappeared in the same direction.

"What does he mean, a state of emergency?" asked Emma.

"Just that," said Mad dryly. "Go and make me a cup of coffee, and tell Dottie to carry on with breakfast. It's exactly 9:35. If that man knew what he was talking about, there may be some announcement at ten o'clock. Switch the radio on in the kitchen, just before the hour. I'll do the same with the television. If there's anything doing I'll give you and the boys a shout. This is something we've all got to share, children and adults alike."

Emma was without appetite, even for cereal. She could not forget the sight of the frightened dog turning at bay, then becoming instantly—nothing. The line upon line of men advancing up the hill. Sam's state of shock . . .

Breakfast was proceeding in the kitchen, but the atmosphere was tense. Terry, sullen because of Mad's brush-off, wore his moody expression, his handsome face dark with resentment. Andy, banished without explanation from the room he shared with Sam, was plainly upset. Dottie, seated at the head of the table, wore her set look. Emma leant over to the kitchen radio and switched it on. They were playing "Land of Hope and Glory."

"Mad thinks there will be some announcement at ten o'clock," she said. "The soldier who brought Sam back told her to keep tuned in. He said there was a state of emergency throughout the country, and everyone has got to stay indoors."

Now I am being calm, she thought, now I'm the one in charge. It's like being deputy for Mad, but not in the ordinary way of every day. This is crisis.

"State of emergency?" questioned Dottie, her mouth agape. "Does it mean we're at war?"

"I don't know. The soldier didn't say. He was American by the way."

"A Yank?" Terry, roused from his sullen mood, sprang to his feet. "Do you mean they were all Yanks there on the main road by the barricade? Well, what the hell were they doing? I mean, if the Russians land what's the bloody use of a road-block? It wouldn't stop me, let alone a lot of Russkies."

"It would stop you if the Yank on the other side of the barricade had a gun."

Andy's interruption was to the point, and for a moment Terry looked discomfited.

"Well, but why should a bloody Yank raise a gun at me?" he queried. "I wouldn't be doing anything."

"You might be running away," said Andy, "like Spry."

There was sudden silence. Everyone, in his or her separate way, was reminded of the morning's unhappy incident. Even Colin looked thoughtful. When Joe had whispered to him, on his way upstairs with Sam, that there had been an accident, and the farm dog had been hurt, he hadn't connected it with the roar of planes and Terry's excited chatter about soldiers.

28

"Emmie," he said slowly, "do you mean that some American soldier carrying a gun shot at Spry?"

Andy answered for her. "Yes," he said, "and what's more, shot him dead."

"It was an accident," said Emma hastily, "the soldier came to apologise."

"The question is, if we're none of us supposed to go out and the telephone's not working, how about letting Mr. Trembath know?" asked Terry. "He'll be terribly upset, so will they all, especially Myrtle." Myrtle was fifteen, and Terry's girl of the moment. "Tell you what, I can slip down across the field, it won't take five minutes."

"No," said Emma, "no . . ." Terry stared at her defiantly, then stuck his hands in his jeans pockets and kicked at the leg of the kitchen table. But before he could start arguing, the music on the radio ceased and a voice said, "In a few moments, after the time signal at ten o'clock, there will be an important announcement."

"This is it," said Emma, snatching up the tray with the coffee. "You can all come through to the library, Mad said so, it will be on the telly. Shout for Joe and Sam, Andy."

She hurried out of the kitchen, closely followed by Dottie and the boys. Her grandmother was seated in her armchair in her sanctum, long-distance glasses on the top of her head, ready to descend instantly upon her nose. The television set was turned on. It showed a picture hitherto unseen, of two national flags side by side, joined together at the base. They were the Union Jack and the Stars and Stripes. Colin settled himself on the stool at Mad's feet, with Ben between his knees.

"What's it going to be, a Western?" he asked.

"Sh!" said Emma.

Joe came in, holding Sam by the hand, and they went and sat beside Terry and Andy on the window-seat. Dottie, with a glance at Mad, drew up a hard chair. Emma perched on the arm of the sofa. The two flags faded, giving place to the face of the announcer, who looked nervous and harassed, unlike his customary debonair self.

"Good morning to all viewers in the south-west," he said. "This is your local station at Plymouth. There has been no transmission this morning owing to circumstances beyond our control. The reason for this will be explained to you by

29

Rear-Admiral Sir James Jollif, acting Commander-in-Chief, Western Approaches, who is in the studio now. Admiral Jollif."

The cameras switched to the bald-headed Admiral who sent Mad Christmas cards and had once been to lunch. He appeared more forbidding in his uniform, with decorations, than he had done two summers ago, in shorts and a floppy T-shirt, playing badminton on the side-lawn with the boys.

"It's Madam's old buffer friend," cried Colin delightedly, and Ben, between his knees, began to clap. This time it was Dottie who said "Sh!" Mad's face was inscrutable, but she placed her glasses firmly on her nose.

"Good day to you all," said Admiral Jollif. His tone was grave, but not unduly so, and at least it must mean, thought Dottie, that Buckingham Palace had not been bombed and the dear Queen was safe. "It is my duty to inform you," he continued, "that since midnight the country has been placed in a state of emergency. Measures have been taken throughout the United Kingdom to ensure the safety of all members of the community, and to maintain power supplies and essential services. There will be no postal services, however, and after midnight trains will not be running for at least twenty-four hours, possibly longer. Telephone switchboards will be manned only for emergency calls. Except for those engaged upon essential work, everyone is instructed to stay at home until further notice, or to return there immediately if they have already left for work, or for any other purpose.

"I am not, I regret, empowered to tell you any more at this moment. I do, however, want to impress upon you all that there is no cause for alarm. I repeat that, no cause for alarm. The aircraft you have seen and heard passing overhead this morning are friendly to us. The American Sixth Fleet is in the English Channel. The troops you may have observed in the towns and ports belong to the combined armed forces of the United States, and are here in the United Kingdom with our full knowledge and co-operation. Keep calm, keep tuned in to the radio and television, and may God bless you all."

His face faded. The two flags reappeared. And instead of "Land of Hope and Glory," the music started up with

"The Star-Spangled Banner." Mad rose to her feet, removed her glasses and switched off the set.

"Is that all?" asked Colin, disappointed.

"For the present, yes," said Mad, "and quite enough too."

Everyone stood up. Somehow it was an anti-climax, for the younger members of the household anyway, as it was after the Queen's speech on Christmas Day. What do any of us do now, Emma wondered. Sam came forward from the window-seat and knelt beside the ancient Folly, who from the only comfortable chair in the room, apart from Mad's, was endeavouring to scratch a lump of canker out of her left ear.

"It's all right, Fol-Fol," he said, "nobody's going to shoot you. If any soldier as much as tries, Andy will get him first."

"Quite right," said Mad, and her lips began to frame her soundless whistle. Oh no, thought Emma, don't say she's going to start that line with the boys, because if she does we'll all be in trouble. God knows what will happen. She raised her eyebrows at Dottie, who began to marshal the little boys out of the room.

"Can I go to the farm and tell them about Spry?" asked Terry.

Mad threw him a look. A look Emma mistrusted. It spelt duplicity between her grandmother and the earliest of Mad's adopted brood.

"Not yet," she said. "Wait till I give the word."

Emma wondered how long it would be before the telephone would work again, before the world returned to normal, or approximately normal, because the first thing to do then would be to ring up Pa in London and ask what was happening. He would know, he was in touch with so many high-up people, not just bankers but Cabinet Ministers, the Lot, and then he could be firm with Mad and warn her not to do anything outrageous. Because the frightful thing was that where her grandmother was concerned you never knew.

The infant Jesus, his hand firmly clasping that of his small black brother, paused an instant before he left the room.

"What I want to know is this," he said. "Are the American soldiers baddies or goodies?" His question was directed at Mad.

She did not answer immediately. She began to whistle under her breath. Then she threw Colin a smile. Not the familiar picture postcard smile that her fans remembered, but the slow, craftier one of the Roman legionary.

"That, my boy," she told him, "is what I intend to find out."

3

The day wore on, but it followed no sort of routine pattern. Chores were done, half-heartedly or unwillingly, everyone was on edge. Mad had gone back upstairs to her bedroom window, but she was in an uncommunicative mood and just sat there, humped, the field-glasses on her knee. The warship was still at anchor.

"What do you suppose is happening?" asked Emma at length.

"Darling, if I knew, I'd say," replied her grandmother. "Don't ask silly questions. Get something to do."

Emma didn't know how Mad could sit there, with the terrible spattered remains of Spry still lying in the middle of the ploughed field. Every time she put up the field-glasses to watch the ship she must see them.

Old people and young children, thought Emma, they don't feel things as we do. One begins to feel at eight or nine; like Sam, and everything goes on hurting until one's about fifty; when it eases off, the person goes numb.

But this meant that Mad had been numb for nearly thirty years, which couldn't really be true. And Pa, who would be fifty in a year's time, was on the brink. It must depend upon the individual, she decided. Numbness is inherited perhaps, like going grey at thirty and getting cancer, like her mother, whom she could barely remember because she was always in and out of nursing-homes, wearing a pink bed-jacket.

"If she had lived," Emma used to ask Mad, "would I have been different?"

"No," said her grandmother. "Why should you be?"

"Well," replied Emma, "that thing of a mother's influence, a mother's love."

"You've had that from me."

"Yes, I know, but still . . ." That poor woman in her pink bed-jacket who surely must have been fond of her husband and child and was dragged panting out of life like Emily Bronte . . .

"You've never really said," Emma asked one day, "but what was she like? I don't mean in looks, but in ways?"

And Mad, with the fearful directness that was so much a part of her, looked her grand-daughter straight in the eye and said, "She was a pretty little thing, darling, but, quite frankly, terribly stupid. I never knew what Pa saw in her."

And so forever after, whenever Emma did anything foolish, or said something silly, or broke a plate or ran out of petrol, she felt she was being like her mother and that Mad despised her for it. Which made life difficult.

Later on, when she went through to the dining-room to clear away Mad's lunch (they generally had it together, but today it had seemed wiser to have it in the kitchen with Dottie, and help with the boys), she found that the dishes were still on the hot-plate untouched, and the dining-room was empty. Her grandmother must have gone back again to her bedroom, and with pangs of conscience—perhaps she wasn't feeling well—Emma ran upstairs to see. The bedroom was empty too. Emma glanced out of the window, and saw the stooping figure of Mad out in the ploughed field. She had Joe's garden spade and she was digging. At least, she had been digging. She was turning the earth over now, and the thing that had been Spry was no longer there. She paused when she had finished, and, leaning on the spade, looked out to sea. The warship was at anchor still, and some of the helicopters had returned to their base aboard. A glimmer of sun peeked through the bleak

November sky. The ensign at the quarter-staff in the stern was plain to see now, and it was the Stars and Stripes.

Mad turned, and began to walk slowly back to the gap in the field leading to the orchard. Emma went downstairs. Better to say nothing. Better to pretend she had not seen. She went and hid in the downstairs lavatory until she heard her grandmother come into the house, and kick off her boots in the cloakroom. Then she waited until she heard her calling to Folly in the library. Emma knew what was going to happen. Mad would cut up her lunch for Folly and say nothing about it, so that Dottie would think she had eaten it herself. Emma was right. When she emerged from her hiding-place and went into the library, Mad was looking for her spectacles and Folly was licking her chops.

"Oh, there you are, darling," said Mad. "I've been looking for you."

Liar, thought Emma. Infuriating, deceitful, beloved liar.

"Tell Dottie the steak was delicious, but I couldn't manage the veg—I'm not very hungry."

Nor would I be hungry, thought her grand-daughter, if I'd just buried a mangled dog . . .

"There was nothing on the one o'clock news," Emma said. "Just a repeat of that statement by the Admiral, so we switched to the news from London and it was the same. Only this time the statement was made by the Commander-in-Chief Land Forces, General Something. Slightly different wording, but otherwise unchanged."

"I know," said Mad, "I heard it."

"I wonder if things are frantic in London. What do you suppose Pa is doing?"

"Treading the corridors of power. If there is any power left," said Mad.

Emma always found it curious that her grandmother indulged her adopted boys to the limit, aiding and abetting them in all misdeeds, but when it came to her only son she frequently disapproved. She used to say Pa boasted. And he didn't, she insisted, get his conceit from her, or from his dramatist father who was always so original and amusing, but from a parson great-grandfather who had failed to become a bishop. Her son Victor, she insisted, always made out that he knew everyone and kept his finger on the pulse of the world, and that people at the top asked his advice about everything from banking to politics.

"Perhaps they do," Emma would say in defence of her father.

"Nonsense," said Mad. "If I ever ask Vic's advice about anything it's invariably wrong. He once made me buy some shares on the Stock Exchange and they immediately fell in value. I've never gone by him since."

"But that was years ago."

"I don't care. His judgement's unsound."

They went together into the music-room. It was called the music-room because of the piano which nobody ever played, but it was also Mad's favourite room, which she kept filled with flowers even if they were nothing but dried hydrangea heads. There were also photographs of herself dotted about the room, in various roles, which Emma secretly thought was rather conceited, but perhaps when you were old you like to be reminded of your young days when you were famous.

"I'll tell you one thing," said Mad, as she threw one of Joe's carefully sawn logs on to the fire. "I have the feeling that your Pa knew something was in the wind."

"How do you mean?" asked Emma.

"When he telephoned a few nights ago it was rather odd. I meant to tell you at the time, and then I forgot. He kept on saying he wanted you and me to go up to London for a few days and stay at the flat with him, there were a lot of things to discuss, and when I suggested he come down here instead he said it was difficult, and he was—well, I can only say cagey. I told him it was out of the question, you and I couldn't possibly leave Dottie all alone to cope with the boys, especially over the half-term, and he said, 'Damn Dottie and the boys. Well, I hope you don't regret it.' Don't regret it . . . That's the odd thing. Then he rang off."

Emma considered the matter. "Oh, I don't know," she said slowly. "Pa does get fussed from time to time. Thinks you do too much. And you know he's always been bored with the boys, that's why he comes down so seldom."

The helicopters were passing backwards and forwards again. One was much lower than its fellows, and its roar made further speech impossible.

"Look," said Mad, or rather shouted, "I do believe it's going to land."

The helicopter had come in low over the ploughed field, and had now skirted the hedge and was hovering above the

36

grazing-field which adjoined the garden and ran parallel with the drive. It came lower, lower, hovering like a hawk, blades whirring, the noise deafening, and then slowly, very slowly, descended and landed in the centre of the field. The blades rotated for a few moments, then ceased. The door of the helicopter opened and six or seven men got out.

"They're coming here," said Emma.

Two of the soldiers began walking across the field towards the drive. The rest remained by the helicopter. The two men climbed over the wire and crossed the lawn towards the gate. Emma glanced nervously at her grandmother. At least she hadn't got her peaked cap on, so she didn't look too much like Mao Tse-tung. Actually, with her white hair brushed upwards like that she looked rather good. Formidable, in fact. On the other hand, it might have been better if she had been dressed to suit her near-eighty years, perhaps in a sensible skirt, and worn a soft cardigan around her shoulders, preferably pale blue, instead of that Robin Hood jerkin with leather sleeves.

"What are we going to do?" asked Emma.

"Play it by ear," said Mad.

They advanced together to the steps before the front door, as they had done that morning, and the two soldiers passed through the gate and walked up the path. "Officers," murmured Mad under her breath, "you can always tell." The soldiers, officers, whatever, came to a halt and saluted. One had what Emma imagined to be a typical soldier's face, long, rather lantern-jawed, his hair beginning to go grey under his service cap. His companion was younger, round-faced, with smiling blue eyes. Emma found it natural that he should look at her rather than at her grandmother. It was the elder man who spoke.

"Colonel Cheeseman, ma'am," he said, "U. S. Marines. This is Lieutenant Sherman."

Mad did not attempt to acknowledge the introduction, or to give her own and Emma's name. She plunged at once into the business at hand.

"Have you come to apologise about the dog?" she asked.

Colonel Cheeseman stared. "Dog, ma'am?" he repeated. "What dog?"

"A posse of your men," said Mad (and surely, thought Emma, posse was a term only used in Westerns), "a posse of your men cross the ploughed field early this morning,

37

and one of them deliberately shot and killed the extremely valuable collie-dog from the neighbouring farm, which, frightened by the appalling noise of the helicopters, was running for its life. The scene was witnessed by a household of young children under my care. They were deeply shocked."

The officer looked taken aback. "Make a note of that occurrence, Lieutenant," he said. "I'm extremely sorry, ma'am, to hear of your distress. There will be an enquiry into the incident, of which I had not been informed. I have come about quite a different matter."

"Yes?" enquired Mad.

"You heard the announcement over the radio?"

"No, on my television. I know Admiral Jollif very well. He has lunched here several times."

"Ah well, ma'am, that makes my request much easier. You have a stable-block right adjacent to your property here, it appears."

"I have."

"We should like to make use of it, ma'am, with your co-operation, for twenty-four hours, possibly longer, depending upon the situation becoming stabilised, which it will undoubtedly do very shortly."

Colonel Cheeseman's tone was courteous, even deferring, yet firm.

"What you mean is," said Mad, "you want to requisition it. As the owner, I have no choice in the matter, I take it?"

Colonel Cheeseman cleared his throat. "That's putting it rather baldly, ma'am," he replied. "There would be no inconvenience to yourself or to your household. It is a matter of communications. My intention is to set up a temporary post in the building, with Lieutenant Sherman here in charge."

"I see."

The colonel was clearly getting little encouragement. The younger officer glanced apologetically at Emma, who smiled nervously.

"There's no telephone in the stables, and only one electric light bulb," said Mad, "and my car is kept in the garage alongside. If your men intend to sleep in the stables they must watch out for the garden manure which is stored there. It wouldn't make very comfortable bedding."

Emma had a sudden vision of scores of American sol-

38

diers coming to the side-door with requests for a bath, or even asking Dottie to wash their clothes.

"No problem, thank you, ma'am," said Colonel Cheeseman, "We have our own equipment."

"I see," repeated Mad.

"I am sure," continued Colonel Cheeseman, risking, for the first time, a brave attempt at a smile, though it was more in the nature of a grimace, "that I am extremely obliged to you, and that your good friend Admiral Jollif will feel as I do when he hears of your co-operation."

"I presume," said Mad, "that Admiral Jollif, like me, has to do what he's told."

The colonel stiffened. And now, of course, Emma thought, she's doing her fatal thing of going too far, of putting his back up, and instead of everybody being friendly and polite it will get awkward, the man will start requisitioning the house and we shall be put in the stables.

"Ours is a joint enterprise, ma'am," replied Colonel Cheeseman. "Our forces are in this together, as you will have heard on your television. The state of emergency will not last one moment longer than is considered necessary for your safety, and for the safety of your fellow-countrymen. Meanwhile, I will not detain you. Good day to you."

He saluted, and so did his companion, but as they turned to go Mad did a dreadful thing—she was always doing it, in front of shop-keepers, or people who asked for autographs, or anyone who suddenly bored her, and that was to say something derogatory about them before they were safely out of earshot. "Pompous ass," she said, her voice much too loud and clear. Emma went scarlet and withdrew to the hall, while her grandmother continued to stand by the front door until the two American officers had closed the gate behind them. Then she returned to the house.

"Call Joe, darling, will you," she said to Emma, "and tell him to get my car out of the garage and tuck it away in the corner under the kitchen window?"

Emma shouted for Joe, who was still steadily chopping wood in the basement. He came up the little stairway that connected with the hall, closely followed by Terry. Mad explained briefly what had happened, and Joe vanished at once to obey her instructions. Not so the Byronic Terry, his eyes bright with excitement.

"What do you want me to do?" he asked. "Shall I take

39

out the fuse that works the stable light, and turn off the outside tap?"

"No," said Mad thoughtfully, "they'd know what to do. Anyway they're self-contained. I tell you what, though. Go to the stables after Joe has brought round the car, wait there until they arrive, and then put on your charm act and say you are there to be of any assistance. Don't overdo it. Just play it cool. Try and find out what's going on."

"O.K."

Terry vanished as quickly as Joe had done and Mad went through to the kitchen, followed by her grand-daughter.

"Dottie?"

"Here, Madam."

Mad's one-time dresser, who had barely finished stacking the dish-washer and laying the kitchen table for the next repast, turned a flushed and harassed face in their direction.

"It seems those American soldiers want to camp in the stables," announced Mad. "They've just landed in the pad-dock in a helicopter."

"Oh dear," said Dottie, "however are we to manage? Will they want tea? And what about blankets? There'll never be enough to go round."

"Don't be idiotic, Dottie. These men have their own equipment. Iron rations, or whatever soldiers have, ground-sheets, field-telephones, radios, everything . . ."

Mad gestured largely, shrugging her shoulders. Anyone would think she was enjoying the situation. The other boys had dispersed to their various quarters, all but black Ben, who was hunting for crumbs under the kitchen table.

"Thank goodness," said Dottie. "We couldn't possibly have managed to feed a lot of soldiers. The baker's never called as it is, with all this emergency, and we've run out of bread. I don't know what to give the boys for tea."

"Give them cake," said Mad. Shades of Marie Antoinette, thought Emma. "I tell you what," said her grandmother, "you go and lie down, Dottie dear, you look worn out. It's been a tiring day and it will probably get worse. I will make a cake for the boys, and they can have tea with me. Find me a basin, and lots of flour and butter and sugar, and all the necessary. Eggs, have we any eggs?"

Dottie raised her eyebrows at Emma, and Emma shrugged. The thing was, Mad's cakes were terribly hit or miss, generally miss, and the net result, as Pa used to say, was like molten lead. Her one or two successes had gone to her head, but usually the effect upon everybody's digestion was damaging to the extreme, and the cakes had to be crumbled up the next day and given to the birds.

"Come on, come on," said Mad impatiently, "let's get started. If it turns out well, I've half a mind to go against my principles and ask that Colonel Cheesering or whatever he calls himself in to tea, if he's still here. I haven't heard the helicopter take off yet."

It will be his finish if you do, thought her granddaughter. She took a peep out of the kitchen window. Terry's charm was working. He was engaged in conversation with both Colonel Cheeseman and Lieutenant Sherman. They must have been discussing the household, because the two officers glanced up at the windows, and the colonel, whose voice had carrying power, said something like "You don't say? I thought there was something familiar about her face, but her costume had me puzzled." His words could mean one thing only. Terry had spilt the beans about Mad. Emma could not decide whether this was in their favour or not. Possibly it was. Americans always liked well-known people. It must help, too, knowing Admiral Jolliff. Perhaps the colonel had forgotten the remark about being a pompous ass, or if he still remembered it he would gloss it over, putting it down to Mad's great age.

"I think it's going to be all right," said Mad later, inspecting her creation, which, on emerging from the oven and being turned out of its tin, looked like a semi-inflated, khaki-coloured balloon and exuded a curious smell of burnt almonds and bitter chocolate. "It's risen, anyway. They don't always. I shall tell that American colonel it's a dough-cake. They live on dough over there. Terry's just gone out to ask him to tea."

Emma caried the silver tray through to the music-room. Mad always used the silver tray when, as Dottie expressed it, they had company.

"Where on earth are the boys?" asked her grandmother, having spread a crumpled lace table-cloth on a card-table with a rickety leg. "Call them, darling, will you?"

But only Folly, also on a rickety leg, emerged from her chair in the library. She had smelt Mad's cake. She knew, with age-old dog cunning, that most of it would fall from the company's hands on to the floor. Before Emma could summon the reluctant brood, there was the sound of the gate clicking by the front lawn. It was Terry, escorting the American officers to the front door. Flushed and self-important, he threw open the music-room door.

"Colonel Cheeseman, Madam," he announced, "come to say goodbye before taking off in the chopper."

The colonel, with the lieutenant at his heels, looked less formidable than before. His teeth were bared in a smile. Terry had evidently done his stuff.

"I won't detain you, ma'am," he said. "I just want to thank you for your courtesy. This lad of yours has been of real assistance."

"I'm so glad," answered Mad, and Emma noticed she had assumed her false voice, the one she used for answering the telephone. "You must both have a cup of tea before you go, and a slice of my home-made cake."

Her smile was gracious, the wave of her hand indicated the easy chairs close to the tea-table.

"Well, ma'am, it's hard to refuse you," said Colonel Cheeseman, "and I reckon we can spare five minutes just to taste that cake."

Terry, with a swift glance from the inflated balloon to Emma, darted from the room. "Oh, has the laddie gone?" exclaimed the colonel. "I meant to thank him too for his time and trouble."

"Don't worry," said Mad, "he'll be back. He's probably gone to tell the others that tea's ready. We're quite a large household, you know."

"So I've heard, ma'am, so I've heard." The colonel looked arch and shook his head gently at his hostess. "I said to Lieutenant Sherman just now back in your stable yard, the assignment we've been given, which, please God, will turn out to the advantage of all of us, British and Americans alike, will be doubly interesting to me personally, now I know who is the owner of the stable-block." He paused, expecting perhaps that Mad would at least incline her head. She was intent, however, on cutting a slice of the cake to proffer to her admirer.

"Oh, really," she said, frowning, "the knife must be blunt."

"I don't suppose you'll credit it," continued the colonel, "but one of my fondest boyhood memories is of your

42

whirlwind tour of the United States. It made the most profound impression on me."

Emma watched the knife finally succeed in its task. The piece of cake, like Shylock's pound of flesh, fell on to the plate. She wondered, at the same time, what Colonel Cheeseman meant by a whirlwind tour. Her grandmother had been to America several times in the past, but as far as she knew had only performed in New York.

"I'm so glad," said Mad, passing the plate to her victim, while Folly edged close to the colonel's boots. "Can you remember the play? Was it one of my late husband's?"

"No, ma'am," answered Colonel Cheeseman. "The play I am talking about dates back three centuries or more and was written by William Shakespeare. And I've never forgotten your first entrance as Lady Macbeth."

Oh heavens, thought Emma, he's boobed, he's absolutely done it. Mad had never been a Shakespearean actress, and had certainly never played Lady Macbeth either in her own country or in the United States, though she frequently imitated those of her contemporaries who had done so, as a parlour-trick to amuse the boys. She watched her grandmother, waited for the knife-edge riposte. It did not come. Mad smiled. A smile so genuine, so unforced, it seemed to embrace the world, not only the colonel.

"Then it's a memory we can share, Colonel Cheesering," she said. "I've never forgotten it either. Have some of my cake."

The impact of the one upon the other was short-lived, however, for the march of great events broke up the tea-party. The colonel had made two attempts to bite into the toy balloon, and at the third, as an unblended almond slipped from between his lips and Folly upon her rickety hind leg leapt for it, the door burst open and Terry came into the room once more.

"Dottie's just told me," he said. "She heard it on the radio that the Prime Minister is making a statement on television. He's in the middle of it now."

Everybody stood up. Mad brushed past the tea-table.

"Come through to the library," she commanded. "All of you. Terry, switch it on fast."

They grouped themselves around the television, and as they waited for the picture to appear, the colonel murmured sotto voce to his hostess, "If he says what I think he's going to say, this is a very great day for our two countries." Right on cue, as if in answer to Colonel Cheeseman, came the voice of the Prime Minister in full spate, bang in the middle of a sentence.

". . . we had no alternative, and we ask for no alternative; for the union that has been offered to us, and that we have gladly and gratefully accepted, is one which will bring new strength, new determination and new hope for the future, not only for our two peoples but for the whole of the free world." His face and shoulders appeared on the screen as his voice dropped to a more solemn note. "You will ask yourselves why we have kept silent up to now, why, in fact, we did not take you into our confidence days, even weeks, ago. My friends, we have been living through troublous times.. The breakdown of our partnership within the European community and our withdrawal from it, due to no failure on our part, brought great economic difficulties, as I feared would be the case and as I warned you at the time, and our political autonomy and military supremacy were also endangered.

"Now, thanks to our old allies and new partners, we are threatened no longer. The great combination of the United States and the United Kingdom, to be known henceforth as USUK, need fear no one. What we have to give is theirs, what they have to give is ours. We are a great and common people. I am proud to tell you that Her Majesty the Queen is at this moment on her way to Washington, to stay at the White House with the President of the United States, not only as his guest but as co-President of USUK. The President, in his turn, will enjoy a short period of office in Buckingham Palace.

"Once again, you may ask, why were the people of this great nation not informed that these momentous changes were to take place? Because"—and his voice dropped lower still—"it was essential, for the success of our enterprise, that no word of the project should become public knowledge until the union had come into being. Every loyal citizen will welcome this partnership as one of the greatest advances in our long and glorious history. But within the last few months a small minority—prompted by powerful groups in other countries with opposing interests to our own—have succeeded in causing grave disruption to our economic stability and to the peaceful rhythm of our daily

44

lives. The damage caused has been out of all proportion to the insignificant numbers of those involved, and their cunning is such that few people outside their ranks have understood the perils to which their actions were exposing our nation. We could not run the risk of allowing this small body of malcontents to jeopardise the success of our great project. This is why you have woken up this morning to find our new allies already gathered on this island. I would ask you, wherever you meet with either our own armed services or those of the United States, acting singly or together, to give them your full co-operation. More than this, give them your friendship too. Citizens of USUK— long live the President of the United States, long live the Queen, long live our great and glorious people and the heritage we share."

The Prime Minister's voice rose to a higher note, he threw back his head and squared his shoulders, and as his image faded the picture of the two flags, the Union Jack and the Stars and Stripes, took its place, accompanied by the strains of the joint national anthems.

The silence in the library was profound. The two American officers were standing to attention, or rather endeavouring to do so, for both held between their hands, like an offertory at church, the plates on which lay the uneaten slices of Mad's cake. Emma did not know whether to laugh or cry, and she looked to her grandmother for a lead. For the first time, however, this was not forthcoming. Mad's expression was inscrutable. She continued staring at the television long after the picture had dimmed and the music had died away.

The tension was broken by the sounds of children's excited laughter coming from the hall. Colin ran into the room, dragging Ben by the hand, his angel face triumphant, his eyes like stars.

"Ben can talk!" he cried. "Ben can talk! He heard the anthems on the telly and he's spoken his first word!"

Mad held out her arms to both boys, but for once they disregarded the gesture.

"I taught him," declared Colin. "It's all my doing."

Emma turned to the two American officers. "He's three years old," she explained hurriedly. "We were afraid he would never learn to speak, although he understands everything."

45

Colonel Cheeseman smiled. "I guess this is doubly an historic occasion," he said, "and I'm proud to be in on it. Come here, little fellow, and let's hear what you have to say."

Ben rolled his eyes towards Colin and Colin nodded his head. Ben wiped his mouth with the back of his hand and walked slowly forward to the colonel.

"Sh . . ." he began, "sh . . ." then paused, as though to summon greater strength.

"Come on, son don't be afraid," said Colonel Cheeseman. "This is the finest moment in your young life, and maybe in all of ours as well."

"Shit!" said Ben.

4

Officially, the state of emergency lasted through the whole of the long weekend, from the Thursday to the following Tuesday. No reason was given other than that announced by the Prime Minister, that "a small body of malcontents" had caused "grave disruption to our economic stability." The expression, Emma could not help feeling, was sinister but vague. Perhaps he meant demos in Trafalgar Square or outside the Houses of Parliament, but then there hadn't been any demos for months, because the mass of people, having voted overwhelmingly for the present Coalition Government after the referendum about withdrawing from Europe, couldn't very well demo about anything without losing face. Unemployment was still acute, prices were rising all the time, but this seemed to have become a way of life. Did union with the U.S. mean that everything would change and everyone be happy? In which case, who were the "small body of malcontents" who would wish to prevent it? It was all very puzzling. It was useless trying to discuss the matter with Mad, she refused to do so.

"I withhold comment," she said icily, "until the state of emergency is over."

Which means, decided Emma, she disapproves of the whole thing. She thinks it's phoney. Well, perhaps she is right. But one can't exactly treat it as phoney while the marines occupy the stable-block, there are barricades on the main road and the telephone is cut. The only thing you can do is to sit glued to the television and hope something will happen in between the succession of old American and British films. There were news flashes, of course. The Queen being greeted at the White House by the President, Prince Philip being welcomed by a tribe of Red Indians with whom, somewhat surprisingly, he was suddenly going to camp. The other members of the royal family were also scattered, the Princess Royal doing something with Girl Guides in Australia, the Prince of Wales commanding his destroyer in the Indian Ocean, the Duke of York seconded from his regiment to serve with the Mounted Police in Canada and Prince Edward on a mountaineering course in Scotland.

Terry, whose technical school had also closed down for the half-term, spent his time eavesdropping on the marines in the stable-block. He inferred darkly that they spent most of their time listening to pop music on a short-wave radio.

"They did let Mr. Trembath know about poor Spry," he told Emma. "The C.O. who came to tea sent the Corporal down. Corporal Wagg."

"How do you know?" asked Emma.

"The Corporal told me himself, when he came to the side-door to return the bucket," said Terry. So there *was* to-ing and fro-ing, despite Mad's instructions to the contrary. Only a matter of time, thought Emma, before they were creeping up the back stairs for cups of tea. "The Corporal said they were very pleasant to him at the farm," Terry went on, "and asked him in, and he said that if all the Cornish girls were as hot as Myrtle he's stay put when the alert was over and to hell with the marines."

"Go on with you," laughed Emma, "that was just his talk."

"Maybe," said Terry, "but I know Myrtle. You've only got to flash at her once and she's had it."

Glowering, he lumbered off to the shrubbery, where Mad had set him and Joe to cutting down the dead trees, "to keep them employed," she said. Mad herself, when not supervising the lumberjacks, had formed an association

48

with Andy and Sam in the basement, and all three of them were engaged in cleaning and sharpening the stacks of lethal arrows and restringing the bows.

"But, darling," remonstrated Emma, when the boys had run off to find fresh emery paper, "you shouldn't encourage them."

"Why ever not?" asked her grandmother, looking from her task, the weapon in her hands more dangerous than a pygmy's spear. "Andy will make a first-class shot. I wish I knew what's become of that old straw target we used to have. I'm certain he would hit the bull's eye every time."

Andy, his thatch of hair more unruly than ever, came running back again from the old scullery, and smiled when he heard Mad's remark.

"I can do better than that, Madam," he said. "I can hit an orange on a bamboo stick at fifty yards. I know, I've tried it from my watch-tower in the chimney."

"Good for you," said Mad, "but don't waste the arrows."

Oh, heavens, thought Emma, you might as well ... you might as well go stand upon the beach and bid the main-tide cease its angry flood ... Was she quoting aright? Anyway, she knew what she meant. Her grandmother was inflexible. She went up to the kitchen, hearing voices, and found, to her great surprise, that Dottie was engaged in conversation with Lieutenant Sherman. Emma felt her cheeks go red, and was furious with herself in consequence.

"Good day to you," he said, smiling.

"Good day," replied Emma, but it was not an expression she ever used and she felt a fool doing so.

"The officer has come to tell us that the state of emergency will be over tomorrow," said Dottie, "and we shall all be free to come and go as we please. That's a great relief, isn't it?"

"Yes, indeed," said Emma. "Does it mean we shall have our telephone working again and the boys can go back to school?"

Lieutenant Sherman stroked his chin. "Well, now," he replied, "as to your first question, yes, your telephone should be working normally from 6 A.M. onwards. As to the second ... I fear I've not been briefed. But I rather think your schools will remained closed until next week."

"What a nuisance," said Emma. "It's such a bind to keep them amused."

Lieutenant Sherman smiled again. "You find it so?" he asked. "I wouldn't have thought it. They seem fully occupied to me."

He winked at her, which was rather fun, she thought—though she hoped he was thinking of Joe and Terry in the shrubbery rather than Andy with his bow and arrows in the chimney. It was nice that he had a sense of humour, though actually it hadn't exactly been apparent the other day when Ben uttered his first word—Ben hadn't spoken since—but then the commanding officer had been present, and everyone was under strain, what with the P.M.'s announcement and having to eat Mad's cake. Emma wished she could ask him to come in later for a drink, but Mad might not like it, or, if she did, then she might come and pour out the drinks herself and hog the conversation.

"We'll be seeing you, then?" she said casually.

"I hope so," he answered. "By the way, my name is Wallace Sherman, known to my friends as Wally. My respects to your grandmother. I hope she's been able to rest these last days and we haven't disturbed her."

Disturbed her, you little know . . . She's sharpening arrows this moment below in the basement. Emma watched the lieutenant return to the stable-block with reluctance, but she was slightly put off by the name Wally. One couldn't imagine saying to Mad, "I'm going out with Wally tonight . . ."

There was no question of Lieutenant Wallace Sherman coming in for drinks or offering Emma iron rations in the stables, because later that evening they heard continual coming and going between the main road and the stable-yard. A couple of jeeps had now appeared on the scene, and the marines were evidently clearing up their equipment in preparation for moving off.

"Good job too," said Terry, peering out of the kitchen window into the dusk. "We don't want them hanging about here any longer."

"They'll not be going far," said Joe quietly, "only down the bottom of the hill. Corporal Wagg told me there are two commando units in our district, and they're taking over all of Poldrea sands and the docks as well. The sands are to be roped off, and they're to requisition the bathing-huts and caravans as living quarters."

"But what the hell for?" exploded Terry. "That Lieutenant Sherman said the state of emergency would be over by tomorrow."

"He didn't tell me why," replied Joe, "and I don't for a moment suppose he knew."

"It's the Communists, depend upon it," said Dottie. "I expect they'll be parachuted down from Russian aeroplanes dressed as nuns, as they did in the last war."

"I know what the Communists will do," said Colin, who had suddenly emerged from the playroom where, so it appeared from the state of the wallpaper later, he had been teaching Ben to write. "They'll swim in to Poldrea beach disguised as mermaids, lashing great rockets to their tails that are full of T.N.T. At least that's what I would do, if I were a Communist."

Ben, who was clinging to Colin's hand as usual, nodded his head vigorously in agreement, and to show he meant business pursed his lips to frame the dreaded Sh . . . Emma escaped just in time to spare herself hearing Dottie's outraged cry and Terry's shout of laughter.

That evening, when she and her grandmother were thinking of going to bed, the telephone suddenly rang.

"I'll get it," said Emma quickly. "It might be some sort of message from the stables, they could have fixed up a house-to-house line."

For lack of anything better to think about, her mind had been full of the lieutenant. She tore through to the lobby where the telephone was installed. It wasn't the lieutenant, it was Pa.

"Oh, it's you!" she exclaimed, not sure whether to be sorry or relieved. "We were told the line wouldn't be working until tomorrow morning."

"I got priority," said Pa, "no problem at all." Which was typical, of course. He liked to sound important. "Well," he asked, "how have you weathered the crisis? I don't mind telling you, things have been humming up here."

"I dare say," said his daughter. "They've been humming down here too. Helicopters roaring overhead, soldiers, Americans, everywhere—we've even had them in the stable-block, but they say they're going tomorrow. Rumour has it they've taken over all of Poldrea beach and the docks as well."

"That's right, that's right," said Pa, "a very sensible move, in the circumstances, nobody wants a lot of hooligans trying to upset the nation, not that they'd succeed. It's wonderful news, isn't it?"

"What is?" Emma asked.

"Why, the two countries forming a union. Should have happened years ago. Some of us have been advocating it ever since we boobed it in Europe. Now we've all got to make it work. There'll be some dissenters, of course, but we can soon shut them up if they try to make trouble. Tell me, is Mad behaving herself?"

"More or less," said Emma guardedly. "I mean, she's not done anything dreadful. We were all upset the first day because one of the soldiers shot poor Spry, Mr. Trembath's dog, who happened to be loose."

"Oh well, if that was the only casualty, count yourselves lucky. These chaps can be trigger-happy, you know, and you want to take damn good care not to obstruct them when they're on duty. I hope you've got that gang of yours under control."

"Yes, they're being very good."

"Well, if I'm not under too much pressure up here I might slip down to see you all, though I can't say when."

Emma wondered what the pressure could be. Floods of money either coming into, or going out of, the Bank of England, and Pa with his finger on the pulse. Her grandmother came into the lobby. "Vic?" she said, seizing the receiver from Emma.

Mother and son started talking at once, neither listening to the other, both expostulating, both arguing, which was standard practice when they were on the telephone together.

"I shall never forgive you," Mad was saying. "Of course you knew all about it, and so did Jimmy Jollif, one of you should have warned me, and then we shouldn't have been taken by surprise. Nonsense, you know how discreet I am, I wouldn't have shouted it from the roof-tops or gone round Poldrea telling everyone I met. What? I can't hear a word you're saying. No, I thought the Prime Minister was very sinister, but then he always is. And who are all these people who are going to create trouble? I don't mind telling you, I shall be amongst the first."

They banged on, parry and thrust, like a couple of prize-fighters. But time was precious and Pa's five minutes of priority evidently ran out, for Mad, clamping down the receiver, made for the stairs and bed.

"Vic will go on and on," she said, never realising that it was precisely what she did herself. "I can't think who he gets it from, certainly not from me, and his father was so quick and to the point. He's talking utter nonsense, of course. Such a ridiculous name too, USUK, makes us the laughing-stock of the world, but then we've been that for years. Em darling, if those roadblocks are down tomorrow you and I will go and do the shopping. I must find out how everyone is taking this business."

The following morning, soon after ten, Emma brought the car round to the front gate, and discovered, somewhat to her dismay, that Andy, Colin and Ben were ranged before her grandmother on the steps.

"Must we take them too?" she asked.

"Why ever not?" Mad, in full battle array, navy-blue from top to toe, Mao Tse-tung to the life, told the boys to climb into the back seat. "I see the marines have left us," she observed with a glance at the stable-block. "Well, that's a relief, at any rate. I hope they haven't gone off with the manure."

She settled herself at the driving-wheel, and Emma resigned herself to the inevitable in the seat beside her. Mad's first motion as chauffeur was generally to crash into reverse. The boys were used to it, and invariably braced themselves for the jolt.

"I feel as if we've been imprisoned for months," Mad declared, as they swerved out of the lane at the top of the hill and on to the main road, taking the corner like the driver of a bob-sleigh at St. Moritz. "Thank goodness there's nothing on the road and we've got a clear run."

It was clear, fortunately for the bob-sleigh team, until they reached the bottom of the hill, when Mad, with great presence of mind, slammed her foot on the brake and brought her craft to a halt almost immediately beneath a road-block that barred further progress. A hut had been erected at the side of the road and beside it a soldier was positioned as sentry.

"Your pass, please, ma'am," he said.

"What do you mean, my pass?" asked Mad, outraged. "Everybody knows me here, I don't have to have a pass."

The soldier—not one of their stable-block marines but American nevertheless—looked apologetic. "Sorry, ma'am, it's a regulation, came into force this morning. Where do you come from?"

"I live three minutes from here, at the top of the hill, the house called Trevanal. Your men have been quartered in my stables for the past five days."

The sentry stared. "I beg pardon, ma'am," he said. "I was there myself last night, helping to remove the gear. I didn't realise you were the lady. I'll issue you with a pass." He disappeared into his hut and came out again with a yellow sticker and two tickets. "It's just a precautionary measure, ma'am. They are being issued to all the local inhabitants. This is for the car, I'll paste it on your windscreen. These are the tickets for yourself and your companion."

"What about us?" asked Andy.

The soldier smiled and shook his head. "No one has a pass under eighteen, son," he said, "but it's O.K. if you're accompanied by an adult. Thank you, ma'am."

He lifted the barrier, and for the first time Emma could remember, her grandmother shot into the right gear and accelerated, nearly cutting off the soldier's foot. He backed swiftly into his hut.

"I've never heard such utter nonsense in my life," exploded Mad. "Who do they think they are, ordering us about on our own highway?"

"Look," said Colin excitedly, pointing to the sands, "they've got a barrier there too, and wire all round, and there are soldiers everywhere."

He was right. Poldrea sands, the delight of tourists in mid-summer and refuge of local inhabitants in winter as an exercising ground for dogs, had become an encampment over the weekend, with notices everywhere saying "U. S. Marines. No Admittance."

Mad brought the car to a standstill outside the Poldrea supermarket. She got out of the car and swept past the swing-door, Emma and he boys behind her. The supermarket was full and the clatter and noise were deafening, like the bird-house at a zoo. Inevitably, as on every occasion when there has been crisis, all wished to give an account of his or her own experiences during the weekend.

"I was just sitting down to tea, and I said to Father . . ."

"Sleep? I couldn't close my eyes. And the roar . . ."

"Takes me back to wartime, I said to Jim, seeing all

these fellows around, and they say they're going to be here weeks. It's the threat, you see, of what might happen if they packed up. Jim says . . ."

Mad swept purchase after purchase into her wire basket, and ended up beside the salesman who sliced the ham—when in doubt, Mad always said, one can live on cold ham. She fixed him with a cold blue eye. He was not a local man, but had been sent down from Bristol when the supermarket first started.

"Well," she said, "what do you make of the invasion?"

"Invasion?" he queried, then smiled. "Now, you mustn't call it that. I've been telling my wife it will be the saving of the country. We should have done it months ago, years ago, even."

"Oh, really?" asked Mad. "Why?"

"Well . . ." He considered the matter as he sliced the ham. "It stands to reason, doesn't it? They're like our own people, aren't they? We all speak English. It's a wonderful thing for the English-speaking countries to get together. America, Australia, South Africa, ourselves . . . you won't get the foreigners trying to push us around now."

"Aren't we being pushed around at the moment?" said Mad. "I've just been issued with a pass coming down Poldrea hill. No one to be allowed to move without a pass."

"Security," said the Bristol ham-slicer, and looking over his shoulder dropped his voice to a whisper. "You'd be surprised the things they say. Oh, not just that the continentals might be slipping over to make trouble, but our own people, folk like you and I, just biding their time to upset the Coalition Government, or make things awkward for the Americans. We must all be on our guard."

"Yes," said Mad, "I think we must."

Emma, who had been keeping a close watch on the boys in case they slipped something into their pockets and not into the wire basket, followed her grandmother out of the supermarket. Mad was looking rather grim.

"Where now?" asked Emma.

"I think I'll have a word with Tom," said Mad. Tom was the fishmonger, and had fished the waters of Poldrea, man and boy, for fifty years. "Well, Tom?" This time Mad's eye was not so cold. She was fond of Tom. "How do you like living in a state of siege?"

"Don't fancy it one bit," was the answer from the grey-haired skipper of the *Maggie May*. "They'm turning the country upside down. And what's more, tryin' to boss we. I don't hold with it. And what do they think they'm to out there in the bay—diggin' for sand-eel?"

Mad smiled. "We used to do it half a century ago," she said. "They call it showing the flag. It's to impress the natives."

Tom shook his head. "It might impress some folk," he said. "It's don't impress me. I've lived too long." He looked down at his flabby wares displayed on the slab. "Nothing here to tempt you, my dear," he said. "Caught Wednesday and been on the ice ever since. They've lost their bite, like the speakers up Whitehall. Will you go to the meeting?"

"What meeting?"

"There's notices posted round the town. Meeting at town hall seven o'clock. Questions from the general public to be answered by our Member and this Yankee colonel who's in charge."

"Ah ha!" said Mad, and she turned to her grand-daughter. "I've a very good mind to attend."

Emma's heart sank. She knew exactly what would happen. Mad would make remarks under her breath, or not under her breath, the entire time people were asking questions. And the M.P. for the constituency was one of her bêtes-noires. She was a woman, for one thing, and had called at Trevanal a few years previously before the bye-election, supremely confident that Mad would be willing to make large contributions to the party. She was duly elected, but she did not succeed in bringing Mad to the polls.

"Two more calls," said Chairman Mao to her followers. "The post office and the Sailor's Rest."

The queue at the post office was almost as long as the one at the supermarket, but Mad never minded queues. She said it gave her a feeling of solidarity. Also she adored getting her pension. "It makes me feel rich," she told Emma, and kept it inside a money-box shaped as a pig, then doled it out to the boys as pocket-money on Saturdays.

Feelings about the state of alert over the weekend were mixed inside the post office. Some of the queuers, like the ham-slicing salesman in the supermarket, thought it a very good thing, others shook doubtful heads. The district nurse, who was sister-in-law to Mr. Trembath at the farm adjoining Mad's domain, was one of the doubtful ones. More than this, she was angry.

"They cut my phone," she said to Mad, "and Mrs. Ellis's baby was due, and when I tried to get across the valley Saturday night they wouldn't let me through. Apologies, of course, this morning. Issued with a pass. Luckily the baby didn't arrive, but if it had . . ."

"It might have been born with two heads," said Colin, who had a habit of butting in on adult conversations.

"Have you been in touch with your brother-in-law?" asked Mad, ignoring the interruption.

The district nurse nodded. "Spoke to him just now," she said, then lowered her voice. "They're very upset about poor Spry."

"I know," said Mad, "so are we."

She left the post office with her wealth, and they proceeded by car to the Sailor's Rest. Originally erected as a public-house for seamen, dockers, clay-workers and locals about a century ago, it had transformed itself into a trendy pub for the two-car, coloured-television types, who would drive over of an evening and swap wives. Mr. Libby, the landlord, had made a good thing out of it since the licensing laws had been relaxed, and positioned as the pub was, near to the sands, it would be interesting, Mad observed to Emma as they parked outside before picking up their crate of cider, to discover Mr. Libby's sentiments. The pub was already filled with American marines and they turned as one man and stared at Emma, who felt relieved that her grandmother had remained in the car. The landlord, from behind his bar, seemed in high spirits.

"Come for your cider, love?" he called. "I'm a bit pressed right now. Send Joe down for it later."

"We want it now," said Emma firmly, and turned on her heel. She could hardly believe her own voice. She might have been Mad herself. One of the marines whistled as she made her exit. In a few moments Mr. Libby emerged carrying the crate of cider. Mad put her head out of the car window.

"Busy?" she asked.

He winked. "I'll say," he answered. "With these chaps at my door I'll do a roaring trade, better than I ever do with the tourists. I hope they stay forever."

He lifted the crate into the boot and waved his hand.

57

"H'm," said Mad as she turned the car towards the hill. "I can only count two for certain who are on our side, and that's dear old Tom Bate and the district nurse."

"What do you mean, on our side?" asked Emma.

"Well, it's pretty obvious, isn't it?" replied her grandmother. "The situation is rapidly becoming one of Them and Us."

5

The town hall was packed. The notice on the outside said that householders only would be admitted, and this foresight on the part of the organisers had eliminated many of the possibly rowdier elements, and certainly the younger age-group, who were being turned away disconsolate. Mad, sizing up the scene instantly, held on to Emma's arm and began to limp.

"I'm seventy-nine," she explained to the attendant at the door, who failed to recognise her—he must have been one of the Member's minions from Truro. "I can't manage without help from my grand-daughter."

The attendant waved them on respectfully, and pushing forwards, the limp lessening with every step she took, Mad glimpsed the familiar faces of Mr. and Mrs. Trembath somewhere in the centre of the crowd. In a moment she was tapping the farmer on the shoulder.

"Let's all sit together," she said. "I want to talk to you anyway."

Jack Trembath was a big man with powerful shoulders, who used to wrestle for Cornwall against Brittany in his younger days. He was still under fifty, and even now would have thrown many a younger opponent. The four of them sat down near to the gangway in the middle of the hall, Mad with Emma on one side of her and the farmer on the other.

"What are they going to tell us?" hissed Mad in a whisper so loud that it carried at least four rows ahead, and people turned round.

"I know darn well what they're going to say," replied Jack Trembath, "and that is that we're to behave ourselves and do as we're told."

"Or else?" queried Mad.

"Or else," he repeated. He hesitated a moment, and then he whispered in her ear. "You know they shot poor Spry?"

"I saw them do it. That's what I wanted to tell you. It was over at once. I went out later and buried him. He's just beyond the gap in the hedge."

He turned and looked at her. "I wish I'd known," he said. "I'd have spared you that job. Never mind, I'll repay you one of these days. My feeling is that there's more trouble to come. It's all been done too sudden, in my opinion. I may be wrong, I hope I am, but I don't like it."

"Nor do I," replied Mad, and she pinched Emma's arm. "That makes three who feel as we do—you, your sister-in-law and Tom Bate."

Jack Trembath smiled. "Ah, Tom," he said. "There's a good man to have to your side in a scrap. Plenty of belly to him."

The hum of voices ceased. The speakers were coming on to the platform. Emma wondered if everyone was supposed to stand, as in church, but nobody did, which was just as well because her grandmother, who had been persuaded greatly against her will to get into a dress at the last minute, under an old tweed coat, had put it on back to front, finding it more comfortable that way, and the zip had snapped coming down in the car, revealing a cast-off vest of Terry's. No such borrowed clothing adorned the Member of Parliament. Mrs. Honor Moorhouse was a very good-looking woman and she knew it. She was escorted by Colonel Cheeseman, smart and erect in his uniform, and another woman whom neither Emma nor her grandmother had seen before.

The proceedings were opened by the Commander of Marines himself.

"Good friends one and all," he began, "I am not here on this platform to detain you any longer than is necessary." (He's so keen on not detaining people, Emma thought—that's what he said to Mad when he arrived from the helicopter.) "I'm just here to say thank you for your steady nerves and your kind co-operation during the past six days. It wasn't easy for you, and we knew it wouldn't be easy, but we had a job to do, and because of the way you've backed us up that job has been completed. It's true that you will have us with you for a while —security precautions make this necessary; but I know, from what I've seen already, that we're going to have a grand time together. I'm ashamed to say it, but only today I learnt your Cornish motto 'One and All.' Now that's just one of the finest mottoes I've ever heard, and it's going to apply to all of us right here, in this little section of your beautiful west country. Friends, this lovely lady doesn't require any introduction from me. Your member, Mrs. Honor Moorhouse."

The gallant Commander of Marines stood back and the Member of Parliament rose to her feet. She had a sheaf of papers in her hand but she did not consult them. She was evidently fully briefed, and indeed it was her confident manner and capable handling of statistics that had won her the seat in parliament.

"Ladies and gentlemen, fellow Cornishmen and women, we live in stirring times . . ."

"Oh God," murmured Mad to her companions, "I know exactly what she is going to say from beginning to end."

The Hon. Member for Mid-Cornwall went over the events of the past weekend, and elaborated on the necessity for U.S. intervention and the forming of the union between the two countries. Everyone had heard it on the radio and television from the Prime Minister, but somehow, because she was a woman, and was speaking to her constituents in their own town hall at Poldrea, she made it all sound more intimate, more parochial, as if the creation of USUK had come about for their especial benefit. After all, London was "up country" and still some distance away, despite the motor-way, and nobody really minded what happened in the east or the north or the midlands, so long as the people who lived there came west for their holidays. It made them all feel they were the centre of attention, beaches roped off, barricades on the main road. It was new, it was sensational, it gave them a feeling of importance. Men squared their shoulders as Mrs. Moorhouse spoke, women lifted their heads and wondered where she had bought her smart lime-green jersey suit; and as their Member continued, with eloquent phrases tripping off her tongue, about the lassitude into which the country had fallen, the lack of backbone amongst the young, the apathy of the middle-aged and the dismal plight of the old, all of which could be changed and whipped into a frenzy of new life through union with "our cousins from across the Atlantic" (rather like the Biblical phrase, thought Emma—was it St. Paul?—"we shall all be changed in the twinkling of an eye"), cries of "Hear, hear!" rang through the hall and a young woman in front of Emma began to cry.

"Wait for it," whispered Mad. "We shall have the English-speaking peoples in a moment, and enemies within our midst who would destroy all tradition, all sentiment, all those things which our forefathers and the Pilgrim fathers strove for when they sailed in the little Mayflower . . ."

Emma waited, and it came. Even the bit about the Pilgrim fathers.

"And so," Mrs. Moorhouse continued, her voice rising to a higher pitch as she wound to her conclusion, "before I introduce our good friend Martha Hubbard, here on the platform beside me, who has flown over from New England especially to talk to you, I want to remind you once again of what the Prime Minister told us last week—that, if we are to survive, we must give the forces of the United States, here in our midst, our full co-operation and our friendship too. More than this, we must be on our guard against subversive tongues, and one and all put our shoulders to the wheel to make our contribution to USUK."

She paused, to be greeted by a storm of applause from her listeners nearest to the platform. The middle rows were possibly more moderate in their enthusiasm, and the stamping of feet from those who were standing at the back could have been taken either way. The clapping died away, and the Member, with a smile of encouragement, looked at her supporters and said, "Any questions?"

Emma, with horror, felt her grandmother move beside her, and before she could tug at the half-zipped frock Mad was on her feet.

"I am sure we are all very grateful to you, Mrs. Moorhouse, for speaking to us this evening, but I would like to know—and I hope you don't think it impertinent of me—but when did you last put a shoulder to the wheel, and what wheel was it that you actually moved?"

There was a murmur throughout the hall; somebody cried, "Shame!" and the voice of a spectator at the rear of the building, sounding uncommonly like that of Tom Bate, the fish-monger, shouted, "Go to it, me old 'and-some."

The Member for Mid-Cornwall, trained to deal with heckling, remained unruffled. She did not immediately recognise the strange-looking elderly woman who confronted her from the middle of the hall. Some eccentric, she supposed, who had come to the meeting after a prolonged session at the nearest public-house.

"A figure of speech," she said, smiling graciously, "not very original, perhaps, but I am sure everyone knows what I meant."

Those standing at the back of the hall were beginning to enjoy themselves and to express their enjoyment in laughter, which was not what the organisers of the meeting had intended. All said and done, it was a serious occasion. Emma, scarlet with embarrassment, stared at the back of the man immediately in front of her. Mrs. Moorhouse turned to Colonel Cheeseman with a little shrug of her shoulder and a raised eyebrow. Colonel Cheeseman, even more embarrassed than Emma because he had recognised, in the questioner halfway down the hall, the figure and features of the Lady Macbeth who had entertained him to tea, whispered into the Member of Parliament's ear. Illumination appeared upon her features. She nodded, and her smile vanished.

"May I remind the questioner," she said, "that I am here to answer questions of a serious and practical nature, and this is not a theatre or a music-hall."

"I know that only too well," replied Mad. "If it were, I should be up on the stage where you are, and you perhaps, though not necessarily, would be down here." (Cheers from Tom Bate and several of his cronies.) "However," Mad went on, "I should like to ask a question of a serious and practical nature, and it is this. If we are to give the gallant forces of the United States our full co-operation and friendship, will they guarantee in return *not* to shoot our farm dogs, and to permit all of us, men, women and children, free access to the roads, towns and beaches that belong to us?"

This time the applause from the back of the hall was deafening. Mrs. Moorhouse made a little gesture of resignation and turned to the Commander.

Colonel Cheeseman stood up, conciliation written all over his lantern face.

"Dear lady," he said, addressing himself to Mad, and his tone was indulgent, suggesting he knew, and the spectators knew, that the question had been put by someone for whom they all had affection and respect, but after all she was touching eighty, was understood to be rather odd, and was possibly suffering from a state of delayed shock.

"Dear lady, I was, and am, grateful to you for your hospitality, as I told you, when I had the pleasure of taking tea with you last week. I also told you at the time that I knew nothing then of the unfortunate incident of the farm dog. The matter was later reported to me, the necessary action was taken, and compensation has been paid to the owner. But—and this I must repeat again and again—we are determined, and your government is determined, that all measures must be taken to maintain law and order in every part of the United Kingdom. Nobody in Cornwall, or in the rest of your wonderful country, wants to see a repetition here of the violence that has taken place in other parts of the world, and it is because of this that a small measure of freedom must be curtailed at the present time. Believe me, it is for your good, for the good of your neighbours. No harm will come to anyone who goes about his business in a peaceable, orderly fashion. We are here to assist you, not to repress you. USUK must be made to work, and we are here to see that in the west country, as well as elsewhere, it works one hundred per cent. I hope, dear lady, that answers your question."

Mad did not reply immediately. Possibly she was reminded of days long past when, standing in the centre of the stage, she had a final line to deliver before the curtain fell. A slow, singularly mocking smile appeared upon her lips. She allowed her eyes to travel the length and breadth of the hall, until they rested once more upon the colonel.

"Yes," she said slowly, "it most certainly does, and, what is more, it confirms me in the opinion which I have held ever since the first helicopter flew over my house on Thursday morning—that the exercise you are engaged upon has been planned by your government and ours, with the backing of financiers in the United States and the United Kingdom, for many, many months, and that it is nothing more nor less than the biggest take-over bid the world has ever seen. Whether it succeeds or fails, the future will show."

She touched Jack Trembath on the sleeve and he rose to his feet, quick on cue like a fellow-actor. So did his wife and Emma likewise, and the four of them walked slowly down the gangway amid a silence only known in days long vanished at the Theatre Royal. It was not until they were safely outside the town hall that the uproar started. Cheers and counter-cheers, protests and whistles, calls for order smothered by the stamping of feet.

"That's cooked his goose for the evening, and hers too," said Mad with satisfaction. "Now we can all go home."

She waited until the noise had subsided, then proceeded towards the car, followed by the Trembaths. Others flocked from the building, amongst them Tom Bate.

"Lovely job, m'dear," he said to Mad. "As good as a play."

Back in the town hall order had been restored, and the salesman from the supermarket who had sliced the ham for Mad earlier that day had risen to his feet. He wanted to know what effect the presence of the marines would have upon the tourist season next summer if they were still occupying the caravans and the bathing-huts on Poldrea beach.

6

When Emma went in to her grandmother the following morning she found Mad sitting up in bed intent upon the local newspaper, which was spread out on the bed in front of her.

"It's here," said Mad delightedly, "bang in the middle of the centre page. 'Famous actress holds floor at local meeting. Pertinent question asked. Is nation being subjected to a take-over bid?' So you see, I've started something, and a jolly good thing too."

She leant back on her pillows triumphant. Emma was reminded of days long past when as a child she had gone into her grandmother's bedroom in London, and found her gloating over the notices of the new play in which she had performed the night before. Now, touching eighty, notoriety in the Poldrea town hall had become an equal triumph.

"What else do they say?" asked Emma, leaning over the bed.

"Read it," said Mad. "I'm going to have my bath. Oh, there's nothing else about our part in it—after all, we're small beer, and so is Poldrea—but read the leader about the state of the country as a whole, and what's likely to happen. Freedom of the press, my eye! The editor's been bought."

Emma settled herself on the bed while her grandmother went into the bathroom. It was true, there was only the very small paragraph about the meeting in the town hall, but the headline did stand out with its "Famous Actress Sensation." If by any chance it got picked up by the national press they would have Pa on the line again. She turned to the leading article. No mention of Mad here, of course, but a great welcome for USUK, which, so the writer insisted, was to be the saving of the country, since the fiasco of the entry into Europe some years previously. "At last we can hold up our heads . . . not a small off-shore island but part of a vast union of English-speaking peoples, etc., etc." Emma skipped through it, because she seemed to have been reading this sort of thing ever since she had started reading newspapers at the age of thirteen, and it was all so *boring*.

She turned to the news itself, and the whole thing of the union certainly was rather overwhelming, because apparently the U.S. troops were everywhere, standing by at power-stations, telephone switchboards, T.V. studios, along with the U.K. forces and the police, in case, so it said, there should be trouble from the mysterious subversive elements everyone kept on talking about. But the welcome from all sections of the population was tremendous. "At last, at last . . ." people were saying, from financiers in the city (Pa, thought Emma) down to the old-age pensioners (not Mad). There was plenty more about free movement between the countries, joint nationality, jobs for all, opportunities open to young people, a common culture; and it seemed that Australia, New Zealand and South Africa were also to have some sort of stake in USUK—the paper did not specify quite what, but there was a rather sinister allusion to the nuclear deterrent, and how USUK could wholly control the present situation. Australia, southern and central Africa, the United States and Great Britain would then have nuclear command all the way from the Atlantic to the Indian oceans.

"I don't follow all this nuclear stuff," Emma called to her grandmother in the bathroom. "Do you?"

"Yes," shouted Mad. "You remember what they wanted to do in Europe—make it a third force? Well, the idea fizzled out, some people blamed the left-wingers, others blamed the right. Anyway, the Europeans didn't agree. Now, reading between the lines, I'd say we have it here, the nuclear deterrent, with the U.S., the South Africans and the Australians. Four compass-points of destruction. Very pretty."

Emma shrugged and began to make Mad's bed. She had grown up with the word nuclear deterrent, and it meant those things rearing out of the ground and blasting off missiles thousands of miles distant that could wipe out whole areas and their populations. There was nothing anybody could do about it, except invent anti-missiles, and then somebody else had to invent an anti-anti-missile. There was no end to it. Perhaps the U.S. forces were going to cordon off Poldrea beach so that builders and technicians could install an anti-anti-anti-missile . . .

Mad came back from the bathroom, dressed this morning as a Siberian peasant prior to the Russian revolution. The baggy bloomers had been purloined years ago—they had formed part of the wardrobe for a provincial tour of *The Cherry Orchard*. She surveyed herself in the looking-glass with satisfaction. The heavy goat-chain round her waist gave the finishing touch to serfdom. (Mad had allowed Joe to keep goats once, but had given them away when the largest had found its way on to her bed.) Alexei Vladavitch was ready for battle.

"Madam?"

It was Dottie at the bedroom door in her usual post-breakfast state of bustle.

"What is it, Dottie?"

"There's that Lieutenant Sherman suddenly turned up, and he has a lady with him, an American lady, he introduced her to me as a Mrs. Hubbard. I had to show them into the music-room but I said I wasn't sure if you were up. I can easily say you are still in bed."

"Let me go," said Emma quickly, "I can cope."

"Nonsense," said Mad, "we'll both go. Mrs. Hubbard . . . Wasn't that the name of the woman sitting between Colonel Chessering and the Member at last night's meeting?"

69

"Yes," replied Emma, "I believe it was."

"H'm," observed Mad, twitching at the goat-chain, "we'll soon get rid of her."

She led the way downstairs with a determined air and, followed by her grand-daughter, advanced into the music-room. Lieutenant Sherman was standing at ease, but he sprang to attention as she entered. Mrs. Hubbard, a pleasant-looking woman of about forty-five with a rush of teeth to the head, was staring in ecstasy at the dried hydrangea heads that filled the vases. She turned towards the Russian serf who confronted her and held out both her hands.

"Martha Hubbard," she proclaimed, introducing her-self like someone at the captain's table on a pleasure cruise, "and many, many apologies for intruding upon your privacy. I'm so enchanted by your flower arrange-ment that I've hardly breath to speak. My, my, what a lovely home you have! And is this dear spotted doggie your especial pet?"

Folly had limped into the room from the library, and advancing towards the stranger smelt her stockings. The result must have been disappointing, for her tail drooped and she turned away to leap into the nearest chair.

"She's a bitch," said Mad, "nearly fifteen years old, blind and deaf, which I shall probably be in a few years' time. This is my grand-daughter, Emma."

"How do you do, dear," smiled Martha Hubbard. She turned once more to Mad. "Now, I don't want to take up too much of your time, but I do want you to know how sorry I am that you did not stay for the rest of the meet-ing last night. I did understand your natural feelings, and my heart went out to you. You are someone for whom I've had a great admiration for many years, if you'll pardon my saying so, and all I want to do, right here and now, is to try and explain our programme to you and win your sympathy."

"Programme?" asked Mad, assuming a puzzled expres-sion. "Are the Forces going to give us some sort of entertainment?"

Oh Lord, thought Emma, she's going to do her vague thing, and deliberately misunderstand every word this Hubbard woman says. She glanced at Lieutenant Sherman, who had coloured slightly and was still standing at attention. "Please do sit down," she said hurriedly. After all, one had to be hospitable.

Martha Hubbard's rush of teeth appeared to stretch from ear to ear. "I don't know what the Forces have in mind," she said, shaking her head gently at Lieutenant Sherman. "I don't represent the Services, and I'm not political either. No, I'm just a member of CGT, the association which is over here on special duties for USUK. We are to form branches right through the country, and this is where you can help us."

"CGT?" repeated Mad, and this time her puzzled air was not assumed. "The letters sound familiar, or have I got them the wrong way round? Didn't we have a GTC some years ago? Girls Training Corps? I can't remember what they did, but it was something to do with Girl Guides."

Martha Hubbard continued smiling. At least, it wasn't exactly a smile but the way her mouth was formed, like the man in the French thriller *L'Homme Qui Rit.*

"No, dear," she said, and Emma felt that the "dear" was a bit daring, but people were inclined to use it to elderly people, "no, dear, this is not GTC but CGT, quite a different thing. The letters stand for Cultural-Get-To-gether. The people of the United States and the United Kingdom. The association is designed to bring us one and all into a harmonious and meaningful relationship."

She paused for breath, the breath that had been taken away by the flower arrangement of the dried hydrangea heads.

"Cultural-Get-Together," said Mad thoughtfully. "Well, that sounds very interesting. Something like the Women's Institute, perhaps? Swapping recipes and showing coloured slides? I have some excellent recipes in the kitchen drawer, and some old coloured slides of my husband's tucked away somewhere."

"No, no," Martha Hubbard hastened to explain. "I feel sure these things would be of interest to our members too, but I was thinking of a more intellectual approach. The reading of plays, books, poems, the interchange of drama, philosophy, the mutual discussion of the great problems of today that engage our thoughts and motivate our lives."

71

"Motivate, motivate," murmured Mad, and then, "Oh, you mean *direct*. The problems that direct our lives?" She still looked puzzled.

"You, with your great dramatic powers and your knowledge of stagecraft," continued Martha Hubbard, "you could bring so much to the movement. There is the problem of increased leisure too. I don't know if it is yet common knowledge, but I understand your government and ours, acting in partnership, are to create a Ministry of Leisure, which will be of special significance to you all in the west country."

"Oh?" said Mad. "Because of our high rate of unemployment? You mean the people out of work don't know how to fill their time? I wouldn't have called that a problem of leisure myself."

"USUK has tremendous plans for all of you," smiled Martha Hubbard. "We know how you depend, ever increasingly, on the tourist trade, and the CGT movement intends to help with that too. Why, take this little bit of Cornwall alone—you haven't started to develop its historical potentiality. Some of our people are highly enthusiastic about it, since they've heard of the association with Tristan and Isolde, and King Arthur too, very naturally. Pageants, displays, the local inhabitants dressed up possibly in the costumes of the times—you could stage the arrival of Tristan with his uncle's bride from Ireland right here on Poldrea beach."

Mad continued to look thoughtful, which Martha Hubbard took as a sign of encouragement. The retired and aged star was evidently impressed.

"Don't you see," she went on, warming to her theme, "that what you have to sell here in the U.K. is not sunshine or bathing beaches, but historical background. Why," she turned to Emma and the lieutenant too, "the whole of the west coast from north Wales down to Cornwall here can be developed as one vast leisure-land. With the good Welsh folk dressed in their old costumes, tall hats and cloaks, serving potato-cakes to the tourists from the States, they wouldn't be talking any more of unemployment. The same in Cornwall. Now, we in the States don't need to purchase your clay, but construct a miniature Switzerland

72

out of your white mountains and train your unemployed as ski instructors and sleigh-drivers..."

"I beg your pardon," interrupted Mad, "did you say slave-drivers?"

"No, dear, sleigh. They run on rollers, very picturesque. I tell you, I'm just bubbling over with ideas for the USUK Cultural-Get-Together, and with your assistance as president of the local branch..."

She broke off in mid-sentence, because the door burst open and Colin and Ben charged into the room.

"Ben has learnt a new word," shouted Colin.

"Oh no," said Emma swiftly, "we don't want to hear that. Come along, boys, I'll take you to the playroom, Madam is busy, she can't have you in here at the moment."

But Martha Hubbard, struck dumb at the sight of a golden-haired cherub holding a small dark boy by the hand, leant forward in her chair and beckoned them towards her.

"You little darlings, you," she said. "Do you eat candy? Does Grandma there allow you to eat candy?"

Colin frowned. He had never heard the word candy in his life. Did the person with teeth mean candles? He flashed a look at Emma, who was plainly ill-at-ease, and then at Madam, who encouraged him with a wink and a brief nod of the head.

"Madam is Emma's grandmother," he said, "not mine. We use candles when there is an electric cut but Dottie doesn't like them, she says they're dangerous and spill grease on the floor. I've never tried eating them."

Martha Hubbard threw back her head and laughed. "Candles?" she exclaimed. "Isn't he cute? No, when I say candy, dear, I mean sugar-sticks. See?" She dived into her bag and brought forth two sticks of pink-and-white rock. "I heard there were boys in this house, so I came well-prepared." She presented a stick each to Colin and Ben, and dived once more into the capacious bag. "And I've something else for you besides candy. In fact, I've brought quite a collection of these, to put on your car and wave in the air when you go walking. All the children in the neighbourhood will be presented with them besides you little fellows."

She drew out of the bag a bunch of flags and shook them in front of Colin's eyes. At first Emma thought they were Union Jacks and Stars and Stripes mixed up together, but as Martha Hubbard spread them out she saw that the flags were of a new design, and bore the Union Jack and the Stars and Stripes side by side. The effect was somewhat dazzling, if hardly harmonious.

"Flown over from the States last night," declared the proud presenter, "thousands of them. In a larger size they'll be erected on all your public buildings, and on ours too."

"Good God!" said Mad.

Luckily she said it sotto voce, and Martha Hubbard was so engaged in pressing the flags upon the boys that she did not hear the murmured exclamation. Lieutenant Sherman did, though. He looked rather awkward and rose to his feet.

"We mustn't keep you," he said. "I know you have a lot to do. Colonel Cheeseman's compliments, though, and to tell you that he understands the local children missed their Guy Fawkes celebrations and their bonfire over the weekend because of the state of alert. He begs pardon for this, and would I tell you we'll be building a bonfire for the local children tonight, and your boys will be very welcome. We will supply the fireworks."

"How kind of Colonel Cheeseman," replied Emma. "I'm sure my grandmother ..."

She glanced nervously at Mad, without the slightest idea what the reaction would be, but to her surprise, and to her relief as well, Mad smiled at the lieutenant.

"How thoughtful of Colonel Cheesering," she said. "As he is supplying the fireworks, my boys and I will bring the guy."

Oh dear, wondered Emma, what on earth will she think up now, but Lieutenant Sherman seemed delighted and thanked her warmly.

But Martha Hubbard had not finished with Ben, who was still staring at her from over the pink-and-white rock. She wished to show that, despite anything Britishers might think, she, Martha Hubbard, Boston-born, had no colour prejudice.

"You haven't thanked me for the candy, honey," she said, "but before you do, you're going to give me such a

74

hug, and you're going to put those little arms right round my neck . . ."

Ben rolled his eyes and drew in his breath. "F . . ." he began, "f . . ."

Emma rushed forward and snatched him up in her arms. "He's terribly shy of strangers," she said quickly, "I'll say thank you for him." And before Ben could utter she had borne him out of the room and into the kitchen, where Terry and Andy waited expectantly.

"Did he say it?' asked Terry, eyes dancing.

"No," shouted Emma, "he did *not*. And if there's any more trouble from any one of you I'll go straight to Madam and tell her what you've been teaching Ben, that is, as soon as the visitors have gone."

"Don't worry," smiled Terry, "she knows all about it."

Emma crashed the kitchen door behind her and found Lieutenant Sherman waiting for her in the hall.

"Your grandmother is very kindly going to show Mrs. Hubbard round the house," he said, "and introduce her to the other kids."

I can't cope, thought Emma. None of the beds will have been made, Dottie will have her face on, and if the little boys don't say something frightful the middle boys will.

"In that case," she said, "my grandmother won't need me. Would you like to come into the garden?"

"I sure would," replied the lieutenant, his relief at getting away from the two women in the music-room almost as great as hers, and then, as soon as they were safely outside, he added, "I wish you'd call me Wally. It sounds more friendly somehow than Lieutenant Sherman."

"All right, I will," said Emma, opening the side-door that led to the shrubbery, and they ran full tilt into Joe with a wheelbarrow full of logs.

"Hi," said the lieutenant.

"Morning," nodded Joe.

He looks disapproving, thought Emma. How ridiculous, it's not my fault if the place is swarming with marines.

"Im's just going to take the lieutenant to the end of the garden to show him the look-out," she said unnecessarily.

A silly remark, considering he had flown over it dozens of times in the helicopter. Joe did not answer, but turned his wheelbarrow towards the kitchen-garden.

75

"Anything wrong?" asked her companion. "He looks put out."

"Oh, Joe's always uncommunicative," replied Emma, "quite different from Terry."

"It could be," suggested the lieutenant slyly, "that he doesn't like you taking a walk with me?"

"Joe?" Emma stared at him, then laughed. "Listen, we've all been brought up together. You've probably noticed, it's a funny household."

They came to the walk overlooking the ploughed field of unhappy memories. There was still a certain amount of activity around the warship in the bay.

"I'll tell you something I have noticed," said Wally, "and that is that none of us are very welcome here with your grandmother. She made it darn clear to everybody last night down in Poldrea."

"Oh, she didn't mean it," said Emma hastily. "What I want to explain is that you know how old people get, so set in their ways, and you must admit that it's all been terribly sudden and overwhelming, this USUK business. You can't really blame her."

"I don't blame her," he answered, "I only regret her attitude. You see, we're here to help everyone to make the whole union go smoothly. And your grandmother is so well-known in this district that a welcome from her would make our work that much easier. People would listen to her, locally."

Emma considered the matter. "I don't think they would," she said. "I mean, she's not that sort of person. She really only lives for the boys nowadays."

"And for you?"

"And for me."

The lieutenant smiled. "I guess when your grandmother was young she looked a lot like you," he said.

"Thank you," said Emma, "you couldn't pay me a greater compliment."

They retraced their steps and waited in front of the house for the tour of inspection to finish.

"Tell me," asked Emma, "without giving away security or anything, is it really necessary to have those road-blocks, and passes, and the ship out there, with the helicopters buzzing about, and all your men so thick on the ground? I mean, if we're united now, what's it for?"

Lieutenant Sherman looked grave. "For just exactly that," he said, "to ensure that the union is solid, right from the start. We can't afford to let it go wrong. There have been too many half-measures taken between nations during the past decade. See the mess they've gotten into in Europe, falling out amongst themselves, although it hasn't come to war yet."

"They're only in a mess economically," said Emma. "That's why we ratted on them, I suppose."

"I don't think you ratted on them, if that's the way you put it, for economics alone," replied the lieutenant. "You had strategic misgivings, or rather your government did. As I understand it, USUK is your only hope. We could get by on our own, but you couldn't."

Emma was silent. He seemed to be saying what she had read in the newspapers that morning. She felt suddenly perplexed, uncertain of everything. It sounded very much like what Mr. Trembath had said in the town hall to Mad the night before. "We've got to behave ourselves or else . . ."

"Anyway," said Lieutenant Sherman with a smile, "you're far too young and far too pretty to concern yourself with grim things that may never happen. Will you come to our firework party down on the beach? We'll give you a fine display, I promise you that."

"Yes," said Emma, "I'll come, if it's only to keep an eye on my grandmother."

Mad and the lady from Boston came out of the house on the path, and it seemed to Emma that Mrs. Hubbard's smile was not quite so broad as it had been before the tour of inspection. She looked rather fatigued, and she was scribbling something in a notebook.

"Just one more thing," she said to Mad. "Now, the name of your lovely home is Trevanal. You tell me Tre is the prefix for home, then what does vanal mean?"

"Oh, tithes," explained Mad with a lavish gesture. "A tithe-barn is a skybervanal, but I thought skyber rather an ugly word, so I just kept the vanal. It was a barn, of course, in olden days."

"But," said Martha Hubbard, still scribbling in her notebook, "I thought you told me when we were upstairs that

King Mark slept in your guest-room, and the recess in one corner used to hold Isolde's bridal bed?"

"It did," said Mad, "but that was before the place became a barn. The recess was full of sacks when I bought the house twenty years ago. Grain everywhere. Oh, hullo, darling . . ."

She stared defiantly at her grand-daughter. She knew, and Emma knew, that the lady from Boston had been accepting every word as gospel truth.

"I do hope and believe," said Martha Hubbard earnestly, shaking her hostess's hand, "that you and I have entered into a meaningful relationship, and if there is any further explanation you need about the work of our movement within USUK, you have only to let me know."

"And you'll bring the boys to the fireworks, and Emma too?" asked Lieutenant Sherman. "Not forgetting the guy?"

Emma's grandmother smiled as she escorted them to the waiting jeep. "Not forgetting the guy," she said.

No sooner had they disappeared up the drive than Mad called out, "Terry? Where are you?"

"What do you want Terry for?" asked Emma suspiciously. "He's supposed to be helping Joe in the kitchen-garden."

"Then he can help me instead," replied Mad, "and so can the rest of the boys. Didn't you hear Lieutenant Sher-_an remind me to bring a guy?"

She looked suddenly thoughtful as Ben came into the hall, a piece of pink rock still in his mouth and a bunch of flags in one hand. Martha Hubbard must have given him a cracker, too, for in the other hand he grasped a sparkler that fizzed and emitted little bursts of light.

"H'm," said Mad.

Emma glanced at her grandmother. There was always an inner meaning to her "h'ms." Sometimes it meant that she was miles away, caught up in the past or else it could have some practical significance, a clue to a crossword, the answer to an acrostic.

"What are you thinking?" she asked.

Mad watched the youngest of the brood advance towards her, his ebony face glowing with joy.

"You could train that child to do anything," she said.

78

7

The marines had cleared a piece of the waste ground between the marshes and the wire surrounding their encampment on Poldrea beach. A pile of driftwood held the centre of the space. Crowds had already gathered to watch the entertainment that the troops had so generously offered to provide for them. Parents with their children, older boys and girls, the local traders, clay-workers, dockers, people from outlying villages and, of course, the marines themselves, good-humoured, smiling, patting the various children on the head, chaffing the girls, and showing by their easy bonhomie what get-together meant, even if it was not so cultural as Martha Hubbard's movement. The USUK flags were everywhere—Mr. Libby, the landlord of the Sailor's Rest, had run up one of them on the pole beside the inn, and as it was a fine, clear evening, and mild for November, he had even brought out chairs and tables on to his frontage of mown grass, for his clients to drink their beer and enjoy the fireworks.

Excitement filled the air. Even Emma, who had felt rather superior before leaving home, and half-inclined to remain with Joe and Dottie, who had decided to stay behind, found the atmosphere stirring, somehow foreign, as though she was suddenly in Italy or Spain. All those marines, moving in and out amongst the local people, their uniforms, their faces, had a foreign cut about them —no, it wasn't Italy or Spain, it was more like an old movie, an old Western, where there was talk of the "frontier," and the Sailor's Rest was the saloon bar with its swing-doors. At any moment someone in a cowboy hat would come out with two guns slung in a low holster belt. Local youths, friends of Joe's and Terry's, called, " 'Lo, Emma" as they passed, and she said, " 'Lo" back to them, but she was used to them, they were just local boys, but these marines, they stared at her, they were . . . well, somehow aware. The look in their eyes, their slouching walk, the laugh and the nudge to one another, and the accent, it wasn't like a great bunch of tourists visiting Cornwall, it was foreign, it was the swagger and appraisal of invaders, of conquerors. And somehow this wasn't entirely displeasing.

She felt someone touch her shoulder and it was Wally Sherman, the lieutenant—the name no longer quite so absurd—and then he put his arm through hers.

"The boys have made a grand job of it, haven't they?" he said, and he pointed towards the pile of driftwood.

For a moment she was muddled, thinking he meant their boys, Mad's boys, but of course he was alluding to the marines.

"Yes, it's terrific," she replied. "I only hope the guy doesn't collapse at once. My grandmother and Terry have been at work on it all afternoon. I wasn't allowed to watch, needless to say. I imagine it's dressed up in all the boys' cast-off clothes, and my grandmother's too."

"Where is your grandmother? I don't see her, or the kids either."

He scanned the heads amongst the crowd behind, and so did Emma.

"She was by the inn a moment ago," she told him, "waiting for the Trembaths—those are our farmer friends. Terry and Mr. Trembath were bringing the guy down in the Land-Rover belonging to the farm. Apparently it was too big to get it into the boot of our car."

The lieutenant laughed. "Some guy," he said, and then,

steering Emma towards the fringe of the crowd, where the ground sloped away and the beach began, he murmured in a lower voice, "And some girl."

The thing is, thought Emma, if he wants to start something, which he obviously does, now is the moment either to fob him or let it rip. The question being, what do I want? A few wet kisses and a mutual fumble, and will it have to happen every time we meet, because honestly . . . She glanced to her left and saw two figures in the shadows under the overhanging cliff—there was a handy cave nearby—who were obviously one stage further advanced in the universal game. Oh well, why not, and Wally put both arms round her and the clinch began. It made for stimulation, because of the crowds and the feeling of excitement. And then bang . . . crash . . . the first rocket went up in the air, splintering the sky, lighting up the world around, and everyone stopped what they were doing and said, "Ah . . . !"

The lieutenant loosened his grip, the two figures to their left unclasped, and as the fragments of the rocket fell Emma saw that one of them was Myrtle Trembath, Terry's girl-friend, and the other Wally's subordinate, Corporal Wagg. All four suffered simultaneous shock of recognition but feigned ignorance, the corporal with tact born of experience leading his prey yet further towards the cave, amid giggles and protests, but Emma, stuffing both hands into her anorak pockets, was aware of a sudden feeling of reluctance, of distaste. What she had been allowing to happen wasn't exciting at all, it was offputting, cheap, and she couldn't decide whether the distaste had come about because of seeing Myrtle doing the same thing, which she knew was a snobbish reaction, or because Corporal Wagg and Lieutenant Sherman—Wally —had both taken the girls for granted and it was held to be one of their perks, the dues, to put it bluntly, of territorial occupation.

"Come on," she said briefly, "we'd better rejoin my lot," and she began to walk away out of the sand on to the firmer ground with the lieutenant saying nothing, just stumbling in her rear, and all the while the rockets and the showering stars kept blazing overhead.

It was certainly a fine display—the marines had done

them proud. There were blue stars and red stars and green stars and white stars, the whole mass showering down upon the upturned faces of the watching crowd. It lasted a full twenty minutes and then slowly began to peter away, as is the nature of all firework festivals, and heads turned towards the bonfire which, once lighted, would become the grand finale to the evening's entertainment.

"There's your grandmother," said the lieutenant, "standing over there with the little boys." He realised he had somehow boobed, and he wanted to make amends.

"So she is," replied Emma with relief, and to show she bore no ill-feelings she linked arms once again with her companion. "And there's Terry," she added. "He's got Andy with him, and some of his friends from the technical school. They're carrying something pretty big, it must be the guy."

It all happened very quickly. One moment the half-dozen boys were walking across the piece of waste ground bearing their load, and the next the stuffed figure was straddling the top of the driftwood pile, fixed firmly in position. It stood about six feet high, and it was not stuffed with Terry's or Joe's worn-out clothes, it was dressed as a soldier, in camouflage jacket and tin-hat, with imitation rifle at the ready, and Emma, catching her breath, remembered the old dressing-up box that had lain stored in the basement for years, holding relics of heaven only knew what timeless past.

"Your grandma's sure gone to town this time," said Wally, in a tone half respectful, half ominous. "Where in the name of Moses did she raise that outfit, and what's the little fellow going to do?"

Ben was advancing, or rather marching, to the base of the pile. He carried a flare in his left hand. He stood still for a moment and saluted. Then he bent, put the flare to the bonfire and retreated six steps backwards. A gasp of admiration rose from the crowd, the locals admittedly, with cries from the women of "Oh, the little dear, see the courage of him!" The marines were silent, crowding together on the fringe, ready to snatch the child from harm should any sparks from the fire blow towards him. As to the guy itself, well, if this was British humour, fair enough. But more was to come. Nobody had noticed that from the rear quarters of the soldier image protruded a USUK flag, and when the flames licked the seat of the guy's pants the flag was revealed in all its glory. There was a splutter, and an explosion, and as the flag shot into the burning pile a rocket blew with tremendous force from the guy's backside, and the guy itself toppled over into the flames.

The roar of laughter that rose with the rocket and followed it as it burst must have rung, as Jack Trembath said afterwards, from one side of the Cornish coast to the other, but best of all, he declared, was the sight of that litle black fellow standing so solemnly at attention, for all the world like a general at a saluting base, and after that the expression on the face of the Marine Commander, who had arrived just in time to watch the finale.

Then, as parents and the middle-aged moved away, still wiping tears of laughter from their eyes, making for their cars parked outside the Sailor's Rest or starting to walk back to Poldrea along the beach road, another series of explosions filled the air. Minor ones, it is true, but effective enough. Some joker had thrown lighted fireworks into Colonel Cheeseman's staff-car—his driver had evidently had his back turned to watch the bonfire—and there was a hiss and a splutter, and a smell of burning as the fireworks flared inside.

"Now see here," said Lieutenant Sherman, letting go of Emma's arm, "this just isn't funny, it isn't funny at all," and he started running towards the car, followed by a handful of marines. The scuffle started when a marine saw a youth bending down to tie a shoe-lace and, thinking he was lighting up more fireworks, booted him over into the gutter. A yell of protest rose from the youth's friends. Somebody picked up a stone and threw it haphazardly. Unfortunately it smashed a window of the staff-car. Then a bunch of marines charged, scattering people right and left. Women screamed, an old man was knocked over, and the tables and chairs outside the Sailor's Rest went flying in all directions. Mr. Libby, white to the gills, tried to shepherd his clients inside the inn for safety.

"It's those damn hooligans of boys," he kept saying. "It's not the marines at all. They deserve to be shot, the whole bloody lot of them."

Men were clutching their womenfolk and children. Stray dogs, already frightened by the fireworks, barked and ran across the road. There were shouting and whistling and angry voices raised, more scuffling and thumping between the marines and a further bunch of boys, and then somebody started throwing not stones but sand, the loose, grey-brown sand that was the feature of Poldrea beach from end to end. In a moment the sand was flying through the air, without point or purpose, blinding the eyes, filling nose and throat. It was chaos. It was hell.

"Mad," shouted Emma, "Mad," and she ducked her head to avoid the shower of sand flung by some boy. "Andy," she called, "Colin, Ben..." but they were nowhere to be seen, nor her grandmother either. There was nothing but a swaying crowd, bewildered, angry, none of them knowing why they were angry except that somebody said an old person had been knocked down, a child had been smothered, a dog had been run over... And all the while the remains of the bonfire glowed and spluttered, while the blackened tin-hat of the guy hung from the iron spike that had formed its base.

"You all right?"

It was Mr. Trembath, his hair blowing, a great smear of dirt on his left cheek, his raincoat torn, and he put his arm round Emma and gave her his own handkerchief to wipe the sand out of her eyes.

"Oh, thank heaven for you," she said, clinging to his arm. "Where's my grandmother, where are the boys?"

"Don't worry," he told her, "they're safe in your grandmother's car behind the Sailor's Rest. I'm going to drive you home, then come back for my own family."

He led her past the gauntlet of onlookers to the car-park. Mad was sitting in the front seat, and the four boys, Andy, Sam, Colin and Ben, were packed together in the back. Mad was smoking a cigarette. She hadn't smoked for twenty years. Directly she saw Emma she threw the cigarette away, out of the open window of the car.

"Oh, darling," said Emma, near to tears, "I've been so worried about you. I called and called, and there wasn't a sign."

"We did the same," replied Mad briefly, "and when someone shouted that a girl had been knocked down I

84

feared it was you. All over now. Jump in, you'll have to sit on my lap, you've done it before in days gone by. Mr. Trembath, I'm more than grateful to you. Shall we go?"

Neither had reckoned on the road-block, and instead of one sentry to examine passes there were four, and an officer in charge. The crowds by the beach were quieter now, but no one was permitted to leave without a rigorous examination of their passes. Men and youths had to turn out their pockets, women and girls their handbags.

The officer by the barricade examined the yellow ticket on the windscreen of the car. Then he asked for the adults' passes. Then the names and addresses of everyone else in the car. Tonight Mad allowed Jack Trembath to answer for her and give the details.

"Out of the car, please," commanded the officer. "We want to search it."

No one said anything as they all got out. The officer stood by while two of his men turned up the seats of the car, examined the pockets, lifted the floor-rug, and finally inspected the boot.

"What are you looking for?" asked Jack Trembath.

"Explosives," replied the officer. "O.K., you may go."

They climbed back into the car and the farmer started up the engine.

"Explosives!" he exclaimed. "Where in the world would we find explosives? Weren't we asked to their darn firework party?"

"Perhaps," said Mad, "according to their way of thinking fireworks are explosives. They can use them but we can't."

"That's about the size of it," replied Jack Trembath. "Well, I'll say one thing. We may all have had a bit of a scare just now when things turned ugly, but when the guy exploded in the hind-quarters I had the biggest laugh I've had in years. And the Yanks didn't like it either."

He began laughing again as he turned off the road and into the drive, and when he set the party down before the house he said to Mad, "Don't worry about that practical joker Terry. I'll pick him up directly when I pick up Myrtle. He can sleep at my place tonight and bring your car back in the morning."

It was not until he had driven out of sight up the drive

that Emma remembered Myrtle had not been with Terry, but with the corporal on the beach. After the fireworks started both had disappeared towards the cave, and during the mêlée that followed anything could have happened. Should she tell Mad, or wasn't it her concern? Mad went into the cloakroom to take off her boots, and the boys ran excitedly into the kitchen to give an account of the evening to Joe and Dottie. All but Andy, who appeared thoughtful.

"What's on your mind?" asked Emma.

Andy looked up at her, mischief lurking in his soft brown eyes. "I know why they searched the car," he said.

"Oh why, pray?" Emma knew that the word "pray" following upon a question often elicited information, if spoken severely.

"They were looking for gely, not fireworks," he answered.

"But we haven't got any gelignite."

"No, but Terry knows where to get it. Some of his friends work up at the clay-pits and they know where it's kept."

He stuck his hands in his pockets and smiled, then strolled off to the kitchen after the smaller fry. Emma waited for her grandmother to come out of the cloakroom. She looked exhausted and small wonder.

"You," said Emma firmly, "are for bed."

"I know, I know." Mad stretched out her arms and made for the stairs. "A very satisfactory evening's work, but for the mess-up at the end. So typical of those marines to lose their heads just because someone threw a few harmless fireworks into Colonel Cheesering's car. No sense of humour."

"It wasn't just the car," protested Emma. "Somebody started throwing stones, and then sand and gravel. You can't blame the marines."

Her grandmother paused from halfway up the stairs. "The only thing I regret is that Martha Hubbard wasn't on the beach beside me and the colonel when Terry's rocket shot into the air from the guy's behind. She would have wanted to know what motivated the action."

She disappeared into her bedroom humming a song at least thirty years old. Emma went into the kitchen. Sounds of protest from the little boys' bedroom suggested that Dottie was scrubbing their faces before puttting them to bed. Andy had gone to his lair. Only Joe and Sam remained, and Sam was still giving Joe an account of all that had happened . . . "Madam was worried 'bout Emma," he was saying, "but Colin told her not to worry, he had seen Emma go off with that lieutenant ages before the fireworks started."

Both boys looked up as Emma came into the room. Sam's cross eyes seemed to be staring at some point above their heads.

"Isn't it time you were in bed?" she asked.

"Yes, Emma. I'm just going. I was only thanking Joe for seeing to the squirrel and the pigeon."

Why, though, did Joe have to look at her in that strange accusing way? Why did his clear grey eyes make her feel younger suddenly, rather than two years his senior? Instead of staying behind with Dottie he might at least have come with the rest of them to Poldrea beach and kept an eye on Terry. Usually, before going to bed, she and Joe would sit up to see one of the late programmes, or they would go over the events of the day, laugh at the misdeeds of the younger boys, plan chores for the following morning. This was before the coming of the marines and the state of emergency. Everything had changed since then, and now tonight . . .

"Well, I'm off," she said. "Turn out the lights."

As she went out of the kitchen she knew he was standing there still, staring after her, that baffled, wounded expression in his eyes. Anyone would think . . . anyone would think . . . what? It's absurd, she thought, he's just one of the boys, a makeshift for the brother I never had.

Emma slept badly, her night a turmoil of stupid dreams. She was arm-in-arm, and then in a clinch, neither with Wally Sherman nor with Joe but with the guy in the tinhat, and, waking early, she went downstairs to make herself a cup of coffee. It couldn't have been much after seven, it was barely starting to get light, and suddenly the telephone began ringing in the cloakroom. She rushed through to answer it, because it would be ringing also beside her grandmother's bed upstairs, and Mad hated answering the telephone unless she knew who it was and before she was properly awake.

"Yes?" she said.

"Is that Emma?" came the voice. "It's Jack Trembath here. Look, my dear, I don't want to make your grandmother anxious, but Terry never turned up last night. Myrtle was waiting for me down on the beach, and she said she hadn't seen him for the evening, except when he and his friends put the guy on the bonfire. We all came back home, and we thought Terry would turn up—you know what the young people are, they have this understanding—but he never appeared. Is he with you?"

"I don't know," said Emma. "No one seems to be awake yet. I'll go and see."

She went along to the elder boys' room and knocked on the door. There was no answer. The room was empty. She looked out of the window and there was Joe already at work, bless him, though it was almost too dark to see the logs he was piling into the wheelbarrow. Terry's bed had not been slept in. She went back to the cloakroom. But when she lifted the receiver there were voices talking, and with a sinking heart she realised that the bell had awakened Mad after all, she was speaking to Mr. Trembath.

"He could have gone home with one of the boys from the tech," she was saying. "I saw two or three of them on the beach last night. Unless he's sleeping soundly in his own bed. Do you say Emma's gone to look?"

"He isn't there," put in Emma, joining the conversation, "his bed hasn't been slept in."

"Well, don't worry," her grandmother said from upstairs. "Terry can look after himself. He'll turn up."

"I hope so," came the answer, but the farmer sounded anxious.

There was a click from the bedroom extension and Jack Trembath said, "Hullo? Are you still there?"

"I am," replied Emma. "I'm downstairs. My grandmother has rung off."

"The reason I telephoned," he said, and his voice was lower than before, "is that I've just been listening to the seven o'clock local news. There was quite a bit about the scuffle last night between our local lads and the marines.

88

The marines set up these road-blocks everywhere, and it seems they've taken a number of lads into custody, but they don't say where. I'm only hoping your Terry isn't amongst them."

"Oh, no . . ."

"I wouldn't have your grandmother worried for the world, but if she listens to the radio it's bound to be repeated at eight o'clock. Peggy will bring your car round for you. One of my heifers has gone sick and I have to see to her. We'll keep hoping Terry will turn up."

Emma replaced the receiver. Mad would be bound to turn on her radio at eight o'clock, and then what? Supposing the marines had picked up Terry, what would they do to him? She went upstairs to her bedroom, dressed hurriedly, and then ran down and out into the garden to tell Joe. He threw down his hoe.

"Madam mustn't hear of this," he said. "I'll go and look for Terry."

"But Mr. Trembath said they've got road-blocks everywhere, and you've not been issued with a pass yet. They might pick you up too."

"Not if I go by the cliffs," he told her. "Terry may have got wind of the search, and be sheltering down by our beach in one of the caves."

"But why should he do that?" Emma asked. "He could just as well have gone to the farm or come back home?"

Joe shook his head. "I don't know. Some of them might have spotted him down on the beach and gone after him, and he had to hide. He knows those cliffs. Could travel them blindfold. Not like those fellows."

He followed her back into the house. It was beginning to rain. Emma looked out to sea, and saw the weather was coming up black and grey from the south-west. The warship at anchor in the bay was almost blotted out.

"Don't go," she pleaded. "Please, Joe, don't go. We just don't know what's happening. If they've got Terry they could get you too. What would we all do then? We can't be left alone in the house without you."

The stubborn expression vanished from Joe's face, and in its place came a kind of serenity, as if whatever burdens might be put upon him they could be shouldered. The weight would never be too hard to bear.

"I'd never leave you and Madam alone, you know that," he said. "You and she are the only things I have."

They stood for a moment in the porch, debating silently whether he should go or stay, while the rain pattered down on the glass roof overhead, and this is one of those moments I shall remember, Emma thought, no matter what happens, and when I'm nearly eighty, as old as Mad is now, I shall think of Joe standing here, his future all uncertain, and forever limited because of being unable to read or write, he depending upon us and we on him. This is union, this is love, it's something to do with trust and being brought up together without ties of blood; we share a common faith, a common home.

"Emma?"

It was Dottie from the kitchen, already astir, and laughter and chatter from the little boys on the move, the turmoil of the long day had begun.

"Wait," said Emma to Joe, "wait until I know what Mad is doing, she must have rung for her orange juice."

The radio was already blaring as she went into the kitchen. "Several youths and young men," the announcer was saying, "have already been picked up on suspicion of having taken part in last night's disorderly scenes after the fireworks display on Poldrea beach. Colonel Cheeseman has stated that he is assuming full responsibility for dealing with the incident. Anyone who is believed to have taken part will be held in custody until they can give proof of their innocence. The parents or relatives of any missing persons should apply to Colonel Cheeseman personally or in writing, and information will be given to them."

Dottie, who knew nothing of Terry's absence, handed Mad's tray into Emma's hands.

"That will teach them a lesson," she said. "A lot of young hooligans from St. Austell, I suppose. Do them good to have a touch of marine discipline."

Emma did not answer. She went quickly upstairs with the tray to her grandmother's bedroom. Mad was already dressed and she had the telephone in her hand.

"I want the Commander-in-Chief at Devonport," she was saying. "Rear-Admiral Sir James Jollif."

She waited, nodding meanwhile to Emma to put the tray on the table beside her bed.

"I tried the police first," she said, "after I heard the eight o'clock news. They don't have any information. I asked how one could get in touch with the U. S. Commander. They gave me a number, which I rang, and the American voice that answered said the Commander was taking no calls himself, and if there was anything I wanted to know, would I apply in person or in writing. So I'm trying Jimmy Jollif. He at least will give me some advice."

There was a long delay before she got him. At first some subordinate tried to make an excuse. Finally the Admiral himself came on the line.

"Yes," said Mad, in a voice that must have rung through Devonport headquarters, "it *is* me. Didn't they tell you? Listen, I think one of my boys, Terry, may have been picked up by the marines last night. We were all down on Poldrea beach, and as you may have heard there was some sort of skirmish between local boys and their lot. I can't get any sense out of the American Marine Corps or whatever they call themselves. Can you find out for me whether they're holding Terry? What do you mean it's nothing to do with you? Aren't you in touch with the Commander? Serious offence? How can throwing a few fireworks around be a serious offence? I've never heard of anything so ridiculous in my life! You mean to tell me that you, Admiral Sir James Jollif, can't have a private word with that jumped-up American marine and tell him where he gets off? What? I don't believe it!" A look of incredulity appeared on her face and she made large gestures at Emma. "Colonel Cheesering has complete jurisdiction in this area and it wouldn't be either polite or right to question his motives? Yes, I should think you are sorry. More than that, if I were in your place I should feel humiliated. USUK, indeed! Right, don't say another word. Good luck to you. Goodbye."

She slammed down the telephone.

"Now we know where we are," she said to Emma. "It isn't just a take-over bid, it's capitulation. We're on our own. Thank God I've got my health and strength, though I may be touching eighty. Give me a piece of paper and pencil, Em, and my specs. We've got to organise."

8

The council of war was held in the library. Mad insisted that everyone should be present, from Dottie to Ben. "I don't believe," she said to Emma, "in children being told to run away and play when serious things are going on all round them. They should take part in decisions. Even if their opinions are immature, they very often see things clearer than we do." So briefly, while they gathered around her, some on the window seat, the younger boys on the floor, Dottie on the inevitable upright chair, Mad explained what had happened. Her task was made all the easier because they had heard the news over the kitchen radio, and the very fact that it was about Poldrea, their own territory, and they themselves had witnessed the scenes described, made solidarity firm amongst Andy, Sam and Colin. They were outraged. So was Dottie, who had instantly switched sides once she knew Terry might be involved. Dottie, when she was baited by Terry, as she frequently was, would allude to him as "that boy"; but if he was in any sort of trouble that did not concern her, then her first nurseling became "my boy."

"If they try to do anything to my boy," she said, "I'll send a telegram to the Queen, even if she is staying at the White House."

Ben nodded his head and began to purse his lips. "C . . . c . . ."

Emma reached for a lump of sugar, intended for Folly's broken molars, and pushed it into his mouth.

"I don't really think, Dottie dear," said Mad, "that we should gain anything by appealing to the Queen. She's probably being held as a hostage herself. Yes, Andy?"

Andy shook his mop of brown hair out of his eyes and lowered the hand that had shot into the air. He was a rapid thinker, but he spoke deliberately.

"Talking of hostages," he said, "I don't see why we can't take one of our own and make him talk. We have two possible choices. That Lieutenant Sherman or that Corporal Wagg. It's only a matter of luring either the one or the other up here, and then . . ." He made a karate gesture, followed by a thumb slice across his throat.

"Oh, Andy!" exclaimed Dottie, horrified. "What a thing to suggest!"

"I don't know," said Mad thoughtfully. "It isn't a bad idea. We wouldn't have to cut his throat necessarily, but a little gentle persuasion . . ." She glanced at her granddaughter. "You spent some time on the beach with him last night," she went on, "Lieutenant Sherman, that is. How do you rate yourself as an inquisitor?"

"Not very high," replied Emma, blushing—when would she outgrow the infuriating habit. "What I mean is, it would depend upon the circumstances, what was happening at the time. He's rather nice, just to talk to casually, but it was he who got angry last night when someone threw those fireworks into Colonel Cheeseman's car."

"Incidentally," interrupted her grandmother, "who *did* do that?"

Nobody answered.

"H'm, I thought so," said Mad, and her eyes drifted towards Colin. His ingenuity was almost as great as her own.

"Have you got something to say?" she asked. "I don't mean about the car, but about the situation as a whole?"

"I think what Andy suggested is very good," Colin said,

"but it would be better to get Corporal Wagg here, and not the lieutenant. Emma would give the show away if the lieutenant came, she would go red. Besides, Corporal Wagg isn't so tall as the lieutenant, he'd be easier to handle. Now, Dottie can ask the corporal to tea . . ."

"I'll do nothing of the sort," interrupted Dottie.

"She will ask him to tea," continued Colin, "and put a little nip of whisky in the tea to loosen his tongue. Then she'll take his arm and say, 'Come for a stroll in the shrubbery, my dear' "—Colin did a fair imitation of Dottie's voice—"and in the meantime Joe will have dug a pit, like the brethren did in the Bible, up at the top of the shrubbery where Madam throws the dead flowers, and wang! down will go Corporal Wagg to the bottom of it, his cries unheard. He'd soon talk after a night down there."

Ben had finished his lump of sugar and he shouted applause. His speech might still be unformed, but there was nothing wrong with his lungs.

" 'Scuse me," said Sam, who was sitting huddled beside Joe on the window-seat, "but I don't quite see *what* we want either that lieutenant or the corporal to talk about. If they've got Terry they've got him. And he'll be guarded, with all the other boys. Why doesn't Madam just go down to Poldrea and call at the camp and find out?"

How obvious, thought Emma. After all, it's what the announcer said on the news. It's what Mad was told herself on the telephone. Could it be—and it seemed disloyal even to harbour the thought—that Mad was too proud, that she felt it would demean her to go down and possibly sand in a queue wih a number of anxious parents and fill in a form and wait to be given information from some clerk in the Commander's office?

"No," said Joe firmly, "if Madam goes down to Poldrea and signs a form to say that Terry is missing, then if he isn't amongst the boys they've picked up they will know he is absent from home. This will look suspicious. Whereas if we don't say anything, the marines will never know that he isn't here."

Everyone was silent.

"I know one thing for sure," Colin announced. "They're the baddies and we're the goodies, and it's going to stay that way, so we may as well make up our minds to it.

Come on, Ben, and I'll teach you the word that Joseph said to his brethren when they bowed down their heads before him."

"Mad," said Emma suddenly, "I wonder if it would help if I went down to the farm and had a chat to Myrtle. She might know something about Terry that she hasn't told her mother or her father. After all, I'm more her generation. And," she hesitated, "I did see her on the beach last night with Corporal Wagg. She might even have made a date to see him again."

"And then she could help by luring him here as a hostage?" suggested Andy.

Mad stood up. "The council is over for the moment. You boys go with Joe and do some work in the garden. All right, Em, go down to the farm and see what you can achieve. I shall ring up Bevil."

Bevil was her doctor, and a family friend of many years' standing.

"Why, darling?" asked Emma, alarmed. "Aren't you feeling well?"

"Never felt better in my life," replied her grandmother, "but by telling him I've got a sudden pain under the left ribs I shall get him out here. He's the best source of reliable information I can think of."

It was rather awful, Emma thought as she walked across the fields down to the farm, how this business is leading us all into subterfuge and deception, and we can't really tell who is friend and who is enemy. Admiral Jollif, for instance, who might have been sympathetic and at least given Mad some words of advice, was evidently useless, and indeed probably forced by his position as C.-in-C. Devonport to connive with the American forces. He had said it was a joint enterprise and there was no getting round it. The same with Pa in London. If Terry really had been taken into detention, Pa would say, "Serve the young blighter right. He was always too big for his boots." Secretly, Emma felt that Pa was jealous of Terry. Mad had been in the full flush of her acting career when Pa had been a boy and away at school. He probably thought that, in retirement, she gave much more thought and time to Terry than she had ever given to him.

People's motives were always mixed, she decided. You

took one side or another depending upon how it suited you, how it affected you. Mr. Libby at the Sailor's Rest only welcomed the marines camping on Poldrea beach because they flocked into the inn to drink his beer. If they commandeered the inn as a headquarters and turned him out, he would be the first to want to blow up the entire beach. The man who sliced the ham in the supermarket had visions of bigger and better hams stacking up his counters so that he could dispose of them to the Americans. Yet old Tom Bate . . . Old Tom Bate didn't care about selling the fish he caught to the marines on shore or on board the warship in the bay. "Let them leave us be," he would say, "we don't need they telling us where we'm to." The old mocked, the young threw sand and stones. It was only the middle-aged and the up-and-coming who collaborated with invaders.

The rain was driving into her face as she climbed the gate into the yard and made her way round to the farm kitchen. Peggy Trembath was rolling pastry. She was a bright, cheerful looking woman of about forty, with her daughter Myrtle's soft green eyes.

"Hullo, dear," she said, "have you come for the car? Jack told me to drive it up to you an hour or more ago. I do apologise."

"As a matter of fact, I'd forgotten all about the car," confessed Emma, which was true. "No, I just came to report that we've had no news of Terry. I suppose you haven't heard anything, or Myrtle?"

Mrs. Trembath shook her head. "I only wish we had," she said. "I just pray to God he hasn't been picked up with those other boys. Jack's as baffled as I am. What we can't understand is that if the Americans are supposed to be our friends, and we're all one and the same, it's a queer way to go about it, seizing a few high-spirited boys and taking them away goodness knows where. It just doesn't make sense. Here, sit down, I'll make you a cup of tea. Take your mac off and let it dry."

""Where's Myrtle?"

"She's upstairs. I'll call her down." She made towards the stairs, then added confidentially, "She's just as upset as we are. That shindy on the beach quite unsettled her last night. She was as white as a sheet when she came back with us in the car and hardly said a word. But whether it was all the noise and shouting, or worrying over Terry, I can't make out."

"I'll go up to her," said Emma quickly. "I don't want any tea, truly. She might feel like talking to me."

"All right, dear. I'll put the kettle on anyway. Jack and Mick will be in directly."

Myrtle was lying on her bed, a transistor beside her. She looked startled when Emma appeared, and switched it off.

"I thought there might be some fresh announcement," she said, "but there's nothing. Is Terry back?"

"No," said Emma, "he's not. And none of us set eyes on him after he put the guy on the bonfire—he just disappeared into the crowd. Then it wasn't long before the fireworks were thrown in the staff-car, and the marines started getting angry. What happened to you? I saw you on the beach earlier."

Myrtle threw herself back on the bed and began fiddling with the transistor.

"I saw you too," she replied. "Did you have a good time?"

"Not particularly," said Emma. "Did you?"

Myrtle shrugged. "All right."

There was silence between them, the only sound coming from the transistor. Myrtle hadn't tuned it right and the singer's voice was out of key. Then she said, "Did you tell Mum you saw me on the beach with . . . you know?"

"No, of course not," replied Emma. "Why should I?"

"Well, only that Austin—that's Corporal Wagg—has kept calling here ever since he came to apologise about one of the marines shooting Spry, and Dad and Mum didn't look too pleased, so when he told us about the firework party we made a date to meet down there."

"Fair enough," shrugged Emma.

"I suppose you did the same with Lieutenant Sherman. Well, I mean, they're different, aren't they? They've seen a bit of life. You get fed up with the boys round here."

"Even Terry?"

Myrtle's slightly sullen, half-defiant expression changed. She looked suddenly troubled. She switched off the transistor, and slipping off the bed crossed the room and shut the door. She turned and faced Emma.

"Look," she said, "I don't know whether to tell you this or not . . ."

"You've started, haven't you?"

Myrtle's eyes filled with tears. "Everything's such a mess," she said. "I'm all mixed up. I don't want to get Terry into trouble, or Austin either. You see . . ."—and now she began to cry in earnest—"I wasn't speaking the truth when I told Mum and Dad I hadn't seen Terry last night. I had. He must have guessed I'd gone round the back of the beach, because when all that shouting and sand-chucking started he came to the cave and found me there with Austin, with Corporal Wagg."

"And so?"

"Well, he was wild. He started calling me names, and Austin too, and then Austin got wild, and before I could stop them they were fighting, not just scrapping, really fighting. Austin's nose started to bleed, and then he winded Terry, and was going to lam into him when Terry did a Rugby tackle and got him on the ground. They were both swearing like anything, it was awful."

She fumbled up her sleeve for a tissue, and Emma patted her shoulder. "What happened then?"

"That's just it, I don't know," said Myrtle. "I saw Austin blow a whistle, to summon his friends, I suppose, and Terry jumped up and began to run along the beach. And suddenly the marines seemed to be everywhere, you know how it was, and Austin ran out on me completely, all he wanted to do was to go after Terry and maybe beat him up with the help of his mates. I just lost my head and scrambled back to the car-park behind the Sailor's Rest. I knew Dad and Mum would be there. And we came back home, and I've scarcely slept for the night wondering what happened."

The two girls sat down together on Myrtle's bed, and Myrtle blew her nose and wiped her eyes.

"If they got Terry it will be my fault," she said.

"No," said Emma, "not entirely. It's all our faults."

She had a sudden vision of Mad and Terry and the other boys making the guy between them. Wasn't it the guy that had triggered off the laughter, and the laughter

99

the resentment, and the resentment the antagonism between invaders and invaded? Wasn't the making of the
guy a thumb-to-nose gesture on Mad's part, because
ridicule angers your opponent and there isn't a come-
back? And wasn't Mad's anger due to the fact that a dog
had been killed because, through age-old instinct, it had
tried to defend its territory? The clue to the fight between
Terry and Corporal Wagg was territorial too.

"Myrtle," she said, "you've played Terry off before
with several boys. He's never been the one and only. He's
often said so. But I don't remember him ever having a
fight about you."

"Well, he wouldn't, would he? I mean, the other boys
are local, they all know each other. Corporal Wagg—
Austin—may speak English, but he's foreign just the same.
Not one of us. That's why I thought it would be fun to
play him along. I wish I hadn't now. And if he calls up
here later today I don't know what I'll say to him."

"You could ask him," suggested Emma, "how the fight
ended, and if he and his mates took Terry into detention."

"I couldn't in front of Mum and Dad," replied Myrtle,
"that is, if they even let him in. And I don't think I want
to see him alone again, not after last night. It wasn't just
the fight, it was . . . everything."

Yes, Emma thought, it was everything. She put herself
in Myrtle's place and thought of being in a cave on
Poldrea beach with Lieutenant—Wally—Sherman. And
someone she was fond of, like Joe, coming along and
seeing her. And Joe and the lieutenant getting into a fight.

"This union thing," said Emma, "I don't think I believe
in it, do you?"

"I don't even know what it means to people like us,"
said Myrtle. "Dad says it's the last in the Coalition Government's bag of tricks. But if it means the Americans
can go round beating up our boys then they can all go
back where they came from, as far as I'm concerned."

"Yes," said Emma, "but you didn't think that way when
you made the date on the beach with Corporal Wagg."
She was thinking of Lieutenant Sherman.

"No," replied Myrtle, "but you don't think, do you,
not when you're all steamed up and a fellow's new?"

Then they heard her mother calling up the stairs that

the kettle had boiled and didn't they want some tea? Myrtle dabbed her eyes again and combed her hair.

"Not a word, mind," she said, "nor at home to your gran."

"No," replied Emma, "but if you should see Austin— Corporal Wagg—try and find out if he knows what happened to Terry."

The two girls went downstairs. Jack Trembath and his son Mick, a boy of about Andy's age, had just come into the kitchen, and were hanging up their wet oilskins on the back of the door.

"Well, Emma," said Mr. Trembath, "any word of Terry?"

Emma shook her head.

"I'm afraid there'll be nothing for it," said the farmer seriously, "but for your grandmother to go down in person and try and see that Marine Commander. I'll drive her down there. It would help maybe if she had a man with her."

"That's very kind of you, Mr. Trembath, but we're not so certain at home it would be a good idea. If they haven't picked up Terry they won't know he's missing, and it might make them try to look for him, especially if..." she hesitated, "if he's in any kind of trouble, been scrapping or anything."

Jack Trembath looked doubtful. "You may be right," he said, "but if they haven't got him, how will you find out where he is? I tell you one thing. If that corporal fellow comes up here after Myrtle I'll darn well get him to talk and see if he knows anything."

He stared at his daughter, who had turned very white.

"Look," said Emma, jumping to her feet, "thanks for the tea but I ought to get back. You never know, they might have some news."

"Tell you what," Jack Trembath rose at the same time, "I'll run you back in your car and have a word with your grandmother, see if there is anything I can do. She doesn't need to go down to Poldrea if they're being fussy still with the roadblocks, and asking questions of everyone. Being a farmer, I can get by and explain my business where it might be awkward for her. I've got to go down

101

anyway, I've to call in at the vet's for something he's made up for Marigold." (Marigold was the sick heifer.)

"How is Marigold?"

"She'll do . . . she'll do."

Emma said goodbye to Mrs. Trembath and Myrtle, and was halfway up the track in the car when a thought suddenly struck her.

"Would you mind very much," she said, "taking the car back by yourself? I've just remembered I dropped a scarf coming across the field, and I'd better find it before it gets soaked in the rain. It won't take me long."

"Just as you like, my dear," he said, "but don't you get wet through looking for it."

Emma jumped out of the car and he drove on alone. Lies and subterfuge again, thought Emma, who hadn't dropped a scarf at all, but couldn't forget what Myrtle had said about Terry running away along the beach with the marines after him. Supposing they had beaten him up? Supposing he was crouching in one of the caves, or halfway up the cliff, above high water, unable to move, not daring to shout?

She waited until the car was out of sight, then turned to the right, away from the farm buildings, and across the hill where the grazing ground sloped steeply to the cliffs below. She was wearing jeans and boots, but her light raincoat was small protection against this blow from the south-east and the stinging rain. White rollers were scudding into the bay to spend themselves on Poldrea beach, sucking at the sand-banks that formed there when the tide ebbed. She could see small parties of marines straggling along the foreshore, or drifting down from the huts and caravans they had commandeered. No smoke came from the chimneys behind the docks, and the docks themselves were bare of shipping. There were naval boats inside the harbour, and the warship itself seemed further out than usual, hardly discernible against the rolling sea. An unpleasant berth, thought Emma, with a lea-shore astern of them, and she wondered if Wally Sherman was aboard and possibly seasick—serve him right—or snugly ashore in one of the harbour offices, sitting at a desk and interviewing parents of missing boys.

She reached the old coastguard footpath above the cliffs

and looked down at the boiling cauldron below. It was about half-tide, and the stretch of beach where she and the boys bathed in summer was deserted. The cliffs between here and Poldrea were not high; anyone who knew his way like Terry could easily have scrambled over the rocks at low tide, even at night, and made his way to safety. She climbed down to the beach and walked to the further end. There was a cave here where they sometimes picnicked after swimming, and the overhanging ledge gave shelter from a shower. Not today, though. The rain drove inside. There was nothing on the beach but seaweed and broken bottles, and a dead gull smothered in tar. She had come on a useless mission.

She climbed back again to the cliff-path, and walked along it and over the stone stile that led to a continuation of Mr. Trembath's grazing ground above the cliffs. The land sloped very suddenly here in places. Mr. Trembath used to say that in his grandfather's day there had been some mine-prospecting hereabouts which came to nothing, but the soil had loosened since, and in winter when rains were heavy it could be dangerous to walk too near the edge, the ground might crumble under your feet and you could pitch headlong to the beach below. Emma turned to the higher ground. The rain was driving straight into her face and it was pointless getting soaked to the skin in an impossible quest, besides, Mr. Trembath would be talking to Mad by now, and telling her that Emma had only gone to pick up a scarf in the top field.

Then she saw a little figure running towards her out of the rain. He came from the direction of the wood that hugged the cliffside further to the east, a wood that had once formed part of the farm acreage but was now a sort of no-man's-land, a bone of contention, if the truth be told, between Jack Trembath and a summer visitor who had bought up three deserted cottages at the bottom of the wood and wanted to develop the site. Lawyers argued and so far had come to no decision, and meanwhile a curious character known to herself and the boys as the beach-comber had established squatter's right in a hut built on a promontory at the far end of the wood. The summer visitor did not know of his existence, and though Jack Trembath knew he did not care.

"Let him live there if he likes," he said, "it doesn't worry me. He keeps an eye on the sheep, what's more, if they stray."

Emma stood still as the small figure paused in its headlong flight, and catching sight of her ducked behind a gorse bush, as if to avoid being seen. Emma waited. The figure did not move. It was one of their own boys, she was certain. Too big for Colin. Too small for Andy. What was he doing out here all alone, without the others, without Joe, in the driving rain? She ran quickly up the hillside to the line of gorse bushes, and she was right, it was Sam crouching there, wet through.

"Sam," she said, "where have you been? You know you're not allowed out here on your own, especially after what's happened, and in this weather."

She dragged him to his feet and held on to his hand. Sam, despite his friendship with his room-mate Andy, and his reverence for Joe, was sometimes odd-man out. His kinship with wild animals, with birds, was stronger than his feeling for fellow-humans. Perhaps it was his eye affliction that made him seem, at times, an outsider in the family circle. Perhaps it was subconscious memory harking back to the days when he had been a battered baby.

Sam did not answer immediately. He allowed his hand to remain in Emma's, he did not attempt to pull it away. Those eyes of his, wherever they pointed, seemed to penetrate.

"I know where Terry is," he said.

Emma swallowed. I mustn't scare him, she thought, I mustn't say anything hasty or stupid; I must remember what Mad has always said, that Sam is more sensitive than the others, that you have to weigh every word or he shies off.

"That's good," she said slowly. "I went looking for him on the beach but he wasn't there. I hope he's hiding somewhere safe."

Sam nodded. "He's got a broken leg but he'll be all right."

He mustn't be rushed, he mustn't have questions flung at him. Joe should be here, he would know what to do. She waited, and then she spoke again.

"A broken leg. Then he can't walk."

"No, that's why I was running up home. I thought I could get some as'prin out of Dottie's medicine cupboard, it would ease the pain. I wasn't going to tell Dottie what it was for."

"Why not? We've all been so worried about Terry. Madam ought to know about the broken leg."

"It's not that I mind Madam knowing, or Dottie either, but I don't want the soldiers to know. They might come and take Terry away. Or they might shoot him, like they shot Spry."

What must I do, Emma asked herself, to try and make him talk? Terry may be lying out there on the cliff somewhere, not only with his leg broken, but perhaps ill, dangerously ill.

"Listen, Sam," she said, "you know how you look after the squirrel, and the pigeon, and all sorts of other animals, but they have to be somewhere warm and sheltered, they can't be left out in the rain with a broken limb or a broken wing. The limb has to be set."

Sam considered her for a moment, or, rather, considered the sky.

"Mr. Willis has set the leg," he said. "He used to know first aid, though he says he's a bit rusty. But he doesn't want the soldiers to know where Terry is either. He hates them as much as I do."

Mr. Willis . . . Mr. Willis . . . ? Emma had never heard of a Mr. Willis.

"You know," said Sam, suddenly impatient, "the beachcomber. I thought of him directly we all stopped talking. He's a friend of mine. So I went to tell him about Terry. And Terry was there, in his hut. Mr. Willis found him on the beach last night and carried him there. Come and see."

9

The hut in the woods had been a summer-house originally, erected before the 1914–18 war by a former land-owner
who had lived at Trevanal and was a keen bird-watcher.
During the Hitler war it was taken over by the Home
Guard as an observation post. It later fell on lean times,
the planking began to rot, and the whole structure might
have fallen in had not the beachcomber appeared on the
scene, established his squatter's rights and made the summer-house weather-proof, dry, and comparatively snug.
Emma now learnt, as Sam led her through the wood to the
promontory, that he and Andy had frequently called on
the beachcomber but had kept the fact secret.

"He doesn't much like people," confessed Sam, "he
says they're nosey, and I agree with him. He's been all
sorts of things in his life. A ship's carpenter, a farm
labourer, he's worked in a zoo, in an electric shop—he's
got his own radio he made himself."

Emma wasn't interested in the life history of the beachcomber, all she wanted to know was how Terry had broken
his leg and if he were in pain.

"You must be polite," urged Sam as the roof of the hut emerged through the trees. "He doesn't like girls or women, he says they're nosier than men."

Emma had visualised a dark, broken-down, makeshift sort of dwelling, shrouded by overhanging trees. She was mistaken. The beachcomber had cleared a fair space around his home and had tilled a vegetable plot behind it. The spring running down the side of the cliff formed his water supply; and he was filling a pail of water as Emma and Sam came upon him. He turned at bay, then relaxed at the sight of Sam.

"This is Emma," said Sam, "I met her in the field. She was looking for Terry and I had to tell her. She's very trustworthy."

"How do you do?" said Emma.

She had only seen the beachcomber in the distance before. He had his own way down to the shore from his lair, a steep path which he had cut himself out of the cliff-face, and when she and the boys had come upon him on the beach he was generally bent double, filling a basket with seaweed or driftwood. Winter or summer he would be dressed the same, in an old jacket green with age, flannel trousers thrust into sea-boots, and a peaked cap pulled low over his craggy features. Colin had had the effrontery to say last summer, when they were all on the beach and the recluse had appeared at the further end poking about the rocks with a long-handled stick, that he looked like Mad.

"You know what," he cried delightedly, "he's Madam's brother, and she lets him live in the hut in the woods and it's a great secret."

This story had gone the rounds for a time at home, to Mad's amusement. She would allude to it as her "guilty secret," but then as the summer passed, and the treks to the beach became less frequent, the man who was squatter, beachcomber and hidden brother was forgotten, except, so it now seemed, by Andy and Sam. That his name was in reality Mr. Willis came as something of an anti-climax.

He looked less formidable without his cap. He had mild eyes and was wearing spectacles. He had a shock of white hair, and must be well over seventy. He looked fixedly at Emma for a moment, and then he said, "Do you want to see the boy?"

108

"Please."

"Come in, then."

He turned and led the way into the hut. Emma was struck by his voice. It had a sort of lilt to it, was it Welsh? And then, once inside, after a rapid glance about her—the place was neat and dry, with a glowing log-fire—she had eyes and thoughts for no one but Terry. He was lying on a camp-bed against the wall, near to the fire. She ran to him and knelt beside him. His eyes looked enormous in his white face.

"Terry darling," she said, "what happened? We've been so worried. Thank God, you're here . . ." She glanced up at the beachcomber standing in the doorway. "We were afraid the marines might have picked you up."

Terry tried to smile, but she could see he was in pain. Happy-go-lucky Terry, who never had anything wrong with him, he seemed so vulnerable suddenly, and so much younger than herself or Joe.

"I'd be a stiff by now but for Mr. Willis," he said. "I don't know how he did it, but he brought me up here on his back, at least that's what he says. I don't think I was conscious half the time."

"Nothing to it," put in his rescuer. "I've borne heavier loads than you on my back and will do so again."

It *was* Welsh. The lilt was unmistakable, the upward turn at the finish of a sentence. Emma turned back to Terry.

"I've seen Myrtle," she told him. "I was at the farm just now. She told me about the fight between you and Corporal Wagg. Nobody else knows. Is that how you broke your leg?"

"No, not exactly," murmured Terry—speech came slowly, because he was in pain. "They came after me, he and about four others, and I ran as fast as I could to shake them off. The tide was beginning to flood, which was my saving, really, because they started to flounder about in the shallows and I gave them the slip by scrambling up Little Hell and hiding there by the gully in the cliff-face, so they lost me and must have gone back to Poldrea beach. Then like a fool I slipped, and went crashing down about twenty feet to the bottom of the cliff. I couldn't move, and guessed by the pain what I'd done.

I lay there for nearly an hour, or so it seemed. Then Mr. Willis turned up."

The beachcomber took up the story. "No, boyo, it wasn't an hour, it was thirty minutes, more like. I was watching the charade on Poldrea beach from the cliff-path above, and I saw them give chase to you. I was planning to come down and face them myself, when they turned on their heels. I thought you'd packed up and gone home. It was only that I keep a store of driftwood near the gully that made me turn aside and saw you lying there, with the tide coming up on you. I couldn't leave you, could I?" He pulled aside the blanket and showed Emma the left leg with the splints around it. "I was an orderly in a naval hospital once. I know this is only a rough job, and the boy should by rights be in hospital. But how to get him there? And what of these road-blocks they have all over the place? They gave it out again, not half-an-hour ago. Picking up boys, they say, for questioning."

Sam had joined the bedside consultation. "Terry's better here with Mr. Willis than he would be at home," he said. "The marines are always coming up to our place. That Lieutenant Sherman is a friend of Emma's."

"He's not," said Emma fiercely, "truly he's not." She turned to the beachcomber. "We had to be civil to the officers when they called. They used our stables over the weekend, we couldn't refuse. But my grandmother, far from making them welcome, was, well . . . almost insulting. She says it's a complete con on the part of the government to pretend it's a union between ourselves and the Americans, that it's a take-over bid or, worse, a full-scale invasion."

Mr. Willis stared at Emma with interest. "Your grandmother said that?"

"Yes, she did."

He scratched his white head and smiled. "I've not been inside a theatre these forty years, but I remember her well. She'd have been in her prime. A comedy it was, I've forgotten the title . . . Now, boyo, what's to be done with you? I'd keep you here until your leg mends, but it should be in plaster."

"Wait," exclaimed Emma, "our doctor is coming to see my grandmother some time today. I'll have to tell him."

"She's not ill, is she?" interrupted Terry anxiously.

"No, she wants to find out what he knows, what rumours are flying around, what's true, what's false. He's a personal friend besides being a doctor, Mr. Willis. You know Andy? Andy's parents who were killed in an air-crash were friends of Dr. Summers, that's why my grandmother adopted Andy. He knows Terry, he knows us all."

Mr. Willis looked thoughtful. "He may be your friend, but how would he react to these circumstances? Road-blocks, passes and the like. The U.S. forces are in control. They may be keeping a watch on the hospitals too. I can give you my word no one will come looking for Terry here. And if they did . . ." He looked up at the wall above Terry's camp-bed. There was an old shot-gun hanging there. "No American marine would cross my threshold."

He almost could be Mad's brother, thought Emma, he has the same determination, the same territorial pride. She squeezed Terry's hand, and with sudden understanding of her thoughts he squeezed it back and smiled despite the pain.

"Mr. Willis," he said, "I don't want to get you into trouble. We seem to have caused enough as it is. I'm pretty certain Dr. Summers can be trusted. But it's for you to say. This is your place, not ours."

Mr. Willis looked at each of them in turn. Then down again, at the leg in splints. "Whichever way it goes, you'll be a casualty for some weeks. No scrapping or bonfires for you. Maybe you should see that doctor."

It was decided that Emma and Sam should return to Trevanal, and Emma would tell her grandmother that Terry was with Mr. Willis.

"Mind how you go now," he warned her outside the hut. "You can't tell what those fellows would be up to, they might be around. I've some broth here simmering I'll give the boy directly, but he hasn't much appetite."

"I can't thank you enough," Emma told him. "Terry was the first of what my grandmother calls her blood. He means so much to her."

"He does her credit, then," said the beachcomber. "Terry has plenty of guts. There's life in him still for many more scrapes."

Emma and Sam threaded their way through the wood and up to the ploughed field above, and so home. It was still blowing hard, and raining too. They shed their boots

111

and raincoats in the porch, and Emma heard the dining-room clock strike eleven. So much had happened since Jack Trembath had telephoned around seven, half the day seemed to have gone already. The television was on in the library, an unusual thing for Mad—it must be she wanted to hear the latest news bulletin. Her grandmother was standing in front of the set, and when Emma appeared she switched it off.

"More complications," she said. "Two explosions near Falmouth. There's a contingent of marines down there too, apparently, and of course they're blaming the dockers. Where on earth have you been? Jack Trembath brought the car back ages ago, and he's gone back to the farm for his Land-Rover, and is going to scout around Poldrea to get more news. He said you'd lost a scarf or something."

"I've found Terry," said Emma.

Her grandmother stood very still. Then she suddenly seemed to shrink, and her eyes went misty and small. She put out her hand to Emma.

"Oh, thank God," she said.

They sat down together on the sofa, and in a moment Mad had recovered.

"It was really Sam's doing," Emma explained. "He had the brilliant idea where to look."

She poured out the whole story, and before she had finished Mad was quite herself again, and began her thing of walking up and down the room, a habit of hers when deep in concentration.

"It must have been instinct that made me telephone Bevil," she said. "He probably won't be here till some time this afternoon, but I didn't expect he would. Do you think Terry will be all right until then? Is he in frightful pain?"

"I don't think so." Emma spoke uncertainly. "He's being very plucky and Mr. Willis has put the leg in splints, but he obviously needs to be seen by a doctor."

"Mr. Willis," Mad said. "Extraordinary name for a beachcomber. It doesn't suit him at all. Welsh, do you say? I shall call him Taffy."

"Mad, you can't . . . He's rather a dignified old person, once you see him with his cap off, in his own lair. The hut was very tidy too."

"What on earth has that got to do with it? Taffy was a

112

Welshman, Taffy was a thief, Taffy came to my place and stole a piece of beef . . . Oh yes, he won't mind, he'll take it as a compliment."

Emma thought otherwise, and she hoped to heaven her grandmother would not advance upon him quoting that insulting old rhyme. Now Terry had been found, broken leg and all, Mad's spirits had risen to their usual heights.

"You know what?" she announced, looking out at the streaming rain. "I shall go down to the hut now, before lunch. You stay here and hold the fort. Sam's already been, I'll take Andy."

"But Mad . . ."

She had already gone out of the room, though, and was shouting to the whole house that Terry had been found. It was so unwise, thought Emma, it ought to be kept secret until after the doctor had called and given his advice.

". . . a terribly nice man," Mad was saying to Dottie. "Not eccentric at all, he was trained as an orderly in a hospital, he just likes living by himself, that's all. What? Oh, retired, I suppose. He's a Welsh bard or something."

Emma went into the kitchen. "Mad, we've got to be discreet about this. No one must know Terry is there, or has broken his leg. There are road-blocks everywhere, as you heard on the news, and the marines are still looking for boys and young men who might have been involved in that fracas last night on Poldrea beach. And now since the explosions they'll be doubly watchful."

"I know, I know," said Mad impatiently. "Call Andy for me and we'll be off."

She had been gone about half-an-hour when Emma, who for want of anything better to do was dusting the music-room, heard the sound of a car. She looked out of the window and her heart missed a beat. It was the marine staff-car and Lieutenant Sherman was driving. Oh no . . . Oh, please, no . . . He climbed out of the car, opened the gate and walked swiftly up the garden path. Emma stood in the hall, uncertain what to do. She had better face him. Dottie might lose her head.

"Hullo," she said, but rather coldly, without enthusiasm.

"Hi," he said. Then smiled, and saluted. He looked very professional. "I'm sorry to hear about your grandmother," he said. "I called to enquire how she was."

113

"My grandmother?" repeated Emma. What on earth did he mean?

"Bush telegraph. News travels fast in these parts. I hope she wasn't too much shaken by the events of last night. We got quite a number of the hooligans, I'm thankful to say."

"On the contrary," replied Emma, "she wasn't shaken at all. Mr. Trembath drove us all home and she was in excellent spirits."

"Oh," he said, looking surprised, "then her heart attack came later? Well, I hope it's not too serious, and we can absolve ourselves from blame."

Emma continued staring. Was she going mad, or was he?

"I'd better explain," he said. "The fact is, we've got road-blocks everywhere, there have been several incidents throughout the county, and we're stopping all cars and examining passes. I'm in charge of a post five miles from here, on the main Poldrea-Liskeard road, and a Dr. Summers showed his pass to me and said he would be calling here later on, that your grandmother had sent for him, a suspected heart condition. So, as I was relieved shortly afterwards, I thought it only courteous to enquire. Has the doctor seen her yet?"

"No," said Emma, "not yet."

Suppose the oilskin-clad figure of Mao Tse-tung should suddenly emerge from the ploughed field beyond the garden?

"I guess he won't be long," said the lieutenant kindly. "You seem rather shocked yourself."

"Yes," said Emma, "I am."

She held on to the front door for support.

"Gee, it's tough," continued the lieutenant. "I do hope he won't find much wrong. She'll need to lie up, no doubt, and she won't like that."

"No," said Emma, "she won't."

The rain was still lashing down. He obviously hoped he would be asked inside.

"Do forgive me," said Emma, "but we're rather rushed off our feet with this . . . this happening. She's rather demanding. I have to sit by her bed." She backed away from the doorway.

"I understand." He seemed disappointed, though. "Just

one thing. You're not mad at me for last night, are you? I guess I got . . . maybe I was too free."

"No . . . no, not at all." Oh Lord, what was she saying?

"Fine . . . Then I'll call again, to enquire after your grandmother . . ." He smiled, "but on you too." The look of self-assurance had returned to his rather square face, his smile suggested that he and Emma were in league. "We'll get together and have a good time."

Then he saluted again, and walked back to the staff-car in the drive. Conceited ass, she thought, have a good time indeed . . . Does that means he expects a clinch down in the basement?

She was definitely off him. Had never been on. Thank heaven for one thing, which was that Mad and Sam had not returned during Wally Sherman's call. There was no doubt it was an idiotic name.

Scarcely had the lieutenant disappeared up the drive than Dr. Summers's Peugeot came rolling down it. He had evidently taken Mad's telephone call in all sincerity, because he only saw urgent cases in the morning after surgery. He's not going to be too pleased, thought Emma, and I don't know what I'm going to say to him. Dr. Summers did not ring the bell. He walked straight into the hall and threw down his raincoat. He was a man in his late fifties, stoutish, with a good head of hair. Patients thought his manner brusque until they had learnt to trust him.

"Hullo, Emma," he said. "How is the patient? Shall I go straight up? I told her to stay in bed."

"Look," said Emma, "I think you'd better come into the music-room." She shut the door behind him and drew a deep breath. "Mad sent for you on false pretences, but we do need you."

He did not blink an eyelid. He went and stood over by the fireplace.

"False pretences?" he echoed. "Oh well, it's not the first time. She might have chosen a less inconvenient day. What's she up to now?"

"It's Terry," said Emma, "he's broken his leg."

"Right. Why didn't she say so? I've brought something for a heart condition in my bag but nothing for a broken leg. Too bad."

"It's not that easy. She didn't know about the broken leg when she rang you up. The fact is . . ." Emma paused

115

—must she embark on the whole story yet again? "The fact is," she continued, "it all started at the firework party last night."

"Oh, that," Dr. Summers smiled. "I heard all about that. I gather your lot produced the guy. Did they throw the fireworks in the Commander's car too?"

"Well . . ."

"Listen here, Emma." He glanced at his watch. "I'm pushed for time. Does your grandmother want to see me or not, and where is Terry? Is he in his room? How do you know the leg is broken?"

"He's not in his room," said Emma, "nor is Mad. They're both in a hut in the woods with the beachcomber."

Dr. Summers stared at her steadily. "I've sorted out a few of your family troubles in my time, but this is a new one."

Emma embarked upon the case history, and was winding to her conclusion when Dr. Summers, who hadn't sat down but was looking out of the window, observed, "Here she comes now, but she's on her own. I'm surprised she didn't try carrying Terry on her back like your beachcomber."

They went out into the hall to meet her. Mad took off her cap and shook herself like a shaggy dog.

"Hullo, Bevil, I didn't expect you so soon, how splendid. Em darling, that Welshman is heaven! He's been telling me all about how he used to sing in a choir at Abernethy. He's got a beautiful voice. I asked him why he had never trained professionally, but apparently he had a sad love affair and ran away to sea. Dottie? Let's have lunch right away. I'm starving. Dr. Summers will be staying."

"Dr. Summers will do nothing of the kind." The doctor put his hand on Mad's shoulder and pushed her before him into the music-room. "I must say that for a woman of nearly eighty with a heart condition you look remarkably well. If you'll only stop talking for a moment we can sort things out. Terry has a broken leg, right? Your broken-hearted Welsh choirmaster has put it in splints, right? He hasn't informed you what type of break it is and he probably doesn't know, and a car can't get through that jungle down there so Terry must be brought up on a stretcher. Finally, and this seems to me to be the crux, you're afraid

116

the marine commandos may be after Terry because of what happened last night, hence the cloak-and-dagger business. Now tell Dottie to serve your lunch, and ask Joe to come with me to the hut. He's got more common sense than the rest of you. When I have seen Terry I shall decide what is to be done."

Mad smiled across at Emma. "What did I tell you? Didn't I do the right thing by sending for Bevil?"

"One of these days," said her doctor, "I shall disoblige you. And you can sort out your own mess."

It was after two before Emma and her grandmother sat down to lunch, and Mad switched on her radio to hear the news headlines. The announcer's voice sounded excited, his patch of country was in the news.

"Following explosions in the Falmouth area, there have been two more, one near Camborne and a second in the clay district, a mile from Nanpean. Other disturbances have been reported from South Wales. It is believed that Celtic factions amongst the population are taking this opportunity of giving vent to their dissatisfaction with the Coalition Government and the formation of USUK. Elsewhere the country is quiet. The President of the United States—I beg your pardon, of USUK—gave a dinner-party and reception for Her Majesty the Queen at the White House last night . . . Football. The match between Exeter University and Plymouth has been postponed owing to weather conditions. The next news bulletin from the south-west will be at three o'clock."

Nanpean . . . Emma remembered that one of Terry's friends from the technical school came from Nanpean. What was it Andy had told her last night about Terry's friends knowing where to find gelignite? Best forget it. And anyway, Terry was not involved. That broken leg, in the long run, might save them trouble. Which, unless you could be dispassionate, was a pretty hard-hearted thing to acknowledge.

As they got up from the table after lunch footsteps suggested that the doctor had returned.

"Come on, let's hear the worst."

Her grandmother made for the stairs leading to the hall, Emma following. Dr. Summers was already in the cloak-room, standing by the telephone. He nodded at them both.

"The leg's broken all right," he said. "I'm going to have

117

a word with Matron at the hospital. She'll fix him up with a bed."

"How do we get him there?" asked Emma.

"Leave that to me," said the doctor. "By the way, I brought Andy back with me, he's breathing fire and wants to get every marine on sight. Find him something to do. Hullo, Matron?"

Emma grabbed hold of Andy and marched him through the kitchen towards the playroom.

"Help Sam with the pigeon, he got loose," she told him.

"The pigeon's not priority," said Andy fiercely. "I'm going to sharpen my arrows."

"Don't be an idiot. You can't have archery practice this weather."

"Who said anything about practice? Emma, do you know the beachcomber has a short-wave radio he made himself and can get frequencies that we can't? He was telling Terry and me all about it, after Madam left. And Terry told me about the fight. He gave that Corporal Wagg a terrific bashing."

"Probably. It didn't do Terry much good, though, did it? Now run along."

By the time she returned to the hall Dr. Summers was already on his way down the path towards his car.

"Where's he going?" asked Emma.

"He's got to give Terry an injection," replied Mad. "He hasn't the right stuff in his bag. He says he won't be more than a quarter of an hour, and he'll be back."

"How is he going to get Terry to the car?"

"Oh, he fixed that with the beachcomber. I called him Taffy, by the way—he was delighted. He and Joe are rigging up a stretcher between them."

I'm beginning to sympathise with Dottie, thought Emma. Things happen too fast in this house. The rain was easing off, which was one good thing, although it was blowing just as hard. She wondered if she should put on her mac and boots and go down to the woods to help with the stretcher, and then, just as she had made up her mind to do so, she saw the little party advancing through the gap in the hedge by the ploughed field.

"Taffy's a genius," declared Mad, "he can put his hand to anything."

Terry, covered with a blanket and the beachcomber's

118

oilskin, was being borne along on a hurdle—or was it an old bedstead? Joe in front, Mr. Willis behind. They came to rest where there was cover under the lime trees by the drive, and Emma and her grandmother went down to meet them. Mr. Willis was hatless and so was Mad, and with their shocks of white hair blowing in the wind they could easily be brother and sister, Emma thought, and she was thankful Colin was safe in the playroom.

"He's stood his journey well," said Mr. Willis. "I don't think we've shaken him up too badly, have we, boyo?"

Terry tried to smile. He looked very white. Joe said nothing. He was arranging the blanket so that it didn't rest on Terry's leg. Mr. Willis stared critically up at the house, and Emma realised that despite the fact that he only lived at the bottom of the wood it was probably his first sight of it.

"You feel the wind up here," he said. "Nothing like as snug as my place."

"Oh, this is nothing," replied Mad. "When it really blows we have to batten down just as if we were on board ship. The whole house rocks."

"I can well believe it," he answered, staring at Mad with —was it astonishment or respect? Emma wondered if he was making a comparison with the star of forty years ago. She wished Bevil Summers would hurry up. They formed such a curious group huddled here under the lime trees. Joe looked disapproving and Terry whiter still.

"Of course in old days," said Mad, "it was a regular smugglers' haunt. We have a basement where they used to store the kegs of rum. There's one old wall, you can't see it from here . . ."

She seized the beachcomber by the sleeve and pointed, and she's off, sighed Emma, there'll be no stopping her. Further revelations, luckily, were cut short by the welcome arrival of the doctor's car.

"Ah," he said, "you've got him here intact. Well done. Now, Terry, show what you're made of. Stand back, everyone."

He advanced with his bag and proceeded to kneel beside the makeshift stretcher.

"I got through the road-block," he continued, glancing up at Mad, "by telling the chap on duty that I had to return to the surgery for a very strong sedative to quieten an old lady who was giving me trouble. I don't consider I was telling a lie. Incidentally, I understand from my secretary that the marines are picking up and questioning all youths between the ages of seventeen and twenty-one who have any connection with the technical school. Gelignite has been found on a couple of them. So, Terry, my boy, you slept at home last night, and unfortunately, when you opened the gate to me just now, as I was driving hurriedly in to bring the sedative to your ailing parent by adoption, I somehow succeeded in knocking you down with my car. My guilt is such that I insist on keeping an eye on you myself in the local hospital rather than have you transferred to Truro, where I don't mind betting, the commandos would sit at your bedside with notebook and pencil. Now then, this won't hurt."

He gave the injection, while Emma, who disliked jabs on principle, looked away. It was no use, however. She felt a buzzing in her ears and the world went black. The next thing she knew was that she was sitting on the drive and Mad was forcing her head between her knees.

"I might have known," her grandmother was saying. "She never could stand injections."

Emma raised her head and saw that all was over. The doctor and Mr. Willis had lifted Terry into the back of the car, and the doctor was patting Mr. Willis on the shoulder. "Good work," he said crisply. Then the beachcomber picked up the bedstead stretcher and began to plod away towards the orchard.

"Taffy," shouted Mad, "come back. I haven't thanked you for all you've done."

But Mr. Willis took no notice. Like Folly, the Dalmatian, his hearing was not what it had been.

Dr. Summers, with Terry comfortably arranged, looked down at Emma. "You told me when you were ten years old," he said, "that you'd like to be a nurse. If you want to make the grade you'll have to do rather better than you're doing now. As for you . . ." he turned to her grandmother, "you're supposed to have a serious heart condition, and I warn you that if I get another S.O.S. from Trevanal to say you're in trouble I shall ignore the signal. Look after them, Joe. Goodbye."

As his car went up the drive the telephone started ringing. Emma, stung by the doctor's allusion to her childhood fancy, went to answer it, despite her feeling of weakness below the knees. It was Myrtle Trembath.

"Emma," she said, "it's about Corporal Wagg. He's off duty and he's just been here." She sounded troubled and was speaking in a whisper. "He kept asking questions about Terry, and I couldn't say he was missing. I just told him I hadn't heard a word from Terry since last night and he must be at home."

"Don't worry," Emma replied. "Terry's all right. We know where he is. I can't explain over the telephone. I'll come down and see you in the morning."

"Oh, thank goodness . . . But Emma, the trouble is, Corporal Wagg believed what I said and is on his way to your place to see Terry."

"Well, too bad. He won't find him."

"I thought I'd better warn you . . . He was quite nice, actually, and said he was sorry for what happened last night, and hoped there'd be no hard feelings. I don't think he wants to pick Terry up, or anything like that, I believe he just wants to shake hands and apologise."

"All right, Myrtle. Thanks."

Apologise! A bit late in the day, and Terry in hospital with a broken leg. Not that slipping down the cliff had been the corporal's fault, except indirectly. Emma decided to keep Myrtle's information to herself. When the corporal turned up she would deal with him, and indeed take pleasure in telling him that Terry was in hospital under the doctor's care.

Corporal Wagg must have thought better of his good intention, for he never appeared. The rain ceased and the short November afternoon turned dim. Emma lay on the sofa in the music-room with her eyes closed. Bevil Summers had rung to report that Terry was "comfortable" in hospital, which was something, but the house felt empty without him.

It was about half-past five, curtains drawn, fire burning, when Joe came into the room. He was deathly pale.

"Emma," he said, "come with me."

"What is it?"

He shook his head. He could not speak. Softly he opened the front door and beckoned Emma after him. It had stopped raining, the clouds had parted, the evening was fine and clear. He took her hand and led her to the look-out and down to the ploughed field beyond. She saw then that there was something lying a few yards distant, a dark shape, spreadeagled. Joe, still holding her by the hand, led her to the body. It was Corporal Wagg. He was lying on his back, dead, with one of the lethal arrows between his eyes.

10

They stood there side by side staring down. Joe did not let go of her hand. The arrow's jagged tip must have pierced some vital point behind the corporal's right eye, because part of the eye lolled out, horribly, and the blood that had flowed at first was now congealed. Neither of them spoke. Emma tried to remember when it was that Myrtle had telephoned. Was it half-past three, was it four? Corporal Wagg had been on his way, having already left the farm. He might have wandered about the fields first, he might have gone on to the main road from the farm track and then cut back. He was off duty. Time was no object.

Emma looked away from the body and up at Joe. She felt strangely calm.

"He was coming to the house," she said. "He wanted to apologise to Terry for the fight."

"How do you know?"

"Myrtle told me. It was Myrtle on the telephone. I didn't tell anyone, there seemed no reason why I should. When the corporal didn't turn up I thought he had changed his mind. It didn't seem to matter much."

"You could have told me. I would have come to meet him. It wouldn't have happened then."

"I know. I didn't think." Numbness that had been shock was wearing off. Horror was seeping into her, taking over.

Although it was dark, the visibility that had been poor all day had cleared now that the rain had ceased. Lights showed from the warship at anchor, she no longer seemed so far away. Across the bay the lights of Mevagissey shone brightly too, as they always did on a fine night. The beam from the lighthouse glowed, then faded, then glowed again.

"When he doesn't return to camp it will be reported," said Joe.

"Yes."

"Some of his mates may have known where he was going. He may have told them he was thinking of calling on Myrtle at the farm." Joe bent down and gently, very gently, seized the arrow and tried to pull it away from between the corporal's eyes, but it wouldn't move. "I can't shift it," he whispered, "it's too deep."

"Oh God," said Emma, "what are we going to do?"

The night was becoming clearer all the time, and the lights from the warship seemed brighter too. In the first glimmer of morning the ploughed field would be like an open map beneath a helicopter flying overhead.

"We've got to get him away," said Joe, "we've got to get rid of his body. I might dig a pit up in the shrubbery, where there's all that dead wood lying around." He stared up at her, his face haggard.

"No," said Emma, "it wouldn't be any use. Once he's missing, and they come for him, surely they'll bring tracker dogs. Wouldn't they trace him as far as here, and then to the shrubbery, no matter how deeply you dug a pit?"

"Perhaps they would," said Joe. "I don't know . . ." And then, in desperation, "We've got to tell someone. We've got to have proper advice. Couldn't you ring Dr. Summers?"

"No . . . Joe, we can't. Look what he's done for Terry today, lied, taken the blame on himself. Besides, how could he help with . . . with this?"

So little time . . . Mad would be wondering where she had gone, where Joe had gone. And a further problem lay ahead. There was Andy to consider. Andy must be their prime concern.

"Joe," she whispered, "how did he do it? Could he have let fly at random and never even seen the corporal?"

Joe shook his head. "No," he said grimly, "Andy's aim is far too accurate. He knows what he did all right, no mistake about that. My guess is that he came out to the pile of logs by the wall, just for practice maybe, and then spied Corporal Wagg coming across the field, and took aim and got him."

"Oh God . . ." whispered Emma, "oh God . . ."

It seemed to her then that the events of tonight, last night, the preceding days, had all been foredoomed. They dated back to that first panic shot by the unknown marine who had taken fright at Spry. Since that fatal moment the world about them, safe, secure, had become threatening to all the boys, to Terry, to Sam, to Andy, even to Joe himself; born to insecurity, then loved and cherished, the shadows whence the boys had sprung were steadily closing in on them again. And Mad, with the power she had over all of them, had not helped. She had encouraged fantasy, built up their imaginations, and this, for Andy certainly, had now proved his undoing. How could a child tell truth from falsehood, reality from make-believe, when she who had nurtured him from babyhood had fed him with images of her own creation, phantoms from a grease-paint world? The fascination of her puppet-show had driven Terry to bravado and pseudo-gallantry, and Andy to murder.

"It's Mad's fault," said Emma. "Andy's not to blame."

Joe stared at her, outrage in his eyes. "How can it be her fault? She doesn't know."

Emma gestured, hands spread out, and even as she did so, the gesture instinctive, she realised that this was what her grandmother did when urged to explanation, that her stance was the same, feet a little apart, chin jutting forward, and it was like being imprisoned in a net—or could it be a shroud?—from which there could never be escape. Not for her, at least, but surely for the boys?

"It's the way she's brought us up," said Emma, "you, me, all of us. Now we're going to start paying for it, first Terry, then Andy."

The outrage in Joe's eyes turned to pity, then disgust. "There's a saying, isn't there, about biting the hand that feeds you? I never thought you'd say a thing like that.

125

What we've discovered here is beastly, yes, and we're both of us shocked, you specially, I can't blame you, but don't put the fault on her . . ."

He bent down once more, and seizing the corporal's body by the heels, dragged it from the ploughed earth to the brambled ditch beneath the wall. The bare head bumped the soil as it was moved, the arrow stuck between the eyes jerking to and fro, and Emma, staring, hypnotised, thought this was a man once, breathing, smiling. Last night he held Myrtle in his arms and made love to her down on Poldrea beach. Vomit rose in her throat, and retching, she spat away both venom and fear. We fear the living, not the dead, the body lying in the ditch is nothing, a husk, whatever indignities we inflict upon it now doesn't matter, the flame is quenched.

"I know what we must do," she said, "we must tell Mr. Trembath. He's embroiled anyway, because of Myrtle, should the marines go to the farm tomorrow and ask questions. But Myrtle mustn't know Corporal Wagg is dead or what has happened. She'd break down at once, under questioning."

Joe thought for a moment or two, then nodded. "He's got his Land-Rover. We could lift the body into it, for a start. Cover it with manure, maybe. Then decide what to do. I think you're right, Emma." He looked back towards the house. "What's the time?"

Emma glanced at her watch. "Just on six."

"I'll go to the farm," Joe told her. "They'll be sitting to tea now milking's over. I can easily get Mr. Trembath outside, tell him one of the ewes in lamb has strayed from their home pasture, anything. Then I'll bring him up here. You'd best nip back to the house, and if Madam asks for me tell her the same story about the sheep."

He strode off at once, keeping under the lea of the hedge that defined the Trevanal boundary. Emma watched his figure disappear over the rim of rising ground, and looking down once more at the body in the ditch she tried to imagine how she would feel if instead of Corporal Wagg, barely known, it had been Joe lying there, or Terry. You don't suffer, she thought, until it hits you, or you may suffer but you have to train yourself to stand it, that's why doctors remain calm, and nurses too; but for their training they'd crumple. And that's why Mad is brave in times of

126

stress and keeps a bold front, because she is acting a part, she is trained to be someone else, and you can't touch the core underneath. She went into the house just as Colin and Ben were coming out of the library on their way to bath and supper.

"Hallo," said Colin, "where've you been?"

"Just for a breath. Do you know what Andy and Sam are doing?"

"They're in the playroom, I think. At least Sam was. He was starting to write a letter to Terry to cheer him up in the hospital. All right, coming, Dottie."

Colin sighed, as though the impatience of elderly adults was a burden to be borne with resignation, shrugged, raised his eyes to heaven and wandered into the kitchen after Ben like an old man of ninety. At least he knows nothing, thought Emma, he could never have kept it to himself. She went into the library. Her grandmother was watching the news.

"If only that man wouldn't wear that appalling spotted tie," she exclaimed. "Somebody ought to tell him it clashes with his hair. They're making the most of the explosions, I knew they would. Turn it off, Em. I can't take any more." She threw herself back in her chair and removed her glasses. Then she stared at Emma. "Anything wrong, darling?"

"No . . ." Her voice wasn't right, though. Unconvincing.

"Oh yes, there is. You're not feeling faint again, are you?"

"Of course not. Just a bit tired."

Joe would soon be at the farm. What if Mr. Trembath wasn't there, had gone to Poldrea, and Myrtle answered the door?

"There *is* something wrong," said Mad, leaning forward. "Emma, what is it?"

Very well, then. Take it, cope with it, you are responsible, Andy's future is in your hands. Am I my adopted brother's keeper? No . . .

"Something terrible has happened," said Emma. "Joe and I have just found a body in the field outside the wall. It's the body of Corporal Wagg. He's been shot between the eyes with one of the arrows. The arrow is still there, so is the body. Joe has gone down to the farm to tell Mr. Trembath."

127

She realised she was trembling all over, but her voice was steady. Speaking had brought relief from tension. Mad looked puzzled. The expression of someone slightly deaf, who hasn't heard distinctly. But this time it was not an assumed expression, it was genuine.

"Corporal Wagg?" she repeated. "That marine who was over in the stables when they were all here. Do you mean he is dead?"

"Yes," said Emma. This time she spoke more slowly. "He is lying dead out there in the field, shot by one of the arrows you gave Andy."

This time the message got through. Perplexity gave way to wonder, wonder to realisation. But not to horror. That was the frightful thing.

"Then Andy obviously did it," said Mad. "How careless of him not to bring back the arrow, and why didn't he come and tell me?"

Emma looked at her grandmother incredulously. Had the shock been too much for her? Was this the beginning of senile decay?

"Mad," she said, "that corporal has been murdered, and by a child of barely twelve years old. Do you realise what this means?"

Mad gestured impatiently, spread her hands. "Of course I do, what do you take me for? Don't be so melodramatic. We have to keep our heads, and thank heaven Joe has kept his. He couldn't have done anything more sensible than to go down to the farm and get hold of Jack Trembath."

"That," Emma told her, "was my idea."

"Good for you. A pity it couldn't have happened when Bevil was here, then he could have coped. He and the beachcomber between them. We can always call Taffy in if Jack Trembath wants extra help, which he well might do. It's not so easy to dispose of a body." She got up and began to walk up and down the room. "No use just dumping it over the cliff as if he had fallen, because of the wound from the arrow—shot between the eyes, did you say? Was there an awful mess?"

Emma did not answer. She just went on staring at her grandmother.

"Darling Em . . ." The hand on her head, the caress, the warmth in the voice was loving, sympathetic, yet

128

curiously detached. "Why not have a stiff drink? There's some brandy on the sideboard in the dining-room. I may need it later, but not yet."

Emma walked like an automaton into the dining-room and poured herself a brandy in a sherry glass, neat. The taste was revolting. She hated brandy. It gave her a sensation of strength all the same. She went back to the library.

"What now?" she asked.

"Go and call Andy," said her grandmother. "The little ones should be in the bath by now."

The brandy had brought courage as well as strength. If Andy was to be cross-questioned, wouldn't he break down, cry, possibly deny all knowledge of what had happened? Wouldn't it be better, perhaps, if nothing was said, if everyone, she, Joe, Mad, all pretended ignorance, and then in the morning, when the body was no longer there, mightn't Andy think it had been a dream, that he had imagined it all? They were not geared to such a situation. Neither she nor her grandmother. Maybe they should get in touch with the doctor after all.

"Mad," she said, "you must be terribly careful what you say. I know he's not sensitive, like Sam, but on the other hand he may be absolutely terrified of being found out. He might try and run away, he might . . ."

"Oh darling, do get a move on, time is all-important."

Emma went through to the boys' quarters, but she did not trust herself to penetrate the middle boys' bedroom.

"Andy?" she called.

"Yes?"

"Come through to the library, will you? Just you, not Sam. Mad wants a word with you."

Coward-like, she did not wait for him. She went on ahead, and returning to the library sat down on the sofa, pretending to look at the *Radio Times*. She glanced up furtively as Andy came into the room. He did not look any different. His hair was more rumpled than usual, perhaps.

"Yes, darling," said Mad. "You've given poor Em an awful fright. She went out for a breath of air by the lookout and saw Corporal Wagg lying dead in the field with one of your arrows stuck in him. She came in to tell me and I had to give her some brandy."

"Did you want me for something?" he asked.

129

Andy turned to Emma in consternation. "Oh, Emma, I am sorry. I didn't want you to see. I was going to wait until Joe came up to the playroom and then explain to him what had happened."

Emma did not say anything. There was still some of the brandy left in the sherry glass. She reached out for it and drank it down.

"Why didn't you come and tell me?" asked Mad.

"I couldn't very well," explained Andy. "Colin and Ben were just coming through to you here, and I didn't want them to know any more than Emma. So I told Sam, as we couldn't find Joe. We tried to pull the arrow out but it was stuck hard. I got him in one shot, and it must have killed him at once, because he didn't seem to be breathing."

"I see," said Mad. She waited a moment, and then she asked, "How did it happen? Did you mean to hit him?"

"Oh yes," replied Andy. "I was crouching by the pile of wood at the look-out, and he came walking up the field. I knew it was Corporal Wagg, the marine who had been fighting Terry, and I guessed he was on his way to look for him, not knowing Terry was in hospital. So I thought, I'll settle you, my man, and I took aim and got him. He didn't even cry out, he just fell."

"H'm," said Mad. She began to whistle softly under her breath. "The trouble is," she went on after a moment, "the marines will realise he's missing and may come and look for him, seeing that he knew his way about here."

"Yes," said Andy, "Sam and I thought of that. We've hidden the bow and the rest of the arrows up my hiding-place in the chimney, so they'll never find the weapon. It's the body that's the difficulty. We can't just let it lie there."

"I know," Mad agreed. "Well, Em discussed it with Joe, who's gone down to tell Mr. Trembath. We can trust him. They'll think of something out between them."

"Oh, what a relief." Andy sighed. "I was really rather worried. Of course, when one of the sheep dies Mr. Trembath digs a pit and buries it. I've watched him do it. He might do the same for the corporal."

"He might," said Mad, "we shall have to see what he says. Anyway, the little boys mustn't know about it, and of course not Dottie."

"Of course not."

"And tell Sam not to say anything either . . . What did he do when you told him?"

"Sam? He said it was a very good shot, but a shame I couldn't have got the marine who killed Spry, then it would have been real justice."

"Yes . . . Well, darling, I'll let you know in the morning what Joe and Mr. Trembath fix up. Oh, by the way, Dr. Summers rang up earlier to say Terry was all right and comfortable in hospital."

"Oh, super. Poor old Terry, he'll hate being stuck away there, out of everything. Still, he's had his revenge. Good night, Madam, good night, Em."

Andy went out of the room. There was silence. Granddaughter stared at grandmother.

"Do you realise," said Emma slowly, "he doesn't even know he's done wrong?"

Mad picked up Emma's glass, saw it was empty, then put it down again. "I do," she replied, "and if you think this is the moment to impress the fact upon him then you don't understand much about Andy." She got up and walked over to the electric fire and switched it off. "If," she said, "as a small child you are sole survivor of an aircrash, and are found lying unhurt shielded by your father's body, it has a traumatic effect. Some day you hit back. Unfortunately for the corporal, the opportunity came tonight."

"But, Mad . . ." Emma stood up as well, the session was evidently over, "do you mean to say Andy would have killed someone anyway, that—well, he's some sort of psychopath?"

Her grandmother looked at her compassionately. "Darling, of course not. Andy's a perfectly ordinary child with a wound deep down that won't easily heal. Normally he wouldn't hurt a fly. What you forget is that these are not normal times. He looked upon that marine as an enemy, an invader, who had tried to beat up Terry. To be brutally frank, I agree with his point of view."

She walked into the hall and through to the cloakroom, and began dragging on her boots.

"Where are you going?" asked Emma.

"To find out what Joe and Jack Trembath have decided. Do you want to come?"

They went out together to the look-out. The dark hump

131

of the Land-Rover was parked near to the hedge a little higher up the field. The two figures, the farmer and Joe, were standing beneath the wall, close to the ditch. Jack Trembath was bending down. They couldn't see what he was doing, but Emma knew. He was trying to extract the arrow from its embedded position between the eyes. She wondered why she felt neither sick nor faint, yet earlier in the day, when Bevil Summers had given Terry the injection, she couldn't take it. She supposed the reason was obvious. Terry was family. Corporal Wagg was not. Corporal Wagg was one of an invading force, as Mad had tried to insist, and by ill-chance Corporal Wagg was dead. He might have a wife back in America, he might have children, parents, he had been coming to the house in all honesty to shake hands with Terry; instead, Andy had killed him. I don't seem to mind any more, she thought, I'm not shocked or even sickened. Perhaps I'm being trained for something . . . but for what?

"Ah! Got it . . ." Jack Trembath, with a grunt of satisfaction, had succeeded in pulling out the arrow. "Not broken neither," he said to Joe. "Lucky job." He reached out for a tussock of grass from the overhanging bank and wiped the barb and the shaft, letting the tussock fall to the ground afterwards.

"I wouldn't do that," Mad called softly. "There'll be blood on it, won't there?"

The farmer looked up and saw them both watching him from beyond the wall. "You're right," he said, "it won't do to be careless." He picked up the tussock, and going to the Land-Rover came back with a sack, and put the tussock and arrow into it. "Easy enough to get rid of that. The body's more of a problem. Don't you think you and Emma had best go back to the house and leave us to it?"

"No," said Mad, "I want to know what you decide."

Jack Trembath looked over his shoulder and stared out to sea. "No use just heaving him to cliff and letting them think he's slipped over the edge. There's this damned great wound between the eyes. You wouldn't get that from falling."

"We could carry him to the beach," suggested Joe, "and let the tide get him."

"What's the tide doing, then?" asked the farmer. "It must have gone high water about an hour ago. Top of
132

springs was yesterday, I believe. The tides will be taking off again tonight. No good just carrying him down and leaving him on the beach, it wouldn't fool anyone."

"There's another thing," put in Joe. "If they should trace the corporal as far as this—Emma suggested earlier, you never know, they might even bring tracker dogs—it would look odd if the scent suddenly stopped, and then the marks of your tyres were just above. We can't put him in the Land-Rover. They could trace him to that too, if they were doing a thorough job."

Silence fell. Jack Trembath stroked his chin and stared down at the body. The wind began to freshen once more and clouds scudded across the sky. A spot of rain fell.

"Watch out," said Emma, "someone's coming up the field."

Joe and the farmer backed against the hedge. Instinctively Emma dragged her grandmother behind the shelter of an ilex tree nearby.

"Wait," said Mad, "isn't it the beachcomber?"

The figure plodded slowly up the ploughed field. He was coming from the direction of the wood.

"Yes," said Joe, "it's Mr. Willis."

Jack Trembath cursed under his breath. "Don't worry. I'll get rid of him somehow."

Mad stood out from behind the ilex. "No," she said, "he's all right. He's already helped us today, and if I'm any judge of character he'll help us again."

She climbed down into the field, assisted by the farmer, and then as the beachcomber approached, for he lifted his head and obviously perceived the little party beneath the wall, she raised her hand and beckoned.

"He's a queer old cuss and gives no trouble," murmured Jack Trembath, "but with the fix we're in now . . . are you sure?"

Mad did not answer. She waited for the Welshman to close up on them, and allowed him to speak first. He was carrying Terry's pullover.

"The boyo left this behind in all the excitement," he said. "I thought he might need it in the hospital. I didn't mean to intrude, just to drop it in at your back entrance. Evening, mister." He nodded to the farmer. "One of your sheep strayed?" He glanced across at the Land-Rover.

"No," said Mad, "I'm afraid we're in trouble again. Bad trouble, this time."

She took the Welshman by the arm and led him to the body lying in the ditch. He stared down at it. Then gave a low whistle under his breath.

"Trouble it is," he said. "How'd he come by the gash, then?"

"It was Andy," said Mad. "He was up behind the wall here with his bow and a particularly deadly arrow, as the marine was coming down the field from the farm. He took aim, and the arrow found its mark."

"It did that all right," said the Welshman. "What became of the arrow?"

"I have it in a sack," replied Jack Trembath. "No problem there. It's the body, isn't it?"

Mr. Willis did not answer. He walked round the dark form lying on the ground as though he wanted to view it from every angle, then bent down for a closer inspection.

"The blood's caked," he said. "Some of it on the soil, though. We can turn that in. What was he doing here anyway?" The events of the preceding hours were explained to him. He nodded, and did not interrupt. "No one knows of his visit to the farm excepting your daughter?" he asked Jack Trembath.

"Not as far as I know," answered the farmer. "Mick and I were milking at the time. My wife was home. She never mentioned the corporal. I take it Myrtle saw him off pretty quick. She knew how we felt."

"The difficulty is," said Joe, "we don't know if the corporal told his mates where he was going. He was off duty, you see. Myrtle knew that."

"We have to make it seem as if the fellow came up here and altered his mind," Mr. Willis said. "Turned off down the path in the centre of the field, and then down to the cliffs and the beach. If they came looking for footprints they wouldn't find them on the path anyway, the ground's too hard despite the rain. There'd be scent, though."

Jack Trembath was listening attentively, but he seemed puzzled all the same.

"I don't follow your drift, mister," he said.

The Welshman looked once again towards the Land-Rover. "How many sacks have you got in there?"

"About half a dozen, could be more."

"Very well then, fetch them, also some twine and a length of rope, if you have it."

Mad moved back towards the wall and held up her hands to Emma, who leant forward and pulled her up from the field.

"What did I tell you?" Mad whispered. "I knew he'd take charge."

Jack Trembath came back from the Land-Rover with the sacks, and some twine and rope. Mr. Willis knelt down and began wrapping the head, shoulders and trunk of the corporal's body in the sacks, tying each part in turn with the twine. When he came to the feet he did not hesitate; he removed the boots from the dead man, and taking off his own sea-boots, which he strung round his neck, he placed the corporal's boots on his own feet.

He glanced up, winking at the farmer. "It's not that I fancy them, but the scent will be on the ground, like the fellow was walking himself. Better be sure than sorry."

The corporal's body now looked like a package, and Mr. Willis looped the length of rope about it and hoisted it over his shoulders. His own boots were hanging in front of him, the long trussed package, from which protruded a pair of stockinged feet, was slung across his back. Then he looked up at the group watching him so intently.

"Last night," he said, "I brought a living boy up from the shore on my back. Tonight I'll take a dead boy down to it. Easier altogether, I shan't have to worry about breaking bones." He paused a moment, glancing from one to the other. "You get in the Land-Rover," he said to the farmer. "Circuit the field, I'll see you presently." Then he smiled at Mad standing beside Emma above the wall. "I've done many jobs in my time, more unpleasant than this one. If a man can't help his neighbour, and she a female, life wouldn't be worth living, would it?"

He started walking back the way he had come, turning off by the path down the centre of the ploughed earth towards the grazing ground below and the cliffs beyond. As he walked the package bobbed on his back and the hanging legs dipped the ground. They stood there watching him until his figure vanished out of sight. Jack Trembath jerked his head at Joe and the pair of them moved towards the Land-Rover. In a moment or two he had started the engine, and the Land-Rover began to circuit the field, keeping close in to the edge. The lights from Mevagissey across the bay continued to flicker, with those of the warship steady and bright.

"That's it," said Mad, "we must leave it to them."

She turned away from the wall, back through the garden to the house. They took off their boots in the cloakroom.

"I think," said Mad, "I might have that brandy now. Only a splash, mostly soda."

"Do you think," said Emma, "I ought just to slip through and see if Andy is all right?"

Mad considered the matter. "He will be," she said, "but go if you like. Just tell him everything is under control and give him a kiss from me."

Emma went through the kitchen to reach the middle boys' bedroom. Dottie was standing by the stove cooking supper.

"Everyone gone down like angels," she said. "Peace be upon this house, that's what I say. It's not often like this."

Emma softly opened the door of the boys' room. It was in darkness. One of them stirred.

"It's all right," she whispered. "It's only me."

Andy sat up in his bunk and flashed his torch in her face. "Sam's asleep," he whispered back, "don't wake him up."

Sam with his eyes closed looked quite different, his expression calm and serene. The pigeon in the lair close to him was also roosting, feathers fluffed, head hunched. The squirrel had rolled itself into a ball.

"Everything's all right," said Emma. "Mad said to tell you. Under control. And I was to give you a kiss from her."

She did this and Andy patted her shoulder. "Sorry I gave you a fright," he said. "I hope you won't have nightmares. Is Joe still with Mr. Trembath?"

"Yes. And the beachcomber turned up with Terry's pullover. He took charge. Joe will tell you about it in the morning."

"That was good. I'd trust Mr. Willis with anything. He's really Sam's friend, but now I shall make him mine too."

He looked suddenly thoughtful, and Emma, anxious,

136

wondered if possibly, deep down, the realisation of what he had done was at last breaking through.

"You know," he said, "I was thinking just now, before you came in, it's very sad my father isn't alive, so I could tell him about this."

Emma took hold of his hand. "Why, darling?" she asked.

"You wouldn't understand," he said, shaking his head. "After all, you are a girl. I think Madam realises, but then she's old." The slow smile that was Andy's most endearing feature spread across his face. "A boy likes his father to know when he's made his first kill," he said.

He put out his torch and turned on his side.

11

There was nothing about any missing marine on the local news the following morning. Newspapers, radio and television featured as the big story of the day a new monetary arrangement between USUK and its allies, pointing out that the trade implications of this wide association of nations would be enormous. A new defensive alliance between the English-speaking peoples, to be known as ESPDA, would play the role that NATO had attempted to do in the past, but in a far wider context, having nuclear bases on both sides of the Atlantic from north to south, as well as in the Pacific and Indian oceans. The actual method of defence and attack, should war ever come between ESPDA and foreign powers—which, editorials and spokesmen fervently hoped, would never happen —would probably be by nuclear-powered submarines, carrying missiles of tremendous range.

Plans for Great Britain herself would take some little time to formulate. It must be recognised that her heyday as a great industrial nation had now ended, but a new future lay ahead for her as the historical and cultural centre of the English-speaking peoples. Just as some years previously people on holiday had gone in their thousands to the Costa Brava in Spain for sea and sunshine, so now tourists would flock in their millions to explore the country that had given birth to Shakespeare, Milton, Lord Byron, Lord Olivier, Nelson (the order of priority seemed rather odd), Florence Nightingale and others. The scope was literally tremendous. "There is not a county in England or Wales," wrote an enthusiastic supporter of the scheme, "that is not steeped in history. King John signing Magna Carta at Runnymede . . . Richard III losing his crown at Bosworth Field . . . the Wars of the Roses . . . all these scenes and countless others could be enacted for our visitors. Hotels and restaurants could be transformed into old coaching inns as a further attraction. Bear-baiting, cock-fighting, jousting, duelling, masked highwaymen on horseback—the tourist could watch them all from the comfort of a roofed-in stadium, or even from his car."

This was one of the extracts that Mad read aloud to her grand-daughter. She threw the paper across the room and took up the local weekly. The message was the same, if slightly less enthusiastic. "We have suffered from a high level of regional unemployment for some time," said the editorial. "Possibly becoming members of USUK will help us to solve this problem. Our partners from across the Atlantic have pointed out that the Cornish china clay industry is on the decline. Therefore we must turn to tourism in a far more concentrated way." There was a brief report on the explosions in various part of the country. Lawless elements would be stamped out, and all members of the community must go quietly about their business. If the weekend passed off without incident the schools would open again on Monday.

"Well, that's a relief anyway," said Emma. "We shan't have to wonder what to do with the boys from nine till four. The only trouble is . . ." She was wondering about Andy. Could he really be trusted to hold his tongue, or would the desire to show off to his school companions prove too much for him?

"Dont worry," said Mad. "I know what you're thinking. I shan't talk to him but Joe will, if he hasn't done so already. Have you seen Joe yet?"

"No, he wasn't in the kitchen when I went to breakfast. Dottie told me he had had it early and had gone out."

"My instructions," said her grandmother. "I sent him down to the farm to check that our story and the Trembaths' are one and the same, remembering, of course, that Myrtle and her mother know nothing. Everything else has been taken care of. Joe reported to me when he got back last night."

So that was why the light from Mad's corner of the house had remained on until nearly midnight. Emma, who had gone early to bed, had seen it from her own bedroom.

"What happened?" she asked.

"Ask Joe," replied her grandmother. "Taffy disposed of his burden. I knew he would."

The telephone rang and Mad reached out for it.

"Wait," said Emma, "don't forget you had a heart attack yesterday. We don't know who it is."

Mad handed over the receiver. "Take it easy," she said, "and be careful. If it should be someone asking after me tell whoever it is that I'm much better. The heart attack served its purpose, but I don't want to be stuck up here all day."

Emma nodded. "Yes?" she said. "This is Trevanal."

A strange voice the other end saying, "One moment, please." She raised her eyebrows at Mad, shrugged, and listened again. Then a familiar voice came on the line, demanding, slightly imperious. It was Pa.

"Oh," said Emma, "it's you." (She mouthed the information to Mad.)

"Can you hear me, you sound very faint," he said, and, not waiting for an answer, went on. "What's all this I hear about Mad getting up and making herself objectionable at some meeting or other and insulting your local M.P.? Oh, never mind how I found out, I have my informers. She's made a great deal of trouble. You really must stop this sort of thing. And that's not all. Weren't you all conspicuous at a firework party down on Poldrea beach? If she's not damned careful she'll be put under house arrest for attempting to disturb the peace, or, worse, bunged into a looney-bin. Is she there? Let me speak to her."

"Hold on," said his daughter. She put her hand over the mouth-piece. "Go on, you'd better," she whispered, "he sounds very angry. Knows about the meeting and the fireworks."

141

She handed the telephone to her grandmother. Mad smiled and settled herself against her pillow.

"Vic darling?" she said indulgently. "How sweet of you to ring. I'm a lot better, thank goodness. Bevil came out and gave me some pills. It was rather unpleasant while it lasted, all the same. A horrid stabbing sensation under the heart."

Emma could hear a torrent of questions at the other end of the line. It sounded like a tape-recorder being played backwards very fast.

"Oh? Oh, I thought that was why you were ringing," Mad continued. "You seem to get the news so quickly. No, as I said, I'm much better, Bevil advised rest for twenty-four hours. I hardly think a second opinion is necessary. Well, naturally, should I have another attack . . . Yes, I've masses of pills." (She made a delighted face at her grand-daughter.) "Doing too much? No, I'm taking life very easy. More than you seem to be doing. But we have had one wretched accident that has upset us all." (Emma's heart missed a beat.) "Darling Terry has had to go into hospital with a broken leg. Such a stupid thing to happen. Bevil turned into the drive too fast on his way to attend to me and his bumper hit Terry, who was waiting for him at the gate. Yes, I suppose it was careless, but it was only his concern for me that . . . No, darling, there's absolutely no necessity for you to come down and sort us all out, as you put it . . . Well yes, of course we want to see you. How can you say such a thing . . ." (She's done it, thought Emma, she's gone too far, she's made Pa hot and bothered, and as he's as determined as she is, we're for it.) "Well, of course, any time you like, you know your room is always ready for you, we'll expect you when we see you . . . No, I shan't be staying in bed . . ." The tape-recorder continued at the other end of the line and Mad raised her eyes to heaven. "Yes, yes, you'll come by car . . . road-blocks won't prevent you, you have a special pass? You're lucky, it's more than we have . . ."

The session ended, Mad turned to her grand-daughter with a gesture. "What was I to do?" she said. "He insisted on coming, you know how he can be. Turn on the electric blanket in the spare room, Em, there's an angel, and tell

142

Dottie to ring up Tom Bate and see if he has any lemon sole."

It wanted but this, thought Emma as she went about her duties, that we have a missing boy one moment and a deliberate killing the next; and now, to crown all, Pa, who knows nothing of any of it and is obviously hand-in-glove with the authorities, the government, Members of Parliament, USUK, the lot, is about to descend upon the household, today, tonight, tomorrow—he was in such a fever of pressure he hadn't even said when. Life is too complicated, she decided, as she drove the car down to Poldrea to do the necessary shopping, showing her pass at the road-block and casting a furtive glance at the wired-in beach. She had not yet seen Joe, she knew nothing of what had transpired between him, the beach-comber and Mr. Trembath after they had all disappeared the evening before, except that her grandmother had told her all was well. The boys, Andy and Sam, whom she had glimpsed for a brief moment during the snatched meal of breakfast, appeared perfectly normal, and talked of letting the pigeon out to try his mended wing. The little boys had decided to enact David and Goliath, which on second thoughts held sinister overtones of the true events of the preceding day.

The first person Emma ran into in the supermarket was Peggy Trembath. Her instinct was to dodge out of the store to avoid questioning, but she moved too late. Mrs. Trembath had seen her.

"Have they been up to your place yet?" she asked, putting her hand on Emma's sleeve.

"Who? What?" replied Emma, startled.

"That marine officer," said Mrs. Trembath, lowering her voice, "with two of his men. They've been up asking us all sorts of questions; poor Myrtle was in tears until her father took over and spoke to the officer straight. 'You bully my girl,' he said, 'and I'll go right to your commanding officer. All I can tell you is that if one of your corporals has gone missing it's because he doesn't want to be found. He knew better than to hang about here after a girl under age. Myrtle's not sixteen, you know.' Well, after that I took Myrtle upstairs and came away down to do the shopping. But I heard the officer tell

143

Jack they were going to Trevanal after he'd made a thorough search of our fields."

It was happening much too soon. Emma had believed herself prepared, but it wasn't so. Her heart began to beat more rapidly.

"We can't tell them anything," she said. "We've had our own troubles. You heard about Terry?"

"Yes," said Mrs. Trembath. "Knocked down by the doctor, wasn't he? Joe was helping Jack round up one of the sheep last night and told him. Whatever made him stay out and hide, though, after the fireworks?"

Emma swallowed. She had forgotten Mrs. Trembath knew nothing of Terry's real accident and the night passed at the hut in the woods.

"Oh, I don't know," she said, "just silliness. Look, my love to Myrtle, and tell her Terry's O.K. I must get on . . ."

She walked through the supermarket like an automaton. Meat, bacon, cheese, sugar, she consulted the list Dottie had given her, and nodded or smiled to familiar faces milling about her, without recognition but from force of habit. Then she walked along the narrow pavement to the fishmonger. Tom Bate was alone in his shop. There didn't seem much demand for his wares.

"No lemon sole, my dear," he said to Emma. "Some nice fresh plaice."

Plaice was the end, thought Emma, but it was Pa's fault, he always demanded fish. Dottie would doll it up somehow. She waited while he filleted the fish.

"Was it the boys' idea or your gran's to dress up that guy?" he asked her.

Emma stared. The firework display seemed a long while ago. She forced a smile. "I think it was a bit of both," she told him.

Tom Bate chuckled. "Best darn thing I ever saw," he said. "We won't forget that in a hurry. Nor her speech at the town hall neither. You tell your gran from me there's plenty more in Poldrea thinks the way she do, and who'll back her up, what's more, if need be."

"Thank you, Mr. Bate, I will," replied Emma.

"This new idea," Tom Bate went on as he handed over the wrapped plaice. "Turning us into a fair ground, with all this talk about going back to the old days. Before we know where we are, they'll have us all dressed up as

144

smugglers and pirates and the like. I tell you one thing. If I catch any Yankee tourist in a frog-suit after my lobster-pots when the season comes around, I'll use him as blinkin' bait."

Them and us, thought Emma as she left the shop, them and us . . . There seemed to be more marines about in Poldrea than there had been on Tuesday, when she had come shopping with her grandmother. It's no good, she decided, it isn't just a visit from friendly allied forces, it's occupation. And on the return journey she wondered if it was imagination only that made her feel the marine on duty at the barricade scrutinised her pass more closely. It was either imagination or a guilty conscience.

"O.K.?" she asked, smiling pleasantly.

"O.K.," he said, and waved her on. He didn't smile.

She turned down the drive and put the car away. Colin and Sam were playing behind the disused stable-block and came running out to greet her. Colin, whether in the guise of Goliath or a commando, was wearing one of Dottie's colanders on his head. He had a piece of bamboo stuck in his belt. It looked uncomfortably sharp.

"Hullo, Emma," he said, "your lover's waiting for you."

"My lover?"

"Yes, Lootenant Sherman," he mimicked. "He's back at the house, talking to Madam. Ben and me were in the kitchen getting our elevenses and he rang the bell and said to Dottie, 'Is your Miss Emma at home?' " Colin smiled. The inflection in his voice was perfect. "So you'd better get along quick and see what he wants." He touched the bamboo at his waist. "If you find yourself in trouble, call on me. Come on, Ben."

"F . . ." smiled Ben, and the pair ran off again behind the stables. Emma walked slowly across the yard and into the house by the back door, and dumped her purchases on the kitchen table.

"That Lieutenant Sherman is here," Dottie said. "I told him you were out shopping and he was going away, but Madam called through from the music-room and said she would see him. So I had to show him in, though I could see he didn't want to go. Whatever's this? Plaice? I can't do much with plaice."

"You'll have to. Where are Andy and Sam?"

145

"In the kitchen-garden with Joe, being useful for once," she replied.

Emma took a quick look at herself in the cloakroom mirror. A bit dishevelled, but no matter. A flick of the comb and she was ready for action. More important, had Mad remembered she was supposed to have a heart condition? She went into the music-room. Lieutenant Sherman was sitting on the edge of a chair, patting Folly, who wore a sly grin on her spotted face, salivary tongue lolling from her open jaw. Mad had not forgotten her heart condition. She was lying on the sofa, propped up with cushions. Her face seemed different. Intuitively Emma realised she hadn't put on her usual foundation cream and powder, but was wearing one of a much lighter tone, to make herself look pale.

"Ah, darling, there you are," she said as Emma entered. Wally Sherman sprang to his feet. "It was so very kind of Lieutenant Sherman to call and enquire after me. I've been telling him our troubles. Poor darling Terry in hospital with a broken leg, and all because he was waiting at the gate for the doctor to arrive. I feel so terribly to blame. But apparently they have troubles of their own down at the camp. That nice Corporal Wagg who was in the stables last weekend has disappeared, never returned to camp last night, and Lieutenant Sherman wondered if any of us had seen him. I asked him to wait until you got back."

"Corporal Wagg?" Emma shook her head. "No. He hasn't been here since they all went off on Tuesday. Wasn't he down on Poldrea beach the evening of the firework display? I have a feeling I saw him then. You remember, I was with you at the time."

She looked across at Wally Sherman. He had the grace to show faint signs of discomfort.

"Sure," he said, "I remember. Corporal Wagg was on the beach with the girl from the farm, Myrtle Trembath. We've made enquiries at the farm but nothing doing." He turned to the recumbent figure on the sofa. "Look, ma'am, I don't want to bother you with all this, especially as you've not been well, and you have the added anxiety of the boy in hospital. Perhaps Miss Emma . . . ?"

He looked to Emma for help, and as he turned his head

towards her she caught the imperceptible nod from her grandmother. The nod suggested, "You're on your own."

Emma smiled. "Of course," she said. "If there's anything I can do please say so. Come into the other room and we'll have some coffee. Will you be all right, darling? Do you want me to get you anything?"

The invalid shook her head. "Don't worry about me." She patted the sofa for Folly to struggle up beside her. "The aged pair will look after each other," she added, smiling at the lieutenant. "We'll probably both take a nap before lunch. My son may be down this evening and I have to be in good form for him."

Emma and her companion left the room and Wally Sherman turned to Emma.

"How bad is she?" he asked. "She sure looks pale. Did you have to send for family?"

"My father is rather worried," confessed Emma. "He's coming down through the night, or so I understood over the telephone."

"I guess she ought to be hospitalized," said the lieutenant.

"Oh, no . . . one of the household is enough. Such a chapter of acidents, it never ends. What is it actually about Corporal Wagg? Missing, did you say?"

They had passed into the dining-room. It was laid for two. Emma wondered if Wally Sherman thought it odd that an elderly woman who had suffered a heart attack should be thinking of sitting down to lunch.

"Well, that's what I didn't want to say in front of your grandmother," he said. "The fact is, we have reason to believe the corporal was intending to call here yesterday, in the late afternoon, at least according to Myrtle Trembath. He did have a word with her, you see. We've established that."

"I must be crazy," Emma smote her forehead. "What can you think of me?" she asked. "I remember now, but what with the worry over my grandmother and then with the doctor knocking down Terry, the whole thing went out of my mind. Of course, yes. Myrtle telephoned me, soon after the doctor had carted off poor Terry, to say Corporal Wagg wanted to see Terry, and I told her it was no use, he wouldn't be here, he would be in hospital. Then I think I lay down in the music-room and had a rest,

147

I'd been on the go all day, and, frankly, forgot all about the telephone call until this moment. Anyway, he never turned up. He must have changed his mind."

"I guess he did," said the lieutenant. "I've already asked your Joe, and the two other lads, who were in the vegetable plot at the back of your house, and none of them saw him. Well, I guess it's not your problem. We'll have to make enquiries round the whole district. It's possible he took a walk after leaving the farm, and twisted his ankle or something, but that's very remote, and anyway we've got a chopper up looking, they'll report if there's a sign of anything." He began walking back towards the hall.

"Coffee?" Emma asked.

"No, I must get going. Thanks all the same. Oh, by the way, what is the name of the old boy who lives in a shack in your woods? I thought I'd check with him before reporting back to base."

"Mr. Willis," said Emma. "He's a bit of a recluse."

The door of the music-room had come ajar—Folly had pushed it open with her nose.

"What's that about Mr. Willis?" called Mad from the sofa. She seemed to be struggling to her feet.

"Don't move, ma'am," cried the lieutenant. "I just had the idea I'd call on your tenant and ask if by any chance he had seen the corporal yesterday."

"He's not strictly my tenant," replied Mad, lying back against the cushions, "but such a dear. He has a wonderful voice, you know, and used to sing in a choir. He's been retired for some years but I think he had connections with the Presbyterian Church. Em darling, why don't you go down with Lieutenant Sherman and see if Mr. Willis is at home? There's plenty of time before lunch."

Emma got the message. By playing go-between she might avert possible danger. On the other hand, she might walk into it. The beachcomber, despite his invaluable assistance the night before, was of unknown calibre where lying was concerned. Taffy was a Welshman . . . Taffy was a thief . . . Taffy came to my house, and stole a piece of beef.

"If he'd like me to go with him, of course," she said.

"Like it," said Wally Sherman, as they walked across the orchard a few moments later, "I didn't dare hope I'd be

148

this lucky. Know something?" He smiled down at Emma. "Your grandmother is on our side."

Our side . . . The path we're going to descend together was where the beachcomber walked last night, carrying the dead corporal trussed in sacking. If you look over your shoulder, Wally Sherman, you'll see where Andy shot the corporal dead. Oh please, God, let everything be all right . . .

"Once things settle down," Wally Sherman was saying, and he would hold on to her arm, which made walking more difficult, "you and I are really going to get acquainted. Would you slap my face if I asked how old you are?"

"Twenty."

"I can give you five years. You don't look it, you know. You're more like sweet seventeen. The trouble with our girls back home is they're all spoilt."

The trouble with me at the moment is that when we cross the stile and walk along the cliff-path we might see the corporal's body lying there on the shore, or splayed out amongst the seaweed on the rocks at the far end, because the tide's going out and it won't be low water before one o'clock, judging by what Jack Trembath said last night, and if we see the body lying there then I can't cope any more, I shan't know what to say, what to do . . .

"I don't ask you to believe me," Wally Sherman was saying, "but that very first day I met you, after the landing, when Colonel Cheeseman and I came to your house to fix up about a communications post, I said to myself, 'That girl is really something, and you'll have to look a long while before you find another like her.'"

Emma did not answer. They were drawing nearer to the stile. If I play along with him, she thought, ten to one it will mean another clinch in the woods and I just can't take it, but if I give the brush-off he'll be hurt, he might even turn sour. None of this would matter if he wasn't one of them, if the helicopter wasn't scanning the sea out there beyond the point.

"I haven't scared you, have I?" he asked, putting up his hands to jump her over the stile.

She was reminded of an illustration in an old Edwardian novel in the bookshelf at home, where a young man in hunting costume, twisting his moustache, was asking the

149

young woman of his choice, "Have I done anything to offend you, Nellie?" The only reply was to turn his query into one of her own.

"No, of course you don't scare me," she said, "but I think you ought to realise that a great many of us in the neighbourhood, perhaps throughout the country, are in a state of shock. I'm not talking about personal affairs, my grandmother, Terry, but about what all of you have done by just appearing amongst us, setting up barricades, that warship at anchor there in the bay. The circumstances just aren't normal, for you, for me, for any of us."

"I know, I know," he said, "you're so right," and he looked suddenly vulnerable, like one of their own boys, Joe, Terry, even Andy. He helped her over the stile (unnecessary, she usually vaulted it), and they walked down to the cliff-path in silence.

"There are my chaps," he said suddenly, "down there on the beach."

Her heart jumped, as she saw two of the marines poking about amongst the seaweed. Wally Sherman put up his hands and hailed them. They looked up, and raised their hands in a negative gesture.

"I'm going along to the woods," he shouted. "Meet you back here in about a half-hour. Nothing so far."

Supposing, she thought, the beachcomber had gone out? Supposing Wally Sherman wants to break into the hut on his own? Supposing there is something there? A sick feeling of apprehension returned. The responsibility seemed overwhelming. She mustn't let him sense this, she must keep up a pretence of calm.

"I still don't see," she said, "why Corporal Wagg couldn't have gone in quite another direction, after leaving the farm. Mightn't he have taken a walk inland, for instance, or gone into St. Austell, or along the coast the other side of the bay?"

"He'd have checked in at the road-blocks," replied the lieutenant. "We have barriers on the road to St. Austell, and along the coast road too. We've tried these. No, that's the puzzle. The Trembath girl at the farm was the last to see him. At least, as far as we know. I'm just hoping your old recluse in the woods may give us a lead."

They came to the edge of the woods and climbed

through the opening the further side of the hedge. The trees closed in upon them.

"Someone's been along here," he said. "Those are footprints in the mud, though it rained plenty in the night."

"It's always muddy here," she told him. "People come up from the cottages a mile or so away to look for kindling. You see, it's a sort of no-man's-land. It belongs to nobody, there are endless legal arguments about it."

"Spooky sort of place," he said. "I guess you don't come here on your own by night?"

He squeezed her arm. She prayed for patience, and for courage too. The roof of the hut appeared through the trees. A thin wreath of smoke was coming from the chimney.

"I'd say the old boy was at home, wouldn't you?" asked Wally Sherman.

Emma halted before they reached the clearing. "Look, we can't frighten him, poor dear. He does at least know me. Shall I go ahead and knock on the door, and then you follow?"

"Okay."

Emma advanced through the clearing. The door was firmly shut. She knocked, but there was no answering shout. She remembered that Mr. Willis had seemed a little deaf, and nervously, reluctantly, she moved round the hut to the window at the side and peered through. The interior looked different somehow, viewed from this angle, or possibly what furniture she remembered from yesterday had been moved. The bed Terry had lain in was against the further wall, and the table too. There was an old-fashioned tin-bath in the centre of the room and Mr. Willis was standing in it, wearing only a pair of underpants, his torso nude. He was scrubbing himself with what looked like a brush. The sight, which, had the little boys been with her, would have brought instant mockery and stifled laughter struck her, at this particular moment, as painful, and in a peculiar way horrific; here was an old man, barely known to her, who had committed a dangerous act for all their sakes, being spied upon within his own four walls, believing himself safe, alone; and to burst in upon him suddenly, while he was washing, was like breaking into his thoughts, known only to himself, close-guarded.

151

Timidly, she tapped upon the window. Her shadow must have warned him, more than the sound, for he looked up startled, the eyes without spectacles wide open, alarmed, and with a protective gesture he hunched his lean shoulders, clasping the scrubbing-brush against his belly. It's no good, thought Emma, one hasn't the right, and she turned away from the window, shaking her head at the lieutenant, gesturing with her hand.

"What's wrong?" he called softly. "Isn't he at home?"

That was the trouble. He was at home. The squatter's hut, the four walls, the plain interior, the tin-bath upon the floor, belonged to the beachcomber alone. Nobody else had any rights. Least of all the lieutenant, waiting there under the trees. Why am I making such an issue of this, she wondered?

"He's home," she called back, "but we can't go in. He's taking a bath."

Wally Sherman laughed. "Is that it? I thought he was hanging from a beam at least by the expression on your face. I'll go."

"No," said Emma, "no . . . wait." She went back to the door and knocked again. This time the summons was answered. The door opened and Mr. Willis appeared on the threshold. He wore a towel round his waist covering his under-pants, and had put on a long cotton vest. "Who is it?" he asked. Then recognition came. The startled expression went, but his face remained guarded, curious.

"They're looking for the corporal," whispered Emma, "been to the farm and our place. Asked us who lived here. I told your name, offered to show the way. Officer suspects nothing."

Mr. Willis nodded. He narrowed his eyes, peering towards the trees. "Would you mind if I fetched my spectacles?" he said. "I see very little without them. I was just taking a bath, you see, I'm not dressed for a visit." He spoke up so that the lieutenant could hear. He waved a hand in his direction. "Please to walk in," he called. "Excuse my appearance. It's bath-day and washing-day all in one for me."

He vanished into the interior and Emma waited for her companion.

"You go in," she told him. "I'd better wait outside."

Wally Sherman lowered his head and passed inside the

152

door, winking at Emma. It isn't funny, though, she thought, it isn't funny . . . She thrust her hands in her pockets and stared around her. The vegetable plot in the clearing was carefully raked. He had winter greens there, and brussels sprouts, and in the far corner a compost heap, mostly seaweed. He had been burning dead leaves, too, and what looked like an old sack. A sack . . .

Someone touched her on the shoulder. It was Wally Sherman. "Mr. Willis says come in out of the cold. He's perfectly decent."

She followed him into the room. Yes, the bed was in a different place from yesterday. But the most conspicious change was not so much the bath in the middle of the room but the garments spread around the fire to dry. She recognised the grey trousers he had worn, and the navy sweater. The oilskin too had been given a soaking and was hanging from a clothes-line fixed from the ceiling. Another thing, the gun had gone from the wall . . .

"Always the same on a Friday," Mr. Willis was saying. "I give the place a thorough scouring, and myself as well. It's the lesson my mother taught me. Ten we were in family, and I the youngest. Three of my brothers emigrated, two to Australia, one to Canada. I've never visited America, though I've long had the wish to do so. Have I left it too late, do you think?"

He smiled at the lieutenant and polished his spectacles. Oh, well done, thought Emma, Mad couldn't have improved upon it. It must be that the Welsh, like the Cornish, were natural actors.

"Never too late to visit the States, Mr. Willis," said Wally Sherman. "We'll get you on a flight just as soon as everyone settles down to the new arrangements. There are going to be flights, you know, between our two countries, that all can afford, not just the wealthy. That's part of the schedule."

"I'm very glad to hear it," replied the beachcomber. "I've been a rolling stone most of my life, and have come to anchor here for the time being, but that doesn't say it has to be permanent, now, does it?"

"No, indeed," said the lieutenant heartily, with another wink at Emma. "Well, Mr. Willis, to the business in hand. I . . ."

He was cut short, however, either because Mr. Willis

was truly deaf or because he enjoyed his role as narrator.

"I could kill two birds with one stone, couldn't I?" he went on. "Visit my brother in Canada first, perhaps, and then on to New York. We correspond, of course, but we haven't seen one another for over forty years. He's been married twice. The first, Edith, a pretty young woman she was too, she passed away with tuberculosis of the spine, a terrible thing, leaving three young children. My poor brother, heartbroken, he reared those three on his own, and then a neighbour, a widow, took pity on him, and they made a go of it together."

The lieutenant's smile, that had become a fixture on his face, began to wear thin. "Sure, sure," he said, "the best thing they could do. Now, I don't want to hurry you, Mr. Willis, but I'm on duty, you know, and I've got to press on." He threw an imploring glance at Emma.

"Lieutenant Sherman is searching for one of his marines," she explained, "a corporal who's gone missing. That's why he's here. He wonders if by any chance you may have seen him."

Mr. Willis put on his spectacles and stared at the lieutenant. "I'm sorry to hear it," he said. "Excuse me for rambling on; when you live alone it becomes a habit. I talk to myself frequently. Would you tell me the circumstances, if you please?"

Patiently and clearly Wally Sherman related the story of the missing corporal. Mr. Willis heard him to the end without interruption. Then he shook his head.

"Had it been fine yesterday, instead of raining and blowing as it did, I'd have been bound to have seen him, that is, if he walked down to the beach. Always, when it's fine, I go to the beach for seaweed for the garden, or driftwood for the fire. The wood burns better when it's been in the salt water, you know, it doesn't get sodden like it does up here under the trees. I give it a miss when it's raining because my object would be defeated, don't you see? Yesterday afternoon I had my pile of driftwood drying here by the fire, knowing I would need a good blaze for wash-day. You see the bit of planking in the corner there? I'd say it came from a ship's boat, and been in the water some time." He got up from the stool on which he had been sitting and showed the plank to Emma and the lieutenant. "That's oak," he said. "Good stuff, too, you can't

154

do better than build with oak, but I shan't burn it yet awhile. Can I make you both a cup of tea? I have a primus stove and it won't take a moment. They laugh at primus stoves these days, and what's more you can't get them easily, but I wouldn't be without mine if you offered me a fortune for it."

Wally Sherman flashed a look at Emma and rose to his feet. "Thanks for your kind offer, Mr. Willis," he said, "but this young lady has to get back for lunch and I must get back to my men. I'm sorry you haven't been able to help us. It's been a pleasure meeting you."

"A pleasure for me too," was the reply. "Had it not been raining the way it did yesterday I would surely have seen your fellow. I hope . . ." he paused, and stroked his chin, "I hope he didn't take it into his head to try and walk by way of the beach round what we call Crane Point and so to the bit of beach the other side, especially with the flood tide. Tourists try it in the summer, and often enough I've had to turn them back. It's the youngsters, you know. They think they have only to see a cliff to scale it. Bad enough holiday time, but in winter, after heavy rain, parts of the cliff fall away, and . . ." he shook his head slowly, "I wouldn't want to try and scale those cliffs myself, either up or down."

They had come to the door of the hut. The lieutenant held out his hand.

"Many thanks for the information," he said. "We've had a helicopter out, and I think if Corporal Wagg had done anything of the sort we'd have known about it by this time. Goodbye, Mr. Willis. Maybe I'll see you again."

"I would like to think so," said the beachcomber. "You'd be welcome at any time. And I'd be dressed for the occasion too. I wish you luck in your search for the missing fellow."

"Goodbye, Mr. Willis, and thank you," said Emma.

No sign of understanding passed between them. He waited a moment, then withdrew inside the hut.

"Well," exclaimed Wally Sherman, once they were away from the clearing, "he's a real old character, but Jesus, does he talk!"

"It's living alone," said Emma. "It does it to everyone."

The lieutenant put his hand under her elbow once again as they trod the muddied path back through the wood.

"Then let's you and I make a pact right now," he said, "never, never to be solitary."

They came to the edge of the wood where it bordered the ploughed field.

"I'll take a short cut up to the house," said Emma. "I'm afraid the visit to Mr. Willis was a waste of time."

"Time's never wasted when I'm with you," he replied predictably, "but you're right, I've not got any information out of the old boy, except not to scale cliffs when it's raining. Well, Emma, I guess I'll have to get moving, back to the beach. I'd like to tell you we'll be seeing each other again soon, but I can't make promises on duty."

"No," she said, "of course you can't. Anyway . . . good luck."

He climbed through the wire that separated the ploughed field from the grazing ground below, and, turning once to wave, was soon out of sight. Emma did not immediately strike towards the house. She hesitated on the bank, and on the brink of decision, too, whether to walk straight home or to have a final check with Mr. Willis now that the lieutenant was no longer with her. The latter seemed the wiser course, though instinct warned her not to plunge yet deeper into conspiracy—they were involved enough as it was—and it might be better to know too little than too much.

She retraced her steps through the wood to the hut, and he must have read her thoughts for he was standing there fully dressed, trousers, sea-boots, grey turtle-necked sweater, oilskin over his arm, and she sensed he had waited there for her return. He let her approach right up to him before he spoke, and when he did it was in a half-chant, softly.

"Full fathom five thy father lies,
Of his bones are coral made . . ."

Emma had the same feeling of discomfort she had known earlier when peering through the window, but now for a different reason.

"I just wanted to thank you," she said quickly. "The lieutenant's gone to rejoin his men."

The grey eyes glowed at her behind the spectacles. "We

156

fooled him, didn't we?" he said. "You and I between us. Tell your grannie we're in the running for an award."

She summoned a smile. "Yes, I will."

"Never had a desire to visit America in my life," he said. "Wouldn't go there if you put the money for the fare into my hand."

He locked the door of the hut with a key, which was threaded through a piece of string, and slipped the string over his head and down under the turtle collar of his sweater.

"I'll see what they're up to down under. They won't find much today, but tomorrow I wouldn't put it past the fellow turning up a little worse for wear." He smiled again. "Had to smash his head in a bit more before putting him in the water, and the sea will do the rest. Whatever the verdict, they won't pin it on us."

The horror that had been upon her the evening before, when she had her first sight of the dead corporal with Andy's arrow between the eyes, came upon her once again. It wasn't over yet. It had only just begun.

Mr. Willis moved towards the path at the edge of the clearing that was his own way of descent towards the beach. He was carrying his old canvas bag for driftwood in one hand and his peaked cape in the other. He bowed, made a little flourish with the cap, and put it firmly on his head. Then he held up one finger, jerking it towards the rear of his hut.

"If you see the boy Terry in hospital," he said, "tell him all's well. And I have the gely hidden where they'll never find it. It might come in useful sooner than we think, you never can tell, can you?"

He was laughing to himself as he went down over the cliffs.

12

If there could be somebody, Emma thought, to whom one could tell everything. If, when one was in doubt, afraid, unhappy, when things were going wrong, had gone wrong, someone had infallibility, so that one knew, intuitively but logically too, that the right answer would come. This, in days past, was what people had from God. Thy Will Be Done, and if you were burnt at the stake you died for the God you had served in the belief that He had once died for you. It was a kind of celestial tit-for-tat. When people no longer believed in God so much, chiefly because it became more and more difficult to visualise God's day, where He lived, how He spent His time, possibly under such pressure from all that was going on in the world and in other solar systems that He really couldn't take it any more, belief in "isms" took His place. The particular ideology of the day held for a time amongst groups of people and then they got bored with it and passed on to something else.

The point was, even when two people loved each other, even when marriages were happy, when parents loved children and children loved parents, there was this separation, this division, there could never be complete union. That was why the USUK thing would never work. That was why even now, at home at Trevanal, there couldn't be total understanding amongst them all. Terry, in hospital, did not know that Andy, back at home, had shot his arrow through the air and killed the corporal. The Trembaths did not know that Terry had spent the night at the hut, and that, without a doubt, he had been as careless of Myrtle's "under-the-age-of-consent" status as had been Corporal Wagg. Mad did not know that she, Emma, had been what her grandmother lightly called "permissive" on Poldrea beach with Lieutenant Sherman. Nor did she know that Terry, her lamb, her first-adopted, had apparently been carrying gelignite when the fracas took place the night of the firework display. The Matron and staff at the hospital did not know that Dr. Summers had deliberately concealed from them the real truth about his patient's broken leg.

So we all hide something from each other, she decided, we all have secrets we cannot or dare not share, and it's no use asking advice from God who doesn't answer; and even when people did believe in God and thought they received an answer, the net result was the same muddle and chaos that we get today. You're on your own... you're on your own. That was the lesson to be learnt from every encounter. Mr. Willis, last night's saviour, was also a little old man with a grudge against society, a chip on his shoulder from some long-buried past. Emma returned to the house and lunch with her grandmother hiding a questing heart under a flippant exterior.

"I deserve an Oscar," she said, "and so does your Taffy. We both lied like troopers—and who invented that expression, one wonders? Anyway, it seemed to work. They're now all down on the beach, and for the moment it's not our problem."

Mad, who had apparently left the sofa as soon as her granddaughter and the lieutenant had crossed the orchard, helped herself to liver and bacon.

"You missed the one o'clock news," she said. "Rationing is to start, it seems."

"Rationing? Whatever for?"

"Some difficulty with supplies, until USUK has established the new method of distribution, and God knows what that will be, they haven't told us. Also, no doubt, they've got in a fine mess during the state of emergency, with food supplies piling up all over the country and no one to shift them. Therefore it's to be rationing as a temporary measure, and you can bet that the urban areas will get first pick. Wasn't this what drove the French peasants wild after the French revolution, when the city dwellers got all their produce and they themselves had to go hungry?"

"Oh well, cabbages forever," sighed Emma. "Joe has rows of them in the kitchen-garden. Colin will get as thin as a match-stick."

"He'd eat cabbages raw if he were really hungry," replied Mad.

Which went once more to prove, Emma thought, the correctness of her theory that the old didn't care, or felt emergencies less keenly than the young. She herself had little appetite for the liver on her plate. She kept being reminded of what Mr. Willis had said about smashing the corporal's face . . .

Later, when lunch was over, she went down to the basement in search of Joe. He loked up as she entered. He was laying out beetroot and onion in rows.

"We could get by on these for a time," he said. "Onions are good for you, I heard that somewhere, and you can make soup with beetroot. Then I've got sacks of potatoes in the old scullery. You can't starve on 'tatties, onions and beetroot, with some greenstuff thrown in. The apples will last us through till apples come again, I told Madam that when we were picking them."

He gazed around him with pride. The root vegetables might have been prize exhibits in some tent at an agricultural show, or even trophies won in a sporting contest.

"I wish now," he said, "I'd put in a late crop of 'tatties to keep, but you know what Madam is, she likes to eat them when they're new."

She comes first, Emma thought, nobody else really matters. He'd die for her, as people in old days died for God.

"Joe," she said, "what happened on the cliffs last night?"

He turned his back on her and began sorting some of the onions on a shelf. "I don't want to think about it," he said. "Please, Emma . . ."

"You have to tell me," she pleaded. "I know it must

161

have been awful. When Lieutenant Sherman came before lunch Mad made me take him to see Mr. Willis. He was going anyway to make enquiries, and I thought it best because of the possible danger. It passed off all right, Mr. Willis let on absolutely nothing. But after the lieutenant had gone he said . . . he said he had to smash . . ."

She couldn't finish. Joe turned round and looked at her.

"When Mr. Trembath and I had circled the field, like he told us, we got out of the Land-Rover and looked down over the beach. Mr. Willis was there already. The tide had turned. He walked over to the rocks at the far end, beneath where we were standing, and began scrambling over them—there was just enough light for us to see him. He did what we all of us do in summer, started to climb up Crane Point, and when he reached the top he took the sacks off the body, and just squatted there . . ."

"Yes?" said Emma.

"I asked Mr. Trembath what he could be doing, and he said he thought Mr. Willis was taking off the boots and putting them back on the corporal. We saw him pick up something, you know how some pieces of shale have jagged edges sharp as an axe, then Mr. Trembath said, 'My God!' and I suppose I was a coward, I couldn't take any more, I looked away. There was a sound of a splash a few moments later, he'd chucked the body off the point into deep water, it was still blowing, if you remember, and the tide-drift is easterly there. Then he put on his own sea-boots and began scrambling back, carrying the sacks under his arm. I said goodnight to Mr. Trembath. Somehow I didn't want to see Mr. Willis again. I came back home, and I went indoors and was sick. Then later I went up to say good night to Madam and to tell her what had happened."

Joe leant against the shelf where he had stored the beetroot. There was a small window beyond, grimey, with a cobweb stretching right across it. He stared through the window at his vegetable garden away up the rising ground behind. Emma took his arm, and they looked past the cobweb through the glass together. They saw nothing. They shared an image, each in a different way.

"What's going to happen?" she asked.

"I don't know. I think they'll find the body."

"Mr. Willis said the same. He said it would turn up."

"They generally do."

"What's so frightening, Joe, is having got Mr. Willis into it, and Mr. Trembath. And there's another thing, did you know Terry had gelignite on him when he fell? Mr. Willis has got it hidden somewhere by the hut."

"I didn't know," said Joe grimly, "but I'm not surprised. I wouldn't put anything past a few of Terry's friends."

"We won't tell Mad."

"No."

Not that she'd mind, thought Emma, she would even say, as Mr. Willis had done, that it might come in useful some time.

"Whatever happens," she said impulsively, "don't let's have any secrets from each other, Joe. We must have implicit confidence, that if one of us hears something, or knows something, we tell the other. Don't you agree?"

"But of course," replied Joe. "It's always been like that, as far as I'm concerned." He seemed surprised at the question.

"Well, perhaps not always," said Emma. "What I mean is, when things are trivial it doesn't matter. We've never been in this sort of situation before. There has to be someone to trust, someone who never lets you down."

Joe was silent. He was never a rapid thinker, and he must have been turning her declaration over in his mind.

"That's what children feel about their parents," he said at last. "I remember I did when I was small. I couldn't make it out when mine suddenly went away to Australia and left me. I felt it was my fault, and so it was in a way. I'd let them down by not being clever like them. Do you know, Emma, sometimes I try to remember their faces, and I can't, and it worries me. I think if they were dead it wouldn't worry me so much."

"I wonder," said Emma, "I wonder . . . dear Joe," and impulsively she held on to his arm. Perhaps he was right. It had never worried her much that the photograph of her poor pretty mother in her bedroom, which she still kissed every night from long custom, lacked reality and might have been a character in fiction out of an old book; but supposing Pa, instead of being a widower, had been divorced, and her mother was still alive, a pretty woman well preserved, married to someone else and living in

Switzerland or America even. Would she have, as Joe did, a feeling of being let down, of abandonment, and that it had all come about through some fault of her own? This is the awful thing, she told herself, we can't put ourselves into other people's shoes. The only one to do that, and quite literally, too, was Mr. Willis last night, when he undid those laces and put on a dead man's boots. But it was the corporal who went into the water, not Mr. Willis. We throw away things that might harm us, bodies, memories, dreams . . .

There were shouts and whoops from the sloping ground beyond the window and Colin and Sam ran past above, with Andy and small Ben in hot pursuit. Missiles flew through the air. Black Ben, his shining face grim and determined, hurled an enormous fir-cone with a twig on the end of it straight into the back of his boon companion, Colin. Colin, with a dramatic stagger, put his hand up to his heart and fell.

"Got him," yelled Andy, and seizing his three-year-old companion round the waist he embraced him, tugging at his hair, in imitation of members of a football team when one of them has scored a goal. Colin was lying spread-eagled as the corporal had done the day before, and little Ben, the marksman, ran forward, picked up his weapon and brandished it above his head. Andy wandered over and kicked the recumbent Colin on the ground.

"He's a gonner," he shouted. "Let's leave him to the crows."

He ran off after the more fleet-footed Sam, tailed by Ben, while Colin, miraculously restored to life, seized the missile Ben had dropped and chased all three of them.

"Joe," whispered Emma, "it's not right, we shouldn't let them."

"No," agreed Joe, "I'll have to stop it. They're treading down all my young seedlings up there, they must play somewhere else."

Angrily, he brushed past her and out of the room to the back door to drive off the young fry from his territory, and it's no use, thought Emma, he didn't see the point, that was not what I meant at all. I'm still on my own . . .

It was dark once again, with curtains drawn, the boys in their own quarters, their bath-time approaching, when there came the sound of an approaching car down the drive and three prolonged blasts on the horn.

"It's Pa," cried Emma, and ran from the music-room where she was sitting with her grandmother, out through the front door and down the garden path to meet him. The tall, rather burly, familiar figure was getting out of the car, blond hair as Mad's had been once but starting to go grey, her same rather beaky nose but more prominent, and then she was enveloped in his arms. He was wearing his hairy, clumsy old driving-coat, she knew the smell of it so well.

"Hullo, hullo, hullo," he said, kissing her on both cheeks —Pa always repeated words and actions—"Well, well, well, what a drive, what a drive. I left at ten, no, ten-thirty, and it's now seven, continual hold-ups, if I hadn't had my special pass I should never have got here at all. How is Mad? Is she upstairs? Is she in bed? Has Bevil Summers been again?" Pa never waited for one to answer his questions. He was always on to the next before you could frame your reply. He was lugging his bag from the back seat as he spoke. "Where's Joe?" he asked. "Will he put away the car! I want a drink, I'm dying for a drink, I must have a bath too before eating. How's Dottie, is she in good form? Those horrible children won't be feeding with us, will they?"

"No, Pa darling, of course not. The little ones are probably in bed by now."

"Thank the Lord for that. One doesn't want to drive nearly three hundred miles non-stop and be met with a gang of shouting young." He put his arm round his daughter's shoulders, and they walked up the path together to the house. "Everything's so quiet here. I can't understand it, I thought you said you had commandos under every bush, helicopters springing from the trees. It's all nonsense, nothing appears to have happened at all. Mother?"

His voice boomed through the house. She was waiting in the hall, arms open.

"My darling Vic."

Emma, watching, was struck, as always, by the family likeness. Hair, eyes, noses, chins, exuberance, and then finish. Not one thought, one ideal in common. Only a mutual determination, and, when thwarted, bloody-mindedness.

They embraced on both cheeks, another family custom (Mad said it was French), and then Pa stepped back and looked at his mother.

"But you look very well," he said, "you look better than when I saw you last. I don't believe there is anything the matter with you, the whole thing is a plot to get me here. Emma, is it a plot? Hullo, Folly, still alive, good heavens, what is she now, fifteen, sixteen? I suppose when she dies you'll embalm her. Mother darling, I'm exhausted, isn't someone going to minister to me, pour me a drink, is there any ice?"

"If you'd only stop talking for one single moment, you'd see it was all here," said Mad, "whisky, soda, gin, tonic, ice forever. You've got the most frightful bags under your eyes, I hope it's driving and not toping. I often wonder how you manage alone in that London flat, if you are alone, which I've never believed for a moment, there must be rows of women waiting in queues to come in and cook your meals and darn your socks, don't tell me . . ."

"It isn't true, it isn't true, I'm the most solitary of creatures, so exhausted when bedtime comes I literally drop between the sheets, I . . ."

Emma went from the room, reeling. The trouble was, when Pa and Mad got together in the flesh it was even worse than when they spoke to each other on the telephone. Other people became worn out. The sheer noise of it deafened you.

She went into the kitchen to warn Dottie. "Pa's here."

"I heard him," replied Dottie.

"And you know he'll want a bath after his drink, and that means dinner about eight-thirty or after."

"In old days," said Dottie, who had rescued the colander Colin had been wearing earlier in the day and was rinsing it under the tap, "Madam had a staff in her kitchen, and they used to run round circles when Master Vic came home for the school holidays. Those days are gone. And praise be, she did not include me amongst the staff."

Oh Lord, Emma sighed, Dottie was in one of her status moods. Give her an inch and she would start naming the stars who hung about the dressing-room at the Theatre Royal, and those who had accompanied some cast or other on tour, all of which must have taken place at least thirty

166

years ago, probably more, and she would proceed to hint, furthermore, that it was not everyone who would condescend to lose face and turn her hand to every sort of menial chore when they had once hobnobbed with the famous.

"The soup can stand on the hot-plate when it's ready," Dottie continued. "Madam can say it's bortsch if she likes, but you and I know it's got nothing in it except Joe's beetroot. As for that plaice . . ."

Emma disappeared from the kitchen and returned to the music-room. The ding-dong argument between mother and son was going full steam ahead.

"But I don't understand, I don't understand," Pa was saying. "However did Bevil Summers manage to knock down Terry, who must have been standing in full view at the top of the drive? Was the man drunk? Doctors should never touch alcohol. Or was Terry himself high on some drug? I wouldn't put it past him. These boys need an iron hand, they are completely out of control. As for that disreputable business on the beach with fireworks . . ."

"You forget I might have been dying," Mad interrupted. "Darling Terry was distraught, I think he tripped over the bumper, I don't know, and Bevil had no other thought in his head but to get to me in time. As it was I had to have an injection, a sedative, don't ask me what it was, I don't know, but it worked miracles, here I am perfectly well. As for the fireworks, none of those marines had any sense of humour, typical of Americans. I remember once in New York . . ."

Pa was banging on, though, not listening. "The Minister rang me up himself, or rather his secretary, tremendous offence given, really tremendous, wanting to know who was trying to throw a spanner in the works in the west country, was there some underground movement. 'I don't know,' I said, 'I haven't the slightest idea, my mother will be eighty any moment and has been bats for years, you must totally disregard her . . .' "

" . . . Always lose their heads in an emergency. I remember a snow-storm on Long Island, a few telegraph poles down, the President had to intervene because chaos broke out . . ."

Meanwhile Joe, who had slipped quietly into the hall while no one was looking, seized Pa's bag and took it upstairs to the spare room, while Colin and Ben, who had followed in his wake, ran through to the music-room washed, brushed and in their dressing-gowns. They looked like cherubs minus the wings.

"Hullo, Vic," cried Colin, never abashed in adult presence, and to show equality smote his elder on the backside. Pa whipped round as if stung.

"Hullo, you horrid little boy," he said. "Why aren't you in bed? When I was your age I was tucked up in my cot and asleep by six o'clock."

"No, you weren't," replied Colin. "When it was your bedtime you used to lie on the floor and kick, Madam told me."

"It's a lie, a complete travesty, I did no such thing." Pa appealed to his mother. "I protest, you bring up these children to believe the most appalling fantasies, I can't allow it. Ask Dottie, ask anyone, I . . ."

"You know perfectly well you kicked and screamed," said Mad. "You frothed at the mouth like a horse, you . . ."

"Vic," interrupted Colin, "I've taught Ben to speak. He knows several words. Do you want to hear them?"

He whispered in Ben's ear, who grinned and nodded his head.

"Yes, yes," said Pa, snatching at a chance to turn the conversation. "Let me hear what Ben has to say. Then the child isn't a moron after all? He'll grow up to be a leader of Black Power yet and murder us all. Come on, Ben, say your piece, I'm all ears, I'm all attention."

The flow of words confused the three-year-old. He frowned and concentrated hard, but the exclamation that was to astonish his audience wouldn't come forth."

"Sh . . . sh . . . sh . . . or f . . . f . . . f . . ." urged the mentor Colin, taking his hand, "it doesn't matter which."

But Ben, bewildered, muddled his instructions. "Shuck," he said, "shuck, shuck, shuck," and started to run round in circles.

"The child *is* a moron," declared Pa. "What's he pretending to be, a hen that has just laid an egg? Cluck, cluck, cluck, is that it? Run along, child, run along. Nobody wants an egg. Emma darling, has anyone remembered to turn on the heater in the spare bedroom? I don't want to freeze. I must go and say hullo to Dottie. Has somebody taken up my bag? Mother dear, shouldn't you be resting? I can't think why Bevil Summers didn't order you to stay in bed. He doesn't know his job. I shall ring him up."

Emma managed to propel her father out of the room and towards the stairs. "Say hullo to Dottie after you've had your bath," she urged. "Joe has taken up your bag and he's putting away your car. I'll bring you up another drink."

"No, no, no, I'll have one when I come down. What's the hurry? Everyone's always in a hurry in this house, nobody ever relaxes."

He was still protesting as he entered his room, and throwing open his overnight bag he emptied the contents on the floor. Emma, from long habit, picked everything up. Ivory brushes on the dressing-table, silk pyjamas on the bed. Pa, at forty-eight, was shockingly trained. All Mad's fault, of course.

"Did Summers take her blood pressure?" he asked, going into the bathroom and turning both taps full on. "We all suffer from high blood-pressure in our family. I must say, she doesn't look particularly ill, but then she has immense reserves, like me. If I didn't, I couldn't survive. You've no conception what these past days have been like. Meetings, conferences, never getting to bed until three, I have no business to be here at all."

"Tell us all about it at dinner, darling," said Emma, and closing the door behind her went along the passage to her own room to fling herself on her bed for five minutes. My reserves can't be as strong as Pa's, she thought; if they were I wouldn't be lying here now, I'd be taking his visit in my stride. It's just that so much seems to be happening, hour by hour ...

The hot bath, the change of clothes, slippers, a second drink, all had their calming effect upon the traveller. Even the whirl-wind visit to the kitchen and the salutation to Dottie, with a quick inspection of the middle boys' room, did not bring the rise in temperature that might have been.

"Something must be done about that boy's eyes," Pa was saying when Emma, who had also changed, came into the music-room. "He must see an expert, an operation may be necessary." (He was referring, of course, to Sam.) "One

169

should always take the highest advice. And isn't there some terrible infection one can catch from squirrels? Yes, yes, I'm sure I'm right. Or is it parrots? Probably both. Weil's disease, or psittacosis, I can't remember which. Emma, my lovely daughter, how exquisite you look. You're wasted down here. Come back with me to London."

Just at that moment Dottie gave a blast on the gong and Mad led the way into the dining-room. Dottie had lighted the candles to give a festive air. Mad peered at the hotplate and turned round with a radiant smile.

"Bortsch," she said, "your favorite soup, and delicious sole to follow. Em, isn't Joe going to join us?"

"He asked to be excused," said Emma. "He had high tea with the boys."

The truth was that Joe, loyal and devoted though he was, found Pa overwhelming and, silent by nature, became mute in his presence.

"Oh? Oh, well..." Mad seemed disappointed. She enjoyed an audience round the dining-room table when there was a chance of confrontation with her only son by birth and not adoption. Terry was usually her mainstay, giving as good as he got. Emma couldn't help feeling relieved that he was in hospital and not poised here, like an athlete, ready to leap into action.

"Joe knows his place," said Pa, spooning his soup with relish—he was a noisy eater, Mad's poor training again. "He's a natural hewer of wood and drawer of water, an excellent lad, but dim. Salt of the earth, nature's gentleman, however you care to put it, we have to have them in society today, pity there are not more like him to wait upon the élite like ourselves."

"Who says we are élite?" countered Mad. "Just because I entertained millions in my time it doesn't put me in some top bracket. And as for you, fiddling the bank balances of Argentine tycoons..."

"I do nothing of the sort, I do nothing of the sort. Fiddling doesn't come into it. It so happens that it requires a certain type of intellect to deal with a certain type of problem. Monetary matters are my speciality, always have been, always will be, and not thanks to you, may I say; if anyone has made a hash of her finances through a long and successful career than my revered mother..."

170

"Pa," Emma broke in, "what we really want to know is, can you tell us what is happening in the world, or rather to this country? Is USUK going to work?"

The topic of the hour should surely bring them on to neutral ground.

Pa wiped his mouth with the table napkin. "It has to work," he declared. "If it doesn't we might as well all cut our throats tomorrow, no, tonight. The only hope for existence in this island lies in union with the U.S., economically and strategically, there is no argument about it, no argument at all. We may not like it, historically we may feel ourselves outraged and raped, but *tant pis*, there is no alternative. The entry into Europe was a flop, a disaster, prices rose nearly fifty per cent, do you remember? We had a political storm and near-revolution. So what happened? A general election with the country hopelessly divided, then a referendum, and finally the Coalition Government we have today, which has seized on the idea of USUK as a drowning man clutches at a straw. The only difference is that the straw is not a straw but a bloody great plank, my darlings, which will carry us all, if not to El Dorado, at least out of the threat of extinction."

He paused for breath. Mad did not seem to be listening. She was pouring the remains of her soup into a saucer for Folly to lap.

"I don't feel myself raped," she said, raising her head, "but I do feel outraged. An economic association, well, fair enough, even a partnership. But not a take-over bid, which is what USUK amounts to, Vic, surely?"

"Darling mother, take the analogy of the shipwreck again. You are in a small boat, a storm is brewing, the boat may upset any moment, and a thumping great liner comes alongside and suggests taking you on board. You accept, but on reaching the deck you don't expect that you and your boatload of survivors will steer the ship, do you? No, you sit back grateful for the rescue, and do as you're told."

Emma removed the soup and stacked the saucers. Dottie had disguised the plaice with a white sauce. Emma wondered if this was wise, it made it look like invalid food in hospital. Still . . . She helped her father generously.

"I think I'd rather brave the storm," said Mad. "The small boat wouldn't have to be leaking. If the planking

171

was sound, and people had oars, you could keep it head to wind, or merely let it drift before the gale. You'd be bound to come to land some time."

"Or hit a reef," said Pa, "if you hadn't upset in the meantime. Don't be so absurd, darling. In the world as it is today nobody can go it alone, we have to combine—USUK and its allies, South America, Africa, Australia, Canada, we can say boo to everyone else, strategically and economically. We shall have joint nuclear and air power, and a joint currency. The rest of the world can get on with their own affairs, starve, succeed, make love, blow each other up, it won't matter to us. What's this, Emma sweetheart, it's not the cream from the borsch being served up again?"

"It's sole," said Mad. "You know you always demand fish. Fresh Dover sole caught in the bay by dear old Tom Bate."

"I didn't know," replied Pa, "that it was possible to have Dover sole swimming about in Cornish water, any more than you can have Dublin prawns anywhere but in Dublin. Still, I take your word for it. Where were we? Oh yes, strategic and economic affairs. A tremendous advantage to have the same currency. It hasn't been decided yet whether we stick to the dollar or invent something entirely new. The pound will go, of course, I'm all for reviving the ducat. Shylock, you remember. 'My daughter! O! Three thousand ducats!' The tourists would love it."

"Ducat," mused Mad. "Rather unfortunate rhyming associations. One can imagine . . ."

"H'm, peculiar sort of sole," Pa went on as he shovelled a forkful into his mouth. "Has a strange resemblance to cotton wool. No, no, no . . . I'm not complaining, but this creature never saw Dover in its life. Perhaps the marines have done a swap, dredged up your local fish and substituted something from Long Island Sound."

Nevertheless, he demanded a second helping, washing it all down with a doubtful chablis.

"I must remember to send you down some Californian wine," he said. "Crates of it have arrived already. Not wildly exciting, but new to the palate. Everyone's drinking it in London."

"Oh, Vic darling . . ." protested his mother.

"Why not, why not? The climate in California is better

than anything you get in France. Acres of vines being grown on the west coast of America. It will cost us less into the bargain. I assure you, once USUK is firmly established we shall be eating American fruit, cheese, butter. We shall all grow enormously fat, of course, but it can't be helped—better that than becoming skeletons like the Asiatics."

"I shall keep a cow," said Mad firmly, "two cows. The boys can milk them, or possibly Jack Trembath would let them run with his herd—run is the right expression, isn't it? Thank heaven for all our apples . . . As for vines, I see no reason why we shouldn't plant vines, Em, at the back somewhere. We could all tread them in the autumn, the boys would adore that."

Pa threw back his head and laughed in derision. "The boys, angel mother, will be so busy learning and adjusting to the American way of life that they won't have time to tread grapes. The interchange of visits amongst the young will do a power of good," he continued, cracking an ancient filbert, which, though he did not know it, had been purloined from Sam's squirrel. "I suggest we send Terry, and possibly Andy, across with one of the first flights. No use to Joe, he can't read or write, the exercise would be wasted on him . . . One thing I must impress upon you both," and he looked first at his daughter and then at his mother, "and make no mistake about it— we're all in this thing up to our necks. There's no going back. If we don't co-operate to the full, take everything that is suggested with a good grace, then we are in for trouble, real trouble."

Mad did not say anything for a moment. Then, "What exactly do you mean by trouble?" she asked finally.

"Just that. They're over here in force, you know. They won't stand for any protest marches, demos, armchair critics getting up and shouting the odds at town hall meetings or on radio and television. This business is an enormous exercise in propaganda to impress a world audience, quite apart from its benefits to this country and to themselves. They lost face once, in south-east Asia, and they're going to take damned care they don't lose it again."

Emma glanced at her grandmother, then back to Pa. The expression on both faces was identical. Eyes narrowed, chins thrust forward. Together, she thought, they'd make a formidable pair to thwart, but apart, and on opposing sides . . . ?

"What's our population?" Mad murmured. "Fifty, sixty million? You can't keep a nation of sixty million people down."

"No," replied her son, "because at least forty-five million, probably more, will welcome what's happening. The tiny minority won't count. If they try anything . . ." he snapped his fingers and pointed his thumb to the ground . . . "Finish. Out . . . So, my loved ones, keep cows and grow vines if you like, but don't say stupid things in public or burn any more guys togged up as marines. By the way, when I switched on the car radio and heard your regional news, I gathered a commando stationed on Poldrea beach has been reported missing. Now, that's the sort of thing I mean. If one of their chaps has come to harm, had a row, say, with a local after a couple of drinks in a pub, well, that local will be for it. And no kid-glove method either. The Yanks are a tough lot when they're roused."

Emma stared at her empty plate, then raised her eyes furtively to look at her grandmother. She was handing Folly the last morsel of stilton cheese, which the Dalmatian rejected and spat out upon the carpet.

"So were the Celts, when the Saxons invaded Cornvall," said Mad. "Let's go into the music-room and listen to Tristan."

She led the way out of the dining-room, while her son grimaced and shook his head. Emma went round the table, snuffing the candles. The pungent aftermath of smoking wick tainted the air.

13

It started blowing hard during the night, and by the time it was light a force-seven gale was in progress. Slates clattered down from the roof, a tree fell in the shrubbery, the rain seeped in at the spare room window, and when Emma went to take her father an early cup of tea she found him sitting up in the four-poster bed, shielding himself from the draught with an open umbrella.

"The appalling discomforts of this house," he complained. "I haven't slept a wink since six, I don't know how you endure it. Why don't you come back with me to London? I could take you on as secretary in my office, or as a P.A. I could do with a P.A., with all the pressure. We could fly together to Zurich..." He sipped his tea thirstily, like somebody deprived of sustenance for more than twenty-four hours. "Sit on my bed, I don't see enough of you."

Emma perched cross-legged at the end of the bed that in days long past had been the central feature of one of her grandfather's most successful comedies, in which Mad, naturally enough, had played the lead. The long run over, she had bought it for sentimental reasons.

"You know I can't leave Mad," she said, "especially now, since all this hullabaloo. I do exercise a little restraint, though I admit not much."

"Then both of you come," he urged. "Plenty of room at the flat, I'm out all day, she can do just as she likes, walk in Kensington Gardens, feed the ducks, go to the Zoo . . ."

"Pa, darling," Emma protested, "Mad isn't Ben. Honestly . . . Far from walking in Kensington Gardens she would be more likely to stage a one-woman demo in front of the American Embassy or the Houses of Parliament. Chain herself to railings, or whatever suffragettes did at the beginning of the century."

"No problem," said Pa, filling up his cup, "no problem. Certify her as being irresponsible, a menace to society. There's a wonderful place in Surrey, food out of this world, colour T.V. in every bedroom. Bobby Wilborough's old mother is there, gives no trouble . . ."

"Pa, you know you wouldn't!" Emma hit her father's leg under the bed-clothes, making him spill his tea on the eiderdown.

"Now look what you've done!" he exclaimed. "Dottie will think I have a shaky hand. What's the matter with her, incidentally? Not the usual welcome. I suppose Mad gives her slave wages and expects to be waited on hand and foot. Her cooking's gone off too, the fish last night was only fit for the cat."

"Oh, no . . ." His daughter hit him again.

"Well, perhaps not the cat . . . The trouble is that standards become lower every mile you travel west, I've noticed it for years. Passable in Hampshire, doubtful in Dorset, on the definite down-grade in Devon, and once you cross the Tamar you might as well be in Tibet—in fact, I would think conditions are superior in Tibet, especially with the Chinese in control."

Emma flounced off the bed. "I think you're very unfair," she said, "just because you're always jetting it from capital to capital . . ."

"I don't jet it more than half a dozen times a year, my precious, I spend most of my life on a swivel chair at my office desk. But Tibet will change, Tibet will become civilised at last—by Tibet I am referring to Cornwall, of course. With the USUK Cultural-Get-Together movement

176

we may even have our early morning tea piping hot instead of tepid."

She snatched the cup and saucer away from him.

"No, no, no, give it back, give it back!"

Reluctantly, she handed him the apparently despised brew which had taken her down to the kitchen at an unearthly hour of the morning.

"You don't really take that Cultural business seriously, do you?" she asked.

"Why not, why not? Oh, complete cock, of course, if you mean personally, between ourselves, but for the native, for the rural, the hoi polloi of your precious peninsula, it may well be their salvation. Industry is finished here, you see, no future, been declining for the past few years and totally dead under USUK. What you don't understand is the fact that we are to become the playground of the Americas. They're taking it very seriously indeed, in the States. The Americans won't be encouraged to travel in Europe any more—this is part of the USUK deal. Instead, they'll come here in search of the past. Canterbury Cathedral will take the place of St. Peter's, York Minster will become Notre Dame, and every minor city in the country that can rustle up a fourteenth-century church and a few cobbled streets will be on the map, with the inhabitants tarted up in coloured stockings and pointed shoes. We've had enormous fun working out the brochures. The Mid-Westerners will be here in droves."

Emma's mind boggled. Would the shop-keepers in Poldrea be expected to put on doublet and hose and wear velvet tammies? She was sure Tom Bate would not cooperate.

"But Pa," she said doubtfully, "it would be rather degrading."

"Nonsense, nonsense," replied Pa. "People will do anything for money. Competition will be enormous, one town vying against another—you wait and see. Mock battles, feudal customs, roast swan instead of roast beef, maids in mob caps with warming pans, who will slip between the sheets to give the visitors extra warmth for extra pay. Oh yes, overtime will be recompensed in a big way, the Trades Unions will see to that."

A more vigorous blast than usual from the ill-fitting window caused him to crouch lower under the shelter of

177

the umbrella. "You could do a good trade right here, for that matter," he said. "Try out a Cornish gale at Trevanal. Honeymoon couples welcome. Umbrellas free."

A thumping on the wall between the spare room and the adjoining suite warned father and daughter that the doyenne was awake.

"Don't desert me, I might drown," implored Pa.

Emma hardened her heart and went to minister to her grandmother; after all, she was nearly eighty and her windows, facing seaward, might have blown in with the force of what appeared to be a near-typhoon. She found Mad unperturbed, standing with folded arms looking out upon a storm-tossed bay whose white crests curved in a series of tidal waves.

"Serve them right," she announced with satisfaction, "they've had to shift. Can't take it any longer. Chicken." The warship had indeed weighed anchor and was proceeding in a southerly direction, decks awash, spume frothing from her bows.

"It doesn't mean," replied Emma, "that we can also say goodbye to the marines. It will take more than a gale to drive them off Poldrea beach."

"I wonder." Mad turned from the window. "What's the betting they're all sitting huddled over the Calor-gas stoves in the caravans they've commandeered? I wish Terry were here to see this, he'd adore every moment. I shall ring up the hospital at nine o'clock and ask if he's fit enough to come home."

"Oh, Mad . . ."

"What?" Her grandmother, frowning, looked her most imperious.

"Well, wouldn't it be better if we waited until Pa goes back to London?"

"Why on earth?"

"Darling, you know how they are together, it's worse than a cock-fight."

"What utter nonsense! They do each other good."

A telephone call to Dr. Summers later in the morning unfortunately put the matter not to a vote but to a firm decision. Terry, his leg in plaster, supported by crutches which would make him a hero in the eyes of the younger boys, could very well return home. His bed was wanted at the hospital anyway.

"But don't let him outside the house," warned the doctor. "Any damage he manages to think up must be done under your roof. Incidentally, we had an officer of marines at the hospital yesterday evening checking up on his movements the preceding day. I was able to satisfy him completely. As to the missing commando, neither Terry nor I had a clue what the fellow was talking about, but I take it you're in the clear?"

"Oh yes, absolutely," replied Mad, making a signal to Emma, who was sharing the ear-piece with her. "Extraordinary thing, the man seems to have disappeared off the face of the earth. Probably fallen off a cliff. By the way, tell Terry Vic is here for the weekend. He came all the way down from London yesterday, he was so concerned about my heart."

A sound something between a snort and a chuckle came down the line. "You can tell your son from me he can quite safely go straight back again, then. The quieter you keep, the swifter the improvement in your condition. And don't, I repeat, don't get into trouble between now and Monday. This happens to be my weekend off."

Emma replaced the receiver with a sigh. I wish it was ours, she thought, I wish it was ours . . .

Mother and son departed together to bring back the wounded one from hospital. They had been gone about half-an-hour, and Emma had just swallowed a cup of coffee with Dottie in the kitchen, when looking out of the window she saw an army vehicle coming down the drive.

"Here we go," she said. "It's probably Lieutenant Sherman again. Keep the coffee brewing, I'll have to ask him in."

The officer who descended and walked up the path was not Wally, however, but a stranger, closely followed by two marines. Emma went to the porch and opened the sliding doors, almost blown backwards by the force of the wind.

"Yes?" she said.

The officer didn't salute, he brushed past her and entered the hall. He looked sharply about him, saw the row of walking-sticks on the stand, picked one of them up and examined it. Then he asked for Mad.

"My grandmother isn't here," said Emma. "She's gone

out with my father in the car. I expect them back any time."

He stared at her a moment and then said, "Captain Cockran, U. S. Marines. I have orders to search your house and question members of the household. It's a routine check, we're doing it everywhere within a radius of five miles of Poldrea camp. Okay for my men to go upstairs?"

"Can't you wait until my grandmother and my father return?" exclaimed Emma. "It's a most unusual request, surely you . . ."

"Unusual maybe, but it has to be done," he answered. "You know, probably, that one of our men is missing?"

"Yes, it was on the radio, and anyway Lieutenant Sherman was here asking questions yesterday. He knows very well we haven't seen the missing man."

"Lieutenant Sherman did not search your house," was the reply, "and I happen to be in charge of this operation. O.K., go ahead." He snapped the order to the two marines, who started to go upstairs.

"Wait," said Emma, "can't I go with them? They won't know where to go, and my father and grandmother are very particular about their things."

"Just as you like," shrugged the officer. "They won't do any damage." He began lifting up the walking-sticks one by one. Folly, who had limped into the hall from the library, sniffed at his legs. "Get out of it," he said.

"Be careful," warned Emma, "she's very old, and practically blind."

The officer didn't answer. Emma picked up Folly and took her back to the library, closing the double doors. Her heart was beating fast, not with fear but from frustration and rage. She ran upstairs after the two marines. They had entered the spare room, and one of them threw open the wardrobe, the other the chest-of-drawers. Pa's overnight bag was scrutinised, the bottom tapped. Then they stripped back the bed and turned up the mattress.

"What the hell are you looking for?" she asked.

They did not answer. One of them grinned. The bathroom was also inspected, and then they turned to Mad's suite, dressing-room, bathroom and bedroom. The same procedure followed. Cupboards and drawers were opened, clothes lifted out and put back again, but in disorder.

Thank heaven she isn't here, Emma thought, thank heaven . . . Her own bedroom was the next to be searched, then the second spare room, seldom used.

"That the lot?" asked one of them.

"On this floor, yes," she said. "We've a houseful of children at the other end. You're not going to frighten them, are you?"

No answer. They proceeded once more downstairs to the hall. The officer came out of the music-room.

"All clear?" he asked.

"Yes, sir," was the reply.

He pointed towards the closed door of the kitchen. "What's through there?"

"The kitchen," Emma replied, "and the children's quarters. We've four small boys, the youngest is only three."

"Okay, okay," he said impatiently, and jerking his head at the open door of the cloakroom ordered one of the men to inspect the multitude of oilskins, raincoats, anoraks and boots that Mad hoarded against eventualities. They entered the kitchen. Dottie looked round in surprise at the invasion of her premises as the officer started opening the cupboard doors.

"Now, hold on," began Dottie, her cheeks flaming, but Emma intervened.

"It's no use," she said. "He has a search warrant, at least I take it he has. They've already been upstairs."

"They've been to Madam's room?" she cried, appalled.

"Sure, lady." One of the marines tapped her smilingly on the shoulder. "And we're going to search your room too."

Dottie threw an appealing look at Emma, who shook her head. "It's all right, Dottie," she said, "it's all right." Then she turned to the captain. "Let me explain to the children," she pleaded.

He nodded briefly and she went ahead to the playroom.

"Look, darlings," she said quickly, "there are some marines here come to search the house. Not marines we know, another lot. So don't be frightened when they come in here."

The little boys stared. Colin, who was brandishing a very long and very sharp bamboo, tilted his head.

"Are they baddies?" he asked.

181

"I think they probably are," replied Emma, "so keep quiet."

The captain entered, followed by the marines. He threw a quick look round the room. A cupboard, bulging with broken and discarded toys, apparently offered no prospect of concealment, either for a live man or a dead one.

"Okay," he said, "let's move on."

Colin did not care to be ignored. "Hi," he said, "guess what we've got," and jumping down from the window-seat, he rumaged in the toy-cupboard, effectively blocking the departure of the captain and his force, and brought out a small square box that appeared to be a camera, which he held up to his eye in the fashion of a photographer on television.

"Want your picture taken, honey?' he said in an American accent, and pressing a button let fly a wriggling snake on a spring that leapt into the air and hit the captain in the eye.

"Fuck off," said Ben, clapping his hands.

The captain, to his credit, flung the missile aside and wiped his eye, then strode from the room without a word, Emma in close pursuit.

"I'm terribly, terribly sorry," she said. "Please understand that the children are a little out of hand."

He went straight along the passage to the small boys' bedroom, not deigning to reply, looked at it, and passed on to the next room in the passage. Sam was feeding the squirrel. Andy wasn't there. Emma knew instinctively that despite the gale he had climbed out on to the roof and had entered the forbidden chimney overhead. Sam looked up. The captain, perhaps unable to meet the cross-eyes, turned away. Before they left the room Emma looked at Sam and her lips framed the one word, Andy. Sam nodded.

"You need some help with the squirrel," she said aloud.

Sam nodded again, he understood what she meant. Andy must be alerted as soon as it was safe to descend. The search-party took rather longer over the third room along the passage, after Emma had explained that these were the quarters of the two older boys.

"Terry is the one in hospital," she said. "My grandmother and my father have gone to fetch him home."

182

"Yeah, we know about him," replied the captain, "he's been seen in hospital. Where's the other boy?"

"I expect he's in the basement. He usually is at this time."

Joe was, in fact, busy chopping wood, axe in hand, hair falling over his forehead.

"Ah," said the captain, "how old are you?"

"Nineteen," replied Joe, looking enquiringly at Emma.

"This is Captain Cockran, Joe," she said. "He's been searching the house. I don't quite know what for."

"Drop the axe," ordered the captain, "and stand over by the wall there, your hands above your head. Look lively, now."

Joe, always a slow thinker, blinked. The captain jerked his head to the two marines, who strode over, seized him by either arm and threw him against the wall.

"Look out!" shouted Emma. "What are you doing?"

"Keep out of this," said the captain. "We're not going to hurt him, we just want to ask him a few questions. Search him, corporal."

They started feeling Joe up and down, turning out the pockets of his jeans.

"Keep still, can't you?" said one of them, kicking Joe on the shin.

Joe turned a blank astonished face to the marine beside him.

"What am I supposed to have done?" he asked.

The marine flicked him across the mouth, not aggressively, but it undoubtedly stung. Joe's face turned a dull red, and instinctively he lowered his left arm to ward off a further blow. The other marine wrenched it back again above his head and kicked him on the shin for a second time.

Emma, beside herself, darted forward to intervene, but the officer seized hold of her wrist and turned her round. "See here, little girl," he said, "you run away upstairs out of it."

"You don't understand," she said. "Joe's done nothing. Lieutenant Sherman knows that. Why the hell don't you get on the telephone down to the camp and check?"

"Lieutenant Sherman is on duty today on board ship," he answered. "We're minus one marine, and it's my job to find out all you know. The local boys are giving us plenty of trouble and we're not standing for it."

Emma shook herself free. "Joe has never been in trouble in his life. He scarcely leaves the house or the garden."

The two marines had fastened an iron grip on Joe and she realised that if she screamed, which was an instinctive response, the children would hear from the playroom above and come running to the basement. They would be pushed aside in the same brusque fashion, and if Andy should hear . . . Andy mustn't hear, Andy mustn't know.

"Get up out of it, Em." Joe managed to speak, and she saw for the first time his mouth was bleeding. "I'm all right." He stood still against the wall with his hands above his head, as the marines had told him.

Emma left the cellar and ran up the little stairway that led from the basement to the front hall. At the top of the stairs she collapsed and burst into tears. She could hear Folly whining and scratching at the double doors between the library and the dining-room. She went through to her, still crying, and picking the old dog up sat with her on the sofa. Useless to call Dottie, worse than useless to call any of the four boys. She had never felt more helpless, more alone. Five, perhaps ten, minutes went by, and then Folly, with her curious dog sense despite her deafness, pricked her ears. It was the car returning, the familiar blast on the horn. She leapt from the sofa and ran down to meet them. Pa was helping Terry to the ground, Mad was handing him the crutches. Terry looked up, smiling all over his face.

"Won't your lootenant leave you alone for one moment?" he sallied, pointing to the American jeep with a crutch.

It was not the moment for joking.

"For God's sake come quickly," she said to Pa. "Some marine thugs are down in the basement beating up Joe. You've got to stop them."

Everyone stared at her, astonished. Mad, with her arm about Terry, turned abruptly, and would have fallen had he not supported her instead.

"Who? What?" exclaimed Pa. "What on earth are you talking about?"

"The marines," sobbed Emma, the tears flowing again, "not any we know. Going from house to house asking questions. They searched all the rooms, turned everything upside down, now they've put Joe against the wall in the cellar."

Pa turned to Terry. "Can you manage the steps?"

"Yes, yes, go ahead." The smile had vanished from the boy's face.

Pa took hold of his daughter's arm. "Don't get hysterical," he said firmly. "I warned you this is the sort of thing you'll have to expect. Probably no more than a routine check, they have to do their duty, I'll deal with them . . . In the cellar, you say? Why the cellar? What's Joe been up to, was he being obstructive, was he surly?"

"No," Emma shouted, "Joe didn't go a thing. He was chopping the wood, they just seized him and flung him against the wall . . ."

"All right . . . all right . . . Keep calm, my darling, you stay here, wait for Terry and Mad, look after them. In the basement, you say, I'll go immediately." He called over his shoulder as he descended the stairs, "Go into the music-room, all of you, and stay there. Shut the door. Whatever you do don't let Mad follow me."

Her grandmother and Terry were advancing slowly up the garden path. "Don't hang on to me," he was saying impatiently. "I can make it better on my own. Let me just catch one of those buggers with the end of this crutch . . ."

"No," said Mad, "Vic and I will cope. This isn't your battle."

"It bloody well is," he said, "if they try to rough up Joe."

Emma had composed herself and was standing by the front door. "We're to wait in the music-room. Pa says so. If any of us interferes it will make things a million times worse. I've tried it, I know."

"Who are they?" asked Mad. "A different lot, you said? Not Lieutenant Sherman?"

Emma explained what had happened from start to finish. "They've done no damage," she said. "I almost wish they had. It was the cool, offhand way they set about it that finished me. Picking up your walking-sticks one by one in the hall, going through the coats in the cloakroom . . ."

"By what right?" cried Terry. "What were they after?"

"I don't know," said Emma. "They didn't say."

And suddenly she remembered that Terry didn't know

185

the truth about the dead marine. He did not share their secret. He was as ignorant as Pa. Oh God, she thought, if only we could present a common, guiltless front, but we can't, we can't . . .

"I think Pa will cope successfully," said Mad. "We laugh at his bluster amongst ourselves, but I noticed that when he showed his pass it produced instant results, we were literally waved through the road-blocks."

"If you ask me," Terry said, "the marines have all got the wind up. One of 'em arrived at the hospital and wanted to put me through some sort of third degree, but Dr. Summers saw them off. What *is* all this anyway about Corporal Wagg having gone missing? Who bloody cares? He's probably curling up with one of the local scrubbers. As long as it isn't Myrtle I don't mind."

"He's been missing," said Mad, "for about thirty-six hours."

"Good luck to him," said Terry.

Presently there was a sound of voices. Pa was entering the hall by the basement staircase, and the marines were with him. Nobody spoke in the music-room. Emma, standing behind the curtain by the french window, watched Pa, the officer and the two marines walk down the garden path and through the gate. Pa was talking, but she couldn't hear what he said. The officer clicked his heels, saluted and climbed into the jeep, followed by his men. Then the jeep turned and went up the drive. Pa came back to the house. Mad crossed the room and opened the door.

"Well?" she asked.

"No problem, no problem," replied her son. "Routine check, as I thought. They're damned angry about their missing marine. Joe's not hurt, a bit bruised, he needs to wash his lip with disinfectant."

"Suppose it happens again when you're not here?" asked his mother.

"It won't, it won't. Unless, of course, you go and do something stupid."

Terry's anger seemed to have subsided. He appeared preoccupied. He raised himself with an effort and swung to the door.

"I'll go and see Joe," he said quietly. "Thanks, Vic, for bringing me home. Glad you saw those buggers off."

Mad watched him through the open door, then turned

to her son. "I don't think he can come to much harm, do you? And anyway, now those marines have gone . . . How dared they bully Joe! Oh, if only I'd been here!"

"I'm very glad you weren't," said Emma. "Pa, yes, but not you."

Her grandmother ignored the insinuation. "Can't you get on to somebody higher up?" she appealed to Pa. "Who were those marines, and why didn't they send the ones we know? Lieutenant Sherman has quite an eye for Emma, and although he's rather stupid, he's always very polite."

"Mother darling, if you think the U.S. forces, or our own forces, for that matter, would arrive with a search permit, rumple chests-of-drawers and prop up disgruntled nineteen-year-olds against a wall to question them just for the fun of the exercise, then you're wildly mistaken. I didn't say so in front of Terry, but I gathered from Captain Cockran that there has been no sign of the missing marine for practically two days. They're afraid the worst has happened, and someone has done him in. Also the clay authorities have reported stolen gelignite. These marines who've just been here were perfectly within their rights to do what they did, though maybe they were a bit tougher with Joe than they need have been, and I'm certainly not going to take it to a higher level."

Emma glanced at her grandmother. She hoped she would leave it at that. Argument might undo all that had been achieved. Pa already had two little spots of colour on his cheeks, which meant he was getting rattled.

"I hadn't time," Emma ventured, "to tidy up the bedrooms. There wasn't much in the spare room to mess about, but they opened every cupboard and drawer of yours."

She addressed herself to Mad, who rose to the bait. "Come on," she said, "I may as well see the worst, even if it gives me another heart attack."

"Now for heaven's sake be careful," urged her son. "This excitement can't be very good. Emma will tidy your room for you and it's always a shambles anyway, cupboards crammed with faded old jeans entirely unsuitable for a woman of seventy-nine. Where are your pills? Shouldn't you take your pills? I shall ring Bevil Summers . . ."

"Shut up," said Mad. When they reached the privacy

187

of her bedroom she sat down on the bed and surveyed the disorder. "Could be worse."

"You don't think," Emma asked, "that, with everything that's happening, we ought perhaps to shut up the house and go to London? Pa was saying something of the sort when I was in his room this morning."

"Go to London?" Mad echoed. "Are you raving?"

"No, seriously . . . I know we'd both hate it, but wouldn't we be safer there? You and I in the flat, Joe and Terry to the Trembaths, and . . ."

Mad went into the bathroom to wash her hands. "Go if you like, Em, I won't stop you. But nothing in the world would induce me to leave home, or the boys. Besides, Folly would never settle in Pa's flat. And what would become of Sam's squirrel?" She dried her hands on the towel. "Oh no, quite out of the question. I couldn't bear to be without all the boys. And anyway . . ."

"Anyway what?" asked Emma as she followed her grandmother downstairs, to the sound of the booming gong for lunch. Mad began to whistle under her breath.

"I think it's all rather fun," she said.

They sat down five for lunch. Joe and Terry were both present, with Terry, for once, rather silent. Joe's cut lip was not too obvious, and by a sort of tacit understanding the visit from the marines was not mentioned. Pa, soothed by a gin-and-tonic, held forth on the tremendous advantages that a six-months' visit to the states might bring to those young enough to seize the opportunity. Jet travel free, and the possibility of a job at the end of it all.

"I've seen the brochures," he told his listeners, "I've seen the brochures . . . Everything taken care of, you can't fault it, reciprocal arrangements here, but imagine the difference, damp beds and brussels sprouts, it will be a total loss for American youth, but never mind. This is where our British young will score for once."

The telephone rang and Joe went to answer it.

"Let us hope," said Pa, "that it is not a further question from thick-headed Captain Cockran."

Joe returned after a few minutes. He looked white and strained.

"It's Mrs. Trembath," he said, "she's in a terrible state, she's crying. The marines went to them after leaving here, and they've taken Mr. Trembath and young Mick away

188

for questioning. She wants to know if you can do anything." He looked at Pa at the end of the table.

"Why, of course," exclaimed Mad. "You know, Vic, the dear Trembaths at the farm, they're such friends to us all. Go and speak to her at once."

But Emma, watching her father, saw his expression change, clamp down from the one of joviality he had worn through lunch to something dogged and determined.

"I'm sorry," he said, "there is nothing I can do. I was able to use what influence I have for Joe, but it goes no further than that. I can't speak for anyone outside the immediate family. If Trembath has nothing to hide, his wife needn't worry. I'll have a word with her, if you wish, but I shall have to make the situation perfectly clear."

He threw his napkin down on the table and left the room. No one spoke. Not even his mother.

14

The tempo of the day, temporarily halted on the brink of trouble hastened towards dissension once again. Mad, aghast, argued with her son when he returned from the telephone, but he was obdurate. Influence, he insisted, could go so far before coming to a full stop, and by over-stepping it he could well bring their own household under further scrutiny.

"If Jack Trembath can satisfy his interrogators that he never set eyes on the marine the afternoon he went missing, then they'll let him go home again," he declared. "It's as simple as that. And the same goes for the boy, natu-rally."

"Mick's only two years older than Andy," said Terry angrily. "Imagine if they had got hold of Andy, just as they did Joe, and thumped him around down in the cellar. What would you have said to them then?"

"The question is hypothetical, so it doesn't arise."

There were pink spots in Pa's cheeks again and, lunch being finished anyway, he stalked out of the dining-room to the music-room. The others followed.

"We've got to do something," said Terry, "but what?

Oh, hell ... these bloody crutches." He lunged out in his frustration and hit the leg of a chair.

"Look," said Joe quietly, "I'll go down to the farm at once and see what I can do to help. There'll be the milking at four anyway. I don't think Mrs. Trembath and Myrtle can manage on their own. If necessary I'll stop the night."

"I'll come with you," said Emma. "If you say she was in such a state, and she's not easily upset ..."

"Why not take the car?" interrupted Terry. "Then I can go too. Anyway, I want to find out what Myrtle's been up to, and if she really did see Corporal Wagg that afternoon."

Emma glanced at Mad. Their eyes met. "Terry darling," said Mad, "I'd much rather you stayed here to keep an eye on the younger boys. You can send messages to Myrtle via Emma."

"All right," replied Terry grudgingly, "but if the little ones play up they'll get a taste of this." He lifted his new weapon, the crutch, and it was evident from his mood that he intended to make good use of it should the need arise.

Pa sat himself down in one of the armchairs and began flipping through *Country Life*. Emma knew he wasn't taking in one word or one illustration. She exchanged glances with her grandmother once again. Mad shrugged and grimaced. She knew she was facing a difficult afternoon.

"The frightful thing is," said Emma to Joe as they trudged across the fields down to the farm, "that Pa is within his rights by saying he can't interfere when it doesn't concern his family. And we can't tell him the truth. That it's a member of his family who's to blame for the whole thing."

"I wondered just now," replied Joe, "whether or not we ought to come clean with Vic and tell him the whole story. After all, what could happen to a kid of Andy's age? He's barely twelve."

Emma stopped and stared at her companion. "Oh no," she exclaimed, "it would be disastrous. Pa would inform the marines, he'd feel he had to, and then they'd hand Andy over to the police, ours or theirs, and he'd be sent to one of those Borstal prisons. Oh, Joe ..." she continued, walking by his side, "I love Pa, sometimes I adore him, like this morning when he was sitting up in bed under the umbrella like a spoilt schoolboy, but he's got that hard streak in him, or blind spot, or whatever it is, that just stops one telling him the truth."

The farm already looked forlorn. There was a gate open which shouldn't have been, and which Joe promptly shut. The cows were beginning to stand already in the patient way that was their routine before milking, still two hours off. No Spry to come barking any more. No Mr. Trembath crossing the yard, no Mick hullooing from the cow-shed.

"Damn them, damn them," said Emma savagely.

Mrs. Trembath was coming down the stairs as they entered the back kitchen. "Oh, it's you, Emma dear," she said. "Oh, I am glad to see you. Myrtle is so upset. I had to put her to bed."

Stupid ass, thought Emma, why on earth couldn't she rally round and help her mother? Instinctively she ran across to Mrs. Trembath and put her arms round her, but her sympathy brought back the tears. Mrs. Trembath collapsed, crying at the kitchen table.

"I'll go out," murmured Joe. "Tell her not to worry, I'll see to things."

Emma had the story, little by little. It was all concerning the missing Corporal Wagg. Captain Cockran didn't seem to believe that Jack and Mick had been milking at the time the corporal had turned up, and that they hadn't even known he had come to speak to Myrtle.

" 'You gave the corporal the brush-off, that was it, wasn't it?' the captain kept saying to Jack," Mrs. Trembath told Emma. " 'You gave him the brush-off because you suspected he was after your daughter here. What did you do to him? Come on, out with it.' Oh, Emma, Jack's never been spoken to that way in his life, you couldn't blame him for getting angry. 'You get off my land,' he said. 'You've no right. First you shoot my dog, then you trespass on my property and accuse me of something I've never done. Get out of it!' Well, that did it, you see. They seized him and bundled him into their jeep, with some difficulty, mind you, and then they took Mick . . ." She broke off and looked imploringly at Emma. "Are you sure your father can't do something for us? Terry's always told us he knows so many people up in London, Members of Parliament and others . . ."

This was the worst moment. To admit Pa's negative attitude. To admit defeat.

"He did stop them questioning Joe," she said, "but possibly they weren't going to take him off anyway. Joe didn't protest, you see. He kept pretty quiet. I suppose it was because Mr. Trembath got angry that they got angry too."

"But it was natural, wasn't it? Who wouldn't be angry? And my poor Jack was telling the truth, he was milking when the corporal came."

Not the whole truth, thought Emma, not the whole truth. That's the terrible part about it. He knows Andy killed the corporal. He knows what happened to the body. And you don't, dear Mrs. Trembath, nor does Myrtle . . .

"Pa says he is sure they will let Mr. Trembath and Mick come back very soon," she told her, "so please try not to worry. Look, Joe will do anything outside you need doing. He'll manage the milking, he'll get the sheep into the home field. What can I do for you here? Have you had anything to eat?"

"You're a dear," said Mrs. Trembath, wiping her eyes, "I'm very grateful to you."

Grateful . . . And what are we? Your husband being put against a wall down at the camp, and your son too, because of us, because of us . . .

Emma spent the rest of the afternoon helping Mrs. Trembath around the house. Myrtle recovered herself sufficiently to go outside and help Joe marshal the cows to the sheds for milking—because he's male, thought Emma, she wouldn't do it for her mother. While she and Mrs. Trembath were getting the tea, somebody knocked on the back door.

"I'll go," said Emma. She opened it, and there stood Mr. Willis, peaked hat held in his hand, white thatch of hair upright in the wind. "Oh," she said, uncertain whether to be glad or sorry, "it's you."

The blue eyes glinted at her behind the spectacles. "We're here on the same errand, I'm thinking," he answered, "offering our services to neighbours in need. I was down in Poldrea and I heard Mr. Trembath and the boy had been taken to the camp for questioning. News travels fast, doesn't it? I came to see if I could do the milking. I can turn my hand to anything, as I expect you've noticed."

"Joe's in the middle of milking now," said Emma, then called over her shoulder to Mrs. Trembath. "It's Mr. Willis, come to know if he can help."

Mrs. Trembath came to the door and stood beside her. "It's very good of you," she said doubtfully. "I don't know where we'd be without good neighbours. Joe's nearly through with the milking, but we've still to round up the sheep and count them. There was one missing the other night. Jack found her, though, after he'd been round the field with the Land-Rover."

Emma moved aside. Everything Mrs. Trembath said seemed to implicate them further.

"You stay where you are, missus," said Mr. Willis. "I'll give Joe a hand with the milking, and with the sheep. It's true, then, they took away your husband? I didn't credit it when they told me in the street."

The story had to be re-told from start to finish. Emma couldn't bear it, her guilt was so intense. At least Mr. Willis shared the secret, but in a way this made it even worse. "I knew we were in for trouble the moment they landed amongst us last week," she heard him saying. "Never can let well alone, look what they did in south-east Asia that time. They beat a man up if he as much as speaks his mind."

"They won't beat up my Jack, surely?" asked Mrs. Trembath anxiously.

"Not if he answers them sweetly," was the reply. "You have to know how to handle them. Plenty of lip-service and they'll swallow it. Then, when the right moment comes strike and strike hard, and they'll scatter like starlings at the sound of a rattle. If you'll excuse me, I'll see what I can do to help the lad with the cows." He vanished into the gathering murk outside.

"He's very kind," said Mrs. Trembath, "but he's such an odd sort of man." She peered outside towards the sheds across the yard.

"I know," said Emma, "but I think you can trust him." What is more, you've got to trust him, because there's no alternative, she thought. He's got you and me, sister, in his hands, he's got our whole world in his hands . . .

The gale that had been blowing throughout the day was easing now. You did not feel it so much here at the farm, which was partly sheltered by the brow of the hill, as you did on the high ground at home. Emma wondered what had been happening up at Trevanal all afternoon. Mrs. Trembath had laid the table for all of them, Emma, Joe and Mr. Willis, saying she and Myrtle would be glad of the company and there was plenty to eat with her husband and son absent, but Emma shook her head.

"I can't speak for Joe," she said, "but I ought to get back."

The sound of a car in the yard brought hope to them both, but it was Nurse Bennett, Mrs. Trembath's sister. She too had heard the ill-news by the all-pervading grapevine.

"They've been to all the farms around," she said, "and to the cottages beyond St. Fimbar. And it isn't just the missing marine they're after, it's explosives. What would we want with explosives, that's what I want to know? You know Jim Couch with the ulcerated leg I dress, whose boy works up at Whitemoor? Well, it seems they've taken quite a few of the younger chaps for questioning, and the mood of the men is getting quite ugly."

"The uglier the better," Mr. Willis had reappeared, and he bowed with old-fashioned courtesy to Nurse Bennett. "We don't want it to be a walk-over, do we? It takes more than a handful of fellows up at Whitehall to make a union between countries. You have to have the backing of a whole nation."

"That's all very well, Mr. Willis," replied Mrs. Trembath, "but they didn't ask us, at least not this time. We did have a referendum when there was all that fuss about entering Europe."

"Entering Europe had nothing on this lot," said Mr. Willis. "As easy as going to Lostwithiel market with that one, exchange your cattle for a sow and piglets and everyone happy. No Yankee troops walking over your land and killing your livestock."

"That's true." Nurse Bennett nodded. "All the same, we don't want trouble."

"That's what the French said when the Germans occupied their country in the Second World War. We don't want trouble, they said. We'll do as we're told. Some of them didn't, did they? They blew up railway lines and junctions and prepared the way for the second front."

Emma caught his eyes and looked away again. She

thought of Terry's gelignite hidden securely somewhere in the hut in the woods.

"Mrs. Trembath," she said, "I really ought to go. Perhaps you'll tell Joe when he comes in."

"He's ready to go back with you now," said Mr. Willis. "If there is anything more that I can do here I'm ready to do it. And again in the morning, at milking time." He rubbed his hands with satisfaction. "The harder a man works the better he sleeps—that goes for everyone, doesn't it?"

Mrs. Trembath looked uncertainly at her new farm-helper as she poured out his tea. Emma felt that neither she nor Myrtle would have much sleep that night, not unless their menfolk returned safe and sound.

Joe was standing in the doorway waiting for her. "I'll look in again tomorrow morning, Mrs. Trembath," he said. "Mr. Willis tells me he will be here first thing. I do hope Mr. Trembath and Mick come home before that."

"Please God," she replied.

"I wouldn't count on it," said Mr. Willis. "They like to make you as uncomfortable as they can, otherwise it's wasting their time. Do you good to sweat it out, that's what they say." He nodded to Joe. "Weather's easing already," he said. "We'll have clear skies tomorrow and a beach full of driftwood from below my place right round to Poldrea. A fine harvest for all of us, and for the Yankees too, I shouldn't wonder."

Emma and Joe went out into the night. The clouds had parted, the air was sharper than before.

"I don't know what it is," said Emma, "but he gives me the creeps."

"Me too," confessed Joe, "but I know we can trust him. He was talking to me back in the shed. He said they can't put anything on Mr. Trembath or Mick, because they will be telling the truth. They didn't see Corporal Wagg when he called on Myrtle, and they'll stick to that. Mick knows nothing of what happened later, so he's absolutely in the clear. He also said feeling is rising locally against the marines, especially since this. Mr. Trembath is very highly thought of locally, everyone respects him."

"Perhaps," said Emma, "perhaps . . . but that doesn't get round the fact that we all know, and so does Mr. Trembath, that the corporal is dead."

They arrived back at Trevanal hoping to find a household, if not entirely happy, at least comparatively serene. They were disappointed. As they entered the house they heard the sound of the telephone in the cloakroom and Pa rushed to answer it. For some reason he had changed out of his polo sweater and was in his suit.

"Crisis ... crisis ..." he said, "everything blowing up." He dashed into the cloakroom and shut the door. Emma and Joe went into the music-room. Mad was putting more logs on the fire. She turned, and raising her eyes to heaven, sighed and sat down on the sofa.

"It's gone on like this since four this afternoon. We had a lovely silent hour, he even went to sleep in the chair while I held my breath, and then the telephone rang, his damn secretary from London. Don't ask me what it's all about. Zurich ... New York ... I'm not sure he didn't even say Brazil. Anyway, he's got to get back to London right away."

"Oh no!" Emma's spirits sank to zero.

"Darling, I'm as disappointed as you are. I know he's maddening, but we both adore him." Mad, of all people, had tears at the corners of her eyes. "We don't see him often, that's it, I suppose. Well, it can't be helped. How was it at the farm? Are Jack and Mick back yet?"

"No," said Emma, "but Mr. Willis has turned up to help."

"That's a relief. Dear Taffy. I don't know what we should do without him."

Joe slipped from the room, saying there were things to be done, though Emma guessed it was because he thought they wanted to be alone with Pa.

"The children have behaved like angels, bless them," said her grandmother. "Dottie started to make the Christmas puddings, far too early, I'm sure, and she allowed Colin and Ben to help; she deserves a halo."

"What about Andy and Sam?"

"They made a new hutch for the squirrel, the old one was smelling so dreadfully, one could hardly go into their room. The trouble is I don't think the squirrel gets on terribly well with the pigeon, they don't seem to see eye to eye."

The patter in the cloakroom ceased and Pa came into the room. "I knew it was a mistake to leave London," he said. "Everyone's going round in circles, people completely losing their heads. USUK and Brazil at loggerheads over the new currency arrangements; I see myself flying out there to help sort things out. And some bloody fool put a bomb on the steps of the American Embassy, no damage, they found it in time, but it's bad for propaganda. Emma darling, I can't find my bedroom slippers, what did you do with my bedroom slippers?"

She hadn't done anything, they were under the bed. She helped him sort his few belongings, pack his hair-brushes, his electric tooth-brush, and suddenly she put her arms round him and held on to him.

"I don't want you to go," she told him.

"How very sweet of you," he said, surprised, "how very touching. Darling Emma, how delightful it is to have a grown-up daughter, one doesn't always realise it, this constant pressure. We must see more of each other. I wish you would come to Brazil, you'd love Brazil. Did you sort out your farming friends? I'm sorry I couldn't do more for them. Out of the question."

Typically, he didn't wait for a reply but ran downstairs again two at a time, and was back in the music-room drinking black coffee.

"This will sustain me until I'm through Exeter," he said. "Once Exeter is past I enter civilisation. I might snatch a sandwich off old Digby-Stratton, he's only a few miles from Honiton, it depends on the time, and whether there are these confounded road-blocks everywhere ... Emma, if the operator rings to say the Brazilian Embassy is on the line, tell them to cancel the call, I've left ... No, no, Mother beloved, I don't want a Bath Oliver biscuit, it would give me indigestion hunched over the wheel, I must get organised, I must leave you." He folded his arms round his mother and his daughter at the same time, hugging them to him. "If I do have to fly to Rio tomorrow and am out of touch for a few days, don't let me return and find you both in prison. These are stirring times—put a foot wrong, and anything may happen. You have my office number, and if there's a genuine crisis tell my secretary to contact me, but I shall be in conference continuously ... Don't forget to take your heart pills, take things easy, control those horrible children ... I must go, I must go ..."

Mad stood at the front door watching as Emma accompanied her father down the drive, and this is all repetition of yesterday, Emma thought, only it was then, with his visit ahead which might have lasted the whole weekend, and it isn't then any more, it's now, and he's going, and nothing has been achieved. It's worse in a way than if he had never come at all, because one had got used to the thing of not seeing him. He was kissing her once again, then climbing into the car and roaring up the drive, the headlights pausing at the gates and shining upon them. Then no more. It was all over. Pa had gone.

Mad was standing before the fire in the music-room. She had picked up an old picture postcard of herself from the mantel-piece and was studying it. It had been taken years ago when she was young. The face that launched a thousand ships, her husband used to say. The eyes were very large, the hair rather full, framing the rounded cheeks. Vic, aged about three, a sturdy replica of herself, sat on her knee. Emma went and stood beside her, then put her arms round her grandmother.

"It's still awfully like," she said.

"Of him, or of me?" asked Mad.

"Of you both."

And yet, and yet . . . What was he thinking about, that plump little boy? Had it been laid out for him, planned, that he would grow up to become a burly middle-aged man tearing about in jets to Brazil and believing, or kidding himself, he could control the finances of millions? And that lovely sensuous woman, his mother, with the smile at the corner of her mouth and the looped tresses falling about her face, did she know then that she would live to be seventy-nine, an eccentric, rather imperious old woman? When the photograph was taken the world, if far from secure, still held some measure of stability, and Hitler's war had not been launched. Later, the little boy, of an age to understand, would have heard Churchill's famous phrase about fighting on the beaches, in the streets. Today the country had been taken over, annexed, by another power, with—at least according to the statement of the little boy of the photograph, now grown to full maturity—the consent of almost the entire population. The fighting on the beaches had been done by a boy of seventeen, throwing his marine opponent in a Rugby tackle, and by a child of twelve, not in a street but on a ploughed field, who, turning killer, destroyed the same opponent with a bow and arrow.

Mad put the photograph back in its place on the mantelpiece. "I had a funny feeling when I saw him go just now," she said.

"What do you mean?" Emma asked.

"Oh, nothing, just . . ." Mad spread out her hands in the familiar gesture, "I feel it may be a long time before I see him again."

Emma did not answer. She was wondering whether old people found that time went slowly or, on the contrary, much too fast. It was going fast at the moment because so many things seemed to be happening every day. If the crisis had not come, would her grandmother have had the same sense of boredom, of frustration, that she herself had known during the past weeks? Or did Mad, because of being eighty very soon, want every day to drag, almost to stop still, because each moment must, by the nature of things, bring her closer to the end?

"Pa will only be a few days out of the country," Emma said in reassurance, "and then he's bound to come down for your birthday. We must make a thing of that, crisis or no crisis."

Mad shrugged contemptuously. "My birthday," she scoffed. "Who cares about birthdays at my age? We'll do something when the moment comes to amuse the boys, but the real question will be, shall we have anything to celebrate?"

15

Jack Trembath and Mick were allowed to return to the farm on Sunday morning. It was a special concession, so the camp commandant told him, because of his livestock and the essential nature of his work on the land. He must be prepared to answer further questions should the need arise. The proceedings had been conducted not by Colonel Cheeseman, who had left for Falmouth in the warship during the storm the preceding day, but by his deputy, a Colonel Tucker, who was altogether tougher. One of the first things the farmer did was to come up to Trevanal and report in person.

"I want to thank you," he said to Mad as soon as he entered the room, "for letting Joe come down and take my place. I don't know what Peggy and Myrtle would have done without him, or you either, for that matter," he added, turning to Emma. "Just being there, and talking to them, was what counted."

"You thank us?" Mad put out her hand and pulled him down beside her on the sofa. "What can we say to you? I don't think either Emma or I got much sleep last night

203

wondering what they were doing to you. As for your poor wife . . ."

"Ah well, it's over," he said. "We'll think no more of it. And it might have been worse. I wouldn't have minded, you know, had it been our own chaps in charge down there at Poldrea, sticking us up against a wall and treating us like vandals or something, but what got my goat was to have this Yankee with an accent like a sheriff from some Western film rasping out questions. I lost my temper at home, that's what did it, no doubt, and I took care to keep a hold on myself when they got us in custody."

"Where did they put you?" asked Mad.

"Why, they've taken over all Poldrea harbour," he told her. "You know the offices of the port authority? Well, that's their headquarters now. I was glad . . ." he lowered his voice, although the door was shut, "I was glad Mick knew nothing. If he had he might have broken down. They rap the questions at you thick and fast, it's darn confusing, and for a lad of his age you couldn't expect him to stand it. But don't you worry," he tapped Mad on the knee. "They didn't get a damn thing out of either of us. And never will."

Emma remembered her grandmother's remark on Friday evening about the Celts and the Saxons, and Mr. Trembath might have read her thoughts, for he smiled to himself a moment and then he said, "The old fellow from the woods turned up trumps, didn't he? Maybe the Cornish and the Welsh have more in common than I thought. Let someone come in from overseas and try to push us around, and they'll get more than they bargained for. He was down at the farm first thing this morning, Peggy tells me, beat your Joe to it by a short head. Oh, he's a tough one, all right. Glad he's on our side and not on theirs."

"Our side," said Mad, "that's the way to talk. I wish there were more of us."

"Don't you worry," replied Jack Trembath, shaking his head. "There's plenty around here who gave the Yanks a welcome when they first landed but'd be glad now to see them go. Oh, not all, I grant you. There's some, and I'm naming no names, who'd sell their birthright for easy money, the let's-fleece-the-Yanks-brigade, same as they fleece the Midlanders, but others, who've got a spark of

204

fire left in their bellies, they're not going to take foreign rule lying down."

Emma shifted uneasily in her chair. She was thinking of Pa. And Mad evidently had been reminded of him too, because, with a slight alteration in her voice that only her grand-daughter could recognise, she said, "I suppose we ought not to consider it foreign rule. It's supposed to be a union, isn't it? My son was trying to explain it all to us. I don't understand finance, never have. But it seems without this union we'd be finished, a bankrupt nation. By the way, I was so sorry he couldn't do anything about preventing the marines taking you away. We, Emma and I, felt very badly about it. The truth was, my son Vic knew nothing about the marines and what had happened. We didn't tell him."

"Didn't tell him?" Jack Trembath looked surprised.

"No. You see, Vic in his work as a banker is closely associated with the government and all this business of USUK. Indeed, he is very much for it, encourages everything that is happening. So if we had told him the truth I really don't know . . ." Mad was genuinely searching for the right words, which she had never done in the past when she had forgotten her lines and anything impromptu had sprung to her lips. "I really don't know what he would have done. He might have felt it his duty to tell the Americans the marine was dead, and how he died."

The farmer was silent. He seemed shocked. He shook his head again slowly.

"That's awkward for you," he said at last, "very awkward. Things have come to a pretty pass when a woman can't ask advice from her own son. I don't blame him, mind you, he's got to work for the government, and if this is the way they feel the country should be run, and they can't do it without the Yankee troops, why . . ." He rose to his feet and smote one fist upon the other. "I just can't take it, that's all. And when that boy Andy drew his bow last week, by God, you know I'd have been proud if my Mick had done it instead. It was the first blow struck in defence of this country, and I honour him for it." He stood staring at both of them. "There now," he said, "I've said my piece and I'll go. And don't you forget, if there's anything I can do for you and for your boys any time of the day or night, I'm ready."

Later in the day Joe reported to Emma that he had seen two marines, and police with Alsatian dogs, crossing the ploughed field to the grazing ground below the stile.

"I was up in the shrubbery," he told her. "They didn't see me. They were following the trail all right that Mr. Willis led. They must have gone down to the beach afterwards. Whether they'd lose the scent down there I just don't know. After all, it's three days, isn't it? The tide must have covered where he went."

"Do the others know?"

"Only Terry," he said. "I thought it best, by the way, to tell Terry the lot last night when we went to bed. I knew if I didn't Andy couldn't have kept it dark for long."

"What did he say?"

"He was pretty shaken. More than I had expected him to be. Not so much the killing, but the fact that Andy did it, and, what was more, did it for him. He said if the marines had been British he'd have felt almost bound to go and tell them and take the blame on himself. But since they were Yanks, and invaders, and after the way they'd roughed me up, and Mr. Trembath and Mick, he'd be prepared to get hold of the bow and arrow and shoot a dozen more himself."

There's an expression for it, Emma thought, they call it snowballing. Someone starts something, and it gathers impetus, and more join in, and then there's an avalanche, and people or property or causes are destroyed.

The school bus waited for the boys at the top of the hill the following morning. It was decorated with a USUK flag, so Terry reported—he had swung himself up the drive to watch the departure. His own technical school was still closed. "Too many of us in custody, I shouldn't wonder," he said grimly.

Mad suggested that she and Emma should go down to Poldrea to do the shopping. Emma would have preferred to go alone; Mad let loose in the supermarket could be a danger. However, nothing would dissuade her, and they set forth in the car, past the road-blocks still in position, passes inspected, and so along the beach road to the town. Emma was allowed to drive because, so it was grudgingly admitted, someone with a supposedly weak heart should not be seen at the wheel. When they arrived to park opposite the supermarket they found a line of cars parked

206

all along the road, and a queue of people stretching round the corner of the street waiting to go inside.

"I'm not surprised," observed Mad. "They're all hoping to stock up before supplies run out. Thank the Lord for our beetroot. I'll take my place at the tail of the queue while you find somewhere to park."

Emma had to circle the narrow streets of Poldrea before she squeezed her car into a private turning near the Methodist chapel. As she walked back along the street she bumped into Mr. Willis coming out of Tom Bate's fish-shop.

"Oh, hulló," she said. "Nice morning for once."

He made her a sweeping bow. "Nice morning it is," he replied, "for those of us alive to enjoy it." One eye closed behind the spectacles and the side of his mouth twitched. "Pity it blew so hard last night—our friend fetched up on Kellyvardo rock instead of being taken out to sea as I'd intended. Wedged in amongst the winkles. You'd never credit it, would you?"

Emma was silent. Mr. Willis could be referring to one thing only. Kellyvardo rock was a reef about a hundred feet in length that was only uncovered at low tide. Marked with a pole, it was a hazard to shipping between Poldrea harbour and the anchorage beyond.

He nodded to a passer-by and then continued, "The pole broke with the force of the gale Saturday. It's done it before, they don't drive it deep enough. Tom Bate was fishing out there yesterday, he knows every inch of the place. He keeps a spike in his boat to test the depth around the reef when he cuts his engine, and the seaweed's fresher there than I get it ashore, so he brings me some in for my plot of ground from time to time." Mr. Willis paused, and winked at her again. " 'Hullo, what's this?' says Tom Bate as he pokes something soft near to where the pole had broken away, and he pokes again, and what he jabbed at wasn't very pleasant, I can tell you. So he started his engine up again and returned to the harbour to report. Not a case of finding's keepings, was it? No, not this time."

Emma waited for another passer-by to walk out of earshot before she answered. "So the marines know?"

"They know . . . they know . . . They kept Tom there in the office most of the day asking questions, so he was telling me, no more fishing for him yesterday. That's why you won't find any fresh fish in the shop this morning. Why don't you go in and ask him?"

Emma shook her head. "I think not," she said, and then she added, "There was nothing on the news about it."

"There wouldn't be," he answered. "It's unofficial, isn't it? The only reason I know is because I came to call in at the shop for my batch of fresh seaweed." He showed her his bulging bag.

Unbelievably the eye closed once more, than he flourished his bag and crossed the street towards the ironmonger's. Emma glanced furtively into the window of the fish-shop. Dried kippers and salted cod were spread on the slab, and Tom Bate himself was watching her from behind his counter. He was smiling.

"Anything I can tempt you with today, my dear?" he called.

"No. No, thank you very much," she replied.

She walked along the pavement to the supermarket. Her grandmother had worked her way up the queue and was practically at the swing-doors. She was talking to the wife of the bank manager.

"They're going to call it the ducat," she was saying over her shoulder, "historical associations and all that, rather like the doubloon. But whether ducats are to be based on the dollar my son didn't say. I think he's flying to Brazil to find out. Your husband will know all about it. The ducat, I mean."

"He hasn't mentioned it to me," replied her companion in the queue. She looked bewildered.

"Oh . . oh well," Mad shrugged, "perhaps it's premature. My son's a merchant banker, he's always one step ahead of everyone else."

Other people in the queue were listening. "I've never heard of the ducat," whispered one woman to another, "nor the doubloon. It's too bad, just as we had all got used to the decimal currency too."

"Very hard on pensioners," grumbled an old man.

"Never mind," smiled Mad. "Now this rationing has started, you and I will get orange juice at half price like the babies."

They moved forward through the swing-doors. Bedlam was within, people pushing in all directions. The assistants were flustered. There were notices on the counter saying "Sorry. No bacon, no butter, no cheese." Customers were filling their wire baskets with tins marked "Not Rationed Yet," but each tin was up in price.

"We don't want any of this," said Mad. "It's old stock pushed to the front to catch our eye."

The assistant behind the counter flinched. "I assure you it's not, madam," he said, "but you have to understand we have been put out by the new regulations worse than our customers. This rationing's come into effect so quickly that we just don't know where we are. We've had no deliveries yet, and we don't know when to expect them."

Mad jostled her way ahead, her grand-daughter at her heels, and finally turned away with a curious assortment of goods ranging from a dozen pallid-looking chops and several pounds of sausages to rolls of lavatory paper and some bottles of orange squash.

"Darling, I don't think Dottie had any of these on her list," ventured Emma.

"Never mind," said Mad, "they'll come in useful. And we mustn't hoard. I always remember that from the war, people who hoarded were beyond the pale. What about fish?"

"No," said Emma. She looked around her. People outside the supermarket were still edging forward. I must lie, she thought. "The shop's closed. Tom Bate isn't there." Yet they would have to pass his shop to get back to where she had parked the car. "I tell you what," she said hurriedly. "You go along to the chemist's and I'll bring the car there and pick you up."

"But I don't want anything from the chemist," Mad protested.

"The boys do. They're running out of tooth-paste. So am I. And you know the soap is better there than it is at the supermarket."

Emma fetched the car and picked Mad up in front of the chemist's, and they stopped at the road-block for their passes to be scrutinised once again. Mr. Libby, the landlord of the Sailor's Rest, was talking to the marine on duty. He waited for the formalities to finish, then stepped forward and bent his head to the car window.

"Good morning," he said. "I think I have something that would please you both. I'm not letting on to everyone, mind you." His tone was confidential. "The deputy commander of the camp here is a most obliging gentleman. What I say is this, if you do your best for them, they do their best for you." He glanced over his shoulder. "How about a case of Californian wine?" he murmured.

"Sorry," said Mad, "it's against my principles."

Mr. Libby opened his eyes wide. "No hanky-panky, I promise you. It's all above board. No duty to pay. We're to import it in large quantities, and this happens to be the first consignment. You'll find it much sweeter on the palate than the French stuff you usually have."

"Mr. Libby," said Mad, "when I come to you asking for Californian wine you will know I've got tired of drinking my own bath-water at home. Drive on, Emma." She turned to her grand-daughter as they shot up the hill. "I meant it too. Californian wine, my foot! So Vic was right. What else are we going to be forced to consume, is what I ask myself. Tea-bags forever, I suppose ... and those terrible clams."

It was not until the car was safely parked in the garage that Emma turned to her grandmother and said, "I saw Mr. Willis in Poldrea. They've found Corporal Wagg."

Mad was silent. Then as she climbed out of the car she asked, "Where?"

"Kellyvardo rock. Yesterday. And it was Tom Bate in his boat who found him. That's why I didn't want you to go to the shop." She explained to her grandmother the few details she knew.

Mad was gathering her purchases together. "They'll have done a post-mortem, no doubt," she said. "I wonder what happens in a case like this—whether they hold an inquest, as they would with one of our own people, or whether it's different, being one of theirs."

"I don't know," said Emma, "and there's nobody we can ask."

"We just have to wait, then. And listen to the news."

Emma could not decide whether it was a relief that the body had been discovered or whether it made things worse. On balance, worse. While it was missing, people might still think the corporal had possibly absconded, was in hiding somewhere; and she and the rest of them who knew the truth could hope that the gale that had blown through Friday night and Saturday might have taken the body far up-channel, so that possibly it would be days, weeks, before it ever came ashore, and then perhaps would be unrecognisable. But now now. Wedged fast under a crevice in Kellyvardo rock. She thought of the times she and the boys had walked out there at low water—it was only at dead of spring that the entire reef was uncovered, and they could paddle around it looking for shrimps, for prawns. She shuddered. She would never be able to do it again.

Dottie greeted them with the news that Pa had telephoned during their absence. "He sounded in a great hurry, Madam, leaving for the airport there and then. New York first and then Rio. His secretary has his addresses. I think he was upset not to speak to you."

Mad gestured. "I shouldn't have gone out. I could at least have heard his voice."

She looked dispirited, so unusual for her. Emma unloaded all their packages on the kitchen table and followed her grandmother.

"What do you mean, you could have heard his voice?" she asked.

"Just that."

A feeling of panic seized Emma. "You don't think he's going to crash, be hijacked, something frightful?"

"No, darling, of course not. Forget it. Just a silly pang."

Emma tried to imagine herself sitting beside Pa on the jet to New York. She'd have been borne away from the trials and turmoil here at home. Pa would make a fuss of her, spoil her, introduce her with a show of pride as his "suddenly grown-up daughter." New York, Rio, everything exciting, fresh, but above all safe, and no responsibility beyond the easy one of having to do him proud and look her best. Instead, beleaguered here at home. Mad nearly eighty, the boys dependent too, and every day that dawned becoming more ominous, more of a threat.

She went off for a walk over the fields and down to the cliffs in the afternoon simply to goad herself still further into a feeling of horror and rejection combined, which she knew the sight of Kellyvardo rock would bring. The sea was oily flat. A different bay, surely, from the storm-tossed cauldron of Saturday. No rollers, no curling crests. The slimy surface of Kellyvardo humped above the still water, and the broken spar snapped at the centre looked like the bent figure of a man. On the far horizon, rounding the Dodman, came the distant shape of an approaching warship. Emma stood watching until the grey outline became clearer. It was the warship returning to cast anchor in the bay. Would it help the situation, at least as far as it concerned themselves, or make it worse? Colonel Cheeseman had surely been more understanding than his deputy, but he might have changed his attitude now the missing corporal had been discovered dead. And Wally Sherman? Would he have changed as well? She turned her back on the sea and climbed up the hill to the ploughed field once more. How many hours in that jet across the Atlantic would it have taken, sitting beside Pa? Had it touched down already, themselves forgotten, and was Pa being greeted by his business friends in a V.I.P. reception lounge?

She returned home to find the boys coming down the drive, the school bus having decanted them at the top of the main road. They were all sporting USUK ties, a strident colour-scheme clashing with their skins. Colin, as always, was the first to run ahead with the news.

"We didn't have hardly any lessons at all," he shouted, "a lot of marching and singing to new songs. We've been learning 'The Star-Spangled Banner.' And Miss Birkett read us history stories about America. And guess what?"

"What?"

"Mrs. Hubbard was there, the lady with the teeth. She gave us a Jesus-talk. We're going to have one every week from now on, but not from her. She was just showing our teacher how to do it."

Emma turned to the others. "Did you get the same treatment?" she asked.

"No." Andy looked fed up. "They kept moving us around into different groups, and the new thing is you've got to help whoever's sitting next to you. I kept getting between girls and it was awful. They did nothing but giggle and poke me in the back. Then we had something called a Think-In. We had to keep quiet for about ten minutes and then each one in turn had to stand up and say what he or she had been thinking."

"What did you say?"

"I told them what a stupid idea I thought it was and

212

that was all. So I was passed over very quickly. I didn't get a star."

"I did," said Sam, his thin little face lit up with a sudden smile. "At least, it's a new kind of star, like the ones on our ties. My think-in was all about Spry, and how Mr. Trembath had found him as a pup, some holiday visitor had left him on the beach on purpose, not wanting to take him home. And I said how he had been trained to guard the sheep and the cattle, and everyone loved him, and then he got shot."

Terry, having exhausted all the gramophone records in his repertoire, had hobbled out to join them. "I bet that shook them," he said.

"I don't know," Sam answered. "Mr. Edyvean and the visiting person looked rather solemn, and Mr. Edyvean gave me a star for imaginative description."

"The Jesus-talk was much better than a think-in," insisted Colin, trying to pull away Terry's crutch, "because afterwards we had to act scenes from Jesus's life. The others did loaves and fishes, and went round the class pretending to give each other bread. I thought that was silly. I took my ruler and lashed out at them all, and when Miss Birkett asked what I was doing and said it wasn't right to be rough, I said I was Jesus whipping the money-lenders in the Temple. Mrs. Hubbard went away after that. She said she had to go on to another school. Miss Birkett gave me a star, all the same."

The school news was narrated in turn to Mad by all three boys after they had finished their tea. Rather to Emma's surprise her grandmother, instead of being amused, was outraged.

"I've never heard such **** in my life," she declared, using a word that she had possibly picked up from Ben. "How dare they change the syllabus in this way without consulting parents, grandparents, guardians? If this is the beginning of CGT or whatever they call it, then the sooner there is a row at the Ministry of Education the better. I suppose it's to be a combined affair in future. Some utter fool like Martha Hubbard as Joint Minister at the head of the department. I've a good mind to keep the children at home. Teach them myself."

"It's against the law," said Emma.

"I don't care. Let them sue me. Those ghastly ties . . .

I cna't believe wearing them is to be compulsory. And why not be straight and direct when you teach Christianity? A Jesus-talk, indeed! All the same," she reflected, "I'd have given a lot to have seen Colin whipping them out of the Temple."

She switched on the television, only to be greeted by the inevitable smiling faces of the President and the Queen standing side by side in the White House.

"Oh, surely not," she groaned. "It's positively indecent. What on earth is Prince Philip doing?"

"I suppose he's still camping with the Red Indians," replied Emma.

"If we're going to have the same thing when the President pays his visit here, and we get him swaying in a coach to open Parliament, I tell you one person who will go stark staring mad, and that's Dottie," said Mad. "Switch it off!"

"Wait," Emma warned her, "there might be something about the corporal."

There was nothing. Preparations for a general Thanksgiving at the end of the week hogged most of the programme, and because the United Kingdom would be joined after nearly two hundred years with her former colony the celebrations were to be on a magnificent scale, with a public holiday for all.

Later that evening the telephone rang. Emma went to answer it. It was Wally Sherman. He sounded rather subdued.

"That you, Emma?" he said. "Wally here. We're back in camp."

"I guessed you were," she replied. "I saw the ship come into the bay this afternoon."

"That's right," he said, and after a moment's hesitation, "I heard you'd been in a certain amount of trouble. I'm sorry."

"So were we," she told him.

He paused again. "The reason I'm calling you is that it isn't exactly over," he went on, "at least, I hope it is for you personally, but not for you as a district. Restrictions are going to be tight again. You see, the body of Corporal Wagg has been found. We had a private P.M., and he didn't drown. The injuries to the head were fairly extensive, but how it happened we just can't tell. He could

214

have fallen from the cliffs on to rocks, and his body carried out to sea with the gale that blew later, or he could have been pushed. There's no proof either way." He cleared his throat.

"I'm sorry," said Emma. "What a terrible thing to have happened."

"The point is," he continued, "it won't come over your radio or T.V. or be in your newspapers, because it isn't good for public relations, but our authorities are pretty sore about this. They don't believe it was accidental, but they can't pin the blame on anyone. So your district may be in for tough measures. There's to be no fraternisation on our part with the locals—you're all out of bounds. This means I can't come and see you. I thought I'd just let you know."

"That was very kind of you," she told him.

"Anyhow, there it is. I wish it wasn't so, but there's nothing I can do. It's against the new regulations to be calling you now."

"Wait," said Emma. "When you say tough measures, what exactly do you mean?"

Again there was an awkward pause. "I'm afraid I can't say," he replied, "because, honestly, I don't rightly know. I just wanted to warn you. Good night."

"Good night."

Emma replaced the receiver. Whatever was going to happen now? Mad had already gone upstairs to bed. She switched off the light in the cloakroom and stood there alone in the dark, wondering.

16

She discovered soon enough. The following morning, after the boys had set off for school, Dottie drew her aside and begged her to go down to Poldrea on her own and bring back some of the things on the list that had been omitted the day before.

"It's always the same," she confided, "when Madam has a free rein to do the shopping. No one is going to eat all these sausages, you'll have to take them back, and although all the toilet rolls will come in handy you can't eat them, can you? Here's my list, stick to it, dear, and slip away before she calls you back for anything."

Emma went round to the garage and found Joe waiting for her, carrying an empty paraffin drum.

"Mind if I come with you?" he asked. "I want to fill this up so I can keep the heater going in the greenhouse, now it's turned colder. The forecast said we're in for some hard weather. I'll stick it in the boot."

She was glad of Joe's company. What with one thing and another she had barely had two words with him yesterday, and indeed, as was his hard-and-fast routine, he had spent most of his time in the vegetable garden or, as

Terry tersely put it, "mucking about up back." Emma told him about the telephone conversation the night before with Wally Sherman.

"I expect," said Joe, and he gave a sort of grunt, half-amused, half-disapproving, "your precious lieutenant just meant he was sore we'd been put out of bounds. But for that I bet you anything you like he'd have been up at the house right away yesterday evening."

"I don't know," she replied. "He sounded embarrassed, not just like someone who can't keep a date."

"Had you a date, in fact?"

"No, of course I hadn't."

When they came to the road-block at the bottom of the hill, the marine on duty marked their passes and the yellow car-sticker with a red X.

"What's that for?" Emma asked.

"No more private cars on the road in this district after today," he said, "not for people with local stickers. You'll have to use public transport."

"Who says so?"

"Commandant's orders. You'll be given notice when the ban is to be relaxed." He waved her on.

Emma turned indignantly to Joe as she released the brake. "Surely they can't do this?" she said. "How are people going to manage? You know there are only about two buses a day that come past us to Poldrea."

"Let's fill up with petrol, anyway," Joe replied. "The tank's right down."

The garage where they usually bought petrol was further along the cliff but when Emma pulled in she saw that notices saying "No Petrol" were hanging on the pumps, and the little office alongside, where the attendant sat, had "Closed" scrawled across the window.

"Can we make it into Poldrea and back up the hill again?" Emma asked.

"Just about," Joe told her.

"This," she said, "is obviously what Lieutenant Sherman was warning me about. Can they do it? Legally, I mean?"

"I suppose," Joe replied, "if you are an occupying power—and it begins to seem more and more that this is what they basically are—you can just about do anything."

Today the queues were not so extensive outside the supermarket—doubtless because the majority of people had done their shopping the day before—but inside the building itself the atmosphere was considerably more subdued.

"I'm very sorry," said the senior salesman with a glance at Dottie's list, "but some of the items here we just haven't got. The van we expected yesterday never arrived, and we were told on the telephone this morning it had been held up and they couldn't say when we could expect it."

Emma did not return the sausages. It was evident they were going to be needed. She took from the shelves anything that might be useful for feeding the boys, and then left. Joe was waiting for her outside.

"No paraffin," he said. "They sold the last yesterday and they have no more in stock. He says there's been a hold-up somewhere, nobody knows how or why. Bang go my seedlings, if we get a frost."

Little knots of people were standing about talking. Snatches of conversation came to their ears. "One of them was found drowned, and we've all got to suffer for it . . ." "They say he was drunk at the time, been in at the Sailor's Rest, and then pitched head-first off the cliffs by Little Hell . . ." "I don't know about that. He was courting Myrtle Trembath, by all accounts, and we all know Jack has got some temper . . . Well, you can put two and two together, can't you?" "Why don't someone own up, then? Why take it out on us?"

Emma dragged at Joe's sleeve. "Come on," she murmured, "let's go."

She had the impression one or two people were staring at them, and this was confirmed when a man who had once swept the music-room chimney rather badly, and had never been asked to do it again, muttered to his companion, "It's all right for some . . ." looking pointedly at the sausages bulging out of her shopping basket. The drop in temperature had not only hardened the atmosphere but had done something to attitudes as well. Hostility was in the air, and possibly because of her own acute sense of guilt she felt it was directed against her, or, if not at her personally, then at all the members of the household at the top of the hill. Another thing—there were no marines off duty walking around, as there had been the week before, and yesterday too.

They were crossing the street to get back into the car when a small blue car came in to park just ahead of them. It was Nurse Bennett. She put her head out of the window.

"They can't put a red mark against my pass," she said, "nor the doctor's neither. But I've had to give them a list of all the people I visit so they can keep tabs on me. I tell you one person who will blow his top and that's Jack, my brother-in-law. He says he's not going to allow his milk to be collected for the depot but is going to sell it locally to those around, like his father did in the old days."

"But Nurse Bennett," Emma asked, "who are 'they'?' "

The nurse jerked her head in the direction of the harbour and the camp on Poldrea beach. "Can't you guess?" she countered, and carrying her bag made for a small house where an anxious face was watching her from the window. "Mrs. Williams's baby is due," she said to Emma. "You can't stop children being born for the sake of one dead marine."

Everyone knew, Emma decided. Not how it had happened or why, but that this was the reason for restrictions, regulations, orders, shortages. And it depended on your personal circumstances, your work, your livelihood, whom you blamed.

Another car drove past, or rather tried to pass but was obliged to stop, as Emma opened the door of her car on the off side. It was Mr. Libby of the Sailor's Rest, but a very different Mr. Libby from the persuasive landlord of yesterday who had tried to sell Mad the case of California wine. He was tense, unsmiling and, ignoring Emma, he called to somebody on the other side of the road, whom Emma recognised as a rival publican.

"Are the marines out of bounds to you too, Jim?" he shouted.

The man nodded. " 'Fraid so. It'll hurt me, but not as bad as it will hurt you. No customers will get to your place unless they go on foot, and no one's going to do that these days." He grinned.

"I'm going to see if I can wangle something with the deputy commandant," shouted Mr. Libby. "Why should honest traders like myself be made to suffer for somebody else's misdeeds, that's what I say."

He swerved angrily into the centre of the road and

drove ahead, nearly knocking down an old woman who was trying to cross. Joe stared after him.

"I hope he runs out of petrol before he gets there," he said to Emma.

"He won't," replied Emma savagely, "he won't. He's probably had his tanks filled up by the marines last night before they were confined to camp."

Now it's not only them and us, she reflected, but the community itself divided. Nobody will know who is for what, or where anybody stands. The sentry at the barricade wore an amused smile on his face as he waved them past, having glanced at the red mark on the windscreen ticket.

"Shan't be seeing you for a while, shall we?"

Emma did not answer. The petrol gauge was pointing well into the reserve tank. They made it up the hill and down the drive, and so to the garage doors with the engine spluttering.

"Done it," she said to Joe, "but only just."

Joe, grim-faced, lifted out her shopping basket. The pound and a half of butter that was their ration lay on top of the sausages. "What we want is guns and not butter," he said.

It might have been Terry speaking, she thought, not Joe. Was it a pointer to the future?

"I feel the same way, but it's not much good, is it? Do you realise that there wouldn't have been these restrictions and the local tightening-up of security but for what happened here last week?"

"I know," Joe replied. "It doesn't alter how I feel."

"The marine was killed," she insisted, "and it was our fault. A child did not know the difference between right and wrong."

Joe slammed the car door and walked to the garage entrance. "If you're going to harp on that track it won't wash with me, Emma. You may as well go back to the beginning of history and ask who threw the first stone outside a cave. Andy acted from impulse, the impulse of the first human being who felt his plot of land was threatened by someone who had no right to be there."

"If that's your argument," she retorted, "then civilisation has been a wasted effort. None of us has made any progress at all."

"You're dead right we haven't. I wonder you've never realised it before. I can't read or write, I can only work with my hands, not my head. That's why, if the need should come, I'll use them to defend my home."

They walked together to the house in silence. Oh, what's the use, thought Emma, if the sort of education I had, the books I've read, the conversation I've listened to between adults like Pa, and Mad and others have brought me to see both sides of a question whatever the circumstances? How can I, or anyone, give judgement in the final analysis? The marines were in the right to bring in restrictions. The community was right to be indignant. The balance was even.

"You know, Joe," she said, "we're forgetting one thing, which is probably the basis of everything, if we apply it to our particular crisis now. When poor Corporal Wagg was on his way here last week he wasn't coming to fight Terry but to apologise and shake hands."

"That's right," Joe replied, "so he died with his conscience clear. But Andy couldn't be expected to know why he was coming, could he? So your basis for right and wrong falls flat, like Corporal Wagg."

Emma left him at the side-door to carry up the basket to the kitchen. She did not feel in the mood to explain why she had brought back so few of the things on Dottie's list. Joe must do it instead, and with his new-found ability to argue and state a case would probably do it very well. She walked round to the front of the house and saw her grandmother, with Ben beside her, picking up fir-cones and dropping them into a sack. It was one of the unnecessary ploys that Mad always enjoyed. She would forget to burn the fir-cones unless somebody reminded her. There were stacks of them down in the basement.

"Hullo, darling," she called cheerfully. "Ben and I have been working like blacks."

Unfortunate phrase, if you came to think of it, Emma decided, but Ben at three could not possibly take offence. He wore a woolen cap on his curly head with an enormous pom-pom on top, and looked like an illustration out of an old missionary magazine.

"Well, we've had it," Emma announced. "Shopping, I mean, by car. It's the bus in future, unless that gets cancelled too, or we'll have to hoof it."

222

"What's wrong?" asked Mad. "Did you go into something?"

"No. The permit's been marked invalid. All local cars forbidden on the road. And every regulation tightened." It was curious that, although she hadn't wanted to break the news to Dottie through fear of irritation, she secretly enjoyed watching the effect upon Mad. "As a matter of fact," she added casually, "I knew it would probably happen. Lieutenant Sherman telephoned to warn me last night."

"Oh, so that was it." Her grandmother shouldered the bag and slung it over her right shoulder. She looked, for one rather awful moment, as Mr. Willis had done when he slung the body of the corporal across his back.

"They did the post-mortem on the corporal," Emma went on. "Nothing was proved, but they suspect the worst. Anyway, the long and short of it is that although they can't arrest anyone they're going to make it tough for the local community, and we've got to lump it."

Mad didn't say much. She began to whistle under her breath. When they reached the house she emptied her sack of cones into the log-basket and then went through to the cloakroom and picked up the telephone.

"It's not good trying the Commandant," Emma said. "We must be No. 2, if not No. 1, on his list of suspected persons."

"I wasn't going to try the Commandant," replied her grandmother. "I'm going to see if our respected Member of Parliament is still in her constituency or if she has scuttled back to Westminster."

Five minutes or more of delay before Mad got through. No, the Member had not yet left Cornwall, but she was expected to do so later in the day. What name, please? Mrs. Moorhouse was exceedingly busy, but she might be able to speak to the caller if the matter was urgent. Emma, kneeling on the floor beside her grandmother, could hear the secretary's frigid voice. Mad gave Pa's name, not her own.

"Hullo?" The voice of the Member for Mid-Cornwall was honey-sweet. Emma could imagine the light-hearted bantering tone that Pa would have used had he really been on the line.

"No," replied Mad in answer to the Member's query, "it

223

isn't Victor, it's his mother. I'm speaking to you from Trevanal, Poldrea."

There was a pause as Mrs. Moorhouse rapidly changed gear. She could cope with the merchant banker; the actress was a different thing altogether.

"Oh, yes," she said, cool but purposeful. "And what can I do for you?"

"We're in some difficulty here at Poldrea," Mad replied. "A ban on all private cars has been put into force, the petrol pumps are closed, food supplies are not coming through to the supermarket, and in fact we appear to be in a state of siege. This is particularly hard on the young, the old and the sick, and everybody is extremely worried. I feel quite certain you can give us an explanation, and indeed let us know if this is happening all over Cornwall or only in this particular district?"

There was a pause at the other end of the line. Rather too long a pause.

"I'm afraid I have no information on this," came the answer finally. "It may possibly have some connection with the fact that Poldrea is at the moment a base for USUK forces, and they are in charge of security in the neighbourhood. I don't know if there has been any threat to the installations in the harbour, but I may be able to find out if this is so and ring you back."

"I'd be obliged if you would do that," Mad answered, "but before you go, you said USUK forces. The marine commandos here are all American."

The Member for Mid-Cornwall gave a little laugh. "You must bring yourself up to date," she said. "American, British, it's all the same thing today. We are all USUK. The sooner we become used to this, the better it will be for all concerned."

"And if we don't?"

"Oh come, don't pretend to be ignorant," replied Mrs. Moorhouse. "I feel sure your son has explained the current situation to you. This is a matter of life or death, as you well know. It's not a case of retiring gracefully from a troublesome association that had become burdensome, as we did from the European community. USUK is our life-line, and I am glad to say the majority of the people in this country welcome it. Historically, it's a proud moment for both nations. Union once more, after nearly two hundred years."

"Don't you bet on it," said Mad. "Some of us may make a Declaration of Independence too, and find our own George Washington." She replaced the receiver with a bang and turned to Emma. "That fixed her. Now we'll wait for fifteen minutes and see what she comes back with."

The telephone rang again in twenty minutes. Emma and her grandmother might have been switchboard operators, their reaction was so prompt.

"Mrs. Moorhouse?"

"Yes. Well, it is as I thought. Security measures have been tightened up in and around Poldrea for a very good reason. I'm afraid I can't go into details. It concerns a missing marine—you probably know what I am referring to."

"Yes, I think so," Mad replied.

"In that case you realise it is a very serious affair, and the authorities cannot risk it happening again. It's unfortunate for the many hundreds of innocent people who have to suffer the consequences, but there it is."

"I see." This time the pause was on this end of the line. "How long are the restrictions to continue, Mrs. Moorhouse?"

"I have no idea. The decision lies with the USUK forces in your vicinity. Now, if you will forgive me, I must ring off, I am leaving for London almost immediately."

"Any message, Mrs. Moorhouse," Mad persisted, "for your constituents in Poldrea who returned you to Parliament? I don't speak for myself, because I didn't vote for you, but I know a number of hard-working people who did, and who I am sure would welcome your advice."

The Member for Mid-Cornwall must have turned to somebody at her side, because there was a slight pause and a murmur as if Mr. Moorhouse, exasperated, was making some remark under her breath. Then, "My advice is to co-operate with USUK forces, to put up with any slight inconvenience, and to report to all forces, or our own choice, any further suspicious occurrences that may be noticed in the district."

"Thank you," said Mad. "Enjoy your Thanksgiving celebrations on Thursday." She replaced the receiver with a triumphant smile. "I always enjoy having the last word," she said. "It's been one of my pleasures through life, and thank God it doesn't fade with increasing years."

I dare say, thought Emma, but it doesn't really get us anywhere, and the only people who are going to come out of this comfortably will be those who live on a direct bus route or own a deep freeze.

"I warned Madam last summer," said Dottie later on, "that she should buy one, and it would save running down to Poldrea for every blessed thing we need. But no, she'd done without one all these years, she told me, and she wasn't going to start now."

"Cheer up, Dottie," said Terry, who as a man of leisure had installed himself in the only armchair the kitchen provided. "We're going to live on beetroot and cabbage from now on. You'll be so full of wind you'll be able to act as an extractor-fan."

Mad, wandering into the kitchen, rumpled his hair. "I don't know why everyone is making such a fuss," she said. "Think of people cast away on desert islands with nothing but coconuts."

"We have no coconuts," observed Terry.

"Well, what about snails? One of the most expensive things you can order in a French restaurant. Escargots à la bordelaise . . . I remember once in Paris . . ."

"Go on, go on, I can't wait." Terry, feigning intense excitement, leant forward in his chair.

"Don't be an idiot," she said. "I am serious. There must be hundreds, thousands of snails in the garden. If really pushed to extremes, one could live on them for days."

Dottie, who always disapproved when Terry baited his benefactress, began rattling the forks in the kitchen drawer. "I'm very sorry," she said, "but everyone who thinks I'm going to start cooking snails for a household of nine can think again." The household of nine was Dottie's big thing when pushed to extremes.

Just then there came a sound of heavy boots clumping up the back stairs and Joe appeared at the door. He still wore a determined, even angry, expression.

"Have those kids been playing around with the stopcock?" he asked, addressing himself to Terry. "I can't get any water outside for washing off the car."

"How would I know?" shrugged Terry. "They'll do anything when they're not watched."

"It's hardly likely, Joe," said Mad. "They didn't play outside yesterday afternoon when they came back from school, and they wouldn't have had time this morning. What do you mean, you can't get any water? There's probably an air-lock."

Joe's manner softened as his eyes fell on her. He had not noticed she was standing by the door at the other end of the kitchen.

"No, Madam, there's not an air-lock, there's just no water."

Dottie moved to the sink and turned on both taps. The hot water ran as usual, but the cold, after a sparse trickle, stopped altogether.

"That proves there's an air-lock," Mad declared. "What an added bore. We shall have to send for the plumber unless you can blow it out, but it needs a special pump, doesn't it?"

"It isn't an air-lock," Joe repeated obstinately, "there isn't any water."

Mad narrowed her eyes, then turned and made for the cloakroom.

"What now?" murmured Terry. "The White House?"

Mad's purpose appeared to be more practical. She was about to telephone the Water Board. Emma and the others waited in the kitchen until her call had finished. She returned, her face inscrutable.

"So that's that," she announced. "A fine new regulation. Water to be cut in the Poldrea district except for one hour every day. No reason given. The order to the Water Board came from the port authorities."

"Meaning exactly who?" asked Terry.

"The Commandant, I suppose. According to Jack Trembath they've taken over the port and everything connected with it."

"I don't follow," said the bewildered Dottie. "Why should he want to cut the water? Rationing of supplies is bad enough."

"Punishment, love," answered Terry. "We're all of us bad boys and girls in this part of Cornwall, and that includes you. Anyway, it's splendid news for those who don't

227

want to wash, which goes for Andy, Sam, Colin and Ben. I don't need a bath."

"Shut up," said Joe. He was thinking, and it took a moment or two. Then he turned to Mad. I'm going to get the old well going," he said.

Everyone stared. "You can't, Joe dear, it hasn't been used for years," demurred Mad. "It's concreted over. And the water would be filthy."

"I'll take a pick to the concrete, and the water won't be filthy, there's a spring runs under the house," Joe returned. "Come on, Terry, stop sitting on your backside and give me some help." He clumped back again down the stairs.

"Anyone for typhoid?" smiled Terry as he seized his crutch and followed his elder.

Emma had never known him agree before to one of Joe's hard labour suggestions without loud protestations nor had she known Joe snap an order rather than make a mild request when he needed something done.

Mad turned to Emma with a smile. "I always knew it was there," she said. "It only needed tapping to bring it out."

"The water from the well?" asked Emma, puzzled.

"No, darling idiot, Joe's qualities of leadership."

The ear drum-splitting crashes that came from the basement throughout the day only served to reinforce Mad's faith in the eldest of her adopted brood and his apparently willing henchman as they chipped and smashed at the concrete surround to the old well in the cellar. Folly, her sense of hearing rudely awakened, limped from the most comfortable chair in the library overhead and with a senile whine of protest gave tongue at the top of the basement stairs. Ben, surfeited with a midday diet of sausages, fell asleep in the playroom on top of his own small sack of fir-cones, and by the time his companions returned from school—no Jesus-talk today, no think-in, to Andy's relief but Colin's disappointment—Joe and Terry had not only uncovered the old well but had drawn to the surface three buckets of crystal clear water.

"There," said Joe, as everyone crowded into the cellar to applaud, "I knew it could be done. I knew we wouldn't go short. They can cut us off from the mains forever, we'll survive."

He shook his hair out of his eyes. His face was flushed

from his hours of exertion. How strange, Emma thought, he looks regally handsome, and Terry, leaning on his crutches beside him, somehow almost ordinary in comparison.

Sam was the only one to appear disturbed. "It's all right for us. What about the animals at the farm, the cattle, the sheep? You know the trough between the ploughed field and the grazing-ground that gets piped water? If none comes through, the animals can't drink."

"I hadn't thought of that," said Mad. "Good for you, Sam. We'll have to keep the trough filled."

"They have a well at the farm," Joe told them. "Mr. Trembath won't go short. Anyway, I'll go down there presently and find out."

"You know what," said Andy. "If we're cut off the mains here, and everyone else at Poldrea, the marines will be without water too."

"I'm afraid not." Terry shook his head. "The port has quite a separate supply, from another source. I remember Ron Blewett telling me that weeks ago. I don't know how he knew, except his father used to work there."

"The thing would be," suggested Andy, with a glance at Mad, "to get some gely and blow up the port. Then the marines really would be in trouble."

"Yes," said Joe, "and so would we."

The time had obviously come to call a halt to the discussion. The well had yielded water, that was enough. Every pail and bucket and jug the household could produce was brought into service, and the various receptacles placed where they would be of most use. It was only then that Dottie announced that her own prize possession, a plastic pail that she kept for emergencies under the kitchen sink, was missing. So were Colin and Ben.

"They were downstairs five minutes ago," said Sam. "I saw them. Colin was outside the back door emptying the dustbin."

"Please, dear," implored Dottie, turning to Emma.

The dustbin was on its side, and Emma could hear the prattle of young voices coming from the cellar. Her heart misgave her. The well, covered for so many years, was now open to all. She ran through to prevent some terrible accident that might yet turn the triumph to disaster. The two children were standing side by side. Ben had a piece of old curtain draped over his head and around his shoulders. Colin, Dottie's plastic pride in his left hand, was emptying the dregs from the bottle of chablis that Pa had finished up.

"What are you doing?" Emma cried, her panic subsiding.

Colin looked up, aggrieved. "We didn't have our Jesustalk today so we're having it now," he said. "Ben is my mother Mary and it's the wedding at Cana. I'm Jesus, turning the water into wine."

17

If the new authorities in charge of Poldrea harbour thought
they had the community licked, they reckoned without the
minority in their midst. Jack Trembath had not been a
champion wrestler in his day for nothing. His skill in
throwing a Breton opponent to the ground, as he had done
once, might not stand him in much stead today against the
might of the commandos, but it had taught him to think
quickly, and to organise. The ban on private cars would
not be in force until the following day, the Wednesday,
and on the Tuesday afternoon, while Joe and Terry had
been uncovering the well in the Trevanal cellar, Jack had
telephoned all the neighboring farmers and had bidden
them to an emergency meeting that evening. Some twenty-
five out of the thirty accepted and turned up, three were
willing but could not make it and sent their sons as sub-
stitutes, the remaining two, suspecting trouble, excused
themselves by saying they had no wish to be involved.

Joe had gone down to the farm earlier to find out if
they were all right for water, and Mad, Emma and Terry
were sitting in the library with the television turned on,
hoping for some enlightenment. There was little new, and

certainly nothing about the tightening-up of regulations in a minute portion of the Cornish seaboard. "The whole country is busy preparing for the Thanksgiving celebrations on Thursday," the announcer said. "In Devon and Cornwall, as elsewhere, the union will be marked in various ways. Admiral Jollif will entertain officers of the joint fleets to luncheon at Admiralty House, Plymouth, and there will be a reception in County Hall, Truro, at which the Members of Parliament for Cornwall will be present. Amongst other regional celebrations will be a luncheon party to be given by the officers and warrant-officers of the marine commando unit stationed at Poldrea. Mrs. Hubbard, area representative for the Cultural-Get-Together movement, will be the guest of honour at the luncheon, which will take place at the Sailor's Rest."

Emma switched off. "I can't believe it," she exclaimed, just as Joe came in, his face alight with information.

"Mr. Trembath ought to be in Parliament instead of Mrs. Moorhouse," he said. "You've never seen anything like it, it was terrific. How everyone got into the house I don't know. Half of them were standing up against the wall, and some of us sitting on the floor, and some on the stairs. Most of them came for a laugh, I think, in the first place, but they soon learnt differently, when Mr. Trembath started speaking to them. 'Are we Cornishmen or bloody suckers?' he asked, and there was a great yell, 'Cornishmen!' even from poor Mr. Swiggs, who's as deaf as a post. Anyway, after Mr. Trembath had harangued them for twenty minutes they were all agreed to stand by what he laid down. No more milk to the depot, nothing to the supermarket, nothing to the camp, those who have their own transport will deliver to households within their own radius and be paid at the door. Oh yes, they'll lose a hell of a lot by it, they just don't care. Only those households who agree to protest against the restrictions will be able to buy milk."

He looked about him, smiling. Emma had never known him so sure of himself, Joe of all people, diffident, silent in company, even amongst those of his own age.

"C'est magnifiique, mais ce n'est pas la guerre," murmured Mad. "I wonder. I doubt if they can achieve much except hurt themselves."

"Oh, don't be so damping!" exclaimed Terry. "By God,

I wish I'd been there. Don't you see, if only people who agree to protest can buy milk, we'll sort out those who resist from those who suck up. And everyone will start talking about it."

"What about water?" Mad asked. "How will the farmers manage for water?"

"Most of them, like us, have their own wells," replied Joe. "And if one of them goes short, his nearest neighbour will oblige. The animals won't suffer, that's agreed. Any surplus water, the animals get it."

Mad stretched herself full-length in her chair, Folly humped beside her. "The marines will have powdered milk, thousands of tins of it. It's not going to hurt them at all."

"Don't you believe it," said Joe. "They drink gallons down at the camp, the farmers were saying so. They go around like kids, with straws in the bottles, sipping it in gulps."

Terry got up and began swinging to and fro on his crutches like something caged. "If only we could hatch up a plan that would really hurt them. Send their bloody ship sky-high."

"Terry dearest," Mad put out her hand to stop his crutch, which was hitting her on the ankle, "the Japanese tried that at Pearl Harbour before you were born, and look what they got in return four years later. Bigger and better explosions won't get us anywhere. We must make it a war of attrition and see who cracks first. Have all the farmers gone home yet?" She turned to Joe.

"Some left when I did, but most were getting merry and having a sing-song. I think they were going to have a rush at the last and beat the midnight ban by a few minutes."

"H'm," said Mad thoughtfully, and then, rising from her chair, "I'll have a word with Jack Trembath before he bids them godspeed. When it comes to protest, his Breton associates of old could give him a tip or two."

She left the library for the telephone. Terry flopped down in the vacant chair beside the slumbering Folly.

"What can she do, or a bunch of farmers?" he muttered. "What we need is gelignite, and stacks of it. Andy had a point when he suggested blowing up the port."

"What about the people who live nearby?" asked Joe. "Remember, if the port went, they'd go too."

233

"Was it Dottie," Terry suggested, "who coined the phrase 'You can't make an omelette without breaking eggs?'"

"No," said Emma, "it was a general in World War One, and people seem to have followed his advice ever since. What you two don't seem to realise, and neither does Mad, is that the majority of people down here, and probably in the country as a whole, appear to want this USUK business, and whether we do or not we're lumbered with it."

The two boys stared at her. "You aren't for it surely?" asked Terry.

"Of course I'm not." It was Emma's turn to get up from the sofa and pace about the room. "I hate the whole thing as much as you do. It's just that a handful of people are so helpless, they can't achieve anything on their own. You must have a powerful organisation behind you to get anywhere, that's been proved time and time again."

"I'm not so sure," Joe pondered. "I believe if people formed little groups and just helped each other, became self-supporting amongst their neighbours, they could get by without having anything to do with the world outside at all. We'd grow our own food, burn our own fuel, use wool from our own sheep for clothes . . ."

"Oh, shucks," scoffed Terry. "Catch our own Black Death from the dirt and stink of it. Hell, this is the last quarter of the twentieth century, after all."

They were still hot in argument when Mad returned from the telephone.

"I'm glad I spoke to him," she said. "Apparently from midnight on we shall get our telephones tapped and our conversations recorded. This is official—Jack Trembath had it straight from one of his farmer friends, whose daughter works in the telephone exchange. So . . . the screws are on, or whatever the expression is. Just Poldrea, mark you. We are the scapegoats. I think they, and by 'they' I mean the marines, imagine that by doing this to the neighbourhood somebody is going to turn informer and come clean about the dead corporal. The guilty person will be caught and punished, the informer recompensed, and the scapegoat community revert to normal, or as normal as USUK allows us to be."

All this, thought Emma, because of an arrow. All this

234

because a boy's fantasy world turned him, for one single moment in time, into a killer.

"If that's what they're doing it for," said Joe, "they'll have to wait a hell of a time."

Mad smiled. "That's what I feel," she said. "In the meantime, I think we might have a little fun at the expense of the Commandant and the marines. I made a suggestion to Jack Trembath, and he was going to put it to the vote amongst his farmer friends who were still in the house. If what I suggested goes with a swing, which I hope it does, then he's going to ring me back in a few minutes."

Now what, Emma wondered? Pa at this moment in New York—or was it Rio?—having a bath after his flight and a soothing drink before dining at some flash restaurant with his fellow-tycoons, and saying to them with a laugh, perhaps, "My old mother, you know, bats, completely bats, my daughter has to lock her up in her room." It might come to that yet. Mad couldn't be trusted, ever.

"What was your suggestion?" Terry asked.

"Never you mind," said Mad.

The telephone rang, and in the race to get to the cloakroom Joe beat Emma by a short head. Jack Trembath only kept him a moment. Emma, watching, saw Joe nod his head, answer, "Yes," a couple of times and then replace the receiver, after which he turned to her, shrugging his shoulders, a puzzled expression on his face.

"Well?" she asked.

"Mr. Trembath didn't say anything to me that made sense. It was just a message to Madam to say Operation Dung-Cart full steam ahead, and any of us who wanted a joy-ride would be welcome. Zero hour as agreed."

Emma left her grandmother to unravel the code concealed in Jack Trembath's cryptic communication. Time enough to find out what it meant when zero hour struck. All she wanted to do at the moment was to go to her own room, get into bed, and with luck fall into a dreamless sleep. Pa had been wrong not to stay with them. Pa should have let monetary problems take care of themselves; or at least allowed someone else to fly across the Atlantic and handle financial crises for the country and the English-speaking peoples, instead of deserting his own family in their hour of need. The responsibility was too great for his daughter to cope with single-handed, and even Joe, steady-going, faithful Joe, seemed ready to be carried away by a new-found rebellious urge. If I can't control her, she decided, before dropping exhausted into bed, and by her she meant her grandmother, then there will be nothing for it but to get hold of Bevil Summers and ask him to put her out with an injection. It was a shocking thought, but the image it conjured up of Mad sleeping peacefully for several hours with a faithful Dottie by her side guaranteed Emma's own exit into the unconscious, and proved far more efficacious than the proverbial counting of sheep.

The hard weather, feared by Joe for his un-heated greenhouse, did not materialise, and Wednesday dawned, like so many of its November predecessors, with a rise in temperature, a shift in wind, a mizzle of rain and fog on high ground. Fog on high ground always meant that Trevanal would be bathed in a white mist as permanent throughout the day as low clouds above an airport.

"Splendid," said Terry after breakfast, with the younger boys dispatched once more to school. "Couldn't be better for our exercise if it continues like this until this time tomorrow." And he winked at Joe.

"Why?" asked Emma.

"Doesn't concern you," replied Terry. "Madam and Joe and I decided last night, after you'd gone up to bed, that we weren't going to tell you anything."

Emma felt anger rise. "That's damned unfair! Mad's my grandmother, not yours, and Pa put me in charge of her. Any crazy plan she may get into her head is my business far more than it is yours."

"Listen, Em," said Joe, "I wouldn't let Madam do anything dangerous. You know that. Nor would Mr. Trembath. So stop being class-conscious."

Emma stared at him, astounded. "Class-conscious?" she demanded. "What the hell do you mean?"

"What I say," answered Joe. "You are her granddaughter, yes, and she is, or was, a famous person. We are no relation to you or to her, yet she's all we've ever known, and if it comes to love I dare say we'd give our lives for her before you did. You think your special relationship makes you superior to Terry and me, and to the kids as well. It doesn't."

"Hurrah!" shouted Terry. "Long live the underdogs. I

236

never knew you could be so eloquent, my old buddy. High time Emma knew her place."

Emma, near to tears, went out of the room. Terry she could take, but not Joe. Class-conscious . . . God! What an insult. She had never thought of the boys in that light, never for one moment believed herself superior. Of course being Mad's grand-daughter gave her a special relationship, it was to be expected, it was natural, but that Joe should accuse her of having some sort of snobbish attitude towards him and Terry and the others—it was outrageous. It was Joe who was the snob, Joe who had an inferiority complex, all mixed up with not being able to read and write, and then a kind of hangover jealousy because of that fool Wally Sherman, who, poor brute, was only trying to be friendly when he had come to the house to soften the uneasy truth of being an invader . . .

"What on earth's the matter, darling?"

Emma had run full tilt into her grandmother after leaving the kitchen.

"It's the boys," she stormed. "They drive me wild at times. Just because I'm your relation and they are not, they accuse me of thinking myself superior, of being a snob, and it's not true."

Mad was trying on a variety of hats before going out to gather more fir-cones with Ben. Discarding three in succession she finally ended up with a sou'wester worn back to front that turned her into a coolie.

"We're all snobs," she said calmly, "and we all like to think ourselves superior. If we didn't we'd never have risen from the apes," she called to her small companion, who was helping himself to mint humbugs from the dining-room sideboard. "Ben and I are going to fill one sack, then I propose taking him down through the wood to call on Taffy. Like to come with us?"

The thought of Mr. Willis, alone in his lair, with the gelignite hidden somewhere under the floor-boards and the sacks that had been wrapped round the body of Corporal Wagg still lying black and sodden on the ashes of the compost heap, was the final straw.

"No," said Emma, "I wouldn't. And to be perfectly frank, I don't think you ought to go. He knows too much. He could be dangerous."

"That's why I'm going to see him," replied Mad. "The

237

more he knows the more flattered he'll be to be one of us. I know how to deal with Taffy."

She set forth into the rain with Ben at her heels, and Emma waited until the pair of them had disappeared under the trees. Then she sneaked upstairs to her grandmother's bedroom to ensure she wasn't overheard by Dottie or the two elder boys, and put through a call to Dr. Summers's surgery. It was only after she had dialled the number that she remembered the telephones were tapped. Never mind. She must choose her words, that was all.

"Yes?' The secretary in the surgery had connected her at once, but she recognised the tone of his voice; there's a patient waiting to be examined, I can give you two minutes, but no more.

"It's Emma," she said. "I think we may be in trouble."

"Terry's leg or your grandmother's heart?"

"Both."

"Well, you'd better drive them along to the surgery and I'll have a look at them."

"I can't," she said. "Perhaps you hadn't heard, but all private cars are banned from today in and around Poldrea. Nor have we got any water. And this conversation is being overheard, the telephones are tapped."

As she heard herself speak she could hardly believe it. She was amazed at her own audacity. I'm behaving exactly like Mad, she thought, this wasn't what I meant to say at all.

"Hold on a moment," said Dr. Summers, and the tone of his voice had changed. She heard him put down the receiver, and he must have gone to speak to the secretary in the office, for he was absent quite a few minutes before she heard him on the line once more.

"I was just checking, Emma," he said, "and Terry has had his leg in plaster now a week tomorrow. He's due to come out of it, and have a wedge in the heel of his shoe instead. I'll arrange about getting him to hospital, it will only take about half-an-hour. If your grandmother's heart will hold out I can prescribe for her at the same time."

"That's the trouble," said Emma. "I'm afraid she may overdo it before tomorrow."

"I see."

He didn't, of course, but he knew what she inferred, Mad was getting out of control.

"Has your father gone back to London?"

"Worse that that. He's either in New York or in Brazil."

"That's very helpful. Right, Emma. I'll be along some time today, but I can't tell you when."

Then he rang off. In the meantime, she thought, he will surely find out what is happening to all of us in this area, and if he has any influence he will try and do something about it. Perhaps nothing very much could be done immediately, with the following day a public holiday; nevertheless, word could be passed from one district to another, and the fact that a small community was being punished for the death of one man, a death which had not been proved to be other than accidental, must eventually rouse somebody to action. And yet, and yet . . . If Dr. Summers turned up later in the day, must she tell him the truth? Would he take the line that punishment was deserved? She turned away from the telephone, suddenly despondent. Perhaps she had done the wrong thing after all in getting through to the surgery.

She glanced out of Mad's bedroom window, and saw that Mr. Trembath's Land-Rover was parked in the ploughed field beyond the garden wall, with the farmer himself at the wheel, and then, from the shrubbery, Joe emerged, and Terry on his crutches, making for the steps in the wall. She flung open the window.

"Where are you going?" she called.

"To the farm," shouted Joe, turning his head. "Madam knows, it was all fixed last night. We're going to give Mr. Trembath a hand, we'll be away for the day."

They grinned up at her, Terry waved his crutch, and they began scrambling down the bank to the Land-Rover below. I'm no longer one of them, she thought, I've been cut out of it, told to mind my own business, I'm class-conscious, I don't belong. She was isolated in a sort of no-man's land between her contemporaries and the aged; between Joe and Terry, and Dottie and Mad.

Her isolation became more complete when, some time later, she saw the fir-cone party return from the wood not two but three. Mr. Willis, a large sack bulging over his back, was walking by her grandmother's side and talking volubly. No question of relieving him of the sack and bidding him farewell at the gate with thanks; Mad escorted

239

her helpmate to the porch, told him to dump the sack inside, and called to Emma.

"Tell Dottie Taffy will stay to lunch," she said. "He doesn't mind what he eats as long as it isn't flesh."

Mr. Willis made his customary bow to Emma. "It sounds as if I expected the rest of you to be cannibals, doesn't it?" he said, smiling. "And truly, to see people chewing meat can sometimes be offensive to a vegetarian like myself."

"I don't think you need worry today," replied Emma. "It will probably be beetroot soup and boiled cabbage."

"Full of vitamins," said Mad. "Come along in and have a drink. You're not going to refuse that, surely?"

"No, indeed." Mr. Willis removed his boots, to expose yellow socks. "Take a little wine for the stomach's sake—it was recommended by St. Paul to all of us. Though I wouldn't say no to whisky or even brandy."

"If you like you can have all three," Mad told him.

Emma disappeared to the kitchen to warn Dottie. "I'm afraid we are in for a lengthy session," she sighed. "Sound the gong soon, or it will mean filling up glasses before and during lunch."

"I don't know why Madam had to invite him at all," replied Dottie. "You never know what someone of that sort will bring in with him, living as he does in that old hut in the woods."

When Emma returned to the dining-room Mr. Willis was already standing by the sideboard, and at her grandmother's instructions was drawing the cork from a bottle of chambertin. He proceeded to fill a tumbler to the full.

"The same for you, ladies?" he asked.

"Just enough to drink your health," said Mad. "Emma and I never touch wine midday."

"It depends on your upbringing, doesn't it?" replied Mr. Willis. "I was born and bred in a temperance society and I never had the taste for alcohol until I had turned twenty. I made up for it then, I can tell you, but it isn't often I get the chance to imbibe these days." He raised his glass to his hostess first, and then to Emma, sipped the contents like a client at a restaurant and nodded his head in satisfaction. "Delicious! What the experts call a full-bodied wine. I haven't tasted anything like this since I worked my passage home from South Africa some years

240

ago as a steward in the first-class dining-room. I like the fruity flavour," he told them. "If you drank this twice a day for weeks on end you'd never need medicinal treatment."

The gong boomed, and Dottie entered the dining-room bearing the tureen of beetroot soup.

"I must drink this lady's health as well," remarked Mr. Willis. "I have not had the pleasure of making her acquaintance."

"Mrs. Dottrell, Mr. Willis," said Mad, gesturing towards them both. "Mrs. Dottrell was in the theatre with me for years."

"Indeed? Another actress? Truly, I feel flattered to find myself so surrounded by stars. The theatrical profession is the finest in the world, I've always said so. Were you in tragedy or in comedy, Mrs. Dottrell?"

Dottie placed the tray on the sideboard. Her mouth was pursed tight.

"I was in neither, though I saw plenty of both backstage. I happened to be Madam's dresser for more than forty years. Luncheon is served."

Dottie stalked out of the dining-room, her head high. Mr. Willis turned to his hostess, glass in hand.

"Now that is an occupation that has never come my way," he told her, "and more's the pity. I've always had the wish to handle costumes."

"You may get your wish yet, Taffy," Mad said, "especially if the Cultural-Get-Together movement has its way. We'll see you in doublet and hose pouring wine for the American tourists."

"I'd see them in perdition first," he replied, "unless I had the chance to doctor the wine. Which wouldn't be likely, would it? Though if I had the drawing of the corks it could be managed."

They sat down to the fare of beetroot and cabbage, which at their guest's suggestion, could be made all the more palatable by mushing them together.

"A spoonful of sherry too, if you have it," he added, glancing at the sideboard. "Then it would make a dish fit for princes. Indeed, I feel myself a prince at this moment, sitting down here at the table with you both, and couldn't wish for better company."

Which was all very well, Emma felt, but Mr. Willis was

getting tipsier with every mouthful of chambertin, and what with the beetroot soup well laced with sherry she couldn't help feeling that his inside, unused to such a mixture since his days on board the liner returning from Capetown, might soon begin to feel the strain. She was right. Dottie, her expression more disapproving than ever, had hardly appeared with the second course, apple crumble—a milk pudding would have been wiser, to give bulk —than Mr. Willis rose unsteadily to his feet.

"You'll excuse me, ladies, I'm sure," he said, "but the penalty of increasing years is not only failing eyesight and the formation of wax in the ears, but a desire to pass water more frequently, if you will pardon the expression."

"I know it only too well," Mad replied. "Emma, show Mr. Willis where."

Her grand-daughter obliged, and the guest tottered out into the hall and beyond.

"Dear Taffy," said Mad, refilling his glass during a rather long absence, "how your grandfather would have adored him. I wonder if he plays the piano as well as sings. We might get him to perform directly. The only trouble is that the piano is out of tune, it's so long since it was touched, and Dottie told me some time ago the mice had got into the felt."

The absence became prolonged. "Darling," said Mad, "I think you had better go and see what he's doing."

"I can't," exclaimed Emma. "Honestly, Mad, I do agree with Dottie, you should never have asked him back to lunch. Supposing he's collapsed?"

"We shall have to send for Bevil," replied her grandmother.

Emma was silent. She wasn't going to say that Dr. Summers would appear anyway. Far better that it should come as a surprise, though the doctor might not be too pleased if he found he was expected to attend to a bucolic beachcomber. It was Dottie who finally showed herself at the dining-room door.

"Your gentleman friend is lying on the cloakroom floor, Madam," she said, her voice totally without expression.

Emma and her grandmother went to inspect the scene. The worst had not happened, or if it had, the effect had disappeared in the right place and with the plug pulled, but the effort had obviously proved too much for the guest, who was lying full-length on the floor, as Dottie had warned them, mouth open, snoring loudly, his spectacles askew on his nose. Mad knelt down, loosened the collar of his jersey and felt his pulse.

"He's all right," she said. "We'll put one of the coats under his head and let him sleep it off. What a shame, though. I did want to hear him sing."

Folly, who had pattered after Mad to the cloakroom, sniffed at the recumbent figure on the ground and backed, hackles rising.

"Don't be silly, Folly," said Mad. "It's only poor Taffy had a drop too much."

"And when he does wake up?" Emma asked. "Will he be in a fit state to walk back to the hut in the woods?"

"He won't have to," Mad replied. "Jack Trembath is picking me up from the field in the Land-Rover later, and Taffy can come with us to see the fun. That's why I brought him back to lunch, so that I could explain it to him. He'll enjoy himself all the more after a good sleep."

It rained steadily the whole afternoon, and the mist thickened. Mr. Willis continued to sleep on the cloakroom floor. Dr. Summers did not appear. Emma tried to call the surgery but the number was always engaged. The younger boys returned from school carrying yet more USUK flags and talking loudly of the holiday that was to take place the following day. Emma, who had rushed to their quarters to prevent them coming through to Mad as they usually did, steeled herself to the clamour of three separate voices.

"We had history forever," complained Andy. "Christopher Columbus, Pilgrim Fathers, George the Third, George Washington, Boston Tea Party—all piled one on top of the other, and I don't know yet what the holiday we're getting tomorrow is for."

"I do," said Sam. "It's for union. Once they didn't want to be with us and now they do. And we are supposed to be pleased. And that Mrs. Hubbard came to talk to us again, and she said in America they always eat roast turkey on their Thanksgiving Day and I told her we only had it at Christmas."

"Well, I bet she doesn't get it tomorrow," said Andy, "unless they've had some flown in from America to the camp. The marines are giving a big lunch at the Sailor's

243

Rest and she's going to be there, she told us. And I heard her say that they hadn't liked to ask Madam because of her bad heart. Bad heart, I said? Cor, you ought to see the sacks of fir-cones she brought in yesterday. Where's Terry?"

"He's down at the farm, and Joe," Emma answered.

She looked around for Colin. Missing once more. Instinct led her to the cloakroom. Colin, Ben at his side, had his eye to the keyhole. He looked up as Emma tried to drag him away.

"There's a man in there lying on the floor," he said excitedly. "Has someone killed him?"

"Be quiet," whispered Emma, "he's not feeling very well. Stop it, Ben!"

She was too late, however, Ben had burst open the cloakroom door, and the noise had the instant effect of rousing the visitor, who sat bolt upright like a jack-in-the-box released from captivity and stared about him with wild eyes.

"Its the beachcomber," cried Colin, astonished. "Madam must have taken him prisoner and forgotten to lock him in. Hullo . . ." he addressed himself to the awakened guest, "are you feeling better? Would you like to come and see Sam's squirrel?"

Mr. Willis fumbled for his spectacles and adjusted them, ran his fingers through his shock of white hair and rose slowly to his feet.

"I feel like Rip Van Winkle," he said. "How many years was it that he lay on the mountain top, and when he came down the whole world had changed? These boys were not present at the luncheon feast."

"No," murmured Emma, "they've just come home from school. It's nearly five o'clock."

Mr. Willis shook his head in disbelief. "I only came through to do the necessary, and I must have had a little turn and tumbled to the floor. How very distressing."

The two boys were staring at him, fascinated. The Welsh lilt was new to Colin's ears, and from his intent expression Emma knew he was concentrating hard in order to memorize it.

"Do you often fall asleep in the afternoon?" he asked.

Mr. Willis smiled. "I have not done it these sixty years," he replied, "not since the days I went to chapel Sundays and the drone of the minister's voice sent me to dream-land."

"Now run along," said Emma firmly. "Mr. Willis wants to tidy himself and then go home." She turned, pushing the boys ahead of her, back to the kitchen. "Have your tea and don't come through again," she warned them.

They were not listening. They had run through to the playroom to tell Andy and Sam of the strange happenings in the cloakroom. She returned to the hall and found Mr. Willis putting his boots on in the porch. The music-room door was closed. He put his fingers to his lips.

"The lady may be resting," he whispered. "I wouldn't disturb her for the world. Tell her from me her slightest wish is law. I burn to serve."

"Yes," said Emma, "yes, of course."

"The fir-cones here are for your fire, the sack is mine, but I bequeath it to her as a souvenir of a momentous visit, to be repeated, I trust, at some future time. The lunch was delicious." Not one word of apology for the lapse in the middle. "Your grandmother did mention a possible encounter later at the farm," Mr. Willis added before going down the steps, "its purpose not fully explained. I shall be there."

He bowed, turned and plodded off down the garden path and through the gate.

All was silent within the music-room. Could it be that Mad had also fallen asleep? She generally left the door open so that Folly could wander in and out. Emma decided to wait until Mr. Willis had departed beyond recall, then she would make the tea, arouse her grandmother, and casually announce the fact that the visitor had left of his own accord with messages of gratitude to his hostess.

Mad was not asleep. When Emma brought in the tea, she found her sitting on the sofa with some half-dozen volumes of Shakespeare open beside her.

"Darling," she said, "I've been wading through all these. Which play is it where the man says 'I can call spirits from the vasty deep'?"

Emma sighed and put down the tray. "Do you mean Owen Glendower?"

"Of course. I couldn't remember his name. Such a wonderful part for Taffy. I want him to read it to me when he wakes. Is it one of the Henry plays?"

"*Henry IV, Part One,*" replied Emma. Mad was really very ignorant.

"Ah . . ." Mad was fumbling through the pages, "wait a minute, here it is . . . 'At my nativity the front of Heaven was full of fiery shapes, of burning Cressets; and at my birth the frame and huge foundation of the earth shak'd like a Coward . . .'" Her reproduction of Taffy's voice was superb. "Em, do go and see if he is awake, he must have been lying there two hours, at least."

"Oh yes, he's awake," Emma told her. "What's more, he's gone."

"Gone?" Mad looked up at her, distressed.

"He didn't want to disturb you. He thanked you for the lunch."

Mad closed the volume of Shakespeare with a bang. "It's too bad. I was looking forward to a lovely reading session before Operation Dung-Cart. How was Taffy? Had he recovered?"

"Perfectly. And he didn't even apologise."

"Why should he? He couldn't help himself."

Emma stood in front of her grandmother, her arms folded. "I think I ought to tell you," she said, "that Operation Dung-Cart, whatever that may be, is just not on. At any rate for you. I telephoned Bevil Summers this morning, and he's coming out to see you. He'll be here any time now."

Mad paused in the act of pouring out her tea. "Bevil can't stop me," she said.

"Oh yes, he can."

Their roles were suddenly reversed. Emma was giving the orders. She would have to treat her grandmother in the same way as she treated Colin when he threatened disobedience. Mad was silent. She went on pouring the tea, but the ominous whistle sounded under her breath. Emma poured out her own tea, equally silent.

Suddenly Mad shrugged her shoulders. "Oh well," she said with a sigh, "you're probably right. I might have got in the way, and I'd like to have a word with Bevil, as it happens. The fact is, I believe I strained myself yesterday carrying the sacks of fir-cones. I've got a curious pain in my side."

"Oh, Mad . . ." Emma was all concern instantly. "Where? What sort of pain?"

"Here," frowned Mad, "rather low down, in the groin." She pointed to herself, and when Emma touched her she winced.

"Why on earth didn't you say so before?" exclaimed Emma.

"I didn't want to make a fuss."

"Shall I tell Dottie?"

"Certainly not. What could she do? I tell you what. Be an angel, and go through to the boys when you've finished tea, and keep them amused. I'll lie quietly here and be on the spot for Bevil when he comes. Don't worry, it's not a bad pain, just rather odd and nagging."

Emma swallowed her tea, watching her grandmother from time to time. Her imagination leapt forward to disaster. Probings by the doctor, X-rays, hospital, an immediate operation . . . Nagging pains were always the most sinister, especially for old people. One day a person was perfectly well, or at any rate never compained, and then when it was too late, when you couldn't do anything . . .

Mad settled the cushion behind her head and reached out for *Henry IV*. Emma carried the tray back to the kitchen. She wouldn't say anything to Dottie until after the doctor had been. Then they would know what to do. As soon as the boys had finished their tea she took them to the library, being careful to shut the door so that the sound of the television should not irritate Mad. She switched on the set, and settled in her grandmother's chair just as a programme about the Boston Tea Party was starting. It proved to be a test of endurance, at least for Ben, who preferred to climb on to the window-seat and rattle the shutters.

"Be quiet," said Colin, yawning, in the tone of a weary undergraduate before taking his Finals. "I can't concentrate."

Ben ceased for a time, then started to rattle the shutters again.

"What on earth does he want?" Emma asked, her nerves on edge.

"I think he's saying something about Madam," replied Colin, without taking his eyes off the screen.

Emma leapt to her feet, seized Ben from the window-seat and bore him off, oddly enough without protest, to

247

the hall. To her surprise, he made instantly for the porch and tried to wrestle with the latch.

"Shuck . . ." he said, "shuck, fit!" and pointed to the garden beyond.

"Will you stop it, Ben?" shouted Emma. "Madam is in the music-room trying to rest."

Ben shook his head and stamped his feet, and suddenly Emma saw the headlights of Dr. Summer's car circle the drive below the gate and stop. Ben must have heard the car. This was doubtless what he was trying to tell her.

"All right," she said, "stop talking for one moment, do."

She waited by the porch until the doctor emerged from the mist and drizzle.

"Sorry I couldn't make it before," he said as she opened the door to him. "It's been one hell of a day. Hullo, blackamoor."

"Oh, I'm so glad you've come," said Emma. "It really is urgent this time, though I didn't know it when I rang you. She's complaining of a pain in the groin. I don't like the sound of it. Ben, *will* you leave the porch door alone?" Ben continued to point towards the garden, mouthing expletives. "Don't take any notice of him, he likes to show off," Emma explained, and she opened the door of the music-room. The light was still on behind the sofa, but only Folly lay curled up asleep amongst the cushions.

"She must have gone upstairs," said Emma. "That means she's feeling rotten. I don't care how much she tries to hide it. I'll give you a call."

She ran up the stairs two at a time and went through to her grandmother's bedroom. The light was not on, nor had the bed been turned down. Could she have gone to the playroom or to Dottie? She ran downstairs again to the hall. Once again Ben tried to struggle with the porch door, gesticulating, his mouth working. Misgiving came to Emma. She remembered him doing the same thing when he stood on the window-seat in the library. The window faced the look-out and the ploughed field beyond the wall. She went to the cloakroom and switched on the light. Mad's house shoes were standing neatly against the wall. Her boots, her oilskin and the peaked cap had gone. Oh no . . . She went back to the hall, her hands spread out in a gesture of resignation.

"It's no use," she said. "She's given us the slip. That

whole story of a pain in the groin was a gigantic lie to put me off the scent. Now what in heaven's name are we to do?"

Bevil Summers raised his eyebrows. "Let's leave heaven out of it, shall we?" he said. "Just try and explain exactly what you mean."

Emma barely heard him. "She even winced when I touched her, said she wanted to rest, asked me to keep the children quiet." Emma paused in mid-statement. "It's true, she did say she had a pain rather suddenly . . ."

"Surely," said the doctor, "you know your grandmother well enough by this time to be certain when she is making anything up or not? I do." He sighed. He had had a heavy day, and he looked it. "Anyway," he said, "do you mean she's not in the house? She's gone out, in this weather?"

"I'm afraid so," Emma told him, "boots, oilskin, all gone. She's done it on purpose so that you couldn't stop her."

"Why should I stop her? She's probably taking a stroll in your shrubbery. It won't hurt her."

Emma stared. Of course, he didn't understand. She hadn't told him.

"Mad hasn't gone for a stroll in the shrubbery. She's gone on some terrible assignation with about thirty farmers called Operation Dung-Cart. That's what I couldn't explain over the telephone."

This time it was the turn of Bevil Summers to stare. Then he shrugged his shoulders and reached for the raincoat he had just taken off.

"In that case," he said, "we had better go and find her. Get your own coat and follow me down to the car. If the commandos are out in force we shall all be in trouble."

18

A sea-mist was always at its worst on the high ground where Trevanal stood. Coming out of the gate at the top of the drive Bevil Summers braked and consulted the clock on his dashboard.

"Now, listen," he said, "I hadn't reckoned on a lawless expedition at the end of a day's work. I'd marked down your grandmother and Terry, and then my final call was to a patient a couple of miles on the homeward trek, just short of Pinnock Down. He's bedridden and I can't miss him out. So we'll just run along there first and get him settled. It won't take long."

"Anyway you say," replied Emma. "I feel frightful in any case about dragging you off in this way but I just can't trust Mad, and the two boys are almost as bad."

"It's not your fault," said Dr. Summers. "You are just one of the luckless hundreds, possibly thousands, before we're very much older, who are being put to inconvenience and worse by these damned rules and regulations. I've spent half the day telling the regional hospital board to do something about it, and I think I've succeeded in moving them, finally. You can't cut off people's water and stop them driving cars because some American marine has fallen off a cliff. Union is one thing, but military tactics to put the wind up the local population are another."

So he too had got himself involved. The snowball gathered pace. Them and us.

The car drew up beside a handful of cottages. "I'll try and make it brief," Dr. Summers said, and reaching for his bag, he made for one of the centre cottages. He went inside and the door slammed. It seemed suddenly very quiet. The mist was as thick as ever, and the mizzle of rain made it impossible to see out of the windscreen. Emma rubbed the side-window, but could see little but a couple of tall trees looming from behind a hedge, their branches bare. An owl hooted. She thought of her grandmother crossing the ploughed field down to the farm in the mist and rain, not minding, not afraid, and she knew that this was something she could never have done, even in ordinary circumstances, unless one of the boys had been with her, because when darkness fell all the familiar things of the day became shrouded, remote, taking on a different, even sinister, aspect as if they belonged to another age, more primitive, where Time did not exist. Even now, even here, on the silent road beside the cottages, she only felt safe because of being in Bevil Summers's car, with its human, leather smell. The car protected her, but across the fields, or further along the road, nothing was friendly, the emptiness threatened, just as Trevanal threatened if she tried to walk through it in the dark.

"Nonsense," Mad used to say. "People who are afraid of the dark are afraid of death. We should all take a lesson from the blind. They live with it."

Perhaps someone was dying up in that cottage bedroom, the bedridden person the doctor had gone to see. She suddenly thought of her mother, whom she barely remembered, lying wan and pale, waiting for the fatal illness to take its course. Had she been frightened, had she felt the shadows closing in upon her, drawing nearer every day, every hour?

Emma wished Bevil Summers would come back. Imagination was beginning to take over. She pictured an old-fashioned bedstead in a small bedroom with an uneven floor, a weeping woman holding an old man's hand, the doctor shaking his head and saying there was nothing he could do. How terrible if there really was something called an Angel of Death that hovered overhead waiting to bear souls away, a dark spirit with enormous wings, and you tried to resist but you couldn't, and you saw it looming nearer, the wings spread wide, until you were engulfed, like drowning . . . like . . . Then she saw the marine lying on the ploughed field with the arrow between his eyes.

She started, almost screamed. It was only Bevil Summers opening the door of the car.

"Sorry," he said, "a bit longer than I thought. Had to hear all about the old boy's aches and pains."

"He's not dying, then?"

"Dying? No! He'll live another ten years if he takes care of himself and his wife stops nagging him. Now then, what's our plan of campaign?"

Her morbid train of thought had led her far from the immediate situation that lay ahead. What a fool he would think her if he knew. Worse than fainting when Terry had his injection.

"I suppose," she said, "we'd better turn round and go to the farm. That's where Mad must have been heading when Ben saw her through the library window. Mr. Trembath and the boys will be there, and Mr. Willis too."

The doctor started the engine. "So he's in it too, is he? Quite an organisation. Where are they supposed to be heading for? They'll be stopped at the bottom of the hill by the chap at the road-block."

"Well, would they?" Emma asked. "If they're in the Land-Rover? It's not a private car."

Bevil Summers shook his head doubtfully. "If you ask me, they'll stop anything they see, even a wheel-chair. I tell you what," he continued. "We'll cut down Pinnock Lane and park against the hedge at the bottom, without the lights, and then we'll find out if there's anything doing at the road-block."

"Supposing we're seen and challenged?"

"I've a doctor's pass."

"What about me?"

"You're my secretary and part-time nurse. We've been called out on an emergency."

Well, really . . . he sounded as if he were enjoying himself. And on second thoughts, Emma decided, she was no longer frightened herself. Someone middle-aged, like Bevil Summers, could be depended upon, he would have an answer for everything, like Pa, and if pushed to extremes would lie himself out of a situation. His generation did not suffer from guilt, as hers did, or from a troubled conscience.

"What do you think is going to happen?" she asked him. "I don't mean tonight, but tomorrow, next week, the future?"

He did not answer immediately. Navigation was necessarily slow because of the mist, which was thicker than ever.

"I think the penny will suddenly drop in the minds of millions of people that it's just not on," he said finally, "and there'll be the biggest uprising this country has ever seen since—well, I don't know, since the Conquest, if you like. Nothing to do with Right or Left, or Fascism or Anarchy, or any so-called ideology; just pure, unadulterated, British bloody-mindedness that refuses to be kicked around."

"By 'it' do you mean USUK?"

"Of course I mean USUK, or any take-over bid from whatever quarter it may come. Association with other countries, fine. Domination from one in particular, never. Open your window and keep your eyes skinned, I'm going to switch off the lights, and the engine too."

He had turned down the narrow incline known as Pinnock Lane, which terminated at the bottom in the cliff road above Poldrea beach. Emma wound down her window and peered out. She could see nothing, hear nothing, with the mist and the rain driving into her eyes. It was a strange feeling, bumping slowly down the steep lane in an unlit, silent car. Exciting too. Dr. Summers let the car roll gently almost to the base of the hill, then he eased it into the left-hand side, under the hedge, and braked. Still Emma could see nothing.

"Come on," he said, "climb out this side, after me. And not a word." He held out his hand and helped her out of the car. "Keep your head down," he said, doing the same himself and hunching his shoulders, "and stay close in under cover of the hedge."

He crept ahead, Emma following, and she had a curious, almost hysterical, desire to laugh, because what they were

doing was so incongruous, so out of character, with Bevil
Summers, whom she had always connected with things
like measles and chicken-pox and bouts of 'flu, and occa-
sional tea-time visits to gossip with Mad and talk about
Andy, whose parents had been his friends, now suddenly
turned into a Resistance spy, a revolutionary, a rebel.
There were fields on either side of the lane, and a gate
into the one on the left. He lifted the latch and motioned
to Emma to pass through, then fastened the gate and
followed her.

Now she could hear the sound of the sea breaking on
Poldrea sands and the first light appeared, dimly through
the mist and darkness, the lights from the Sailor's Rest
across the road and the single lights by the sentry-box at
the road-block. Dr. Summers held out his hand again and
drew Emma into cover of the hedge. They crouched there
side by side, watching the sentry on duty, the inn and the
entrance to the beach and the camp behind him. He was
standing inside his box to obtain cover from the rain, now
and again looking to right and left. There was no sound
of any vehicle, no sign either of cars drawn up outside the
Sailor's Rest. The ban had kept Mr. Libby's clients at
home, both his local customers and those from the camp.
Serve him right, thought Emma, no bidders for his Californian wine, nor for his beer either.

She was wrong, though. Some straggler was emerging
from the darkness behind the inn, obviously the worse for
liquor. Whoever it was was swaying on his feet, and singing too. The sentry, on the alert, came from his post and
called, "Halt!" The straggler, unheeding, continued to
advance, waving a hand in greeting and singing loudly.

"Pipe down, buddy, and go home," called the sentry.

Then, with a shock of realisation, Emma recognised the
oilskin and the peaked cap. "Oh God, Bevil," she whispered, "it's Mad."

She heard him draw in his breath, and he put his hand
on her arm to enjoin silence. The supposed reveller hic-
coughed, and caroling "John Brown's body lies a-moulder-
ing in the grave" lurched forwards towards the sentry,
staggered, and collapsed upon the ground at his feet. The
sentry instinctively bent down, and as he did so somebody
sprang from behind his box and dealt him what appeared
to be a karate blow on the back of the neck. The marine

255

lay motionless and the oilskinned figure in the peaked cap rose to its feet.

"Well done, Taffy," said Mad. "I'm afraid I hammed it rather, but it worked."

Dr. Summers withdrew his hand from Emma's arm. "This," he said, "is where we come in."

He was wrong, however—temporarily, at least. Vehicles were coming down the main road, silently, without lights, and from Pinnock Lane, too, the route they had themselves traversed.

"Land-Rovers," said Emma, "and tractors too. It's the farmers."

"Good for them," murmured the doctor. "Stay here and don't move. It's possible I may have a patient in our friend the entry."

Emma watched him return to the gate, speak to the driver in an approaching tractor and go towards his own car. She did not see him reappear but he must have fetched his bag, for a few moments later she saw him kneeling beside the sentry, and he was taking something from the bag. Mr. Willis was with him, and between them they carried the unconscious marine into the sentry post. There was no sound except the sea breaking on Poldrea sands. The farm vehicles were silent. Mr. Libby, the landlord of the Sailor's Rest, ignorant of the assembly gathered so close to his terrain, and sulking perhaps for lack of custom, slumbered conceivably behind his bar. Emma could no longer distinguish Mad from amongst the figures crowding by the barricade, nor Joe, nor Terry, but a tall shape who seemed to be in charge was surely Jack Trembath. It's no good, she thought, I can't stay here, I must join them, and she ran through the gate and out on to the road, and then someone turned, and took hold of her arm, and twisted her round to peer into her face. Whoever it was, he was a stranger to her.

"I'm Emma, from Trevanal," she said, and instantly he released her, grinning, and she realised that he, and all the others, had blackened their faces with burnt cork.

Then she realised the purpose of the mission, what they were going to do. Operation Dung-Cart was well named. The muck and dirt, the refuse, the manure, from every local farm within reach had been loaded into Land-Rovers, trailers, tractors, and was now being disgorged beside the

256

road-block and dumped also at the entrance to the Sailor's Rest, where the Thanksgiving celebrations were to take place the following day. Spades, forks, buckets, pitchforks, every sort of tool had been pressed into service, all in silence, as the crowd of farmers and willing neighbours spread the muck. No tidal wave, bringing a sweep of sand, could have caused greater havoc. The stink of rotting manure filled the damp air. The sentry, covered by a blanket and unconscious in his box, his sleep evidently prolonged by medical assistance, was unmindful of all, and the doctor himself, no longer kneeling by his patient's side, had seized a pitch-fork from an obliging hand and was tossing muck with the best of them.

"There," said Joe, suddenly appearing at Emma's side, "take this," giving her a garden spade, and in a moment, half-laughing, half-exultant, she was helping too, throwing the dirt from a trailer on to the rapidly-forming mountain that made a more effective barricade than ever the military post had done; while across the way she saw her grandmother at the same task, with Terry by her side, and Mr. Willis darting from one group to another with a navvy's shovel borrowed from heaven knows what source.

The fun could not last forever. Someone from the Sailor's Rest must have given warning, for the door opened and Mr. Libby stood on the threshold, then ran forward, shouting, waving his arms, only to stop again, further progress barred by a mountain of manure almost ten feet high. He reeled as someone flung a spadeful at his feet, and Emma caught sight of his expression, horrified, appalled. Then he ran back inside the inn and slammed the door.

"Home, lads," called Jack Trembath, "and every man for himself before they get us in the rear."

Instantly the figures dispersed, people were climbing into vehicles, and the silence was broken by the sudden roaring of engines as tractors and Land-Rovers ground into action for their return journey. Dr. Summers, with Mad beside him and Terry swinging on his crutches a pace or two behind, called out to Emma.

"To the car," he said. "Quickly! We can back up the lane faster than the tractors. Joe's all right, he'll double up the field on foot to the farm and then home."

They crossed the road to the lane, and hardly a moment

too soon, for someone, perhaps Mr. Libby, had given the alarm. Lights were showing in the camp itself, figures were running and orders were being shouted. Somehow all four tumbled into the car, Emma and her grandmother in the back seat, Terry beside the doctor. The engine started and the car shot into reverse, backing furiously up the hill. Grinding in their wake came the slower progress of Land-Rovers and tractors. Caution thrown to the winds, the drivers of the assault force of Operation Dung-Cart blew their horns. The doctor blew his too. The night, hitherto so still, was filled with discordant, triumphant sound.

It was not until Bevil Summers had backed successfully out of the lane and turned into the road beyond that Emma realised the stench of dung filled the confined space of the doctor's well-kept car. She felt slightly sick.

"You realise," said Dr. Summers, "that I shall charge for this expedition."

Mad leant forward and brushed a blob of manure off the doctor's neck. "Nonsense," she replied, "it's on National Health. If you attempt to charge me I shall report you to the BMC."

"I know who is going to summons the doctor for assault," said Terry, "and that's Libby of the Sailor's Rest. I saw you fling the last spadeful of muck at his feet."

"I'm safe enough," murmured the doctor. "He's not one of my patients, and I'm not one of his customers."

"A pity," Mad remarked. "He might have sent you a case of Californian wine."

They had driven almost full circle before they reached the turning to Trevanal and safety, and as the car came to a halt at the bottom of the drive they could hear, away behind them on the main road, the rumble of the farmers' fleet on the journey home. Bevil Summers turned round in his seat.

"Well?" he said. "I hope you're satisfied."

"Not entirely," Mad replied. "That bank of muck could have been a few feet higher. Still . . . the Commandant will have to give his Thanksgiving luncheon somewhere else. I don't see Mrs. Hubbard exactly swimming through the natural barricade, do you? Come on, Bevil, you'd better have a bath before you go home. We'll draw some water from the well and heat it up."

She climbed out of the car. Her jerkin had muck on it, and so had her boots.

"Thanks very much," said the doctor. "I'd rather not risk it. And whatever you do don't drink the stuff, or I'll be sending you all into isolation hospital with typhoid. You, my boy," he added, addressing Terry, who was struggling to descend, "are supposed to have the plaster off your leg tomorrow. But don't count on it. Anything may happen now."

"And what exactly do you mean by that?" asked Mad, tilting her peaked cap and standing with a hand on either hip.

"You don't imagine for one moment the commandos are going to take Operation Dung-Cart lying down, do you?" he countered. "They'll retaliate with sterner measures still, so watch out for it, and everybody stay indoors."

"What about you?" Emma asked. She felt anxious suddenly for his safety. It was as though the curious events of the evening had shown the usually brusque and somewhat impatient medical practitioner she had known from childhood in a new light.

"Oh," he said, "I shall take a leaf out of the farmers' book and refuse my services to everyone but rebels. No milk or dairy produce from them. No pills or potions from me. I may even have a go at closing the hospital and getting all my colleagues in the region out on strike." He winked at Mad and started up the car. "If they telephone from home, tell my family I've been a couple of hours trying to make you take a sedative for a tired heart," he shouted, as he turned the car round and disappeared up the drive.

"He means it, you know," said Mad seriously, as she opened the garden gate.

"Means what?" asked Terry.

"What he said about a strike. Farmers, doctors, nurses, teachers, grave-diggers, sewage-workers, if they all stayed away from work with a placard written on the door saying 'Yankees go home,' USUK might begin to fall apart."

"That's all very well," Emma said, as they walked up the path, "but surely we'd end up in chaos."

"Not necessarily."

The gate through to the look-out slammed and Joe came in panting, soaked to the skin, hair falling over his face.

"I had to climb up over the cliffs," he gasped. "Luckily I didn't break my leg like you, Terry. There's a fine old shemozzle down there by the Sailor's Rest, and I didn't want to get caught up in it."

"Did everyone get away?" asked Mad.

"I think so. The Trembaths did, I know that. By the way, as much milk as we want from them tomorrow, and Mr. Trembath is killing a pig which we can share in. They're going to have a load of wood from me in exchange." He stood by the porch, smiling at Mad, then he turned to Emma. "You see, it does work, community living. Our neighbours support us, we support them. We don't need any money, we can live without it. If everyone did this, throughout the country, there wouldn't be any need for trade outside. We shouldn't get rich but we'd be happy, we'd be free . . ."

He broke off as the sky overhead became suddenly bright, and as instinctively they raised their heads the sound of the explosion came, like the clashing of stars. The glass shattered in the dining-room windows and in the porch beside them, and, shocked, the four of them crouched there on the steps, their hands over their faces for protection. The echo faded, the vibration stilled, the ground no longer seemed to rock under their feet. Terry was the first to move. He said nothing, but he pointed to the sky, seaward. It was yellow bright, like day. He seized his crutches, hobbled to the garden door and flung it wide. Through the bent branches of the ilex tree they could see the dark waters of the bay turned streaky red, and where the warship had lain proudly at anchor was a pall of smoke and a pool of fire.

19

Nobody had much sleep that night. The children, awakened by the explosion, had run in to Dottie, crying. The middle boys, preparing for bed, had done the same, but white-faced, serious, without tears, Sam clutching the squirrel. Poor Folly, trembling, was trying to crawl under the settee in the hall when Mad and Emma and Joe and Terry opened the front door. Everyone gathered in the kitchen. Mercifully the windows had not shattered. Dottie, surprisingly one of the first to recover, stood by the stove in her dressing-gown making cocoa. "We'll all feel better if we have something hot inside us," she said, and Ben, sucking his thumb with his face buried in Mad's shoulder, lifted his head and watched her as she mixed the frothy brew. Colin, seated on Emma's lap, stopped shaking. Terry, puffing nervously at a cigarette, kept tilting backwards and forwards astride a kitchen chair. Sam, kneeling beside his squirrel, stroked its twitching ears. Joe, the only member of the household missing, returned before anyone noticed he had not been there.

"I've been the rounds," he said briefly. "Dining-room windows blown, library O.K. except for a cracked pane.

261

Two panes gone in Madam's bedroom, nothing in the spare room, Emma's O.K. I doubt if anything has blown in the basement but I'll just nip down and see."

He disappeared again. Andy, who had been standing silently deep in thought, jerked to activity.

"I'll come with you," he said. "I don't want any cocoa."

Nobody else spoke. Then the kettle hissed, the milk began to boil, and soon everyone was sipping the goodly mixture out of blue-and-white mugs. It was homely, it was natural, and yet a treat at the same time. If we could stay like this for always, Emma thought, and not go forward . . .

"Do you know what?" asked Colin suddenly, speaking to no one in particular. "When I woke up and heard that bang I thought it was the Judgement Day, and Jesus was coming in the clouds of heaven to divide the sheep from the goats."

Sam looked up from stroking the squirrel. "That's funny," he said, "I thought it was Judgement Day too, but I don't believe Jesus would divide the sheep from the goats, it would be too unfair. I think he would make the lions lie down with the lambs. That's what I should do if I were Jesus."

"I don't know about Judgement Day," said Dottie, "but little boys who run about without slippers on their feet are going to get cut by broken glass and that's for sure. The sooner they are tucked up in bed again the safer they will be."

Normality was returning to the household. Mugs were laid aside, Mad put a sleepy Ben into Dottie's arms, then rose to her feet and stretched. Emma followed her grandmother up to her bedroom. A dust-pan and brush soon disposed of the broken glass.

"The fresh air will do me good," observed Mad. "Get rid of the smell of manure. Funny thing. No one said anything about it in the kitchen, or asked where we had been. Not even Dottie."

"They were too frightened," said Emma. "And I don't mind admitting to you, so was I."

Together they stood at the window, looking out upon the bay. There were lights everywhere, the lights of rescue craft searching the sea, and overhead the roar of helicopters and searchlights too, sweeping the spot where the ship had lain.

"Judgement Day," murmured Mad, "but for how many?"

"It's horrible," whispered Emma, "horrible . . ."

Yet she could not drag her eyes away. The darting lights seemed to bob and circle over a particular patch of oil caught in the searchlight beam, and the lights of the helicopters hovered like gigantic moths, now dipping, now rising again.

"Poor devils," said Mad, turning away. "One thing, they must have gone instantaneously, whoever was on board," and from force of habit she began turning down her bed, switching on the electric blanket.

Why devils, Emma wondered. Was it a term one used automatically when enemies were wounded or killed? Had it been normal times, the ship at anchor a British or a European vessel waiting for the tide before entering Poldrea harbour to load clay, and a sudden explosion had taken place, blowing the ship to pieces in this way, Mad, despite her age, would have been down there on the cliffs, on the beach, and Emma too, and the boys, in hopes of struggling seamen finding their way ashore. Not tonight. No aid from Trevanal tonight. Whoever clung to a burning spar, whoever tried to swim, maimed and helpless in the choking oil, was alien, did not belong. Them and us . . .

"Mad," said Emma, "what do you suppose happened? Could it have been some fault in their engine-room, something that went wrong, a terrible calamity?"

Her grandmother was putting out her dressing-gown and slippers, turning on the bedside lamp, pouring some water into a glass.

"I'd like to think so, but I doubt it," she said. "More likely someone managed to put explosives aboard. And if they can prove it, then they'll believe our little Operation Dung-Cart was nothing but a diversion to distract their attention. Part of a joint plan."

"Oh, my God . . ." Emma turned from the window, gesturing helplessly.

"Yes, I know, but we can't do anything about it, can we? So run along, darling, and try and get some sleep. It's not going to be easy for any of us."

Emma wished she could have stayed. Sat on the end of the bed and gone into everything, her dread of the future, of what tomorrow might bring. She knew it was no use. Mad was not like that. Enough was enough. She preferred to be alone. Emma kissed her good night, and when she paused at the head of the stairs, before turning off the light and going to her own room, she saw a small figure standing in the hall, staring up at her. It was Andy.

"What is it?" she asked. "Why aren't you in bed?"

"Em . . ." Andy hesitated, one foot on the stairs, "can I ask you something?"

"Of course."

"It's the ship that's blown up, Joe told me. They may have lost a great many men."

"Yes, I know."

"Well, here's the thing. If a lot of men get killed like that all in one go, together, does it make the killing of one man by himself less of a crime?"

Emma looked down at him. He was still rather white from shock; the explosion that had frightened the little boys must have frightened him too. He's been thinking about it, she had not realised this during the past days, he's been thinking about it, at school, at play, and he hasn't asked anyone or told anyone, and now he's asking me. And I don't know what to say, because I don't know the answer.

"Yes," she said slowly, "yes, I think it does."

Andy smiled. "I'm glad," he said. "I hoped you'd say that."

"Good night, then. Hurry up and get to bed."

It isn't true, though, she thought as she went along to her room, it isn't true . . .

Thursday morning, Thanksgiving Day, which was to herald a new era for the English-speaking peoples and be celebrated all over the country with toasts to USUK and a public holiday, got off to an uneasy start in Cornwall. It would be fairer to say that it never got going at all. Operation Dung-Cart might have been treated as a local breach of manners, something to be mentioned as an aside or even ignored, but an explosion on board a U.S. ship, lying peacefully at her anchorage in a Cornish bay, with terrible loss of life, this was another matter, and took prior place on radio and television and in the newspapers. The celebrations went ahead as scheduled, but they were muted, and the Prime Minister, speaking after a televised Ministerial USUK luncheon, said, "We do not yet know how this disaster came about. Should there be definite proof of sabotage, should it be found that the destruction of this fine vessel, and the loss of so many loyal and valuable lives has been brought about deliberately, by unknown agents hostile to USUK, then let there be no mistake about it. Those responsible will be hunted down and punished—they will not escape justice. I wish, too, to address myself particularly to some of our countrymen who live in the west country and who, because of their place of birth, imagine themselves to be different from the rest of us—and this applies also to the inhabitants of Scotland and Wales, where there have been reports of minor explosions. I warn such people, do not be misled by evil men, by false propaganda, into thinking you can divert the course of history, block the union of progressive, peace-loving nations, and revert to a narrow tribalism. You cannot."

Roars of applause greeted his remarks, and the Prime Minister of the Coalition Government looked about him, eyes gleaming yet narrowed, the arrogant tilt of the head suggesting triumph. Mad and Emma and the two elder boys, grouped around the television set, stared in silence.

"I feel like Wellington," said Mad when the oration had finished. "He may not frighten the enemy, but by God he frightens me."

"It depends," replied Terry, "on the enemy. Does the P.M. mean a handful of Cornish farmers?"

"He surely hasn't heard about that," protested Emma. "He talked about unknown agents. It sounds like people creeping about in cloaks and masks. I don't understand how a spy could have crept on to the American ship without being seen."

"I don't know," said Joe thoughtfully. "They can't have been entirely self-sufficient on board, they had to take in a certain amount of stores. And we know a lot of the dockers at Poldrea disliked the Yanks. Some of them have lost their jobs and they don't any of them know what the future is to be. Someone could have planted something."

"Tom Bate," suggested Terry. "Sticks of gely stuffed inside some of his local plaice."

Gely . . . Emma remembered the sticks that Terry had passed on to Mr. Willis. Taffy was a Welshman, Taffy was a thief. Evil men, diverting the course of history, reverting to a narrow tribalism . . .

"I'm rather surprised," said Mad suddenly, "that Bevil didn't telephone us last night to find out if we were all right. Or even this morning."

"Don't forget," Emma reminded her, "the telephones are tapped."

"Yes, I know. But that explosion must have been heard for miles around, everyone would have been telephoning neighbours, friends. Joe . . .." She looked towards him. "Bevil will have finished lunch. Get on to him, but be careful what you say."

Joe obeyed, but reappeared almost at once. "No use," he said, "the line's dead. Like it was the morning of the first landings."

"Thanksgiving?" Terry queried.

"Day of Atonement," answered Mad.

They were indeed back to a fortnight ago. The only difference this time was the silence, the absence of troops in their immediate vicinity. Helicopters circled the bay and small craft nosed the disaster area, but from Trevanal itself no wreckage could be seen. Whether debris had drifted ashore, whether detachments of the marines were themselves searching the beach below, nobody from the house could tell, unless someone ventured out across the fields and down to the cliffs. And Mad was adamant. Nobody was to stir from the grounds, not even to the farm. If Jack Trembath considered it necessary to get in touch with them, doubtless he would do so. One thing must be very evident. Quite apart from the successful outcome of Operation Dung-Cart, there would be no Thanksgiving lunch at the Sailor's Rest.

The other very necessary order that Mad laid upon Joe and Terry was the washing-down of all boots, oilskins and other items of clothing that had been at all contaminated by the muck-laying of the preceding night. Minute particles of muck clung even to socks and collars, under-pants and vests. The well in the basement did a thorough job, and Folly's old bath, discovered at the back of the garage, made a fine washing-tub. The stone-flagged floor of the basement became awash, and the old one-time kitchen and scullery began to suggest an indoor swimming-pool.

"Let's get more water from the well and flood it properly," shouted Colin. "Ben, fetch the model boat from the playroom and we'll see if she sails. No, wait, we'll both undress and pretend it's summer."

"You'll do nothing of the sort," cried Emma. "Mad, for heaven's sake . . ."

Her grandmother only smiled. "They can't go out. Let them enjoy themselves. But whatever you do, darlings, don't splash the beetroot or the apples. We shall have to live on them till Christmas."

The fun continued fast and furious, and Mad, her genius for invention increasing as the afternoon wore on, suggested lighting a fire in the ancient grate with some of Joe's dry logs and stringing the wet clothes around it.

"Do be careful," Emma urged as clouds of smoke belched from the unused chimney. "You're not only going to undo all the good of the wash by getting the clothes covered with smuts, you may set the house on fire as well."

"I know," said Andy, who with Sam had jointed the fray, "let's boil a kettle and have tea down here, like proper campers. There's a kettle behind the dresser. The spout has broken, but that doesn't matter."

The fire in the rusty grate burnt bravely after the first gush of smoke, the kettle boiled, and the tea, handed round in old yogurt cartons, was pronounced delicious even by Colin, who never touched it in Dottie's kitchen. It was Dottie herself, not a spectator of the family wash or an assistant at the camp-fire, who came downstairs just as it was getting dark and reported that an army vehicle filled with marines was coming down the drive.

"Oh, really?" said Mad, her voice suspiciously calm. "I wonder why."

"It may be something to do with the electricity," replied Dottie. "It's been cut, like the telephone, and Joe and Terry are out in the garage now, trying to trace the fault."

"Perhaps," suggested Colin, "the marines want to use the garage again, like they did before. If they do, I shall put nails in their tyres."

Ben nodded, applauding loudly, and to show fellow-feeling began splashing everyone within reach with soapy water.

"Better go upstairs and listen for them, Dottie," said Mad. "If they ring the bell and ask for me, tell them they'll find me here in the basement."

Dottie looked shocked. "Oh, Madam, surely . . ." she began.

"Well, why not? With the electricity and water cut, we're past the stage where we sit about in drawing-rooms, and the sooner they understand it the better."

The commandos didn't ring. Some entered by the front door, others by the back. The boys, still sitting in a circle round the old kitchen grate, could hear the loud voices and the tramping of boots on the stairs. Andy leapt to his feet.

"Here, what do they think they're doing?" he said, and Emma noticed that his hand went instinctively to the flick-knife he always kept in the belt of his jeans.

"Keep quiet," said Mad sharply. "Just behave as if nothing was happening, and leave the talking to me."

The voices were joined by Dottie's in the kitchen over-head. She was protesting, and everyone seemed to be speaking at once.

"Put some more wood on the fire," said Mad. "It will give us a little light, but not much."

Sam threw on some smaller logs, and shavings too, that Joe had cut for kindling. As the shavings caught, the shad-ows of the group about the fire grew monstrous on the grimy ceiling. The voices and the clatter became louder, as the invaders descended to the basement and burst into the old kitchen.

"Hi, there, on your feet, and your hands behind your heads," shouted someone. He was carrying a torch, which he flashed on to the faces of the group around the fire. Nobody moved. The only one to obey the command was Ben, who with hands clasped on top of his head moved forward and launched a miniature wave with his foot in the direction of the marines.

"Somebody grab that kid," said the man who was giving the orders.

Emma reached out and pulled Ben beside her. She did not know how many of them there were. It could have been four or five, but the firelight did not reveal the num-ber as they flashed the torches they were carrying upon walls and windows, peering into the old scullery where the apples and the beetroot were stored.

"Nothing but a bunch of kids and an old woman," said

the marine in charge. He sounded disappointed, even disgusted. "Who the hell owns this place anyway?"

"I do," said Mad. Her voice was cold as ice, and very clear. "And if you would kindly turn that torchlight off my eyes so that I'm not blinded, I may be prepared to speak to you."

Whether the man was officer, sergeant or corporal, Emma could not tell. They all looked alike anyway in combat dress. He was certainly not Captain Cockran, who had come when Pa was in the house, or indeed anyone she had seen before.

"Okay, what's your name?"

Mad told him. "This is my grand-daughter," she continued, "and these are four of my adopted boys. Because we have no other light and no water except what we are able to draw from a well, we are obliged to do the family wash here, where you see us. We cannot get to the town as we have no transport, and we are existing on a diet of cabbages and beetroot. Anything else you want to know?"

"Sure, lady." The leader's manner, if somewhat milder, was still offensive. "We have information that you have two boys under your roof who have turned nineteen. Where are they?"

"I've no idea. Probably in the garage, trying to find out why we have no electricity. And the younger boy is only seventeen."

"Right. Go get them." The marine in charge snapped his order to two of his men, who clattered away.

"What do you want with them?" asked Mad.

"All adult males, lady, are wanted for questioning. We're making a house-to-house search throughout the district, and yours is just one of hundreds on our list. The faster a guy tells us what we want to know, the sooner he'll come home."

He was chewing the inevitable gum. Why did they do it, and why the glance down at her, Emma wondered, half-familiar, half-contemptuous, as if he had only to jerk his head towards the cellar and he'd expect her to follow him?

"Do you mean to tell me you are taking away for questioning every able-bodied man in the Poldrea area?" asked Mad.

"You've guessed right, lady. And you're lucky we don't

take away kids younger still. It's time some of them learnt respect."

"Respect for whom?"

The leader didn't answer. He was looking around him at all the clothes hung up to dry.

"Some wash-day," he observed. "Do you always have as much as this in your weekly tub?"

"It depends on who's polluting the air we breathe," Mad replied.

Emma could hear Joe's voice at the side-door. "Ah-ha . . ." exclaimed the commando, "here they come. We'll return them in the morning if they behave themselves."

He and the other marines moved across the room towards the passage.

"The younger boy has a leg in plaster and is on crutches," said Mad. "He's under the doctor's care, and has been in hospital. He was due to go back to hospital today to have the plaster removed, but we couldn't get him there."

"He'll have to wait, then, until your Cornish medicos come to their senses," replied the commando. "Maybe you didn't know they've gone on strike, and your local hospital has shut down, along with others. Public-spirited lot, aren't you, in this God-darn peninsula?"

Joe and Terry, a marine on either side of them, appeared at the turn of the passage.

"I'm afraid we couldn't locate the fault, Madam," said Joe. "The electricity is cut."

"That's right, ma'am," repeated the leader mockingly. "No water, no light, no transport, ma'am, you're back in the old times, ma'am. Maybe it will do you all good to live hard for a time, ma'am, like we did one hundred years ago on the frontier. Come on, let's go."

Colin, who had turned very white, planted himself in front of Joe and Terry. "If you take my brothers away I shall kill you," he said.

"You don't say?" The marine bent, picked up Colin by the collar of his jersey and dropped him neatly in the tin-bath. "They breed killers young in this part of the world. Maybe we'll come back for you tomorrow."

It was the way he pushed Terry ahead of him so that the boy stumbled, one of the crutches slipping from under his armpit, that drove Emma to her feet.

"For God's sake be careful," she said. "Can't you see he can't walk properly? And if you're taking him down to the camp, and Joe as well, they've already been questioned last week. Ask Captain Cockran, no, ask Lieutenant Sherman, he knows them both, he knows my grandmother, he knows us all."

The man turned and looked at her. His companion's torchlight shone on his face. The expression was no longer contemptuous, only hard.

"Listen, girlie, maybe he did, but he doesn't know you now. Captain Cockran and Lieutenant Sherman, along with a couple of hundred more of our buddies, were blown sky-high out of your bay last night and we haven't even recovered the bits and pieces yet. So if we don't love you very much, and have nothing to celebrate on what was meant to be Thanksgiving Day, just remember that when you sit here in the dark."

He and the rest of the marines went along the passage and out of the side-door, driving Terry and Joe ahead of them. The door slammed. In a moment or two there came the sound of the lorry starting up and the grind of the wheels as it backed along the drive. Folly, disturbed from sleep and finding nobody about, began to howl at the top of the basement stairs. Sam crept from the silent group around the grate and went to comfort her.

"Why didn't we stop them?" cried Colin passionately, kicking aside the tin-bath. "Why didn't anybody do anything?"

Nobody answered for a moment. Then Mad threw another log on to the fire.

"Because there were more of them than there were of us," she replied.

Andy came forward and put his hand on her shoulder as she crouched there by the fire.

"Don't worry," he said. "I'll look after things while Joe and Terry are gone. I'll be the man in the house, and Sam and I will do their work, saw the logs, bring in the vegetables. I'm sorry if the marines have lost a lot of men in that explosion, but it doesn't mean we have to give in, does it?"

"No," Mad looked up at him, her face haggard in the firelight. She looked all of her eighty years. "No, Andy, we won't give in. Never . . . never . . . never . . ."

271

20

It wasn't the darkness one minded, thought Emma, nor the doubt about the water lasting—though indeed, as she peered down into the well, the round pool at the bottom seemed to have gotten lower, with a layer of scum—or the now inevitable beetroot or cabbage soup and boiled potatoes, varied by what remained in tins on Dottie's shelves, all cooked on the old basement grate, but the anxiety of what had happened to Joe and Terry, where they had been taken, what was being asked. Nor was it any consolation to know that the Trembaths were suffering too; fourteen-year-old Mick had come running up to Trevanal the following morning to report that his father had been taken once again.

"Mr. Hawkins has been taken from Pendower," he said, "and Bill and Dick Rundle from Hilltown. Mr. Willis is going round every farm he can, offering to help with the milking and anything else. We'd all be lost without him. Not many know how to milk by hand these days. Mother has sent you up these eggs, but Dad didn't have time to kill the pig."

Communications were completely cut. There were no

vans, no buses, no transport other than army vehicles on the road. The shops in Poldrea were closed. There was no question of the boys attending school because nobody knew if the schools had opened or not, and anyway there wasn't a school bus to take them. The only link with the outside world on the Friday, and again on the Saturday, was the district nurse, who walked up to the farm to console her sister, and out of the kindness of her heart crossed the field on the way there to visit Trevanal.

"I had to see if you were all right," she said, "and if there's any message I can take to anyone I'll do so."

"Is it true the doctors aren't on duty and the hospital is closed?" asked Mad.

Nurse Bennett shook her head slowly. "I just don't know," she replied. "My phone is cut like everybody else's, my car has run out of petrol, and the garages are still closed. I can't get to anyone except on foot. Nobody knows what's going on anywhere. People are bewildered. Poldrea is completely cut off from the outside, road-blocks between us and St. Austell and Liskeard. The worst thing is the way they've been going from house to house taking off the men."

"Where are they taking them to?"

"Nobody knows. They say there's a great area up round the clay-pits with barbed wire and dogs, a regular concentration camp, but it could be lies, couldn't it?"

Joe, Terry, Mr. Trembath . . . It wasn't possible, thought Emma, that they, and hundreds of others, could be held prisoner indefinitely, having done nothing, without being able to protest or demand their legal rights. This was the sort of thing one had always imagined only happened in the Soviet Union in the past and years ago, before she had been born, in Nazi Germany in the nineteen thirties.

"If only," said Nurse Bennett, "we could get proper information on the news, but our battery set isn't working, and this goes for lots of others as well, and anyway, I'm told nothing is said on the radio about our plight. It's just ignored."

"The police," asked Mad, "what are they doing?"

"I haven't seen any panda cars on the road," replied Nurse Bennett, "and the local police station is an army post, or marine post, I should say. It's all due to the explosion on the ship. They blame every man, woman and child, and we've got to be punished. None of this would have happened but for that."

"I wonder," said Mad, "I wonder . . ."

Emma knew what was passing through her grandmother's mind. It was Mad's theory that the measures adopted to cut off all news, all movement amongst the local population, would have come about anyway, quite apart from the explosion on the ship. Tighter restrictions had already come into force after the death of Corporal Wagg, and even if the explosion had never occurred the disruption caused by the small episode of Operation Dung-Cart would have triggered off punitive measures and house-to-house arrests, if not on quite such a wide scale as they had turned out to be.

"It's loss of face and loss of nerve," Mad told Emma. "You remember what Vic said when he was here? The marines can't afford to lose either. Nor can our Coalition government, which is backing the whole enterprise of USUK. The population must appear to back the union, they must be cajoled, bribed, coerced, whichever works best. Sabotage must be punished, that's what the Prime Minister said. And I dare say if this explosion had happened in Suffolk, instead of in our own bay, we'd be agreeing with him."

"Some would," Emma suggested, "but not you. You took your stand from the very first day. I've not forgotten the look on your face when Spry was blown to pieces in the ploughed field, and you'd have felt the same whether a farm dog had been shot in Cornwall or on the Isle of Man."

No denial came. Her grandmother had turned away, saw in hand, for tree-felling in the shrubbery had been the order for Friday afternoon, with the older boys pressed into service. A dog had been killed, a man had been killed, a ship had been destroyed, a small township had been isolated from the outside world and its male population had been arrested . . . and for what? So that more and more men like Pa could jet around the world juggling with currency? So that more and more people, frustrated, unfulfilled, jobless, might emigrate, in the vain hope that the grass was greener elsewhere, while those who remained sought never to share but to compete, never to help their neighbour but to go one better? There must be an answer,

Emma thought, but nobody has it. And it's useless going back in history and talking of the fall of Rome and how society was sick two thousand years ago, men and women lolling about quaffing wine and watching gladiators, while Christians crouched in catacombs; the Christians were no better when they became top dog, burning people at the stake, putting them on the rack. Even the Sermon on the Mount got you nowhere; the saying about "Blessed are they who hunger and thirst after righteousness" gave such a picture of crowds of men and women on their knees in a gloomy church praying like mad, and then looking terribly disapproving afterwards if anyone as much as held hands or fumbled in the dark. And suddenly she thought of Wally Sherman, poor, harmless Wally Sherman, who had only meant to be kind, who even on the beach at the firework party had only intended warmth and get-together in the usual fashion of the young of both their countries, Wally Sherman who had taken the trouble, possibly at danger to himself, to warn her about the restrictive measures to come, and now . . . nothing left. One moment talking, perhaps laughing, perhaps having dinner on board and due to go ashore afterwards, and the next . . . fragments, all gone, like Spry. If a lot of men get killed at one go, does it make the killing of one man less of a crime? I don't know, Andy, I don't know. I'm only twenty and they say today the world is ours, but Pa was twenty once and felt the world was his, and long, long ago Mad was twenty too, laughing at applauding audiences, smiling from picture postcards, and when I am as old as she is nothing will have changed . . .

These thoughts, fragmented, passed through Emma's mind before Nurse Bennett's visit and after she had gone. She walked part of the way with her across the ploughed field but not to the farm itself, there was too much to do at home, and as she stared after the blue-coated, rather stout figure who had climbed the muddy track from the cliff road, showing her nurse's pass to a reluctant, sulky sentry, in the cause of family feeling and common humanity, Emma wondered if it was because of women like Nurse Bennett, multiplied a thousand-fold throughout the country, that they would survive, someone who brought children into the world and comforted the dying. Nobody but their neighbours ever knew them, when they had gone they were forgotten, they never became rich, never became famous, these were the meek who inherited the earth, never to hold it themselves but to pass it on, as a sort of trust, as a way of life.

"You're another one," she said to Dottie, whom she found kneading the last bag of flour to make bread for the four boys. And when it had been baked in the cloam oven in the basement that probably hadn't been used for a hundred years or more she would spread some of Joe's apples upon it, stewed in a pot in the old grate.

"I'm another what?" asked Dottie, her usually plump face streaked into lines of fatigue, because how were they going to manage tomorrow, next week, if there were still no supplies, no light, and no water but what came from the stagnant-looking well, every drop of which had to be boiled, and no Joe, no Terry—how were they going to endure?

"You're one of the blessed," said Emma, "you're one of the meek."

Dottie stared at her over the dough. "Meek?" she repeated. "Blessed? What's meek or blessed about trying to make a bag of flour satisfy four growing appetites? I'll go on until I drop, but I don't call it meek. As for blessed, that's for the saints, and I've never been one of them." She shook the flour from her hands and suddenly her body sagged, her face crumpled. "I can't bear to think what they may be doing to my boy," she said.

My boy . . . Terry, the first-adopted, the spoilt one, the nurseling. Emma, stricken, her own tears near the surface at the sight of the older person breaking down, dear, dear Dottie of all people, put her arms around her and held her close.

"They won't hurt him, they won't," she said. "He'll be back mocking and laughing as he always does, teaching Colin worse swear words than ever, I promise you."

"You can't promise, you don't know," said Dottie. "We none of us know. I thought the marines were meant to be our friends, they were here to help us, but the way they spoke to me, the way they pushed through the house, through my kitchen down to the basement, and took our boys off in their lorry as if they were cattle . . . What's our own army doing to protect us, where's our police, what's happened to the government? You hear of such

277

things happening in other countries, but not here Not to us."

It can't happen here, thought Emma, it can't happen here, that's what people in England have always said, even in war-time when they were bombed, because they were all together on their own ground. Not any more.

"We must try and be brave," she said aloud. "We mustn't give way. We've just got to take each moment as it comes, each hour, each day."

Two days only since Joe and Terry had gone. It seemed like two years. The dragging awful fear when one awoke in the morning that something more terrible yet was going to happen, that the news would come that the marines were going to make an example of two out of every dozen prisoners and shoot them, and the two would be Joe and Terry. The fear that Pa would never come back again, would settle in Brazil, believing this country was finished. The fear that one of the children would fall ill, awake in the night with appendicitis, and without a telephone they couldn't send for Bevil Summers. The fear that he too had been taken away in the lorry by the marines and there was no one, but no one, who could come, who could help . . .

Stop it, she told herself, stop it. This was the way to breakdown, to hysteria, and if she, at twenty, young and strong, gave way, what would happen to the very young, the very old?

"Show me what to do," she asked Dottie, putting her hands into the dough. "I have no skills, I've got to learn. If I can't bake bread what use am I to anyone?"

Dottie wiped her eyes and tried to smile. "You put me in mind of a song they used to sing when I was a kid," she said. " 'Poor little rich girl'—Noel Coward, I believe it was. What about those expensive cooking classes your Pa sent you to a few years ago?"

"Souffles and creme brûlée," replied Emma. "Nothing basic."

"That's half the trouble with the world," said Dottie. "Everything frozen and sold in a supermarket, no time any more for people to grow stuff and cook it themselves in their own home. My mother passed on what she knew to me, and I never thought I'd need it working in the theatre all those years, going from place to place, but

278

thank the Lord I remembered when it was needed, and what I don't remember I do by instinct."

This was it. Whatever we do is done by instinct, some pointer from within. Eating, drinking, loving, hating, these were the basic urges driving humanity forward, anything else was transient.

"The thing is," said Emma, speaking half to herself and half to Dottie, "we should all live in small communities, sharing each other's work and needs. The farmer growing grain, the miller milling it, butter, milk, vegetables, fruit, everyone supplying their neighbour and getting something in return, but no money any more."

"I don't think it would work, Emma," said Sam, who had come into the kitchen, his narrow face serious. "There might be someone in the next community who had a bigger and better breed of cow giving more milk, or whose land grew more grain. Then the people who hadn't such good cows or such good land would be jealous, and try and take it over. The fighting would start all over again."

"Not if there was a good leader," said Andy, the kitchen rapidly filling with hungry boys who were beginning to grow restive under a diet of beetroot and apples. "A good leader would have such authority he'd say, 'You just stop talking and do as you're told,' and the people would have to get on with it, and be content with their own cows and their own land."

"No, they wouldn't," said Colin, who had entered dragging Ben after him, "not if the people were very hungry and greedy too, like Ben. They would see the fat cows in some other farmer's field and they just couldn't wait until they got them, and the leader would be killed and a greedy man take his place. That's what you would do, wouldn't you, Ben?"

Ben nodded aggressively, and reaching up to the kitchen table snatched a piece of sticky dough and thrust it in his mouth.

"Now then, none of that," cried Dottie. "You wait until the bread is baked and then you shall have your share. Spit it out, you'll be sick else."

"Nurse Bennett did bring some eggs," murmured Emma, "if he's very hungry . . ."

"Eggs are for lunch," said Dottie. "If they have eggs now there'll be nothing later. That's right, isn't it, Madam?"

Mad, who as far as her grand-daughter knew hadn't breakfasted at all, stood by the kitchen door. "They've been working so hard," she said, "they ought to have something. We've plenty of Folly's biscuits in the store-cupboard, and you know her poor teeth can't get through it nowadays. Suppose we soak some of that?"

Ben's face fell. He looked up at Colin for support, but none was forthcoming. Anything different in diet or daily routine stimulated Colin. Besides, he was never hungry. "Let's try it," he said delightedly, "let's pretend we're in kennels. Let's all get down on our hands and knees and be hounds yelping, and Madam and Dottie can put the biscuit into bowls and feed us."

One word was enough for Ben, and curiously enough for the older boys too. A series of yelps and howls filled the kitchen, the prancing of feet, the pawing of hands, until Mad, her hands over her ears, suddenly ceased laughing, and Emma, following the direction of her eyes, saw she was looking towards the window.

"Who are those men?" Mad said. "What are they doing?"

The yelping stopped. Everyone ran to the kitchen window and looked out. Two men were walking through the small wood bordering the drive. One of them had an axe, another a saw.

"Those aren't marines," Mad said, "they're not in uniform. Andy, go and find out what they want."

There was something familiar about the figure with the saw, tall, burly, humped in a leather jacket.

"It's Mr. Libby," said Emma, astounded, "and that man he has to help him. I'll go and speak to him."

She ran down the stairs and out of the side-door into the yard. Andy was already halfway up the drive. He paused when he saw Emma was following him. He too had recognised the landlord of the Sailors Rest.

"He's by the load of logs Joe stacked for the Trembaths," he told her. "You remember, the load they were to have in exchange for the milk and eggs."

Emma strode through the undergrowth, but Mr. Libby took no notice of her. He and his assistant were throwing the logs into sacks.

"Excuse me," Emma said, "but my grandmother wants to know what you are doing."

280

The landlord stared down at her. He looked unkempt. He hadn't shaved, and the stubble was grey on his face.

"You've more wood here than you use yourselves," he said. "Time some of the rest of us had a fair share of it."

"I'm sorry," Emma replied, "but those logs are promised."

"Oh yes?" he retorted. "Well, first come, first served. It's everyone for himself these days. Why should you people up here keep warm while we go cold? Carry on, Harry, fill up those sacks, and then we'll come back for more."

"Mr. Libby," persisted Emma, "I've told you, those logs are promised. We're only waiting for Joe and Terry to return. They're promised to the farm."

The landlord laughed. It was not a pleasant laugh, but derisive, harsh. Gone was the obsequious manner, the tone adopted for the selling of Californian wine.

"You won't see your lads in a hurry," he said, "nor will Peggy Trembath see her husband Jack. People who obstruct the Queen's highway get punished for it, and when they aid and abet sabotage they deserve to be shot as well." He paused a moment in his task of axing a sapling. "And we are the ones to suffer," he said, striking his chest, "honest, law-abiding citizens with our custom taken away, water and electricity cut, livelihood gone, all because of people like you. All very well for someone like your grandmother with a load of money tucked away in the bank. What about me? No customer has been near my place since the regulations came into force."

"Money's no use if you can't get to a bank," said Emma. "We're no better off than you are—worse, in fact. You can at least get drunk on Californian wine."

Which was an error, for his face turned dark with anger. "You'd better watch your tongue," he said, "or those of us who feel badly treated will take more than wood. We're not getting free milk from Jack Trembath's farm, or free eggs, like I hear you do, and if those who deserve to be punished by the authorities for sabotage get off scot free, we'll take the law into our own hands and raid the farms while the farmers are away. We could all do with some of their pigs and sheep and cattle, to keep our own families from starving. Tell that to Mrs. Peggy Trembath when you see her."

He drove his axe into the sapling ash. It crashed and fell. Emma put her hand on Andy's arm, who had crouched to spring. "No . . ." she whispered, "no . . ." One false move, and Mr. Libby's threat would turn to action. He would go to the farm and seize any animal he wanted, just as he was taking the wood now. There would be no one to stop him, for Mick was hardly bigger than Andy. She looked over her shoulder, and her grandmother was standing in the drive below, saw in hand.

"Hullo, Mr. Libby," she called, "there's another ash sapling just ahead of you. Want me to help you?"

The landlord of the Sailor's Rest tripped over the root at his feet and slowly turned. Embarrassment, resentment, self-righteous indignation all struggled for priority in his bearing, in his face. The memory, too, of cider sold in the past, and what might be sold yet in the days to come.

"No call for sarcasm," he said. "Some aren't as lucky as others. We're living in hard times."

"I know, said Mad. "I wasn't being sarcastic. I'll help you saw up the first tree if you want me to. The question is, without your car, how can you get it back down the hill unless you drag it? Did you bring some rope?"

Mr. Libby was silent. His assistant shuffled the leaves at the root of the tree.

"I tell you what would be fair," said Mad. "You take as much wood as you can carry for your own household, and when things return to normal, if they ever do, let me have a barrel of cider, free."

The soft answer turneth away wrath—but did it? Resentment, and being caught in the act, still left its imprint on the landlord's face.

"It's all very well to talk of things returning to normal," he said. "What this country needs is a dictatorship, I've said it for years, and with the Americans to back us up we'd get it. I wouldn't want to blow up their ship. They've never done any harm to me, only brought custom, which I've now lost."

"Oh, I agree with you," said Mad. "We all stand to lose as things are, but as to a dictatorship, it depends who does the dictating. They certainly have the whip-hand at the moment. Now, do you need any help, or shall we leave it to you?"

282

Training behind the bars of several small pubs had left its mark. The customer was always right.

"We can manage, thank you," said Mr. Libby gruffly. "We'll only take the one tree, and one sack of logs."

"Fine," Mad replied, "then I'll only expect a small barrel of cider."

She turned away, whistling, followed by Emma and Andy. When they reached the garage Andy stopped and said, "How could you let them get away with it? I'm so boiling with rage I can hardly speak. You'd only to whisper and I would have dashed up to my chimney on the roof and got them both with . . . with you know what."

"Yes," Mad answered, "I know. But it didn't help much last time, did it, so I thought I'd have a try at community relations instead. I doubt if that will help much either. Not with Mr. Libby. Besides . . ." she paused, and added, "I really should have let him have all the wood he wanted without striking the bargain about the cider."

"Why?" Andy asked.

"It would only have been fair," she replied, "considering what we did to him the other night."

Andy frowned. "I don't know what you mean," he said. "This is the first time Mr. Libby has been here, isn't it?"

"Yes," said Mad, "but it won't be the last if he finds out that Emma and I and your godfather helped the farmers chuck tractor-loads of manure outside the Sailor's Rest about half-an-hour before the explosion blew up the American ship." She looked Andy straight in the face. "So, you see, we're all of us guilty of some crime or other, and we none of us want to be found out."

Conflicting emotions fought for supremacy in Andy's eyes, just as they had done in Mr. Libby's. But emotions of a different kind. Certainly not embarrassment, nor resentment, nor self-righteous indignation. Possibly wonder, and then envy.

"Was that what you were doing," he said slowly, "when we thought you were talking to Dr. Summers in the music-room, and Dottie told us not to interrupt but to have our supper and go straight to bed?"

"Yes."

Andy sighed, his shoulders drooped. "If only you'd taken me with you," he said at last, "if only I could have been there." Then he looked up, straightened his shoulders, and remembering he was the man of the house with Joe and Terry away, he added, "You'll have to take me next time. You can't do without me now."

Mad laughed and put her arm round him as she might have done Terry, the pair of them walking towards the side-door, while Mr. Libby and his crony shouldered the felled sapling up in the wood, and the sack of logs, and made their way out of the gate on to the road. How does she get away with it, wondered Emma, how does she manage to slide over difficulties and ward off antagonism, and never get caught out herself? Mad isn't one of the meek, like Nurse Bennett, like Dottie, she doesn't go through life unnoticed, smoothing sickbed pillows or baking bread, she's like a bulldozer churning up unwanted earth, pushing everything out of the way. Talk about dictators, Mad was the supreme example, Mad was the one to order everyone else about and command obedience, but not overtly, not so that you actually noticed; in fact, very often people thought they were doing what they wanted to do when they weren't at all; they were bluffed into it, they were conned. Oh Pa, come back and save us, stop things happening, don't stay in Brazil . . .

Turning on the radio for the news was routine but no help at all. Nothing of significance was mentioned. Monetary talks were taking place in various capitals. The Cultural-Get-Together movement had established headquarters in every county town and was to work in close co-operation with the Minister of Education. The date for the visit of the President of the United States, co-President of USUK, had not yet been decided, but plans were well advanced. Meanwhile, units of the American Forces were on guard at Buckingham Palace.

"Haven't you noticed," said Mad, "that with every news bulletin about USUK there's more emphasis on the U.S. and less on the U.K.? I suppose it's the same in the newspapers and on television, but cut off from both we just don't know. More serious, this battery is fading, and so is mine upstairs. We shall have to ration ourselves to listening once a day."

"It won't help much," Andy told her. "Batteries fade even if you don't use them."

"Mr. Willis makes his own radio sets," Sam announced.

"Radio's his hobby when he isn't beachcombing. I bet you anything you like his battery hasn't faded."

"There's our answer." Mad surveyed them all triumphantly. "Taffy will keep us up to date. He shall be our link with the outside world."

Emma's heart sank. She had hoped they had done with Mr. Willis. It was certainly very kind of him to go to the various farms around and help with the milking, but it would have been best to leave it at that. There mustn't be a repetition of that awful lunch and him falling asleep drunk in the cloakroom.

She hoped her grandmother would forget what Sam had said, but her hope was in vain. They busied themselves all afternoon with sawing and wood-gathering, for most of the cooking was now being done by a reluctant Dottie on the music-room fire, as slates were starting to fall inexplicably into the old grate in the basement, and the music-room fireplace devoured fuel like a hungry furnace. It must have been half-past five, and the boys were installed in the kitchen munching Dottie's home-baked bread, when Mad, whom nothing seemed to tire, turned to Emma in the library and said, "Do you suppose they've finished milking yet?"

Emma, who had flopped on to the sofa, missed the significance of the question. "Oh yes," she replied, "they usually milk around four. At least, at the Trembaths'."

"In that case," said Mad, "let's you and I slip down to Taffy's hut and see if he is there, and if he is we can hear the six o'clock news."

Emma stared, aghast. "In the dark?" she exclaimed. "Through the woods to that sinister little hut? Oh no, darling, we can't."

"Why ever not? We've both got torches, and anyway it's a fine night. We're never likely to find him at home in the daytime, with all the farm work he's doing, and who knows, he may have picked up all sorts of things from walking about the countryside. He might even have heard rumours about where they've taken the boys."

Emma looked closely at her grandmother. It wasn't the six o'clock news she wanted to hear; it was because of the chance, the slim chance, that Mr. Willis might know something, have heard a whisper, that would bring a ray of hope about Joe, about Terry. The good humour, the

285

energy, the joking with the younger ones, was all a bluff. More than Dottie, more than Emma, Mad herself was worried sick about her boys.

"All right," Emma said. "I'll get my things on and come with you."

There was no necessity to tramp all the way across the ploughed field and the grazing ground to reach the wood. There was a gap in the hedge bordering the Trevanal paddock that gave easier access and was more sheltered, even if the path was less direct, because of overgrown brambles and ivy and fallen stumps of trees. I don't like it, Emma thought, we shouldn't be doing this, someone might spring out and strangle us, no one is safe today after what has happened, with Mr. Libby and that man on our own domain, carrying axes. What if others should do the same, in this no-man's-land, by night?

Mad strode ahead, her torchlight flashing oddly amongst the trees, and she surely had no nerves at all, or else it was a form of magic, a sort of witchcraft. Emma prayed that Mr. Willis wouldn't be there, and they could retrace their steps at once, but as they drew nearer she could smell the smoke. There was a thin wisp of it coming through the queer stovepipe thing he had for a chimney, and, more proof positive still, a dim light showed through the window, candlelight, or it could be a paraffin lamp. The last time she had come here it had been with Wally Sherman, poor Wally Sherman, who had held her hand along the twisting path, and somehow the memory of this, and the knowledge that he was dead, not just dead through illness but blown to pieces, made the walk more frightening still. He hadn't known that time was running out, any more than Corporal Wagg had . . .

"He's at home," said Mad, "there's a light. Shall we look through the window?"

"Be careful," Emma warned her. "The last time I did that he was having a bath, with hardly anything on. It was rather dreadful."

"Why dreadful? It's a relief to know he does take his clothes off and strip occasionally. Some people who live alone don't wash for years."

The path widened into the small clearing before the wooden shack. They crept together to the window and peered through the curtainless pane.

"There he is," breathed Mad, "sitting by the wall there in the far corner writing something on a pad. And look, Sam was right about the home-made radio. He's got head-phones over his ears. We've caught him just in time."

She rapped loudly on the window-pane. The effect was instantaneous, even more rapid than on the morning over a week ago when he had stood gripping the sponge against his belly. Head-phones were dashed to the ground, and seizing the shot-gun at his feet he whirled round, extinguishing the small lamp at the same time. The hut was plunged into darkness. Everything fell silent.

"Let's go away," pleaded Emma in a whisper. "Please, Mad, please."

"Nonsense." Her grandmother moved from the window round to the door at the front. "We've frightened him. I'd keep a gun if I lived by myself out here." She knocked on the door, then, seeing a hand-bell hanging on a nail, she rang it, pushing it to and fro so that the clapper struck the side, high-pitched, shrill. "Taffy?" she called. "Taffy? Nothing to worry about, it's only us."

Emma had the uneasy feeling that he was watching them from some spy-hole which they couldn't see, some wooden partition in the wall that could be silently removed and then replaced. They waited. Then they heard the bolt withdrawn from the lock. The door opened. He stood there in the darkness, the gun no longer in his hand.

"Excuse me, ladies," he said. "I'm quite overwhelmed. If I'd known you were coming I should have been better prepared. Are you in trouble up at the house? Have you come for assistance?"

"No," Mad replied, "we're managing all right. We just thought we'd pay you a visit and hear your news. The difficulty is our radio batteries are fading and we hardly dare use them, so we're terribly out of touch with whatever is going on. Sam told us you're so knowledgeable with radio and have a set you made yourself . . ."

She paused, for the sudden drawing inward of his breath was unmistakable. He did not answer. They heard him fumble with something, and then he struck a match and lit the small lamp standing on the table beside him. He held it high and the light flickered on their faces, so that he could read their expressions, but they could not read his. Then he bowed and gave a little laugh.

"Will you come into my parlour, said the spider to the fly? But in this case there are two flies to one spider, isn't that so? Walk in, ladies, walk in."

He stood aside and let them pass before him into the hut, and then he shut the door and bolted it behind him.

21

Mr. Willis turned up his lamp and put it on a shelf where it threw more light about the room. Two logs, uptilted, smouldered on the hearth and he darted forward, seizing an armful of kindling, which he thrust into the fire to catch aflame. Emma glanced about her. There was no sign of the ear-phones, no sign of the gun. An ordinary, rather old-fashioned type of battery radio stood on a table, but nowhere near the stool where he had been sitting with the ear-phones on his head and the pad on his knee when they had peered through the window a short while before.

"Sit down, ladies, sit down," he said, dragging forward a rickety chair and the stool. "Not quite the comfort of Trevanal to which you are accustomed, but clean nevertheless. I have a good scrub round twice weekly. There, I'm falling into vaudeville language from very confusion, twice nightly they used to say in the old days, didn't they? What can I offer you for refreshment? Alas, no wine from the grape, but I have a home brew fermented from potato. On a winter's night it can be stimulating."

Mad favoured him with a famous smile and shook her

head, gesturing at the same time. "No, really," she said, "we won't take anything, and we haven't come to stay." For courtesy's sake she dropped into the rickety chair, and Emma perched on the stool. "We just thought, knowing how good a neighbour you are being to the Trembaths while he is in custody, and to the other farmers' families too, that you might have heard a little more of what is happening than we do, isolated at Trevanal."

"Ah!" He smiled for the first time, and the tone was surely one of relief. "I pick up all the local gossip I can, you can rely upon me for that. Whether it is all authentic is another matter, isn't it? There's solidarity throughout the farming community, that seems to be truth and not rumour, it comes by word of mouth from one farm to another."

He sat on the end of his bed, legs crossed, arms about his knees, shoulders hunched. He looks like a gnome, Emma thought, but not one of the jolly elfin ones from children's fairytales, more the sinister goblin kind from myth and legend.

"Do you mean that farmers outside our own area know what is happening here?" asked Mad. "Despite road-blocks and a clamp-down on news and information?"

"They couldn't fail to discover it, could they?" he countered. "When the milk never turned up at the depots and there was no communication between Poldrea and the neighbouring districts, someone had to take action, and it wasn't the National Union of Farmers, they were evasive, they said they were waiting for instructions from some new body within the USUK framework. So the farmers stopped deliveries themselves, and it's a hand-out sale amongst neighbours, like our friend Trembath instigated.

He smiled again, or rather grinned, looking more like a gnome than ever.

"We may boast we've started something in this peninsula," he told them, "for they say there isn't a farmer in Cornwall that isn't protesting at our men being taken into custody. Give them a day or two, and it will spread to Devon and to Dorset. The doctors are doing the same. Communications must be restored to this area, lighting, water, telephone, or they'll practise no medicine, visit no patients, perform no operations. It isn't a strike for money, you see, it isn't a strike at all. It's a protest against domination by the strangers in our midst over one section of a small community."

He leant over from the end of the bed and threw a piece of his driftwood planking on to the fire. The driftwood spat and the flames leapt high, showing blue lights. He isn't a gnome, he's a wizard, thought Emma, and Mad is a witch, and in a moment the incantations will begin, the spells will start.

"No doubt about it," he said, "we have them on the run. You've only to fan the flame, and the chimney roars. Damp wood is sluggish, but the true salt burns."

"You mean the marines, the U.S. forces?" persisted Mad.

"The U.S. forces here locally, and wherever else they've established themselves," said Mr. Willis. "The Coalition Government up at Whitehall will have to think again, or they'll find the population of this country splitting into sections. But there, it's an emotional matter, isn't it? You said you wanted to hear the news. I doubt if there will be anything fresh since one o'clock."

He climbed down from his bed and switched on the set. It was just before six. They heard the weather report and the time signal. Then the regional announcer, after a momentary hesitation, said there had been a few minor disturbances throughout the west country, chiefly amongst the farming community, but that the situation was well under control. He then passed on to the news they had already heard at lunch.

"As I expected," Mr. Willis said. "The usual repetition, with one exception." He looked at Emma and her grandmother, and smiled once more. "They've been forced to take notice, and it's only the beginning. Minor disturbances, they say, and the situation under control. Well, this won't be the last allusion to our activities." He removed his glasses, still smiling. "I wish you ladies would celebrate with me in a glass of potato wine."

Emma glanced at her grandmother. She was watching Mr. Willis closely. Then she suddenly spoke. "Taffy," she said softly, "why were you wearing head-phones when we looked through the window? Does it mean you have a second radio that works differently from this one here?"

Mr. Willis paused in the act of polishing his glasses. He lifted his head and returned her gaze. The fact that he did not stop smiling made the gaze the more sinister.

"When I was a boyo we had an old saying," he murmured. "It takes a peeping Jenny to catch a peeping Tom. You learnt the habit behind the curtain, now, didn't you? Looking down at the men and women in the stalls, and taking a dekko at the boxes too. Will they laugh or will they cry, you must have asked yourself? And adapted your performance accordingly."

"Sometimes," Mad agreed. "It was customary in the profession in the old days, but mostly in the provinces, on the road."

"I thought so. Well, I'm by way of being a performer too, but in a modest capacity. I listen, and sometimes I give tongue. What is it, then, that you would have me tell you?"

"Only if you know more than you've told us already," she replied. "Only if you can give us any information, however slight, about our boys."

Slowly he got off the bed and walked towards the corner of the room where they had seen him first. "There's something I can tell you, which is they've not been ill-treated," he said. "Stomachs rumbling a bit, maybe, but not man-handled. You wouldn't think a tourist paradise could be turned so easily into a milder version of Devil's Island, could you?"

It was as though he was playing with them, Emma thought. His analogy of the spider and the fly was very apt. A feeler stretched out, and then withdrawn.

"Lundy?" asked Mad. "St. Michael's Mount?"

He shook his head. "It's simple, really," he said. "Try further west amid the lapping ocean waves, and if you guess the Isles of Scilly you'd be right. Don't panic, now, with the way things are they'll soon be home again. Mind you, I'm not talking of your boyos only but all the men they're holding for questioning, and it amounts to a fair number since the first landings."

The Scillies . . . Joe, Terry, Mr. Trembath, the other farmers from their own district, the Poldrea and Falmouth dockers who had felt themselves ill-used, the clay-workers who had lost their jobs, anyone, perhaps, who might have questioned, might have demurred—was it possible men could have been picked at random and just removed?

"Taffy," said Mad gently, "where do you get your information from?"

He laid his finger against his nose and winked. "That would be telling, wouldn't it? The air is full of language if you listen for it. Watch, I'll show you something." He stooped, and removed a floor-board from under his feet. There was something there that looked like an oblong box, with head-phones beside it, and wires, and knobs. "This is my box of tricks," he said. "Brimful of magic I am, like Prospero in his cell. Love of music started me off, so I could hear opera from Vienna and Milan. Then little by little I heard voices too." He beckoned to Emma. "Now, let me crown you." She shook her head as he picked up the head-phones. "No need to be frightened," he told her. "You won't hear anything but human voices, I haven't yet made contact with the stars." He was playing with her, joking, yet even so there was something forbidding about the crouching figure, the shock of white hair, the eyes glinting behind the spectacles.

"Crown me, Taffy," said Mad. "Prospero's cell can't frighten an aging actress. Besides, I want to know if the magic works."

He turned from Emma, and as Mad rose, and pulled her chair nearer to the box beneath the floor-boards, he placed the ear-phones on her head with a reverent gesture, as though he were indeed some priest placing a crown or wreath upon the brow of an initiate. Then he bent to the box and turned a knob. Emma watched Mad's face, and the terrifying thought suddenly came to her that Mr. Willis was indeed mad, that he was not a radio "ham" or whatever the expression was for those who could pick up short-wave messages, but an expert in some ultra-high frequency, and Mad would suddenly collapse, her brain pierced.

Nothing so appalling happened. Mad listened, appeared absorbed, then smiled and removed the head-phones.

"It's Welsh, isn't it?" she said. "I wish I could understand it. What are they saying?"

He took the head-phones from her and placed them upon his own head. He nodded once or twice and smiled at her.

"It might be just as well you couldn't understand," he told her. "It is not very complimentary to the English people as a whole. Wait, now, while I translate."

He seized the pad from beneath the floor-boards and began to scribble. Emma dragged her stool next to her grandmother's chair and took her hand. Mad pressed it in sympathy.

"I told you he was Owen Glendower," she whispered. "What a pity we never made him read that scene from *Henry IV*. Next time he comes to the house we must. And *The Tempest* too. The man's a born actor."

Mr. Willis, unconscious of the rôles they were assigning him, removed the head-phones and switched off his box of tricks. "Civil disobedience in Scotland and in Wales," he said. "No striking, no violence, just nobody going to work. The men staying at home, the shops putting up their shutters. They can't arrest people for sitting at home, can they? It will take a little time to spread throughout both countries, but where one starts the next man follows suit, and you'll soon have every country forming a cell of resistance on its own." He smiled, and began stacking the ear-phones neatly beside the home-made radio set.

"Doesn't it work both ways?" Mad asked. "Can you not also pass information on to the people who are informing you?"

"Indeed I can, and do," he replied. "I had finished transmitting a short while before you played peeping Jenny through my window. One local piece of information, however small, however insignificant, can form a link in an ever-widening chain. I transmit in two languages, Welsh and Cornish."

"Cornish?" Mad raised a quizzical eyebrow.

Mr. Willis nodded. "You seem surprised. No necessity. The Celtic languages have many factors in common once you study them, and the Celtic peoples too. Welsh nationalism and Scots nationalism have been irritants in certain governmental circles for many years now, we all know that, but the Cornish are, shall I say, more secretive behind the usual open front. They are strong underground, very strong indeed. But with mining stock that's natural, isn't it?"

Mad appeared to be thinking. Surely, Emma wondered, she didn't take him seriously?

"I never can make up my mind about nationalism," said her grandmother. "It's inclined to turn fanatical, and the fanatics make such a point about where one is born. I was born in Wimbledon, and although I used to adore going to the tennis there in the old days I wouldn't die for it. In fact, it wouldn't worry me if Wimbledon and all its houses ceased to exist. But I've made this corner of this particular peninsula my home for a long time now, and I'd certainly die for it if I thought it would do any good."

Mr. Willis paused in the middle of stowing away the installation under the floor-boards.

"Which it wouldn't," he said. "It's a form of mistaken idealism the way men and women sacrifice themselves, only to be forgotten by their contemporaries and their immediate successors. In a hundred years they may be resurrected as heroes and martyrs but it's a little late then for the project in hand. On the other hand, as an actress you have a fine ear for intonation. One or two practice attempts, and I would have you speaking Cornish, Welsh or Gaelic in the manner born. A woman's voice would make a great impression, and yours especially."

He squatted back on his haunches, staring at her. Oh no, thought Emma, she mustn't fall for it, heaven knows what he mightn't make her say—encourage arson, anarchy, blowing up bridges. Someone would recognise her voice and trace it back.

"H'm," said Mad thoughtfully. "'We must be free or die, who speak the tongue that Shakespeare spake' . . . Who was it said that?"

"Wordsworth," replied Emma hastily, "but darling, honestly . . ."

"Apropos of what?"

"One of the sonnets to liberty. 'Milton, thou should'st be living at this hour.'"

Mad looked over to where Mr. Willis was rapidly uncovering his radio set for the second time.

"I wouldn't mind quoting 'We must be free or die,'" she said, "but wouldn't it sound rather foolish pleading for the tongue that Shakespeare spoke if all your contacts want to do is to spout in Welsh or Cornish?"

Mr. Willis dismissed this with an airy gesture. "It's the meaning behind the words they listen for," he told her. "I like 'We must be free or die,' I like it very much, it strikes the authentic note for all of us." He had placed the head-phones over his ears and had started fiddling with the knobs. Mad was murmuring the phrase over again to herself.

> *"We must be free or die, who speak the tongue*
> *That Shakespeare spake . . ."*

"Mad," said Emma, "you can't do it, you might get into the most terrible trouble, and for all we know these short waves are picked up with the greatest of ease down in the camp. They are probably listening in the whole time for something of this sort, it would be part of their job."

"The trouble is," said her grandmother, taking not the slightest notice of Emma, "the Americans also speak the tongue that Shakespeare spoke, so the point has rather gone. Unless, of course, one followed it up with something ironic and pretend to be Martha Hubbard at one of her Cultural-Get-Together meetings. And even that would be lost on the inhabitants of the Welsh valleys."

Mr. Willis had taken off his head-phones and was beckoning her to his side. "If you think you'd just be talking to the Welsh valleys you'd be mistaken," he said. "Those who listen are in high places, many of them, you'd be surprised, on county councils, professors and students, indeed I would say a cross-section of the entire population throughout Scotland and Wales and the west country. They are only waiting for a rallying call, and who better than yourself to kindle the flame?"

Mr. Willis, flushed with his own eloquence, seemed to have mixed his metaphors a little, but Mad did not appear to mind. She was evidently enjoying the experience, and even looking forward to hearing herself speak in an unknown language to an audience she could not see and who were unable to applaud.

She smiled down at Mr. Willis from the rickety chair, and he isn't playing with her at all, thought Emma suddenly, she is playing with him. They're both seeing who can hoodwink the other longest, and neither of them really believes a word they're saying.

"One moment, please." Taffy held up his hand. "Quoting the whole poem would be very effective. It would reach out to a wide circle." He glanced at Emma, then reached for the pencil and pad. "Scribble down what you remember, and then your grandmother can read it aloud over the air," he said.

"That's no good," shrugged Mad. "I haven't got my specs."

"Borrow mine, lady, borrow mine." He whipped off his glasses and handed them to her with a flourish. The blue eyes without them looked naked, pale.

Mad placed them upon her own face, frowned, and was instantly transformed into another being, someone older, evil, alien. That is what happens to people, Emma thought, bewildered, when they lose their identity, when they stop being themselves; it happens to individuals when they fall in love with the wrong person, the personality doesn't develop, it gets swamped, and it happens to communities, to villages, to countries under invasion, however benign the intention, however all-embracing the ultimate design.

"Take them off," said Emma quickly. "You look ghastly."

Mad turned her head and stared at her through the borrowed spectacles, and it was as though she, Emma, had become a child again, about the age of Ben, and the grandmother she knew and loved, by putting grease-paint on her face and wearing a wig, had damaged or even destroyed the self within. Mad laughed, removed the offending glasses, and gave them back to the Welshman.

"I don't mind what I look like," she said. "The trouble is I can't see through them. They were completely blurred."

And yet, Emma thought, as Mr. Willis replaced them, on his face they are right, they somehow protect him, his eyes just now without them were like an animal, trapped.

"You'll have to teach me the poem," said Mad. "Is it very long?"

"Much too long," Emma replied, "and not really appropriate. We did it for A level at school, and I can only remember lines here and there."

"Such as?"

Such as . . . Emma tried to think. Written in London, 1802, what was Wordsworth doing in London, and was it something to do with the Peace of Amiens or war breaking out again or what? All the lines were jumbled together in memory. Aloud, she quoted,

> *"We must run glittering like a brook*
> *In the open sunshine, or we are unblest:*
> *The wealthiest man among us is the best;*
> *No grandeur now in nature or in book*
> *Delights us. Rapine, avarice, expense,*
> *This is idolatry; and these we adore:*
> *Plain living and high thinking are no more:*
> *The homely beauty of the good old cause*
> *Is gone."*

She paused, concentrating hard. Blank, blank, blank in her mind. Wait a minute.

> *". . . We are sefish men;*
> *Oh! raise us up, return to us again,*
> *And give us manners, virtue, freedom, power."*

And there was something later on, in another sonnet, about a tyrant, how did it go?

> *"There is a bondage worse, far worse to bear*
> *Than his who breathes, by roof and floor, and wall,*
> *Pent in, a tyrant's solitary thrall:*
> *'This he who walks about in the open air,*
> *One of a nation who, henceforth, must wear*
> *Their fetters in their souls. For who could be*
> *Who, even the best, in such conditions free . . ."*

Free . . . Yes, but the bit about freedom came from an earlier sonnet.

> *"We must be free or die, who speak the tongue*
> *That Shakespeare spake; the faith and morals hold*
> *Which Milton held. In everything we are sprung*
> *Of earth's first blood, have titles manifold."*

It was something to do with the Napoleonic wars, must have been, because there was that Anticipation sonnet which came later on:

"*Shout, for a mighty victory is won!*
On British ground the invaders are laid low:
The breath of Heaven has drifted them like snow,
And left them lying in the silent sun.
Never to rise again! the work is done.
Come forth, ye old men, now in peaceful show,
And greet your sons! drums beat and trumpets blow!
Make merry, wives! ye little children stun
Your grandames' ears with pleasure of your noise!
Clap, infants, clap your hands! Divine must be
That triumph, when the very worst, the pain
And even the prospect of our brethren slain,
Hath something in it which the heart enjoys.
In glory will they sleep and endless sanctity."

Yes, that was the bit which she used to enjoy when they had to recite it in class, because of the grandames' pleasure in your noise, it always suggested Mad laughing at the boys.

"*'Tis well! from this day forward we shall know*
That in ourselves our safety must be sought;
That by our own right hands it must be wrought,
That we must stand unpropped, or be laid low."

Phew! It was no good. The whole thing was hopelessly jumbled. No wonder Mr. Willis was exchanging glances with Mad and trying to hide his smile.

"I'm sorry," she said, "I was simply quoting at random from various sonnets." She turned to her grandmother. "You'd best give up the idea anyway," she added.

"I have," replied Mad briefly. "You've done my work for me."

"What do you mean?"

Mad nodded at Mr. Willis. "Show her."

The Welshman laid bare the floor-board close at hand. There was a small tape-recorder amongst the rest of the paraphernalia. The tape was still running. He switched it off.

"You may have thought yourself back in the school-room," he told her, "but I did not. You were staring at the ceiling in such concentration that you never noticed when I signalled to your grandmother and pointed to my little box of tricks, and she gestured in the affirmative. Now we have your voice recorded, and no one will ever be the wiser when they listen except that it is a young voice trans-mitting the stirring message. I shall send it out on the air later tonight."

Wizard and witch looked at her, and laughed.

"You can't," exploded Emma. "It wouldn't be fair, I never agreed to it, and the lines are all mixed up, they didn't make sense."

"On the contrary, they made great sense. They were very inspiring," he said. "Would you like me to play it back?"

"No." Emma rose to her feet and paced up and down the wooden floor. "Mad," she pleaded, "you must prevent it. Please make him give you the tape and we can destroy it."

"Nonsense," said Mad firmly. "Taffy's perfectly right, the lines were most inspiring, and all the better for the purpose by being quoted out of order." She rose from the rickety chair and straightened her Chairman Mao cap. "You were very good, darling," she said generously, "far better than I should have been. I never could speak verse. You must let us know, Taffy, what sort of effect it has upon your Celtic masses and all the other people under-ground. Come on, Em, Dottie will be wondering where on earth we've got to."

She made a move towards the door. Mr. Willis, how-ever, had once more placed the head-phones over his ears. His expression was intent, he was listening hard.

"Wait one moment," he said hastily. "There is some-thing coming through. It's a little confusing . . ."

His face changed to astonishment. He tilted the head-phones and Emma could hear the muffled voice coming through. Whoever it was spoke rapidly, seeming excited, and then as suddenly it faded, was cut. All was silent again. Mr. Willis turned to his visitors, genuine bewilder-ment in the bright eyes behind the spectacles.

"It wasn't expected," he said, "no one was warned. But

300

on the whole, all things considered, it must work to our advantage and puzzle the enemy, which is what we are after, isn't it?"

"If we knew what you were talking about, we might agree," Mad replied.

Mr. Willis stared. The news had evidently so dumbfounded him that he had forgotten he was one step ahead with information.

"Why, the boyos have landed," he said, "one in Scotland, the other in Wales."

Now it was the turn of Emma and her grandmother to stare, first at Mr. Willis and then at one another. How could Joe and Terry have possibly escaped from the Isles of Scilly and be landing in the west and north? Did it mean there had been some sort of mass escape, and their many companions were free as well?

"Who helped them, how did it happen?" asked Emma.

Mr. Willis shook his head. "No details," he said. "Later, perhaps. Just the bare facts that both boys have landed, and want nothing for themselves, no titles, no honours, no pushing themselves forward, they just want to serve, and band themselves together with other youngsters throughout the country to keep the land free. It's time, afer all, they showed some activity and let us older folk sit back." He looked across at Emma. "Your tape may be heard by princes, think of it," he said. "Young Andrew in Scotland and Charlie boy in Wales. You must find it distinctly encouraging, to say the least of it. Put fire into both their bellies, that it will."

Mr. Willis insisted on walking back with them through the wood. He would take no denial. He carried an old ship's lantern which glowed and flickered as he swung it from side to side, plodding a few steps ahead of them all the while. He parted from them at the far end of the wood, where the hedge bordered on their own domain.

"The transmission will go out at 21:30 hours," he told Emma. "First your own voice speaking, then the translation I shall make in the two languages, for it's a pity, after all, not to send it out in all three. I have a busy night ahead of me. Sleep soundly, ladies."

Looking back over her shoulder, Emma watched the flickering lantern disappear, engulfed, all of a sudden, by the ghostly line of trees. She put out her hand and clung to her grandmother's arm.

"Is it true?" she whispered.

"Is what true?" countered Mad.

"Everything. Transmissions on the radio, voices on the air, the princes landing. Or was it all a hoax just to impress?"

Mad opened the garden gate and they passed inside. "I don't know," she said. "But when we looked through the window he had the ear-phones over his head and a gun by his side. He didn't expect us. It wasn't rehearsed."

The house stood out before them, dependable, solid, everything about it homely and safe, lacking only Joe and Terry to give final assurance.

"Then you do believe him?" Emma asked.

"I neither believe nor disbelieve," Mad answered. "Taffy's a mountebank, so am I. Rogues, vagabonds, strolling players, we're all alike. Politicians too. The original mountebank was the Pied Piper, who first of all led the rats out of town, and then the children. Who follows depends upon the tune."

She slid the doors into the porch and walked up the steps through to the hall. Everything was as they had left it. Only Folly had moved and was waiting on the mat, tail slowly wagging, tongue hanging from a salivary jaw.

"I think," said Emma, "that's the most immoral thing I've ever heard you say. You imply that nothing is ever true, that we are all misled, that each one of us, guilty or innocent, follows some will o' the wisp and then vanishes off the face of the earth for evermore?"

"That's right," Mad replied, patting Folly's sleek head and submitting to a wet caress.

"In that case . . ." Emma looked about her, the one candle, left by the faithful Dottie, throwing a doubtful light on familiar things, "why do any of us bother, what's the point of living, why . . . why . . ." she searched desperately for an answer to questions never before put, "why didn't you just go on acting until you dropped, instead of living here in retirement and adopting the six boys?"

"Ah," said Mad, kicking off her boots, "that was just a

302

sop to appease my ego. Haven't I told you I always wanted seven sons? Listen . . ."

She lifted her head. The silence was broken, as it had not been for several days and nights, by the sound of aircraft passing overhead.

22

Something was happening. Above them in the air, and out at sea. Gunfire, explosions, depth-charges, all of these things or none of them, they couldn't tell. Lights flashing on the horizon, lights in the sky. A stench of chemical or oil. No brewing of cocoa this time, no sitting chatting round the kitchen table. They dragged mattresses to the basement and spread them out over the flags, not seeking to rekindle the ashes in the old grate because smoke might attract attention, and the only thing anybody wanted was to stay hidden. Dottie, her back to the wall, a pillow between her and the cold plaster, rocked Ben to sleep. Colin, who at first had shaken from head to foot like someone with high fever, calmed down when Sam hit upon the right solution, which was to stuff his ears with cotton wool and tie a scarf around his eyes.

"It works with animals," Sam explained. "If a stable catches fire you bandage the horse's eyes, so it must work with humans too."

The practical measure diverted attention from the terror outside, and after a while imagination brought its own reward. "I'm a very old man," said Colin. "I'm a very old man starving in a city where they've just had an earthquake," and he smiled as Emma wrapped a blanket round his shoulders, and took off the bandage covering his eyes, but kept the cotton wool in his ears. Sam himself was preoccupied with the needs of Folly, the squirrel, the pigeon, and a new addition, a very old and quarrelsome rook which had tumbled down the chimney of his and Andy's room. Andy was on duty at the cellar door, bow in hand, a sheaf of arrows slung across his shoulder. Mad had given him permission.

"If we're attacked I'll stand by your side and fight with you," she said, "and anyway, we're all together. What a good way to go!"

The thundering of aircraft flying low overhead, the explosions out at sea, and at times the shaking of the walls themselves seemed to threaten not only the roof and the upper floors but the foundations themselves. When this happened Ben stirred in his sleep and clung to Dottie, Colin trembled again, and Andy, with a grinding of teeth and a sigh of exasperation, fixed an arrow at the ready, pointing it at the cellar door and the non-existent foe without. The transistor radio brought no news: the battery was not yet dead, but no voice came from the regional station, nor from any other. Someone spoke from a German source, but nobody understood what he was saying, and a French voice, caught for an instant with the words *"On dit oue les associés de l'USUK sont maintenant . . ."* was instantly jammed.

"The associates of USUK are now" . . . what?

Emma looked at her grandmother. Mad was asleep. The night wore on, the children creeping closer to the adults, the adults creeping closer to one another, and even Andy finally slumped to his knees and lay with his bow beside him, the arrow-sheaf for pillow.

Ben was the first to awake, belly empty, demanding food. He's not meek, Emma thought, wrenching open her reluctant eyes, he won't inherit the earth. Ben, indeed, was the only one to look round about him with an air of cheerful confidence, having slept well, and because he was black he showed little outward sign of strain or weariness; whereas his white companions looked like little old men, grey with fatigue, bags beneath their eyes. And the adults . . . Poor Dottie, poor Mad. Old women with no future, humped, chins dropping. And myself, Emma thought, I know how I look too, and how I feel, a jaundiced yellow, streaky hair, a furry tongue, and frightened still.

She glanced at her watch. It had stopped just after three, she had forgotten to wind it. The light was grey, seeping in through the small basement windows. It must be seven, perhaps later. Ben, fumbling with his brief shorts, looked enquiringly at her. She put her fingers to her lips. It didn't matter about the boys, but Mad and Dottie must sleep on. Ben grinned, and scrambling to the far end of the cellar made water on to a pile of logs. This is what we shall all be doing, she thought, if it continues, if the rumbles in the distance never cease, for, although, the house no longer shook, somewhere, higher than it had been during the night, aircraft were flying, but in what direction, whether inland or out to sea, it was impossible to tell.

Ben pottered to and fro, chewing an apple he had found on the shelf where Joe had stored them, yet keeping silent, intuition warning him, perhaps, that this was no ordinary morning, when he could joke and play with Colin, adding new words to his vocabulary. If we none of us had woken up, Emma thought, but only Ben, he would have fed himself on apples and raw beetroot, and played alone, and somehow got through the day on his own until he felt sleepy again, when he would have yawned and tumbled down in a heap by Dottie's side, the very fact that she was there bringing security. Looking at the sleeping figures, Mad, Dottie, the three boys, the morning light so slowly invading the dark room, she thought that this was how a chamber of the dead must look when discovered by archaeologists after centuries, the only difference being that those who lay buried would be priests or kings or queens, with jewels upon them, and anyone who ventured into the basement of Trevanal after a thousand years would think they had stumbled upon the skeletons of peasants. Folly too, her muzzle between her paws, might be the guardian hound that, cast in gold, guarded Egyptian tombs.

The curious smell, half-chemical, half-oily, which she had noticed the night before seemed more obtrusive now. She got up silently and peered into the narrow court beyond the cellar. In winter abandoned because it had no sun, in summer Dottie used to hang washing out to dry between two posts. A robin was lying dead on the cobbled stones. Something for Sam to bury, she thought with pity, and then . . . the night had not been cold, why had it died? The light became more grey, more pallid, and wiping the streaky window she saw the sea-mist drifting into the court, masking the trees above, and with each passing vapour the smell of oil became stronger, more pungent, coming inland from the sea. Had it happened? Had it started? Had it come at last, the chemical warfare people had warned one another about for years? Was the robin lying there one of the victims? Why were Mad and Dottie and the boys sleeping so heavily? Why did the air itself seem more oppressive in the old basement kitchen than it had been when they all descended to it the night before?

This was it. Not nuclear power but something more silent, more insidious, set loose upon the air from pilotless planes and coming in vaporous form to fall upon the land, to seep into cracks between windows, cracks in walls, down chimneys, up through drains, until breathing was stifled, the good air turned to poison, the heart burst . . .

"Mad . . ." Her cry was panic-stricken, beyond control, and Ben, in the midst of his second apple, turned and stared, his eyes rolling. Everybody stirred. Colin sat up as if shot, throwing off his blanket. Andy grasped his bow. Dottie opened her mouth, not to scream, but to let forth a gigantic yawn. Sam stretched out a hand to Folly, who stood on three shaking legs, the fourth tucked up by her haunch, useless as always after hours of immobility. Only Mad slept on, indifferent to the waking world, peaceful, happy, an oilskin under her head for pillow, a car rug, riddled with moth and unseen since the previous winter, across her knees.

"Madam's worn out," whispered Dottie, "and no wonder. Let her sleep on."

The boys were yawning too, stretching themselves, rising to their feet, looking curiously and rather disdainfully at Emma, who had awakened them with her panic cry.

"I'm sorry," she said. "It was the smell of oil, the smell of chemicals. Don't you notice it? For a moment I thought . . ."

She didn't finish her sentence. The smell had gone, or,

308

if not entirely vanished, was no longer strong. The boys sniffed, shrugged. Andy went to the cellar door and opened it. The vapoury mist still clung to the trees above and drifted inward, but the air was fresh.

"No sound of aircraft," he informed them, "no sound of anything. It must be over. Let's go upstairs and see."

"Be careful," warned Emma. "Don't open doors or windows, we don't know what's happened, it might be dangerous."

She ran after them up the stairs, but they were too quick for her. They had sped through the kitchen and into the hall, and had thrown open the fron door and the porch as well. The morning mood was too strong for discipline. Cramped through the night in the basement, hungry, stiff with fear, morning had brought release, the day had come, and a day like any other day, foggy, still, without explosions, without bangs and crashes and other ominous sounds.

"Come back," Emma called, "come back."

They disregarded her, running out into the garden, laughing down the garden path, flinging wide the gate.

"Let's go to the look-out," shouted Andy. "Let's see if all those explosions meant more wrecks."

Emma followed them, with the vain thought that if there should be chemicals there on the ploughed field the earth would have turned black, and this would prove to them her fears had been well-founded, but when they came to the wall and looked out across the bay they could see nothing but the drifting mist, harmless, odourless, damp as the stems of grass under their feet. A vehicle came looming across the field towards them and Emma gripped the shoulders of the nearest boy, preparing to turn and run back to the house, for this could be the first of ten, of twenty, of heaven knows how many motorised enemy units, even tanks, and then something familiar about the sound of the engine, about the shape, brought reassurance.

"It's the Land-Rover!" shouted Andy. "It's the Land-Rover from the farm, and Mr. Trembath is driving it."

The relief, the wonder of it, the snapping of unbearable tension! And as the boys jumped down over the wall, shouting and laughing, she jumped with them, and there was Jack Trembath himself, climbing out of his seat, setting down a crate of milk bottles and a great basket of eggs. The boys were leaping up and down and he was laughing too, although surely greyer, thinner, stubble all over his chin, and Emma stumbled over the ploughed furrow in the ground and threw her arms round him, as if she were Myrtle.

"There, my dear, there," he said. "You've had it rough, we all have, but I put down we're over the worst of it, things are on the mend. Did you get your windows broken, any slates gone from the roof?"

So many questions to answer, but more important to ask hers first.

"When did you get back, Mr. Trembath? Did you escape? Won't they be after you again?"

"Escape?" He shook his head. "No suggestion of escape, they were letting us go regular, forty or fifty at a time, no reason given, just dumped out on the road and told to hoof it."

"They flew you in, then, by helicopter, to the mainland?"

He stared at her. "Mainland? We were never off it. They had us packed like peas in a pod inside Lanhydrock, guarded, of course, but I don't know what the National Trust will say when they go inside the mansion to clean up after us." He grinned, and began handing out the milk bottles to the four boys. "Mixed bunch we were, I can tell you that. Farmers, dockers, lawyers, clay-workers, the odd parson or two, doctors—yes, your Dr. Summers was there—each one of us hauled in to be questioned and saying nothing, I can tell you. It was the good humour that broke the buggers, nothing else. If we'd turned nasty they'd have had us there still."

The boys were drinking the milk, spilling half of it, the creamy froth running down Ben's chin.

"I don't understand," said Emma, bewildered. "We were told all the prisoners were being held on the Scilly Isles."

"Not us, my dear, not us. There may have been others, I wouldn't know about that. Anyway, they let us go last evening, as I was saying, and your two were in fine fettle. The doctor is only waiting for transport to get Terry to hospital to have his plaster off, and something put in the heel of a shoe. You'll have 'em home today."

He gave Emma a bottle of milk. "Go on," he said, "drink it, you've been living on short commons for the past day or two, according to what Peggy and Myrtle told me when I got back. And what old boy Willis told me too this morning when he arrived to give a hand, not knowing I'd be there. Ah, that reminds me." He fumbled in his pocket and brought out a small object sealed in an envelope. "For you," he said, "with his compliments. It seems he's had enough of it for the time being and is packing up and moving on. Wouldn't say where, and I wouldn't be surprised if he's off and out of his shack by this evening. Peggy told me he'd been very helpful, she and Mick and Myrtle couldn't have managed without him, and yet . . . Well, it doesn't sound kind, but he made her feel uncomfortable, she said."

Uncomfortable, yes. But we couldn't have done without him . . . Emma looked at Andy, who was tilting his head back, and like Ben the milk was running down his chin. He was standing on the ploughed furrow where he had shot the corporal dead.

"Mr. Trembath," she said, one hand clutching the packet he had given her and the other holding the milk bottle, "if the commandos have let everyone go and aren't holding men in detention any longer, what was going on last night? Why all the gunfire and aircraft and explosions?"

"Submarine in the bay, so Mr. Willis said. Unidentified. The Yanks were letting off depth-charges. He got this off his home-made radio."

Emma handed the milk bottle to Ben, who was grabbing for it. "I rather doubt," she said, "if you can believe everything Mr. Willis tells you."

"Pinch of salt? I reckon you're right. But submarine or no submarine, something's shifted them. They've stripped the camp and gone to St. Mawgan to take off. It seems what we started down here in Cornwall is spreading all through the country, and into the cities, all the ordinary folks digging in their toes and saying they don't want to be Yankee-ridden or government-ridden, so the troops will be needed further up the line. I reckon—London and the Midlands, I shouldn't wonder. Maybe we in the west are too small beer for them to bother with right now. Anyway, we're free of 'em. No more road-blocks, no more barbed wire, no more rules and regulations. You'll find your water will have been turned on, and your electricity too, and the telephone back. How long for we don't know, but at least it's a breathing-space. Tell me, is your grandmother all right? How did she stand the strain?"

"Marvellously," said Emma, "but she's tired today. We all spent the night in the basement, and when we came away just now she was sleeping still."

"Lovely job," replied Jack Trembath. "Well, give her my regards, and I'll be up to see her soon."

He turned back to the Land-Rover and climbed once more into the driver's seat. The mist was clearing and the sun was struggling to shine. Already Emma could catch a glimpse of the glassy waters out in the bay.

"Gone," she said to the boys. "I can't believe it. What would be the reason? What would have made them go?"

"Windy," said Andy. "Like when the ship first went to Falmouth because of the gale. Now it's an unidentified sub and they've beaten retreat."

"No," said Sam, "I think they've thought it all over and realised coming here was a mistake. They didn't enjoy it, nor did we. It's like mixing a new flock of sheep on to the grazing ground with our lot, specially if they're a different breed. They don't get on."

"Or p'raps too many people laughed at them," suggested Colin "like when we burnt the guy on the beach, and I let off the snake in the playroom in the officer's face."

"It doesn't matter what it was," said Emma. "The thing to remember is that life is going to begin all over again."

They walked back to the house, Andy and Sam carrying the basket of eggs and the milk. Emma let them go ahead, and when they were out of sight she opened the packet. It was the small recorded tape. There was a note attached to it, written in a curious spidery hand.

"A promising debut," it ran. "Despite the disturbance in the night it was heard by many, and appreciated. I have been sent for elsewhere and so will be moving on, but one of these days I trust we shall meet again. My humble regards to both you ladies." The note was signed "Taffy."

And so it's something I shall never know, Emma told herself, never find out, if he was really working for Celtic nationalism or anyone else and truly sent out this tape over the air to hundreds of listeners in Cornwall, Scotland and Wales, or whether it was all fabrication, fantasy, something to console himself with. Console for what? An uneventful life, one that had miscarried? A sop to the ego, as Mad had said about herself, adopting the six boys because she had always wanted seven sons? Perhaps Mr. Willis had longed to be a leader of men, and in a flash of perception had glimpsed a subconscious desire in Emma herself to show off, to spout verses, to declaim.

Two sounds greeted her as she entered the hall. Normal sounds, belonging to the everyday world that seemed to have been absent for so long. One was the television, which the boys had switched on in the library. The other was the telephone. She decided for the television because it must be just on eight and with luck the announcer would be reading the local news. "Hurry," shouted Andy. "It was a sub, Mr. Willis was right." She went and stood beside them, first of all drawing the curtains to let in light and air, and there was the young announcer, looking a bit paler than usual and wearing his terrible purple tie, and he was saying, ". . . Depth charges were dropped and the combined forces of USUK were put on the alert, but no statement has been issued from joint high command, and it is not yet known whether a submarine was in fact involved and, if so, whether it was identified. It is now reported, but this again has not as yet been confirmed, that the explosion which destroyed the U.S. vessel some days ago at anchor in Poldrea bay with severe loss of life may also have been caused by torpedo action. In any event, the recent security regulations affecting the local population have now been relaxed, and the Marine Commandos have relinquished the port and beach of Poldrea for the time being and handed them back to the local authorities, who state that it may be a few days before things return to normal." He looked down at a piece of paper in his hand. "A Cabinet meeting will be held in Downing Street this morning. It is understood there is some conflict of opinion amongst members regarding policy in general and the future of USUK. There will be a further bulletin at nine o'clock."

The telephone was still ringing. Emma ran from the library to the cloakroom.

"All right," she shouted to Dottie, who was emerging from the kitchen, "I'll get it."

"Praise be," said Dottie, "the electric's back. I'm doing scrambled eggs for everyone, Sam's just brought them in."

Emma snatched up the receiver. "Hullo? Who is it? What do you want?"

Why in heaven a foreign voice, at least it sounded foreign, with its staccato "One moment, please?" Then a pause, and unbelievably, though on second thoughts inevitably, the staccato tones of Pa.

"Is it you? Is it Emma? Why did nobody answer? They've been ringing you for ages, couldn't get through. I've about five minutes before a conference, the pressure's tremendous. What's happening, what's everyone doing?"

"Look, I can't begin . . ." Emma tried. "Where are you speaking from?"

"I'm in Zurich. I flew in from New York last night. I shan't know until the conference is over whether I catch a plane back to London or fly on to Tokyo. Turmoil . . . turmoil . . . and the whole issue of USUK at stake. Everyone seems to be losing their heads back at home, and the rot started, so I'm told, with a lot of pig-headed people down in your part of the world, who didn't know what was good for them. I gather the infection is spreading through the whole blasted country like an epidemic of smallpox, and the Americans may decide to pull out and leave us to it. Bankruptcy, that'll mean, very likely, but why should they care? They've given us our chance. Or else it'll be a complete take-over, and martial law. That'll learn you . . . Incidentally, I rang to wish the old beloved many happy returns."

Many happy returns. Oh God, she had forgotten. They had all forgotten. It was Mad's eightieth birthday.

"Pa," she said, "it's too dreadful, we've none of us remembered, Mad least of all, so much has been happening, Pa . . ."

He didn't understand, he didn't care.

"Give her a kiss and tell her I'll bring her back a cowbell," he said. "You can ring it all in turn to keep yourselves awake. You do nothing but sleep in the west country —or did until you started getting bloody-minded. I've had no sleep for twenty-four hours, I'm worn out, I'm exhausted. Disregard everything you hear on T.V. or the

314

radio or read in the newspapers, rumours abound, they will have to be squashed. But apparently it's true that the youngsters have done a bunk, landed in Wales and Scotland to rally the people and fight beside them if it comes to fighting, disregarded all constitutional advice, put their elders and betters in a jam, it will have to be sorted out . . . I must go, Emma darling, I must go . . . take care of yourself and many happy returns."

He had gone. The one link with sanity wasn't sane at all. Pa was as crazy as Mr. Willis. And even now it was impossible to tell whose side he was really on, what he wanted to happen. Was he still for USUK, or had he turned against it? Why Zurich? Why Tokyo?

Replacing the receiver, Emma glanced out of the window up the drive. What now? Everything was happening at once. It was Bevil Summers's car, and there was Terry in the front seat, and Joe behind.

"Dottie," she called joyously, "Dottie, they're back, they're home. You must go down to the basement and wake up Mad. And do you realise, so awful of us, we'd forgotten about it being her birthday? That was Pa on the telephone ringing to wish her many happy returns."

Dottie, saucepan in hand, stood open-mouthed at the entrance to the kitchen.

"I shall never forgive myself," she said, "and there's no orange juice, what's more. Whatever is she going to say?"

The boys were at the gate, Terry without his crutches, Bevil Summers, Joe. She ran down the garden path and flung herself upon them.

"My boys, my boys," she said, which was rather excessive really, and not her place to say. "If you knew, if you only knew, what we've been through."

"That's rich, that just about beats all," exclaimed Terry, kissing her on both cheeks. "There we've been penned up in bloody old Lanhydrock, threatened with the rope, threatened with torture, all for our womenkind, all for love . . ."

"All for nothing," said Joe, "except to stay home again, and find my beetroot gone."

He held out his arms, and kissed her for the first time in his life without diffidence, without reserve.

"We've done it, we've done it," said Bevil Summers. "I haven't felt so bucked with myself since I passed my first

315

medical exam. Civil disobedience, and the pundits who said it wouldn't work are licked. I know we weren't many as numbers go, but it started the ball rolling. And if you want proof of it, there go some of the stragglers, out of Cornwall into Devon, and by now I'm pretty certain they'll get the same treatment here."

The helicopters were coming out of the north and going east. One after the other, in line astern and then fan-wise, spreading out, engines roaring, blades whirring.

"You never know," said Emma doubtfully, "they may come back."

"Dampers, dampers," mocked Terry. "We'll be better prepared if they pay us a second visit. Anyway, it's another day, and life is for living, isn't it? How's Madam?"

"It's her birthday," said Emma, "and she's asleep in the basement, or was. We none of us went to bed last night." She turned to Bevil Summers. "It's really been rather a strain, but you know how she is, she never lets go. Now Joe and Terry are back all will be well. There, she is awake. What a happy birthday greeting for her."

Mad was standing at the top of the steps by the porch. She was holding out her arms to both the boys. They were laughing and talking together, they didn't see her. They went straight past her and into the hall. Had they done it on purpose, was it a joke? Mad was still standing there with her arms open, smiling at Emma. Then she wasn't there any more.

"What's the matter?" asked Bevil Summers.

Emma did not answer for a moment. What was it her grandmother had said last night to Andy, on sentry duty at the cellar door? "We're all together. What a good time to go." Now it was true—they *were* all togther, for Joe and Terry had come home.

When she spoke her voice was calm. "I think you had better go down to the basement. Mad has been asleep for a very long time."

He glanced at her quickly, then ran up the steps into the house, brushing past a small figure at the entrance. Sam came down from the porch, carrying something in his arms. He stood on the path a moment, then lifted his hands.

"I thought I'd let pigeon go. I had a feeling she wanted to be free."

The bird didn't fly far, though. She circled a moment, then settled on a branch of the ilex tree overlooking the ploughed field. It wasn't misty any more. The helicopters were still flying eastward into the sun.

THE BIG BESTSELLERS
ARE AVON BOOKS:

Facing The Lions Tom Wicker	19307	$1.75
High Empire Clyde M. Brundy	18994	$1.75
The Kingdom L. W. Henderson	18978	$1.75
To Die in California Newton Thornburg	18622	$1.50
The Last of the Southern Girls Willie Morris	18614	$1.50
The Hungarian Game Roy Hayes	18986	$1.75
The Wolf and the Dove Kathleen E. Woodiwiss	18457	$1.75
The Priest Ralph McInerny	18192	$1.75
Sweet Savage Love Rosemary Rogers	17988	$1.75
How I Found Freedom *In An Unfree World* Harry Browne	17772	$1.95
I'm OK—You're OK Thomas A. Harris, M.D.	14662	$1.95
Jonathan Livingston Seagull Richard Bach	14316	$1.50
Open Marriage George and Nena O'Neill	14084	$1.95

Where better paperbacks are sold, or directly from the publisher. Include 15¢ per copy for mailing; allow three weeks for delivery.

Avon Books, Mail Order Dept., 250 West 55th Street, New York, N.Y. 10019